IN THE NAME OF LOVE

"When a man's serious about a woman, he gives her a serious ring," Logan said. There seemed to be a husky caress in his rough voice, or perhaps she just imagined it.

Kelly stared at the breath-taking diamond Logan slipped on her finger. "It's so big!"

"An engagement ring should help convince the Stanfields we're in love."

Love?

She had to pretend to be in love with this dangerous man, not just to fool the Stanfields. The social workers must be convinced they had a stable marriage and could provide a proper home for an adopted child.

What had she gotten herself into? She was marrying a total stranger.

"This isn't so bad, is it?" Logan's thumb moved in lazy circles across her bare shoulder. "To be convincing, touching each other has to be second nature to us."

"I guess you're right."

Something shifted in the depths of his blue eyes. He moved closer and gazed down at her.

He's going to kiss me, Kelly thought. Even though she knew better, knew enough to be afraid, she couldn't believe it. She actually *wanted* him to kiss her . . .

Books by Meryl Sawyer

UNFORGETTABLE

THE HIDEAWAY

TEMPTING FATE

Published by Zebra Books

TEMPTING FATE

Meryl Sawyer

Zebra Books
Kensington Publishing Corp.

http://www.zebrabooks.com

ZEBRA BOOKS are published by

Kensington Publishing Corp.
850 Third Avenue
New York, NY 10022

First Printing: May, 1998
10 9 8 7 6 5 4 3 2

Printed in the United States of America

The best way to love anything is as if it might be lost.

—G. K. Chesterton

I have used G. K. Chesterton's quote on all of my books, and I've tried to live my life, remembering what is important and truly meaningful to me. This book is dedicated to my "stand-up guy." Thank heavens, I had the sense to love him while I had him. Now that he is "lost" to me, I'm blessed with happy memories. Thank you, big guy!

Prologue

Logan McCord drew the line at kissing. Hell, he really enjoyed sex, and he was willing to try almost anything to please his partner. Except kiss her lips.

"Sugar," whispered the woman, moving closer, her bare breasts grazing his chest.

Logan noticed her seductive pout, then her lips parted. Why did women automatically assume because you had sex with them that you wanted to kiss them?

He wasn't going to let her kiss his lips. No way.

He scooted upright, back against the cracked wall, and turned his head. Her moist lips brushed the three days' growth of stubble bristling across his jaw. He put his arm around her, and she rested against his shoulder, her long, dark curls tickling his skin.

"You are very beautiful," Logan said slowly, knowing her English was limited.

Her breath was warm against the crook of his neck. She'd doused herself with perfume. The scent was rising from her hair, almost gagging him. Again, she said, "Sugar."

Some other customer must have taught her that word. She used it constantly along with: "You like?"

Logan had liked her body, but he knew he wouldn't remember her long. Paying for sex made it forgettable, less personal. He preferred it that way.

He checked his watch and saw the Breitling's glowing hands. He would gladly have kissed his watch. The Chronomat Blackbird with the lightweight Titanium band had kept him alive more than once.

3:00 A.M. the infallible Breitling told him.

Shafts of moonlight filtered through the tattered burlap bags that had been nailed up as curtains. Out of habit, Logan checked the dark shadows in the room. Nothing. Even the bar on the floor below was silent now.

He was between assignments, waiting for a high-level security clearance for a new anti-terrorist project. No one was after him.

Still he was edgy, restless. The only time he'd had trouble getting a security clearance had been when he had first applied years ago. Questions about his past had been raised, then overcome by his impressive record while training for the Cobra Force. Why was Washington screwing around now?

It's because you want this assignment so much.

"True," he muttered under his breath. They had already given him the computer he would need, a state-of-the-art laptop no bigger than a paperback book. And an arsenal of high-tech gadgets to fight terrorists. Now all he needed was the security clearance and he could begin.

"Sugar." She interrupted his thoughts as she trailed her fingertips across his chest. "You like?"

Her whispered words almost masked the slight creak. The third stair from the bottom had squeaked when he'd stepped on it while following the woman up to the flea-bag room where he was now trapped.

The stairs were the only way out.

Since he had been a kid, he'd made it out of a lot worse jams. And lived to remember and learn from those miserable lessons at the camp.

"Ss-h-h!" he told the woman. He reached for his Glock, pulling it from the windbreaker he'd dropped beside the bed along with his clothes. He pointed it at the brunette's temple, again whispering, "S-s-h-h!"

It was an idle threat. He wouldn't fire the damn gun and wake half the town. He could kill her with one hand if necessary and not make a sound. He had his pants on and was crouched by the door when another telltale squeak came from the stairs.

No one's after you, he told himself. Okay, so why was someone sneaking up the stairs in the dead of night?

The past has a way of catching up with you, he thought. He had made some very dangerous enemies. One of them could have discovered where he was holed up ready for his next assignment.

Logan turned the knob, attempting to muffle any sound with the hand that held the gun. The warped door scraped open with a sound like a bone splintering. The windowless hall was pitch black, shapes discernible only by degrees of darkness. No one was there, but he sensed someone stealthily moving up the stairs just around the corner out of his sight.

He waited, back pressed to the wall, his finger on the Glock's trigger. The air in the short hallway reeked of stale beer. From the alley behind the bar came the screeching of two tomcats, itching for a fight. The shadow reached the top stair, then hunkered down. Logan cursed himself for not being more careful.

Always be certain there are two ways out.

The shadow darted to one side, then hit the floor, rolling to the opposite wall before Logan could aim his gun.

"Gotcha!" yelled the man.

Logan shoved the Glock into his waistband, instantly recognizing the voice. "Brodie Adams. You son-of-a bitch! What are you doing? Trying to get killed?"

The man surged to his feet, chuckling. "You're in kickass form. I can't even blindside you while you're getting laid."

"Give me a second," Logan said. "Let me get my clothes."

Back in the room, the woman was still huddled in the darkness. Logan found his T-shirt and windbreaker on the floor, then handed her a hundred-dollar bill.

Even in the moonlight filtering through the burlap, the woman recognized the new Franklin one-hundred-dollar bill, a fortune in Argentina.

"Sugar . . . Sugar," she cried as he left.

Out in the hall, Logan asked his partner, "What are you doing here? Don't tell me you were so bored that you decided to see if you could catch me off guard."

Brodie crooked his head toward the stairs, indicating they should talk outside. Logan silently followed him down the wood plank staircase. Brodie probably wanted to tell him the security clearance had finally come through.

Outside the building, the night air was cool and refreshing after the stale room. Brodie Adams turned to him, his expression dead serious.

"Logan, your security clearance is on hold."

From the time he was a child, living at the camp, Logan had tutored himself to show no emotion. Years as a member of the Cobra Force had reinforced those early lessons. He stoically listened while Brodie explained the situation. With those few words, Logan McCord's life completely changed forever.

Just as it had so many years ago.

Brodie waited, obviously anticipating a response to the bombshell he'd just delivered. Logan shrugged off the news. After all, danger had always been his best friend.

Chapter 1

Instead of returning home after the dance, Kelly Taylor drove to her office. A lovers' moon hung over Cathedral Rock, illuminating the magnificent spire and the surrounding red rock formations. The blue-white glow cast deep shadows across the unique pueblo-style buildings, making the adobe appear a shade darker than it did in daylight. At times like this when most of Sedona was asleep and the only sound was the lonely, soul-stirring cry of a coyote seeking its mate, Kelly missed the big city.

Arizona had been her home for most of her thirty-one years. She'd lived in the East for the last decade, attending college, then working in New York City. Returning to Sedona, even though its quaint beauty appealed to her, took some adjusting.

She parked her temperamental Toyota in the newspaper's lot. The only noise came from the rear of the adobe complex where the antiquated press was cranking out the bi-weekly edition of the *Sedona Sun*.

Inside, Kelly dropped her evening bag onto her desk, then rifled through her messages, thinking she should go home. But deeply ingrained habits were hard to break. For as long as she could remember, she had slept until almost noon, then worked all night. Her usual schedule did not allow for time with Pop. And time had become all too precious.

"Go home now," she muttered to herself. "Set your alarm for sunrise so you can have breakfast with Pop."

A sharp, insistent knock interrupted her thoughts, echoing through the deserted building. A warning bell sounded in the back of her brain. Who would come to the newspaper office at this hour? The second knock caused the skin on the back of her neck to tighten.

She walked out of her small office into the semi-dark day room where two reporters shared a desk near the receptionist's bay. Sedona was a safe town, a haven for artists and writers who believed the majestic red rock formations inspired them. Along with the artists came the wealthy, drawn, too, by the awesome landscape and the ambiance of the cultured community.

She paused, her hand on the door knob. What was wrong with her? She wasn't the type who had premonitions. Well, the day after Christmas she would go to the sales, absolutely, positively certain she'd find something she *simply* could not live without.

But that was it, the extent of her premonitions. Even when she should have sensed something was wrong like the time she'd kissed Daniel good-bye or when she'd used an unreliable source, her intuition had failed to kick in.

So why now?

"For heaven's sake, this isn't New York or L.A.," she whispered to herself. "Everything's fine."

The rustle of sound beyond the door unnerved her, and she hesitated a second before she turned the knob. In the shadows stood a tall, handsome man with dark hair and lively brown eyes.

"Matt," she cried, stunned. "What are you doing here?"

He pulled her into his arms and gave her a hug that filled her with bittersweet sadness for the time when they'd been inseparable.

B. D., she thought. Before Daniel.

"Hey, Ace," Matthew Jensen said. "Why didn't you dress like this when we were working together?"

She looked down at the silk slip dress she'd chosen because the splashy violet print emphasized her blond hair and brought out the amber lights in her brown eyes. The dress nipped in at the waist, then draped softly over her hips and thighs. It had been perfect for the dance, but it looked ridiculously out of place in an office reeking of newsprint and ink.

"It's a long way from New York City to Arizona," she reminded him. "I just came from the Sedona Arts Center Ball. It's a must for anyone in business here."

She laughed and he chuckled along with her, his flint brown eyes reflecting the sense of humor Matt always used to his advantage. Still, it felt great to share a laugh. How long had it been since she'd genuinely laughed?

Since Daniel Taylor had died.

"Come in, Matt." She tugged on his arm and he walked into the semi-dark reception area. "What are you doing here?"

"I was in the neighborhood," he answered as they walked back to her office.

"Yeah, right," she said, puzzled about what could possibly have brought him out West. As certainly as her career had eclipsed, Matt's star had risen. He was now publisher of the New York-based news magazine *Exposé*, a major achievement for a man not yet thirty-five.

"Actually, I came to see you, Kelly."

"Really?" She didn't venture a sideways glance at him. The last thing she wanted Matthew Jensen to see was her cubbyhole of an office. Her official title was editor-in-chief, but in reality she did whatever it took to get the bi-weekly on the stands, from selling ad space to writing copy to billing. It was a long, long way from the city desk she'd once shared with Matt.

"Not only did I come all this way just to see you, I've been driving around until you showed up," Matt told her, and she almost smiled, knowing how much he hated to be kept waiting.

"Well, you found me, and this is where I work."

She waved her hand at the small room that had been her grandfather's office for over fifty years. A Timex clock beside an Arizona state flag dominated one wall while the other walls were covered with plaques and photographs, a tribute to Pop's status as a community leader. When she'd taken over his job, she hadn't had the heart to change anything.

Matt smiled or tried to and glanced down at the computer mockup of the next issue that was on her desk. "Liberating chickens? Is that for real?"

She sat on the edge of her desk, one leg slightly hitched up, blocking his view of what had to be the most asinine article she'd ever written. "What can I say? The Society to Liberate Chickens is holding a demonstration this Saturday. That's big news in Sedona."

Matt sank into the chair opposite her desk, sprawling in a loose-limbed way that was endearingly familiar. "You don't belong here. I want you back in New York working with me."

His words brought an ache of gratitude, and she managed to smile as she gazed into his dark eyes and saw he was serious. Of all the people to continue to have faith in her—despite her terrible mistake—it would be Matt.

"Thanks for your support," she said, justifiably proud of her calm tone. "My grandfather is very ill. I can't just walk out on him. Pop needs me to run the paper. Besides . . ." She let the word hang there. They both knew she'd disgraced herself. Matt might want her, but the owner of the prestigious news magazine would be outraged.

"I have your ticket back to the show, Ace," he told her with a smile.

The show. New York. The big time. Last year she'd been there, poised at the pinnacle of success. An ace reporter. It had been a long, hard fall, a descent into oblivion symbolized by this small office and a headline about liberating chickens.

Matt leaned forward, his elbows resting on his knees, his expression serious. "All you have to do is write one story. It'll take a little research. That's all." He smiled as if everything had already been decided. "Then you return to New York whenever you're ready."

"Sounds tempting," she admitted, "but what's the catch?"

He kept smiling, but his head tilted just slightly. Kelly had known Matt since their college days working on the *Yale Herald*. This wasn't going to be easy, yet Matt would never concede any difficulty. That's how he convinced people to work so hard for him.

"Remember the disappearance of the boy Senator Stanfield adopted?"

"Sure, it happened right here over twenty-five years ago. Parents still warn their children about it," she told him, wondering what this old news had to do with a breaking story. "On the anniversary of Logan Stanfield's disappearance, the paper recaps the story."

"I'll bet that issue sells more papers than any other."

"It's one of the best sellers," she conceded. "People are still fascinated. A little boy—just five—goes out for a pony ride and falls into a ravine. His older brother and sister go for help, but when they return, the child has vanished."

"I read the UPI clips on it. Senator Stanfield financed quite a search. Bloodhounds, the Mounted Patrol, helicopters, an Indian shaman, then private investigators scoured the country."

"I guess," she replied, even more confused about Matt's interest in the case. "It happened a few years before my parents were killed and I came to live here with my grandfather."

"Two weeks ago Logan Stanfield turned up."

"You must be kidding. They found the body? How did they ID him after all this time? Why doesn't anyone around here know about it? The Stanfields' estate is just outside of town. They're big news around here."

Matt leaned back in the chair and swung his legs up to her desk, resting his Ferragamo loafers on the wood. "They IDed him by matching his fingerprints with the ones on the adoption records."

"Back then, it was unusual to fingerprint a child. If he hadn't been adopted, I doubt if his prints would have been on record."

"The FBI is using a sophisticated computer with digitized fingerprint analysis. They've just added a lot of older files to their data base. They were running a top secret check for a special project when they discovered Logan is working out of the U.S. embassy in Argentina, using the name Logan McCord.''

She slid off the edge of the desk and paced across the small office. "How did he get there? Where's he been?''

"That's the mystery, the interesting angle on the story. It's why I need your skills as an investigative reporter. Logan McCord didn't officially exist until his eighteenth birthday when he walked into a Marine recruiting office in Northern California and enlisted. The records don't tell us anything about his life before then.''

"Wait a minute! He had to produce a hospital birth certificate to enlist.''

"Not if you were delivered by a midwife. Then all you need is a form signed by a registered midwife.''

The quiver of excitement built in her chest, the way it always did when she was onto a great story. "He must have had a social security number. Parents have to—''

"What if your parents were hippie types who wandered from town to town and never bothered to pay taxes? Logan McCord filed for his own social security card when he was accepted into the Marine Corps.''

She tucked a strand of hair behind one ear. "It still sounds fishy to me.''

"Logan McCord claims he had no idea he was the missing child until the FBI computer matched his fingerprints with a set in the missing persons file. He thought the McCords were his real parents.''

She turned and gazed at the picture of Pop with the governor. "You know, my grandfather was right. He thought a tourist was visiting one of the vortexes in the area. They discovered Logan and took off with him.''

"Two weeks ago Senator Stanfield was notified his son had been found. Logan McCord took a leave and flew here to meet his family. I wouldn't know a thing about this except a top-secret source in the CIA tells me Logan McCord's security clearance is on hold until the legal questions about his name are resolved.'' Matt smiled, unable to conceal his excitement. "I'm wondering why the Stanfields have kept this so quiet.''

Kelly dropped into her chair; the elation she'd experienced just moments ago had evaporated. "This isn't out of character for them. They're a rich, powerful dynasty headed by Haywood Stanfield. When something happens, they call the spin doctors."

Kelly tried to temper the sarcasm in her voice with a smile. She had absolutely no use for the snobby Stanfields. They had done their best to ruin her grandfather's paper just because he didn't share their political views. Granted, Pop often antagonized them with his scathingly critical editorials, but they were rich and arrogant.

"No wonder the Stanfields haven't announced the return of their missing son. Believe me, they're waiting to steal headlines nationwide," she told him. "Senator Stanfield is retiring and his son, Tyler, plans to run for his senate seat. This news will get media attention no other candidate can compete with."

"Maybe that's why they've kept quiet." Matt braced his elbows on the desk and studied her. For a moment it was like old times; they were sitting together, working on a story. "What if I told you that Logan McCord doesn't want to change his name to Stanfield?"

"I'd say he's smart," she replied before she could stop herself. "It's hard to believe, though, coming from a guy whose job it is to guard the embassy. The Stanfields are one of the richest families in this country. Their name alone opens doors that are forever closed to someone like that."

"Sorry if I gave you the impression the man was just a grunt stationed in front of the embassy with a rifle. He's part of the Cobra Force. They're responsible for anti-terrorist activities abroad." He rolled his eyes, then smiled at her. "God only knows what they really do. Cobra Force activities are classified top secret."

The beat of silence following his statement warned her. "Okay, Matt. What aren't you telling me?"

"I have the classified CIA report on Logan McCord out in the clunker I rented. Why don't you read it?" He checked his watch. "I've got to get back to the airport. I have a jet standing by to fly me to Dallas for a meeting. I'll give you my cell phone number."

"Save me some time. Tell me what the top-secret report says."

He turned his head slightly and gave her the half-smile she remembered so well. She couldn't help wondering what would have happened between them if Daniel hadn't come into her life. Then died so tragically.

"Kelly, the file indicates Logan has a psychological disorder. I'm not going to be surprised if the Stanfields want to distance themselves from him. The senator may be retiring, but he's still on everyone's short list to run for president. With Tyler Stanfield running for his father's senate seat, I don't think they want anyone looking into Logan's work with the Cobra Force."

"You're saying Logan was involved in one of those controversial government projects or something?"

"Absolutely." Without warning his hand closed over her right shoulder. "The military breeds certain men—like Logan McCord—who are nothing more than trained killers."

Chapter 2

Kelly sat in the den of the ranch where she'd grown up, reading the file on the disappearance of Logan Stanfield that she had dug out of the newspaper's basement after Matthew had left. Last year when she had returned home to be with Pop, Kelly had moved into one of the guest houses on the property. She wanted to be near her grandfather, but allow both of them privacy. She often worked in the large den that was lined with books and family photographs rather than stay alone in the two-room *casita* where she slept.

There was something comforting about the room where she had done her homework in front of the river rock fireplace on cool winter evenings. Pop would be in his favorite chair, the old leather recliner, reading stories that had come over the UPI earlier in the day. When she was here, it was as if time had stood still and she was just a young girl again.

But time stood still for no man, she reminded herself as she gazed out the window into the darkness. She was grown now, and it was her responsibility to take care of Pop. Not that she minded. Even if her career hadn't just taken a nosedive when she had learned about Pop's heart attack, she would have returned home to be with him.

"Jasper, I wonder what Pop will think about Logan reappearing?" she asked the young golden retriever who was at her feet.

The dog cocked his head as if he really understood, and Kelly stroked his sleek ears. When Kelly had gone away to college and Pop had been left alone, he'd become active with Guide Dogs of America. He'd taken in a series of puppies and kept them until they were fifteen months old, getting them ready to train as guide dogs.

Pop had needed something to fill his life, Kelly reflected. He'd been a widower accustomed to living alone when Kelly's parents had been killed. Suddenly, he found himself cast in the role of being both mother and father to a young girl.

He'd done remarkably well. This room, this house, had been filled with love and laughter. If her own parents had lived, Kelly doubted they could have done a better job. She hardly remembered them now, recalling little more than vague images. Without the family photograph album, she would never have recognized their faces.

"What did Logan McCord feel when he heard the news?" she asked the dog. "Did he remember the Stanfields?"

Jasper licked her hand in response as Kelly stared at the grainy copy of Logan McCord's passport photograph that had been in the top secret file Matt had given her. The only known photograph of Logan McCord revealed a scowling man with close-set eyes and buzz cut that made it impossible to tell the exact color of his hair, but it appeared to be brown.

"Logan speaks three languages fluently, Spanish, Portuguese, and French."

Kelly spoke out loud, knowing how important it was for guide dogs to be accustomed to people talking to them. Relationships between guide dogs and their owners were exceptionally close. To that person the dog was not just a dog, it was a lifeline in a dark world. Jasper put his muzzle on Kelly's knee, listening to every word.

"His personality profile is interesting. His IQ is off the charts. But the word loner is written in caps. The psychologist scribbled 'Haas Factor' in the margin. Matthew thinks its a psychological disorder akin to a death wish," Kelly rattled on, patting the dog. "I'm going to check with a psychologist."

She gazed down at the dozen or more photographs of the little boy the newspaper had used while covering Logan Stanfield's disappearance. He had been an adorable child with blond hair and blue eyes, yet he had grown up to be a very homely man.

"It could be this terrible picture. Heaven knows my passport photo is downright scary," she told Jasper, and the retriever wagged his tail sympathetically. "I'm going to need several current photographs of him for the *Exposé* article.

Kelly could almost hear Pop huffing with disgust and railing about how journalism had become nothing more than mindless images without underlying substance. He had a point, but people adored *Exposé* and had made it the nation's foremost newsmagazine.

"All I have to do is find Logan. I'll snap a few pictures myself."

Kelly concentrated on the photographs used when Logan had disappeared. She was struck by how young and handsome Haywood Stanfield had looked that first year he'd been in the United States Senate. His rich chestnut hair was gray now, but still thick, and his eyes were just as blue, just as compelling.

Haywood Stanfield had a certain bearing, a way about him that someone is either born with or will never possess, she decided, gazing at the photograph of the senator and his wife, Ginger, with their newly adopted son. Logan's light hair and blue eyes reminded Kelly of Ginger and the twins, Tyler and Alyx. Tyler and his strikingly beautiful sister, Alyx had inherited their mother's cool Nordic blond looks.

Kelly preferred "Woody" Stanfield's more masculine appearance. She held up the shot of him with the newly adopted child. The angular planes of the senator's face were enhanced by a square jaw and a nose some might consider too long. But his warm smile tempered his sharper features.

The smile that had won him thousands of votes was highlighted by two unusual dimples. They didn't appear in the center of his cheeks the way most dimples did, instead his smile caused indentations high on cheekbones just beneath the outer corner of his eyes. Time had weathered Woody's face and the dimples were now almost lost among the skein of lines around his eyes.

Still, he was a very handsome, charming man. Pop might berate Haywood Stanfield for his ultra-conservative politics, but people adored him. Even with Ginger's drinking and emotional problems, the man might become the next president.

"Stranger things have happened," Kelly said, but Jasper was now napping at her feet.

From the kitchen beyond the den, Kelly heard the back door open, and Uma Begay came in as she always did before long before dawn to begin cooking. Uma had been Pop's house-keeper since he'd unexpectedly found himself with a young girl to raise. She was part Hopi but mostly Navajo, born to the Falling Rock Clan, for the River Bend People. Begay was a common name like Smith or Jones, and Uma was related to most of the Native Americans in the area either through her Hopi lineage or her Navajo clan connections.

"Yaa' eh t'eeh," Kelly greeted Uma in Navajo.

"Yaa' eh t'eeh," Uma flounced into the kitchen, wearing a traditional dark blue velvet blouse with hand-tooled silver buttons and a pale blue skirt that brushed the beaded tops of her squaw boots. Her glossy black hair had turned a rich shade of pewter over the years, but she still wore it the Navajo way, tied in a sleek bun at the nape of her neck.

Uma was putting on a plaid apron when Kelly came in with Jasper at her heels. It was the Navajo tradition to exchange stories about everyone they knew. It was hard for Kelly to believe Logan's reappearance could have been kept quiet this long since so many Native Americans worked at the Stanfield estate.

"Is there anything interesting going on at the Stanfields?" Kelly asked.

"Get real! Tyler Stanfield is fixing to run for the senate. He's holed up with Benson Williams writing campaign speeches. That's about all that is happening out there."

Kelly banked a smile. Uma was such a kick. She practiced centuries-old Navajo rituals, yet each day she watched soap

operas on the small TV in the kitchen, patterning her speech
after hip Hollywood types.

Where was Logan Stanfield? After Matt had left, Kelly had
called every hotel in town. Logan wasn't registered anywhere,
so she assumed he must be staying with the Stanfields.

"Uma, do me a favor. Call your cousin, Jim Cree. Ask him
if he's seen any strangers at all."

Jim Cree was quite elderly now, but an expert horseman
who was in charge of the Stanfields' prize-winning Arabians.
He was also a *yataalii*—a shaman. According to the files Kelly
had been reading about Logan's disappearance, Jim Cree had
been working at the ranch back then. A very desperate Haywood
Stanfield had asked the shaman to help locate his missing son.

Shamans prided themselves on their ability to locate things
that had been lost. For weeks, Jim Cree had tried in vain to
find the child. If anyone would be acutely aware of his return,
it would be the *yataalii*.

"I'll ask Jim if he's met any strangers," Uma responded.

It took a second for Kelly to realize there was an odd note
in Uma's voice. Navajos rarely lied; it was against everything
they were taught since they could bounce on their mother's
knee. They skirted outright lies by not including every detail.

"Uma, did Jim report anything or anyone unusual anywhere
around the estate?" The broadness of the question was deliberately designed to flush out the entire story.

The older woman concentrated on breaking an egg in half
and pouring the egg into a small bowl to be used later. Like
many Navajos, she scoffed at measuring-spoons, using half an
eggshell instead, the way her ancestors had.

"Uma?" Kelly prompted, positive she was onto something.

"Jim saw someone out at the old hogan near Sand Creek."

Kelly had often ridden horses out to Sand Creek when she'd
been younger. She pictured the abandoned round stone structure
with its domed earth roof and the pole corral behind it. Why
would Logan McCord be out where there was no electricity
and the only water came from a rusty windmill?

"What did Jim see at the hogan?" Kelly asked.

Uma hesitated, looked around, then lowered her voice. "A skinwalker."

"A witch?" Kelly couldn't keep the disappointment out of her voice. No wonder Uma had been evasive. Pop had encouraged Kelly to learn about the positive aspects of Navajo culture. They set high standards for personal conduct and valued family above all else.

Living their lives with honor and in harmony—*hozro*—with the world around them was important. Respect for nature and the environment were cornerstones of their beliefs. But the flip side was a world ruled by the unexplainable and that meant the supernatural. Years ago, Pop had forbidden Uma to discuss witches with Kelly.

Despite Pop's unwillingness to embrace the darker elements of Navajo culture, Kelly had managed to wheedle the Native American superstitions out of Uma when Pop wasn't around. Skinwalkers or witches dominated the dark side of life. A person became a witch by violating a sacred tribal taboo like incest or murder. Once a person had "crossed over" to the nether world, the skinwalker could take any shape. He might be a man one day, an eagle the next.

Or become invisible.

Uma turned her back to Kelly. "The skinwalker is staying in the hogan."

Ten minutes later, Kelly was driving Pop's Jeep across town to Sand Creek. "A skinwalker isn't out there," she told herself. "It's a gulcher."

Sedona, the elite haven for artists and their wealthy patrons, refused to acknowledge a problem with the homeless. Even so, drifters were drawn by the magnificent vistas and the temperate climate. They lived in the numerous gulches and ravines in the area. Locals called them "gulchers" and pretended they didn't exist.

It seemed highly unlikely that Logan McCord would be out at the remote hogan. In a few hours it would be light. She could wait until then, but her reporter's instincts told her to check out every lead now before the trail went cold again. She had her camera with her . . . just in case.

The hills flanking the deserted road jutted upward, ebony and jagged, blocking the moonlight except for places where it glimmered through a break in the red rocks. At the fork in the road stood a crumbling adobe church, a one-room structure dating back to pioneer days. Kelly turned left onto the single lane.

The dirt road was narrower and more rutted than she had expected. Few people traveled this way; there were no homes for miles. It was a vast track of national parkland. Her headlights cut through the darkness, revealing a sharp turn. She braked hard, sending a hail of loose gravel against the fender.

What passed for a road ended a few miles later becoming nothing more than faint grooves in the hard-packed red earth. It was difficult to imagine anyone, even a gulcher, way out here.

But Jim Cree had seen someone.

Kelly glanced down at Pop's forty-five on the seat beside her. Years ago, he'd taught her how to handle a gun, and he insisted she practice behind the barn where he had a target area. Pop had designed the targets himself. They were coyotes with the bull's eye at the base of the neck, focusing attention on the area where the animal could be quickly killed.

Coyotes were the scourge of the area, numerous and brazen. Once Kelly had dispersed a pack of coyotes who were attacking her cat. She hadn't been able to save Muffy, but she had killed the leader.

Knowing she was a crack shot made Kelly feel more comfortable venturing out into the dead of night. True, the area was safe; crime, even petty crime, was rare in Sedona, but common sense insisted that she take precautions. She'd taken Pop's gun out of the secret compartment in the grandfather clock and loaded it herself.

She stepped on the brake and put the Jeep into park where the road ended at the pair of mammoth boulders known as the Two Squaws. Behind the rocks sculpted by the wind was Sand

Creek, a meandering stream that was dry most of the year, but it could be treacherous during monsoon season.

She switched off the headlights, tucked the large gun into the waistband of her jeans, and got out of the Jeep with a flashlight in her hand. She walked around the rocks, her tennis shoes sliding on the loose shale. In the distance, she saw the dome-shaped hogan that had never been occupied since Kelly had moved to Sedona.

It was eerily quiet. The wind came up at dawn, but this early not a whisper of a breeze stirred the branches of the cottonwoods along the creek or turned the ancient windmill that once provided water to the family who had built the hogan.

"This is just a wild-goose chase," she said out loud.

Feeling foolish, she took a deep breath. There was a purity to the air in the West, a clarity of sky that was never present in the city. The dazzling stars seemed closer, undiminished by bright city lights.

"Daniel," she murmured, recalling how much her late husband loved to gaze at the stars. "You're up there somewhere, aren't you, darling?"

Her vision blurred as the vise of sadness cinched around her heart. You could love someone so much it hurt. She thought time and moving out of New York would help. But it hadn't.

She missed Daniel more and more with each passing day. Every night she rolled over in bed, reaching for him.

Waking up alone.

She had always imagined them raising a family and growing old together. Now she had to face the rest of her life without the man she loved.

"Oh, Daniel, what am I going to do without you?"

A star twinkled at her, but it didn't have an answer. Be thankful for the time you had with someone you dearly loved, she thought. Be grateful not sad.

She blinked back the tears and started toward the hogan, her flashlight trained on the ground. It was the time of year the Navajos called "the season when snakes sleep," but the fall nights were still warm enough for snakes to hunt kangaroo rats.

The hogan was in worse condition than she had remembered.

The round building had been built out of *adobe,* mud bricks. The large chinks between the *adobe* had been filled with a mixture of mud and straw. Most of the mud had worn away, leaving wisps of straw sticking out.

Behind the hogan was a pole corral with a rusty water trough fed by a windmill that had tipped to one side since the last time Kelly had ridden past here. How long ago had that been? Kelly decided it must have been five years ago, the summer before she met and married Daniel Taylor.

The bleak, aching loneliness that seemed to be her constant companion swept over her again. She opened her eyes wide to keep back the tears. Another star winked in the sky brightening with the light of a new day. She liked to think of the twinkling stars as those she loved signaling to her from heaven.

It was childish, she knew, but it went back to the days when her parents had suddenly been taken from her. Pop insisted they were in heaven, like the stars above, watching over her. She smiled in spite of the emptiness welling up inside her. It was comforting to think of Daniel and her parents being together. In a way she was jealous she'd been left behind.

"Oh, stop feeling sorry for yourself."

She turned to leave without looking into the hogan or calling out. There was no car or bike or anything to indicate anyone was inhabiting this godforsaken spot. It was utterly stupid to be standing out here with a huge gun in her waistband, waving her flashlight. She should be home; Pop would be getting up soon and they could have breakfast together.

"Time is running out," she whispered. "One day Pop will be a twinkling star who can't talk to you."

She took two steps, then sniffed, inhaling deeply. In the cool, still air, she detected a smell, faint but distinct. Smoke. She turned toward the hogan again, thinking about the firepit in the center and the smoke hole directly above it. The nights were still too warm to build a fire in the hogan.

With a broad sweep of her arm, she flashed the light around the area, checking for a campfire. Not far from the windmill, she spotted a neat circle of stones.

Someone had been here! When?

She walked softly up to the campfire, curious. Most gulchers scavenged in trash cans outside Sedona's upscale restaurants. A logical explanation came to mind. Some hunter had probably shot one of the hordes of jackrabbits that lived out here, then cooked it.

She knelt down by the campfire, noticing it was still slightly warm. The beam of light caught something on a flat rock nearby. She trained the flashlight on it.

"Yuck!" she cried, surging to her feet.

Someone had skinned a large lizard, then roasted the meat. The remnants of the food she'd eaten at the Arts Council gala roiled in her stomach. What kind of person ate a lizard?

The fine hairs across the back of her neck stood at attention. She whirled around, splashing light across deserted area. Nothing. If the lizard eater was still around, which didn't seem likely, he must be inside the hogan.

"What should I do?" She put her hand on the butt of the pistol in her waistband, noticing her fingers were trembling. Going into the hogan, even with the gun drawn, was pure stupidity. Her only choice was to wait for the sun to rise and see if anyone came out of the hogan.

She turned to inspect the lizard. It had been skinned smoothly and cleanly; the pool of drying blood and entrails beside the rock indicated the person had taken care to drain the body fluids and gut the lizard properly before roasting it.

Could it be Logan McCord? What was he doing all alone out here, eating lizards?

"Suppose it is Logan," she whispered to herself. She desperately needed several good photographs of him. She hadn't lugged her camera from the Jeep because she really hadn't expected to find anyone. Before the sun rose, she should return to the car and get her camera.

As she turned, something slammed into her back. The air whooshed out of her lungs with a startled gasp, and she dropped the flashlight. The gun was yanked out of her jeans. The cold blade of a knife was at her throat, the sharp point pricking the skin just under her earlobe. The hot trickle of her own blood on her neck made her knees buckle with fear.

"You're as good as dead!"

The man's deep growl unnerved her even more, but she hadn't lived in New York without taking a self-defense course. She rammed her elbow backward into a rock-hard gut. A rough hand grabbed her throat in a death grip.

The last thing she saw was exploding stars behind her closed eyelids, then the dark velvet embrace of the night.

Chapter 3

Kelly's tongue swept over sandy particles of grit, tasting the dirt coating her lips. It took a second for her to realize she was facedown on hard-packed earth. She squinted, eyes straining and saw a patch of gray light overhead.

She had to be inside the hogan, seeing dawn's light through the smoke hole. In a dizzying rush images came back to her. The deserted hogan. The skinned lizard. The knife at her throat. With trembling fingers she checked and found nothing more than a small scratch. Beneath her ear a sticky scab was already forming.

She hadn't fainted from such a tiny cut, had she? Of course not. He'd choked her . . . or something.

She levered herself up on her elbows, praying he'd gone, but knowing she couldn't be so lucky. If he'd taken off, he wouldn't have carried her into the hogan and dumped her facedown. Was the man Logan Stanfield or just some lunatic?

Or was there a difference?

"I could have slit your throat back there."

The masculine whisper cut through the darkness with a rasp to it like the blade of a rusty knife. Why do people always whisper in the dark? The irrational thought came to her as she turned to face him, every nerve tingling, her pulse throbbing in her ears. As she sat up, a blast of light hit her in the eyes, a light too intense to be an ordinary flashlight.

All she could make out was a large shadowy figure sitting near her holding a deadly knife. The backwash of light revealed powerful hands with blunt fingers and clean, close-clipped nails. The dusting of hair on the back of his hands was dark. He wore no rings, but she noticed an unusual watch on his wrist. It had several smaller dials on the face and glowed in the darkness.

"Why did you drag me in here?"

"I want to know who sent you." His voice was rough as if he were recovering from a bad case of laryngitis.

"No one sent me," she assured him, struggling to keep her tone calm.

He was silent for a long moment, and she wondered what he was thinking. All she could see beyond the blinding glare of the light was the blade of the knife with a ruby red droplet of her blood drying on the gleaming steel.

And the unusual watch with all the dials.

Off to the side, just visible beyond the circle of light was the pistol he'd taken from her. She told herself not to look at it and let him know she'd spotted Pop's gun.

"You are Logan Stanfield, aren't you? I want to interview you for an article for the local paper."

"The local paper?" he repeated in his rough voice as he turned the beam of the flashlight against the hogan's wall.

In one swift movement, he was on his knees beside her. A large hand cupped her chin, and she had the craziest notion that he was going to kiss her . . . or something. This was hardly a romantic encounter. Kissing was out of the question. If anything, he intended to rape her.

"You're lying," he said, his fingers tightening his grip on her chin.

"No, I'm not." She shook her head in a futile attempt to get him to let go. "Your disappearance was big news around here. Your return will be even bigger. People will want to know just where Logan Stanfield has been all these years . . . and who kidnapped him."

His hand slowly slid down her throat, and she nearly panicked, thinking he was about to strangle her. An unsettling silence filled the small hogan. All she could hear was her own labored breathing. She expected the hand circling her throat to tighten and choke the life out of her, but it didn't.

Finally, he spoke. "I never said I was Logan Stanfield."

His voice was hoarse and barely more than a whisper, but the lethal undertone to his words dared her to contradict him.

"What are you doing way out here, packing a gun?" he asked, his warm breath fanning her cheek.

"This place is in the middle of nowhere. I brought the gun for protection. That's all."

He let go of her neck, but in a heartbeat the blade of the knife was at her jugular. "Stop lying! Tell me who sent you."

She didn't dare tremble for fear she might slit her own throat on the razor-sharp blade. She slowly scooted backward so the knife was no longer pressing against her skin. She was breathing far too loudly, making her furious, *furious* with herself because he was so calm and so in control of himself that the beam of light never wavered, the shadow behind it never moved.

"I wasn't sent exactly . . ." She kept her eyes trained on the blinding light, but out of the corner of her eye, she saw Pop's gun. If only she could divert him for a moment and grab the gun.

"I wasn't sent exactly," she repeated, inching sideways closer to the gun. "Jim Cree, he's in charge of the Stanfields' Arabians, you know. Well, he told his third cousin. I mean . . . I think Uma is his third or perhaps fourth cousin." She knew she sounded like a ditz, hoping it would distract him enough to give her the split second she needed to get the gun. "There are sixty-odd Navajo clans and many of them are related, producing a galaxy of cousins. It's—"

"Cut the crap. Who sent you?"

"Ah . . . Matthew Jensen sent me."

She could almost hear the wheels of his brain turning as he tried to make sense of what she'd told him. As well known as Matt was in publishing circles, the average person wouldn't recognize the name. Taking advantage of his confusion, she lunged for the gun.

She grabbed it and spun around toward him. He switched on the blinding flashlight. She stared directly at it. For one insane moment she wished she knew what he looked like before she shot him. The dark shadow behind the light said he was a very large, tall man, but didn't give a clue about the color of his hair or his eyes.

"Drop the knife! Now!"

"You haven't the guts to pull the trigger." He didn't sound the least bit fazed by having a gun aiming point blank at him.

"Don't bet on it." She firmly believed she could shoot in self-defense, but did this man pose the kind of threat that justified killing him? What if he really were Logan Stanfield? How could she shoot a child who had been kidnapped no matter what type of man he'd become?

She opted to bluff, wiggling her hand as though she were terribly nervous, but training the gun to the side so she wouldn't hit him. She slowly pulled back the hammer, giving him time to throw down the knife, but he refused to budge. She pulled the trigger, bracing herself for the powerful recoil, thankful she was still sitting down.

Click! The hammer snapped down on the empty chamber with a sharp metallic sound. She frantically squeezed the trigger again and again—click—click—which made no sense. She had loaded the gun herself. On the third click, the light dawned. He'd tricked her, removing the bullets, then deliberately putting the gun where she could get it.

"You have two seconds to tell me the truth, or I'll cut your heart out."

She truly believed this maniac *would* kill her if she didn't tell him what he wanted to know. Squinting against the glare of the light, she said, "I am with the local paper, but *Exposé* magazine hired me to do a feature article for them. A secret source told them you had applied for a higher level security clearance and the updated check revealed your fingerprints matched those of Logan Stanfield."

The flashlight snapped off and there was a flurry of activity in the hogan. It took a moment for her eyes to recover from the harsh light followed by darkness. The gray light seeping in from the smoke hole overhead helped, and she blinked rapidly, not quite believing what her adjusting vision was telling her.

The dangerous man had vanished. She was alone in the hogan. Her sigh of relief bounced off the adobe walls, and she hugged herself for a moment, not knowing if she should be thankful to escape a killer or curse about losing her chance to interview him.

She spotted Pop's gun, its barrel jammed into a chink in the wall. Even though it was useless without bullets, she scuttled across toward it on all fours. She vaulted to her feet, intending to grab the gun.

That's when she realized the creep had taken her shoes.

Kelly slipped into her grandfather's home, easing the heavy plank Pueblo-style door closed behind her. Through the archway between the back patio and kitchen, Kelly watched the housekeeper take out her silver vial of pollen from her purse. Uma tapped a pinch into the palm of her hand, then blew it into the air. Closing her eyes, the older woman chanted a prayer in Navajo.

The morning blessing. It was the Navajo habit to rise before dawn and welcome the first rays of the new day with the traditional prayer and sacred pollen just as Father Sky blessed Mother Earth with sunshine.

"Kelly?" Pop's voice took her by surprise. She looked into the dining alcove next to the kitchen and saw he was already up and dressed, a cup of coffee in his hand. "What happened to your shoes?"

She stared down at her once-white socks. They were now red from the rust-colored dust along the rocky trail. Ignoring her tender feet, she walked over to the table where he was sitting and dropped into a chair. Slowly and carefully she explained what had happened out at the hogan.

"Do you think the man was Logan Stanfield?" Pop asked.

"I couldn't see his face," Kelly replied, "but when I mentioned *Exposé* and a secret source, the man took off. I'll bet it was Logan, and he doesn't want to be found. The question is why?"

Her grandfather touched the spot on her neck where she had been nicked by the knife, lifting broad yet bony shoulders against the fabric of his shirt. She realized once again how frail he had become. His hair was totally white now, a sharp contrast to the dark eyebrows framing his light brown eyes.

The doctor's prognosis was excellent. Pop just needed to rebuild his strength. She hoped consulting him about this case would rekindle his interest in the newspaper he'd published for almost fifty years.

"I don't know why Logan Stanfield doesn't want to be found." Pop buttered a tortilla as he spoke. "I think he's got a screw loose, threatening you like that. He better not let me get my hands on him."

Kelly could help smiling at the concern in Pop's voice. He loved her so much.

She reached down and petted Jasper, thinking that Pop's illness had nearly sapped his will to live. Even having a new puppy to train hadn't helped. Kelly decided fate had brought her home for a good reason. Until she returned, she hadn't realized how much Pop needed her.

True, this article for *Exposé* would certainly help restore her reputation as a journalist, but she wasn't going back to New York and leave Pop again. She would continue to run the newspaper and write freelance articles when she could.

"Eat your eggs," Pop interrupted her thoughts. "That's what you're always telling me."

She took a forkful of the scrambled eggs laced with mild Chimayo chiles that Uma had freshly diced. "I don't think Logan Stanfield ever intended to seriously hurt me," she said, but Pop shook his head and frowned. "He believed I meant to kill him. Even so, he's a strange man." Inwardly she shuddered, thinking about the lizard.

"Everything about him was strange—right from the beginning."

"Really? Tell me more. If I don't want someone to steal my scoop, I'm going to have to write an article fast and I need an angle. Heaven knows, I'm not going to get a current photograph of the man, or be able to interview him."

"Call it reporter's intuition, but I detected something was wrong from the moment Ginger and Haywood Stanfield adopted that child," Pop began. "Why take a year-old child instead of a baby? They already had a boy and a girl. The twins were already ten years old when they adopted Logan."

"Maybe they'd been trying to have more children," Kelly responded, thinking about handsome Tyler Stanfield and his beautiful sister, Alyx. Who wouldn't want more children like that?

"Bull-pucky!" Pop waved his hand as if swatting a fly. "Ginger has always been obsessed with her appearance. She tolerated the twins, but Luz Tallchief, the nanny raised them. Ginger refused to ruin her figure with another child. It had to have been Woody Stanfield's idea."

"Maybe," she conceded. After all, Pop knew the family much better than she did. He'd been challenging Haywood Stanfield's political decisions for years.

"From the start, Logan was a problem child who always got into scrapes that landed him in the emergency room."

Kelly imagined the cold, calculating man behind the beam of the powerful flashlight. A sense of ruthlessness and unleashed power had emanated from the dark shadow. She could easily imagine what a difficult, problem child he must have been.

"Logan's disappearance seemed odd to me," Pop said. "He went out riding on his pony with the twins even though Luz Tallchief told him not to leave the house."

"A little brat who wouldn't listen. Since the twins were ten years older, going with them must have been quite a lure, so he disobeyed his nanny. He was five and they were almost fifteen. To him they were adults, right?"

"Probably," Pop conceded. "But the twins were too young to handle a crisis. When Logan fell into the ravine, the twins rode off to get help. They returned to the estate and found Ginger was asleep."

"Are you politely saying she had passed out?" Kelly asked. Ginger Stanfield's long battle with alcohol and drugs was common knowledge. Kelly could just imagine two frightened teenagers returning home for help only to find their mother was incapable of comprehending the situation.

Pop reached down and petted Jasper, and the dog stared up at him with soulful brown eyes. "No one ever admitted Ginger was drunk, but the twins lost time waiting for her to wake up. Luz Tallchief found them sitting outside their mother's room. The nanny was the one who summoned the stable hands to search for the child. The twins led them to the spot where they thought Logan had tumbled into the ravine. There wasn't any sign of the boy."

Kelly struggled to imagine herself at fifteen and wondered how she would have handled the situation. "In the late afternoon, shadows become longer in minutes, they might have mistaken the ravine for one of a dozen others."

"True." Pop slowly nodded. "But when they returned to the ranch, Ginger was awake, yet she failed to call the Coconino Sheriff. Instead, she asked—"

"Don't tell me. Ginger ran to Benson Williams."

The look in Pop's eyes told Kelly the answer. During Haywood Stanfield's first senate campaign, Benson Williams had moved in with the family—and stayed. Before the term "spin doctor" had been invented, Benson had mastered the art.

"Right," Pop confirmed. "Ginger called Benson and he insisted the stable hands conduct another search before contacting the sheriff."

"Stupid," Kelly said. "Delaying gave the person who found Logan extra time to get away."

She pondered the situation for a minute, imagining the hordes of visitors who made pilgrimages to the vortexes. Scientists explained the phenomenon as electro-magnetic energy springs. Many people, especially New Age types, believed that by visiting certain rock formations they could absorb the cosmic energy emitted from the earth. Such energy could induce a number of miracles from curing cancer to putting you in touch with the dead.

Kelly had lived in Sedona long enough to know most of the vortex stories were exaggerated, but she'd been so despondent after Daniel's death that she had visited the vortex the Native Americans believed was sacred. They called the huge monolithic rock Changing Woman. Kelly had to admit there was a certain ambiance around the vortex—a sense of inner peace—that could not be explained.

But Daniel Taylor's spirit had not spoken to her. He was lost to her forever. All she had was memories to sustain her until she joined him.

"The boy disappeared around three," Pop said, cutting into her thoughts, "yet it wasn't until nine o'clock when Benson Williams reached Haywood Stanfield in Phoenix at a fund raiser. Woody told him to call the authorities."

"Six hours. That's a long time. By then the trail was cold, right?"

"Yes, it was dark. The Search and Rescue Team spent the night searching the area, finding nothing."

"Weren't there any leads in the case?" Kelly asked, even though she had read and reread the file. She liked the excitement she heard in Pop's voice. It had been missing far too long.

"Sure, Logan was sighted more often than Elvis during the next few months, but none of the tips amounted to a thing. He'd vanished into thin air."

"From a ravine outside a small town in Arizona to the elite Cobra Force in South America. A quantum leap, wouldn't you say?"

Pop regarded her with his most serious expression. "Absolutely. Whatever happened to Logan Stanfield between then and now—that's your story."

"True, but without interviewing him, it'll be impossible unless I have a lot more time to ferret through the records and piece together his past."

"Doesn't his military file give you some place to start?"

"Not really. Logan claims he was never enrolled in school. His mother taught him at home, so I can't do that type of background story." She thought a moment and recalled the psychologist's notation. "In boot camp, the psychologist scribbled 'loner' in caps in his file, then he wrote in 'Haas Factor.' I need to find out more about what it means.''

"I've never heard of it." Pop pushed his plate aside, and Kelly noticed he had eaten more than he usually did. "But let me call Bernard Robinson, my old college roommate. Someone who taught psychology at Princeton should know."

While Pop went into the house to call, Kelly struggled to come up with an angle. She could interview the Stanfields to see how they felt about Logan's return, but she was reluctant to let them use her to hype Tyler Stanfield's senate campaign. She decided she had to write the story today. If she waited any longer, word would leak out and someone else would get the credit.

Jasper nuzzled her leg and Kelly smiled down at the gangly puppy with the soft gold fur.

"Here, boy." She slipped Jasper a little egg, wondering how she was going to give up the dog when it came time for formal training. Jasper reminded her of Peaches, the mutt Pop had brought home from the Humane Society just after Kelly had lost her parents and moved here. Peaches became a lonely little girl's best friend. The sweetie would sit under the table and eat the peas Kelly tossed to her when Pop wasn't looking.

"It's going to be tough to let you go," she told Jasper who was now licking her fingers. "But someone will be thrilled to have you be their eyes for them."

"This time you'll come to the graduation," Pop told her as he came out to the patio again. "When you see how thrilled people are to get dogs, you'll understand how I can keep a dog two years, then hand him over to a stranger."

"I'm looking forward to it," she assured him, feeling guilty for never having gone to previous graduations. She'd used her career and her personal life as an excuse, yet Pop had always been there for her. She should have made the time to attend the graduations of the dogs he'd trained.

"Bernie was really helpful." Pop's eyes glinted with excitement, a look she hadn't seen since the heart attack that almost killed him. "The Haas Factor is a term that's rarely used. It came from research done by Dr. Quentin Haas with survivors of concentration camps. Many of them lost their entire family. They often wondered: Why me? Why did I survive?''

"They feel guilty,'' she blurted out, immediately recognizing the feeling. ''You know, I experienced the same reaction. I had planned to go to Venezuela with Daniel, but I changed my mind at the last minute because I was working on a big story. I should have been with him when the plane went down.''

"No, honey,'' Pop said gently, touching her shoulder. "You should not have been on that plane.'' He remained silent for a moment, then continued, ''The Haas Factor isn't really about guilt, although that is one component of it. The risk aspect is more prevalent. Apparently people with the Haas Factor are willing to put themselves at risk over and over and over in a way that indicates compulsive behavior.''

"What drives these people to keep taking such risks?''

Her grandfather shrugged. ''Bernie says they believe they've lived through the worst life has to offer and are no longer afraid. It can be very positive. Many concentration camp survivors went on to become very successful businessmen. They were willing to roll the dice, taking business risks that paid off.''

Kelly stroked Jasper's ears, thinking out loud. ''I'll bet there's also an element of danger and excitement that someone tries to recapture. It's probably a subconscious thing, but I'll be surprised if that isn't true.''

Pop beamed his approval the way he always had when she said or did something clever. ''That's exactly what Bernie said. Members of certain high-risk professions like SWAT teams and pilots may also exhibit the Haas Factor.''

"Logan Stanfield is part of the Cobra Force. He's spent years in the line of fire doing anti-terrorist work. What happened that made him love danger?''

Chapter 4

Kelly spent the morning in her office struggling to write the article about Logan Stanfield. The Pentagon provides hometown addresses and the names of next of kin for members of the armed services on active duty. Logan Stanfield or Logan McCord was not listed. They did find a Logan McCord on a Marine Corps enlistment roster.

"He went directly from boot camp to Survival School," the information officer at the Pentagon told her when she called.

"Isn't that unusual? Wouldn't most recruits do a tour of duty before being sent to a special school?"

A beat of silence. "It happens."

His hesitation told her it was rare, but he wasn't going to admit this to a reporter. Another thought occurred to her. "Are the members of the Cobra Force listed in your database?"

Two beats of silence. "No. They're Marines, of course, but they go through SEAL training with the Navy, then they're sent through an anti-terrorist program run by the CIA. The Cobra Force reports directly to the CIA. They're in a top-secret database."

Previous experience told her it would be possible to get info from the CIA, but it would take secret sources. That meant time, something she didn't have if she planned to publish this story in next week's issue of *Exposé*. She didn't dare wait one more week to run the story in the following issue. By then some other reporter would get wind of the news and scoop her exclusive.

She tried getting background on the Cobra Force itself, but found little information available. An elite group of anti-terrorist experts, it consisted of less than thirty men. Releasing the men's names would have made them easy targets for the terrorists they were tracking, consequently no roster of their names was available.

The Cobra Force had been created to protect American embassies, but the rise in terrorism expanded their role. They had alerted 10 Downing shortly before the IRA launched a surface missile at the building. They had warned the Army that its barracks were too close to the guard station in Saudi Arabia. Regrettably, the Army hadn't listened, and many men had died needlessly.

"Start at the beginning," she said out loud, popping a coco-nut Jelly Belly into her mouth. She kept a small bowl of Jelly Bellies at her desk for stressful moments like this. For her guests, she had the full assortment of flavors, but she ate only white ones—coconut or piña colada. "Back to Logan's child-hood."

Logan McCord had listed Mapleton, California as his home address when he'd enlisted. According to the last census, the town boasted all of three thousand and twenty-seven people. It was roughly the same size as Sedona, big enough to have a newspaper and small enough for people to know each other's business.

She called the *Mapleton Tribune*. The editor-in-chief owned the paper, and he'd been publishing it for over thirty years. He sounded intelligent and friendly, reminding her of Pop. The man was positive that no one by the name of McCord had ever lived in the town.

When Logan had entered the service, he'd given his home address as a post office box on a rural route. An old codger at the post office informed her the box no longer existed. She asked if it had been there in 1983, the year Logan had enlisted.

"Yep," he proudly informed her. "I was delivering mail on that route myself back then."

He remembered the rusty trailer at the end of a weed choked lane. He believed the place was deserted. There was no name on the box, nor did the family receive any mail except junk mail marked "occupant."

"At least it's something to go on," she told herself as she hung up and selected another white Jelly Belly from the bowl she kept on her desk. "Whoever lived there must have had electricity or a telephone—the bare essentials."

Calls to the electric company and Pacific Telephone confirmed no McCords currently used their services in the Mapleton area. It took some persuading, but Kelly was able to convince both companies to check their records for 1983. No McCords were listed, which didn't surprise her. But she was astonished to discover neither company had ever provided services to that address.

By early afternoon, she was forced to call Matt Jensen on his cell phone. She explained she had too little to write even a one-page article.

"Keep on it," Matt said, disappointment evident in his tone. "I have to have it by tomorrow at midnight—at the very latest—if it's going to run in next week's edition."

"I understand," she said and hung up. This called for another Jelly Belly. She picked through the colorful candy and found another white one as she considered her options.

She had the rest of the day, then tomorrow morning she would have no choice but to contact Haywood Stanfield for a statement. Woody was Pop's archenemy. Her grandfather was devoted to preserving the environment and helping poor people get a chance, especially the Native Americans who lived in the area.

Woody favored development, expansion of tourism and programs that benefited the rich without doing much to help those less fortunate. It was a classic political tug-of-war. But Stanfield wasn't all bad. He'd risen in the senate and had served on several important committees, making a lot of intelligent decisions.

If she called, she doubted that she would be allowed to speak to Haywood. The smarmy Benson Williams lived at the estate, acting as the senator's political advisor and carefully monitoring the senator's exposure to the press. Williams would milk this story for all it was worth, spinning it to foster the career of Tyler Stanfield, the senator's son and fuel interest in Haywood's bid for the presidency.

A child's disappearance was every parent's nightmare, a tragedy that wrenched the hearts of people across America. She wanted to tell the real story, not hype the political fortunes of the Stanfields.

Pop poked his head into her office. He had Jasper at his side, wearing an orange vest with black letters: Guide Dog. "How's it going?"

"Terrible. It appears the McCords took great care to make certain no one discovered their secret. I can't find anything on the family."

"Have you tried locating the Marine psychologist who wrote the boot camp report on Logan?"

"That's next on my list."

"We're going to the bank, then the post office," Pop told her as she reached for the telephone, and he turned to leave.

"Tell Uma to expect me for dinner," she called after him.

This time, luck was with her. Dr. Max Sobell was still with the Marines, stationed at Camp Pendleton. She called there, but he was in a meeting and would have to call her back.

"I might as well select the photographs to submit with the article," Kelly said under her breath.

She spread the various photographs the paper had run of little Logan. The choice was easy. She selected the shot of Haywood Stanfield holding the beautiful child with a smiling Ginger at his side. The perfect American family.

It gave Kelly an idea. She carefully tore the photograph, ripping the child out of his father's arms. **A FAMILY TORN APART WHEN THEIR CHILD VANISHES.**

She propped up the only picture she had of the man Logan

Stanfield had become against her computer terminal, studying his sullen expression.

What had happened during those missing years?

"Awesome, like, totally awesome." Cindi Mertz, the receptionist/classified advertising person barged into Kelly's office as she usually did without knocking. The girl was bright, just out of college, but her vocabulary seemed to be limited to "coo-wull" and "aaah-some."

"A friend of yours is here to see you, and he's, like, awesome."

"Send him in," Kelly responded, knowing Cindi considered anything in pants "awesome." It was probably someone Kelly had known in high school. Old friends had a way of dropping in when they needed her to run special articles for the Little League or wanted her to give them a discount on an advertisement.

She glanced at her desk clock and saw that it was almost five. Never stand between the door and Cindi Mertz when the clock struck five. The two part-time reporters had already left. Kelly should leave soon, too, since she'd promised to join Pop for dinner, but she didn't want to miss Dr. Sobell's call.

"Hello," Kelly said as a tall, powerfully built man walked into her office.

He responded with a nod and a slow, easy smile that was slightly off-kilter, canting intriguingly to one side. But this minor defect only added to its engaging appeal.

He seemed very familiar, but she didn't remember his name.

She knew this man, she decided, as he slung a large military-style backpack off his massive shoulders and casually dropped it on the floor. She kept her eyes on his face, but used her reporter's training to note other details.

His jeans were years old, his Reeboks brand new. His periwinkle blue polo shirt had to be XXL. The University of Arizona baseball cap with WILDCATS in bold letters partially hid what appeared to be chestnut brown hair. Mirrored aviator-style sunglasses reflected her own distorted image back at her, concealing the upper portion of his face and making it impossible for her to see the color of his eyes. She noticed he had a tan, which indicated he spent time outdoors.

The longer she looked at him, the more convinced she became that she knew the man, but she couldn't quite place him. She hoped he would say something, so she wouldn't embarrass herself by asking his name. The moment lengthened as she continued gazing at him, and she was just about to admit she couldn't recall his name when the phone on her desk rang.

She motioned for him to sit at one of the two chairs opposite her desk as she picked up the telephone, praying this was Dr. Sobell. It was the psychologist, but as he identified himself, she looked at the stranger opposite her desk. The man pulled the chair to the side, angling it just slightly, and it occurred to her that he might overhear this conversation and repeat it.

"I'm editor-in-chief at the *Sedona Sun*," she told Dr. Sobell, carefully choosing her words. She picked up a pencil, pretending to be ready to take notes, but kept her eye on the stranger, annoyed with herself because she couldn't place him. "I'm doing an article about rare psychological conditions."

"How may I help?" he asked, but he didn't sound really interested, and she imagined a career Marine psychologist settled into his job, evaluating new recruits, a dead-end career.

"I'm counting on you having a good memory," she said, conscious of the stranger watching every move she made. It made her wish she'd taken more time brushing her hair or had bothered with mascara.

"I'm a Life Master in bridge," the doctor said.

She immediately knew he had an excellent memory. "I'm referring to a psychological profile you did on a recruit in 1983. Do you remember where you were stationed then?"

"Sure. That was my first year in the corps. I remember it well. All that year we selected special recruits for survival school."

Perfect, she thought. This man would remember Logan, and now she knew why he had gone to survival school without doing a normal tour of duty. She phrased her next question carefully. Logan wasn't a common name. If she used it the man across from her might recognize it.

The stranger helped himself to a purple Jelly Belly, placing it between his crooked forefinger and thumb. He fired the Jelly Belly backward and it zinged through his barely parted teeth. A perfect shot.

"Do you remember a recruit named McCord?" she asked, distracted by the man opposite her. Despite his casualness, his body was tensile, reminding her of a cocked gun. "You recommended him for the survival school."

"No," the doctor shot back. "I don't remember him. It was a long time ago."

"Really?" she couldn't help sounding incredulous. "You recommended McCord for survival school."

"Like I said. It was a long time ago."

Obviously, the man had been warned not to discuss Logan with reporters. "You wrote Haas Factor on his file. Does that help?"

"No, not at all. I'm doing sexual harassment counseling now. I don't remember much about Haas Factor indicators."

The stranger fired another Jelly Belly with equal precision. He caught it effortlessly on the tip of his tongue, showed it to her as if it were a precious gem, then sucked it into his mouth.

"I'm sorry, but I can't remember more," the doctor said.

She started to press him even though she knew it would be useless, then something about the stranger clicked. She thanked the doctor for his help even though he'd been worthless, staring at the forearms of the man opposite her. He had them stretched over his powerful torso, an unusual watch with several dials on the face gleaming at her.

She almost gasped, remembering last night. Then anger charged with exhilaration swept through her. "You're Logan Stanfield."

"McCord. Logan McCord."

The fine hairs across the back of her neck prickled. His voice. A distinct rasp like a blues singer in a smoky nightclub. The threatening voice from last night.

Without obviously looking at the clock, she saw it was almost five-thirty. Cindi was gone. She was all alone with the nut who'd promised to cut out her heart if she didn't tell him the truth.

He smiled, obviously detecting her wariness. Again, the smile seemed familiar, which was impossible. All she'd seen of this man was a huge shadow and his forearms with the unusual watch.

She had never seen his face. How could his smile seem so . . . familiar?

"What are you doing here?"

He reached over and unzipped the backpack beside his chair. She told herself she wasn't frightened, and this was her golden opportunity to interview him. But her heart was slamming against the wall of her chest, making so much noise she was positive he could hear it.

He pulled her Reeboks out of his pack and set them on her desk. "Thought you might want your shoes back."

Again the phenomenal smile. He swung long, lean legs across the chair beside him, making himself at home.

She stared hard at him, refusing to smile back. He'd scared the life out of her, threatening her with a knife and knocking her unconscious. Did he seriously believe a sensational smile would smooth things over?

"About last night—"

"Do you always try to kill people who want to talk to you?" she asked, anger punctuating each syllable.

He fished around in the candy bowl until he came up with a purple Jelly Belly. This time he fired it backward in a high arc and caught it between his lips, then chewed it. "Nope. I haven't killed any women that I know about . . . yet."

He swung his legs to the floor and leaned forward, angling himself across her desk before she could scoot back. He touched the small scab below her ear, brushing it with the pad of his thumb. Her neck tingled and she felt the hot rush of blood to her face.

He was much larger close up, a body honed by years in the military, enhancing a superb build. He had a clean woodsy smell, and she noticed he had recently shaven what must be a heavy, fast-growing beard.

"Not too bad," he said, his fingertips, trailing across her neck for just a second too long. The back of his hand brushed her chin, causing an annoying flutter in her chest.

"You might say you're sorry," she said, irritated at the catch in her voice.

"Why lie?"

He treated her to another adorable smile, and she realized he was a very dangerous man. A trained killer who could take charm to the level of an art form. At will.

"You came after me with a gun. What was I supposed to do? Kiss you?"

There was a teasing, flirtatious tone to his voice. He was trying to make a joke out of the situation, yet there was a sensuous undertone that warned her this was the kind of man who would have his hand under her skirt in a second if she gave him the least encouragement. What a jerk!

"How did you make me blackout?"

"I used an *aikido* hold," he explained with the half-smile that seemed to constantly play across his lips. "That's a martial art like karate, but less brutal. I can easily subdue someone without hurting them."

"I see," she said, her voice conveying just the opposite.

She silently conceded that he hadn't overreacted at all. He had seen her gun and believed his life was in danger. He could easily have killed her, but he hadn't. He'd tricked her into going for the gun, and he'd taken her shoes, knowing he would be long gone before she made it up the rocky trail to her car. He was smart and clever, but she wasn't giving him the satisfaction of saying so.

"When I realized what a flake you were, grabbing the gun the way you did, I knew you wouldn't harm me."

She bristled inwardly at "flake," but managed to smile. Forget last night. He was here, giving her the opportunity she desperately needed, an interview.

"I should have known. Reporters are like locusts. I was with a special unit they dropped behind the lines in Bosnia. Two reporters from CNN were waiting for us."

His words had a sarcastic note. It warned her that he was

among those who saw the press as the enemy. She needed to be careful what she said. This story was too important to risk alienating him.

"Breaking news is our job," she told him, unable to temper the anger she felt. "That's why I went out to the hogan. You're big news around here."

"You know, you're cute when you're mad."

Someone less intelligent than she might have read this as a come-on. Kelly knew better. This man was a first class manipulator. He was toying with her, which made her even more furious and uncertain how to deal with him.

His head shifted just slightly, a subtle movement many wouldn't have noticed, and she realized he was watching the door. Evidently he wanted to make certain no one caught him off-guard. It was a conditioned response, she realized, recalling a SWAT team leader she had once interviewed. He'd explained how they were trained to watch their backs at all times. Members of the Cobra Force would be even more highly trained.

"How did *Exposé* magazine know I was out there?" he asked.

"A secret source—"

He surged forward, a lightning quick movement that brought him out of his chair and leaning across her desk before she could even flinch. Her startled expression was mirrored in his sunglasses.

"If you want an interview, then tell me." His gritty voice never rose, but there was a threatening edge to his words.

"Someone, I have no idea who, leaked the news that a security check revealed you were the missing Stanfield boy. The source told Matthew Jensen, editor of *Exposé*. He asked me to do the feature article because I'm right here in Sedona and know the family."

He eased back into his chair and rummaged through the candy bowl. He selected a purple Jelly Belly. "You two were hot for each other until Daniel Taylor stole you away." He pointed to the gold wedding band she still wore. "I bet Jensen's looking for a second chance."

She heard herself gasp as his words stunned her. He'd known

of her existence for less than twelve hours, yet he knew the details of her private life. It shouldn't shock her. After all, Logan McCord's career gave him access to top secret information. All he had to do was make a few calls.

"I suspected you were at the hogan because one of the Stanfield's ranch hands reported seeing someone out there. Since I couldn't find you anywhere else, I decided to check. What were you doing there anyway? Why weren't you staying with the Stanfields?"

"I was practicing survival techniques. I would have been on a plane back to Argentina this morning . . . if you hadn't found me."

"The Stanfields weren't going to have a news conference with you and blow this story around the planet?"

"No, they weren't." A half smile crossed his lips, then vanished. "No way."

"Why not? It makes no sense unless your work with the Cobra Force would embarrass them . . . or something."

"Or something," he shot back, a hint of amusement coloring his words. "Now they are going to tell the world—thanks to you." His rough-textured voice had more than just a trace of resentment. "They contacted the media this morning. It's going to be an 'event.' They're throwing a barbecue where Senator Stanfield will make the joyous announcement: His son is back."

"You would rather return to your old life and skip the fanfare?"

"Damn right, but that'll be impossible with my picture in every newspaper and on television. I'll be killed if I go back to South America. Every member of the Cobra Force has a bounty on his head."

Even though his voice didn't show any emotion, she could tell he was one of those men who lived for his work. It was his life, and now, it was going to be taken away. And he blamed her.

"The Stanfields didn't invite me to the press conference."

"Of course not. It's a party for family and close friends and selected members of the media who can appreciate the pain and suffering good old Ginger and Haywood have been through.'' He shrugged, his broad shoulders stretching the fabric of his shirt in a way that some women would have found extremely sexy. ''You've already caused one person to commit suicide with a story. Ginger almost went off the deep end when I left the hogan and went back to their house to tell them that you knew I was alive and the story was going to come out.''

Her reflection in his mirrored glasses told her the pain she felt inside showed on her face. She'd relied on a source who had been lying, convinced her editor to print the story about a policeman skimming drug money. Before the story was retracted, the man's wife had committed suicide.

And Kelly had never forgiven herself.

''If I don't report your story, someone else will.''

''True. That's part of the reason I'm here. It took a lot of guts to come out to that hogan the way you did. Why allow Benson Williams to orchestrate an 'event' to make the Stanfields look good and hand the story to big names in the media?''

''Thanks.'' She wondered if this could be a trick. He didn't seem the type of man who would protect her scoop.

''No big deal,'' he said, adjusting the baseball cap.

Again Kelly was taken with the familiarity of his gestures. ''Have we met? With the hat and glasses, I can't see what you look like, but I'm positive I know you.''

''Come on, sweetheart, don't you remember?'' His gruff voice stole its way into her body almost as if he were physically touching her.

Experience told her Logan was a dangerous man, yet he was intriguing, striking. His voice alone was memorable. She would never have forgotten someone like him. ''No, I don't recall.''

He leaned forward, and for one mind-blurring moment she had the impression he was going to take her into his arms. Of course, that was an idiotic notion. The desk separated them. Thank God.

He reached for her hand and gloved it with both his. Suddenly, her insides felt like warm honey.

''Kelly, you and I met one dark night in Paris just before the Reign of Terror. We were lovers so hot for each other that no one could separate us except the guillotine.'' He pressed a callused thumb into the palm of her hand, and heat seared through her body. "Death parted us in that life. I think we should take up where we left off, don't you?"

"Be serious," she said as sternly as she could, but it was hard. The thought of making love to such a dangerous yet compelling man unnerved her. She yanked her hand away. "Have we met?"

"Nope. Until last night, we were total strangers."

He pulled off the ball cap and laid it on the desk. His hair was a rich shade of chestnut with lighter streaks from the sun. It was long on top, but cut stylishly close over his ears.

With his hat off, she could see more of his face. His broad forehead complemented an uncompromising jaw and square chin. His strong features projected a threatening type of virility, tempered only by his charming smile.

He was removing his sunglasses, but she could already see he was a devastatingly handsome man. A dangerous combination, she thought, a trained killer with drop-dead looks and a captivating smile. She would have to be very careful around him.

He slowly pulled off the glasses, his searing blue eyes never leaving her face. The impact of seeing him was like a karate chop, and she swayed in her chair. It was several seconds before the dry tightness in her throat abated.

"Oh my God!" she managed to whisper. "I would have known you anywhere."

Chapter 5

Logan watched Kelly as he pulled off his sunglasses, her expression strangely arrested as if she'd seen a ghost. He smiled inwardly. He was a ghost, all right.

Sins of the past had returned to haunt the sinners.

"I—I n-never suspected." Her voice faded to a whisper.

He remembered how soft her skin had felt beneath his fingers and the fresh floral scent that he'd detected each time he'd come close to her. He cursed his body's unwilling reaction to the blonde who had wrecked his life. But if it hadn't been Kelly Taylor, it would have been some other—less attractive—reporter.

Once the secret source had squealed, his story was bound to come out. His gut clenched with impotent fury, and he damned the FBI and its state-of-the-art fingerprint computer.

"You're . . . you're—"

"A dead ringer for Haywood Stanfield." His voice reflected the bitterness burning inside him. "Now you know why the Stanfields didn't immediately call a press conference. They weren't exactly thrilled to have me turn up."

"When they adopted you, didn't Ginger realize you were

her husband's illegitimate son? Didn't it occur to them that you would grow up to look like your father?''

Logan threw up his hands. ''Hey, shit happens. Apparently Ginger had no idea I was Haywood's son. He would have been forced to confess, if I had grown up here, a clone of my old man. But since I had disappeared, he didn't bother telling his wife.''

Kelly picked up a photograph and studied it. From his angle, he couldn't see it clearly, but he saw it was a child.

''This is the picture of you they used on the missing child posters.'' She handed the photo to him. ''Luz Tallchief, your nanny, took it the day before you vanished.''

He gazed at the picture for a second, then tossed it back on her desk. ''What do you know? I was a cute kid. Back then, I looked more like Ginger than Haywood.''

''Surely you've seen other pictures of yourself when you were young.''

He could have shocked her by saying that he'd never seen a mirror until he was sixteen. He had a vague idea what he looked like because he had seen his reflection in the pond behind the camp where he had lived until he joined the Marines. It had been just a glimpse before one Zoe whacked him with the switch she always carried and bellowed at him to get back to class.

Class. Ha! Zoe's ''lessons'' were pure torture.

What doesn't kill you makes you stronger. That had been the camp motto, and in some absurdly perverse way, it was true. He'd survived, but his soul was undoubtedly a sold block of granite incapable of true emotion.

''The only photos that exist are the ones from my days with the Stanfields, and the one on my passport.''

She eyed him with a sympathetic expression. He could almost hear her thinking: You poor thing. How sad. That's why women made piss-poor terrorists, he reminded himself. They let their emotions show. Those rare female terrorists who didn't reveal their feelings needed a chromosome check.

''Who's this?'' She handed him a photocopy of a photograph. Logan shrugged. ''Ugly bastard, isn't he?''

"It's your passport photo."

"Look, when you join the Cobras, records are altered so terrorists don't know who we are." His stomach chose that second to let him know it wanted a Twinkie. Jelly Bellies did not cut it.

Her inner turmoil was etched on her face. She was pissed at him—big-time. But Kelly Taylor desperately wanted his story. She stared at him a moment before regaining her composure.

"Come home with me for dinner. My grandfather would love to meet you."

Aw, hell. The last thing he needed was another family to deal with. Families made him uncomfortable. He'd never been part of one, so he didn't know how to act. Then he'd been hurled into a pit of vipers calling themselves the Stanfield family. Give him a gang of terrorists brandishing Uzis and plastic explosives any day.

"Sounds good," he fibbed.

He checked the door out of the corner of his eye, having already determined the office was deserted, and watched as Kelly gathered her things. She had a mane of blond hair that looked as if she'd just lifted her head off a pillow. Tiers of dark eyelashes framed intelligent brown eyes flecked with amber. Her face was heart-shaped with a dainty chin and sculpted cheekbones that gave her an exotic look.

Her mouth intrigued him and had last night in the hogan even though he'd thought she intended to kill him. Her lips were full and soft-looking. The corners of them tilted upward, making her appear to be on the verge of a very sexy smile.

He was attracted to women who smiled and joked. Happy women. Probably because the women at The Last Chance Camp where he'd grown up had been miserable and it showed on their faces.

"Ready?" Kelly asked with a smile that revealed her white teeth and the tip of her tongue.

He was ready all right. A flare of pure lust ignited in the pit of his gut. He shunted it aside. Reporters were among the lowest life forms known to man—just a cut above lawyers and politicians. She would have kicked his sorry ass out of her office except she needed to interview him. She didn't have squat unless he cooperated.

I'll help you, babe, he said to himself, watching her walk around the desk with a stride that was businesslike yet provocative. He wasn't working with Kelly because he felt guilty about last night. Hell, no. She'd gotten what she deserved. Most members of the Cobra Force would have slit her throat without asking a single question.

He was using Kelly just as she was using him. He wanted his slant on this story. No way was he letting the Stanfields use him to enhance their political goals.

Logan slung his pack over one shoulder and followed her to the front door. She quickly locked it, then turned to him, asking where he'd parked.

"I hitched a ride here. It took a while. People don't like to pick up strange men."

She led him toward her car, a small blue Toyota. He put his backpack on the floor behind the passenger seat. He seldom let it out of his sight, but he knew no one could touch it without tackling him first.

They were driving down the street a few moments later, and Logan realized Kelly hadn't said a word. He'd expected her to fire questions at him, knowing she was a first-rate reporter. Okay, so he hadn't known she existed until last night. After he'd left her in the hogan and returned to the Stanfields' house, he'd made a call.

What he'd discovered pissed him off. She wasn't some two-bit reporter with an imagined connection to *Exposé*. He couldn't slip out of town without anyone discovering he was the missing Stanfield kid.

"I've been lots of places," he said to break the silence, "but nowhere else looks quite like Sedona. It's . . . unusual."

He gazed out the window at the craggy rocks glowing blood-red in the setting sun. A contrast to the flat-topped formations, spires of crimson stone vaulted skyward to catch the last rays of sunlight. From the crevices in the mammoth boulders and towering pillars grew tenacious clumps of golden mesquite. Skirting their bases were cactus with leaves like paddles.

Kelly drove with a casualness that said she could have found her way blindfolded, and she turned down a narrow road just off Oak Creek. Here the vegetation was greener, the red sandstone outcroppings flanked by Goliath cottonwoods, and apple trees with branches drooping from the weight of the fruit.

"You're right," she responded, but she sounded distracted. "Sedona goes from high desert to mountains. It's beautiful, yet there's a mystical feeling here. Some people pooh-pooh the vortexes, but there is a certain . . . something in the air."

He didn't put much stock in the magical powers of vortexes. Some people claimed Easter Island, Machu Picchu, and Stonehenge were vortex sites. They did emit enough electro-magnetic energy to be measured, but Logan refused to buy all the New Age spiritual crap about vortexes.

Kelly turned to him, her remarkable brown eyes studying his face. He'd put the baseball cap on backward and tucked the sunglasses in his backpack. He let her eyes drift over his face for a moment, then he unleashed his killer smile.

His father's smile.

She wasn't impressed, asking, "Do you remember being here when you were a child?"

"How much do you remember from when you were five?"

"Not much. Hazy images." She guided the car around the corner, going down a one lane road.

"Look," he said, spotting a battered cowboy boot on a fence post and changing the subject. "Someone lost a boot."

"It's a signal people use around here. See how the toe of the old boot points toward the house? That means Pop—my grandfather—is home. If the boot pointed the other way, his friends would know not to bother to go all the way to the house because he wouldn't be there."

Everything about this place fascinated him. The unusual, the different called to him. Perhaps, he reflected, because it was an echo of himself.

"You don't remember your life in Sedona. What is your first memory?"

She wouldn't want to know.

Kelly pulled into a driveway near a mission style home. The rambling adobe structure had a flat roof and an overhanging portal. Terra-cotta tiles paved the walkway up to the house. A massive pueblo-style door with forged iron hinges shaded by an ancient cottonwood marked the entrance.

Logan couldn't help comparing it to the Stanfield estate with the clipped hedges and acres of dicondra. Like the Stanfields themselves, the compound had to appear perfect. But the people, their home, seemed pretentious, devoid of real personality.

Kelly switched off the ignition key and looked at him, expecting an answer to her question about his first memory.

"Let's eat," he hedged. "Then I'll give you word-for-word the statement the Stanfields will be releasing."

She hesitated a moment, ready to fire off another question, but something stopped her. They got out of the car and went inside where the air was filled with the mouth-watering smell of roasting chilies and fresh-baked bread.

For once Logan did not crave a Twinkie. His stomach rumbled anticipating a delicious dinner. One lizard—no salt—did not cut it.

A Native American woman gaped at him from the arched doorway that led into the dining room, then she crossed her chest whispering to herself. Hail Marys, no doubt.

Beyond her stood an older man with thick white hair. Although he was extremely thin, Kelly's grandfather held himself erect. The older man's resemblance to Kelly was unmistakable. The high cheekbones, the brown eyes speckled with amber, a certain tilt of the head as he looked at Logan.

"Pop," Kelly said as she gave the older man a kiss on the cheek that made Logan glance away. "I've brought someone special home for dinner."

Special. Sucking up pissed him off big-time. Even though he would like to hop in the sack with her, Kelly was just another reporter after a story. Logan looked the other way as Pop hugged Kelly.

Families gave him the willies. They were always hugging and kissing.

"Logan Stanfield," the older man said as he came toward him.

"Logan McCord," he corrected. No way was he using the Stanfield name. Not now, not ever. "I hope my coming to dinner isn't causing a problem."

"Uma always makes more than we can possibly eat," he assured Logan.

Logan glanced at the Native American woman named Uma. She stared down at her moccasins and crossed herself again. Great! He hadn't managed to wrap Kelly around his little finger the way he did most women. Now this woman wouldn't even look at him.

What the hell. He didn't want Kelly's approval. He needed her to put his "spin" on this story.

"I'm Trent Farley," Kelly's grandfather said, shaking Logan's hand. "Call me Pop. Everyone else does."

Logan found himself smiling, his first sincere smile during what had turned out to be one of the longest, most miserable days in his life. He honestly liked Trent Farley, and gave him credit for accepting the situation instead of gaping at him like a Neanderthal time-warped onto the space shuttle.

Kelly disappeared into the kitchen with Uma, and Logan let Pop guide him into a den filled with family photographs. The older man opened a cedar plank sideboard that served as a bar.

"Scotch?" Pop asked as he pulled out two glasses.

"Got any tequila?"

"Sure," he responded without missing a beat. "Herradura Anejo."

"You're on!" Logan had been in South America long enough to appreciate pure blue agave tequila. Pop understood premier tequila, all right—a stand-up guy.

Kelly sprinted through the kitchen and out to her *casita*. Her Hasselblad was on the table where she'd left it after she'd returned from the hogan. An amateur photographer since high school, Kelly developed the photographs herself.

She picked up the Hasselblad 500 CM, a gift to herself after

Daniel's death, and loaded the camera with a roll of Kodak Tri-X.

"Go find Pop," she told Jasper when he greeted her at the back door. He dashed across the kitchen, tail beating the air, and Kelly rushed after him. She spotted Pop with Logan sitting on the terrace having a drink. Without letting them see her, she opened the door and Jasper bounded out.

"Jesus, Mary, and Joseph," Uma said from the stove where she was making fry bread. "Jim Cree was right. That man is a skinwalker. He looks exactly like Haywood Stanfield looked years ago. Only witches can change themselves like that."

Kelly smiled at Uma's mixture of Native American beliefs and Catholicism. She'd been brought up in the church, yet she retained their own beliefs. It hadn't occurred to Uma that Logan was Haywood's son.

Native Americans did not indulge in elaborate deceptions like the adoption of a child who was actually the man's own son. They were honest and forthright. When something couldn't logically be explained, witches—skinwalkers—were often blamed.

Through the open window, Kelly watched Logan react to Jason's appearance Like most people, Logan grinned at the friendly golden retriever. His smile wasn't the calculated smile he'd unleashed on her earlier. This was a relaxed, genuine smile that lit his face, making him—if possible—more handsome.

Kelly adjusted the lens for a shot that would include Jasper. This was a priceless opportunity to get a series of natural, unposed shots for her story. She hated being sneaky, but there was something so . . . guarded about Logan. After she developed the shots she would show them to him.

She clicked away, thrilled at the pictures she was getting. Now if she could just get his story as easily. Why had Logan McCord come to her? Was it just her "guts" in coming out to the hogan, or did he have some hidden agenda?

The camera loved every inch of Logan's face. It wasn't difficult to imagine one of these pictures on the cover of *Exposé* with a small inset of him as a child. She envisioned the headlines her article would generate. Could Haywood Stanfield take the pressure, or would his presidential fortunes plummet and never recover after the reappearance of his illegitimate son?

She took the camera back to her *casita* and quickly changed her clothes. Later, she would develop the film, then decide which pictures to overnight to Matt with the article. She joined them on the terrace that was gracefully suspended over Oak Creek.

"Honey, you look great," Pop said. "How about a glass of merlot?"

"Perfect," she replied, taking a seat at the table across from Logan. "You said you were hungry. Brace yourself, Uma is serving shrimp and her special fry bread."

There was a seductive quality to the smile he gave her. No doubt, he'd coaxed more than his fair share of women into bed with his adorable grin and sexy blue eyes. Here was a man who knew what he wanted—and he knew how to get it.

"Sounds better than what I had for dinner last night, lizard."

"A lizard tastes like chicken," she said, trying to joke. "Right?"

"Nope. Lizard is chewy like rattlesnake. It's lousy without salt. Last night I didn't have any salt."

Kelly almost gagged. Again she asked herself what kind of man was this?

The sun melted behind an imposing butte, firing the brush-stroke clouds with gold and scarlet while steeping the Red Rock country in shadows. In a few minutes it would be dark, and the exterior lights would automatically come on. Taking advantage of the concealing shadows, the man slipped into the bedroom suite through the patio door.

He eased the door shut without making a sound, but didn't reach for the light switch. The plush carpet cushioned his footsteps and muffled any noise as he walked toward her bed.

Over the years, he'd come into her bedroom countless times. By her body language, he could accurately gauge her mood. Sometimes she indolently lounged across the bed naked. At other times, she would be in one of her expensive Natori negligees that she loved to buy, then wear once.

He squinted, his eyes adjusting to the darkness, and saw she was in one of "those" moods. She was fully clothed and sitting upright, her back against the headboard of the bed.

"You promised Logan wasn't going to be a problem," she said when he sat down beside her.

"You saw how he acted when he showed up here. Logan swaggered in like he owned the place. He claimed he wanted to keep his name, McCord and live his own life. Bullshit! He was just pretending not to be interested in the money."

"I believed him until he returned, saying Kelly Taylor knew about him. Kelly Taylor—of all people!" She punched one of the silk butterfly pillows on her bed. "That is just a little *too* convenient. Logan fed Kelly the information, so he'd have an excuse to come here again."

"I agree. He was lying about wanting to rejoin the Cobras. Who in hell would want to piss their life away traipsing around third-world countries hunting terrorists?"

She leaned so close to him that he could smell the perfume she always sprayed between her breasts and thighs. "What if Logan knows the truth?"

"That's impossible. He was barely five when he disappeared."

She put her hand on his thigh and his cock responded with a surge of heavy heat. "I don't trust him."

He loved her more than any other person on this earth, but she was a bit dense and self-centered. "Neither do I. While you were napping, I phoned Washington. I had to call in a few favors, trying to get Logan's file."

"Good idea. His background might show some weakness we can use."

"If Logan has an Achilles' heel, I couldn't find it. His file has been electronically deleted. It'll take time and money to find a private investigator to work on this."

"Logan is after the Stanfield money. I just know it. He'll stay here and worm his way into Haywood's heart." She squeezed his thigh, her long nails pressing into his linen slacks.

Her graceful fingers inched upward, then traced the hard length of his shaft. "I say Logan should have a terrible accident—before the press conference."

"Logan has disappeared. I have no idea where he is. But if I can find him before the barbecue tomorrow, he's a dead man."

"Be careful," she cautioned, her fingers gloving his sex. He sucked his breath in, then held it.

He let out his breath. "Killing Logan won't be as easy as murdering Suzanne."

Suzanne's name caused her beautiful face to contort with fury. "Suzanne thought she could marry into this family and take over, but we showed her."

"True," he conceded as her fingertips explored his erection. "But this won't be as easy. Logan is a trained killer himself."

Chapter 6

Logan resisted the temptation to stroke Jasper's head, suddenly aware of how much he missed never having had a dog. Actually, he'd never had a pet unless you counted the chickens they raised at the camp.

As a young child, he'd been lonely, desperate for someone to play with him. He made friends with the chickens, and hand-raised one from the time it was a chick. Fancy would follow him around the camp, paying attention to him when no one else did.

Zoe had deliberately chosen Fancy for dinner because Logan loved the chicken. She grabbed the back of his neck and forced him to watch as she lopped off Fancy's head with the rusty hatchet used for chopping wood. Fancy hopped around for a minute, headless, then dropped. As her blood seeped into the dirt, he bawled, realizing his only friend had been butchered.

But that didn't satisfy Zoe. She made him pluck every feather off Fancy, then she cut up the carcass and fried it. Nothing Zoe did could make him take one bit of dinner that night. Nothing.

It had been such a long time ago that it almost seemed as if it had happened to another person. Those years had been miserable beyond description, but he had become stronger than most men because of the experience.

The primary lesson was not to become attached to animals like Jasper. Or to people.

He took a swig of the premium tequila, aware of how intently Kelly was watching him. Unlike most women, she was immune to him. Who cared? He didn't want her to fall for him.

All Kelly had to do was be first with the story—his version— then the Stanfields could go to hell. As soon as they staged their stupid press conference, he was out of here.

"I was just telling your grandfather about my arrival at the Stanfields' place." He couldn't help smiling, recalling his own father standing in the door slack-jawed with astonishment. Okay, he'd been blown away, too, but at least he'd kept his cool. "I'd called from Argentina, and the senator invited me here. He just wasn't quite expecting what he got."

"Hadn't you ever seen a picture of Haywood Stanfield?"

"No. How many state senators can you name let alone recognize?"

"Not many," she conceded, "and I'm a reporter. I probably know more than most people."

"You might have noticed the resemblance if Woody ran for president."

"Maybe, maybe not," he answered Pop. "I work out of the country. Sometimes I go undercover and don't see a newspaper or television for months."

Kelly nodded, then asked, "Was the whole family there when you arrived?"

"Yes. Benson Williams had wanted to have the press there, too, but I talked him out of it."

He didn't add that Williams was a real tight-ass. He'd hated the prick from that first telephone conversation when he'd called from Argentina. At first, Benson had flat refused to allow him to speak to his father.

"I thought I could come here and meet the family, then rejoin the Cobra Force."

"With your picture everywhere, it won't be possible to do that. Terrorists will know exactly what you look like."

The sympathetic tone in Pop's voice told Logan the older man truly understood how difficult this was for him. He might be forced to give up the life he loved all because some computer discovered his real identity and sent him back to a family who didn't give a rat's ass about him.

The Native American woman delivered a platter. She put the warm appetizers in the center of the table, never once looking at him. Kelly explained they were cactus, baked, then rolled in cilantro and Mexican cheese before being sliced into bite-sized pieces.

"Uma, this is Logan McCord," Pop said, then he turned to Logan. "Uma Begay is practically a member of the family."

"Pleased to meet you," the older woman said. She kept her eyes downcast and shuffled off to the kitchen.

"Guess she doesn't like me," Logan said as he reached for a cactus appetizer.

Kelly sipped the wine Pop had given her. "It isn't that Uma doesn't like you. Navajos consider it rude to stare or point. They don't look you directly in the eye until they know you as well as their own family."

"Hum-m-m," Logan muttered as he ate the appetizer. It gave Twinkies a run for their money. He hadn't eaten any junk food until he'd enlisted. He discovered Twinkies in a vending machine at the base, and they'd become his favorite snack. "She's a helluva' cook."

"She certainly is," Pop agreed. "Uma's fantastic. She helped me raise Kelly."

"Who raised you?" Kelly asked him.

"Do you want me to recite, word for word, the statement Benson Williams is going to read at the press conference, or should I explain my past in a way that doesn't make the Stanfields sound like heroes?"

Kelly took the bait. "I want to hear your story, not some spin doctor's version."

"Same here," Pop said. He snapped his fingers and Jasper deserted Logan, obediently going to the older man and sitting beside his chair.

"I don't remember falling into the ravine, or the McCords

finding me," Logan began, looking directly at Kelly. He didn't plan to tell anyone the whole truth, but this explanation fit the situation. "My earliest memory is my mother teaching me to swim in the pond out behind our place. I loved to swim, so I begged her to take me every day."

Christ! Was he good, or what? He actually sounded convincing.

His gaze shifted to Pop, whose head canted slightly to one side as if he didn't want to miss a single word. "I realized other children attended school, but I did not. Mom claimed it was because we moved so often, and she could teach me better."

"What did your father do?" Kelly asked.

"He took any job he could get. He said he had wanderlust and wanted to see the whole country." Logan shrugged. "I was much older before I realized we moved constantly to stay ahead of the bill collectors."

"You never attended school—not ever?" Kelly's tone echoed her incredulous expression.

He leaned forward and helped himself to another appetizer, subtlety craning his neck to get a better view of the gentle rise of her breasts barely visible above the scoop neck of her dress. "I never attended school until I joined the Marines. I got my high school certificate then."

Zoe's "lessons" did not count in his mind. She had taught him to read and write, and she'd even managed to see that he knew a little geography. But she specialized in making his life miserable. Everything he'd really learned, he'd taught himself by reading the books around the camp.

He caught the sympathetic look in Pop's eye and cursed himself under his breath. He didn't mind lying to reporters. They were all bottom feeders, ready to do anything to get a story.

But Pop was different. Just having a drink with him had impressed Logan. Still, he didn't want to tell anyone about The Last Chance Camp where he'd really grown up.

What doesn't kill you makes you stronger.

Hell, he was strong now. Let Amanda McCord live her life. His mother deserved that much. Zoe, his "teacher" had died just before he enlisted—not that he would ever have protected her.

"What about the Mapleton, California address you put on your enlistment papers?" Kelly asked. "No McCords ever lived there, as far as I could discover."

He managed a half-smile, not particularly shocked at her ferreting out this information. Not only was she pretty, Kelly was a crack reporter. "We passed through Mapleton once when I was about sixteen. We spent several nights in an abandoned trailer there. When I enlisted, I used that address."

Kelly frowned. "Recruiting officers are supposed to check the facts."

"How many actually verify addresses? What they're concerned about is legal problems that arise if they accept underage recruits. I had a midwife's certificate, and I looked older than eighteen when I enlisted."

"You never suspected you might not be the McCords' child?" Pop asked.

"The thought never crossed my mind."

"That's a shame," Pop told him. "You could have been raised here and had all the advantages the Stanfield—"

"Forget it. I'm lucky the McCords found me. Do you seriously believe the Stanfield money has made Alyx and Tyler better people?" He couldn't bank the sarcasm in his tone. "Tyler's a cocky jerk and his sister is a total bitch. People think Alyx is window shopping, but she's just admiring her reflection."

Kelly tried to hide her smile, but he noticed it. The Stanfield twins were the epitome of conceit and arrogance. Hard to believe the same blood flowed in his veins.

Thank God for his mother. Amanda McCord's genes made him what he was today.

"I'm happy with my past, and with my life now. I just want to get through this half-assed press conference and go back to my job."

"You said you wouldn't be able to rejoin the Cobra Force," Kelly reminded him.

He concealed how much this bothered him by kicking back

the last of his tequila before answering. "So? I'll find something interesting to do."

"Logan, what about the McCords?" Pop asked. "I don't believe there is a statute of limitation on kidnapping. They could face criminal charges."

No way was he letting anything happen to his mother. Granted, she'd been a piss-poor excuse for a mother. Make it on your own or die trying, she often told him, using one of her brother, Jake's, favorite lines. For the life of him, he didn't know why he was protecting her.

Amanda and Jake McCord had started The Last Chance Camp. They marched to a beat of a different drummer that was for damn sure, but he didn't want a tsunami wave of reporters descending on the camp. If his mother and uncle wanted to rot their lives away out in bum-fuck, let them.

"The last I saw of the McCords, they were heading for Mexico. Dad said you could live on less down there."

"When was that?" Kelly asked.

"Just before I joined the Marines. They gave me a choice. I could head to Mexico with them, or strike out on my own."

"Do you hear from them?" Concern colored every word Pop uttered, and Logan knew this man loved Kelly far too much to ever understand the people who had raised him.

"I don't know where to find them, and they don't know where I am."

Kelly glanced at her grandfather, and Logan could almost hear her thinking how fortunate she'd been to have him raise her. And love her. She hadn't a clue about how lucky she really was.

"Logan, do you know who your natural mother is?" Kelly asked. "Did Woody Stanfield tell you?"

He brushed the hair off his forehead, trying not to appear irritated by her question. "She was some woman who had a short affair with the senator. She blackmailed my old man into adopting me."

They both appeared concerned by his confession. Okay, so it was a half-truth. Close enough for government work.

"I'm going to help Uma serve the main course so she can

go home to her family,'' Kelly said, rising to her feet, giving Logan an enticing glimpse of her legs in the short skirt. ''Should we eat out here or inside?''

''Out here,'' Pop said. ''Soon it'll be too cool to dine outside.''

Logan glanced around the terrace suspended over Oak Creek. The water swirling over the chunky stones in the riverbed produced a rhythmic sound that soothed most people's nerves. Not Logan.

He knew better than to let his guard down. His hand dropped to his side to make certain his backpack was still beside his chair while he scanned the thick bushes along the creek. Craggy vermilion boulders were barely visible through the shrubbery. Anyone could hide in the creek's underbrush, but it would be impossible to spot him without alarming Pop by pulling out the night vision binoculars Logan had in his backpack.

''I'll bet I can guess what happened when the Stanfields saw you,'' Pop said as Kelly disappeared into the kitchen. ''Ginger became hysterical and Benson Williams was downright hostile. The twins kept their distance while their father did his best to smooth things over.''

''Were you a fly on the wall that morning when I knocked on the Stanfield's door?''

''No, but I've known them long enough to realize how they would treat you. You're an unexpected chink in Woody's political armor.'' Pop's crown of white hair glistened in the amber glow of the Spanish lanterns lighting the terrace. ''The twins are scared spitless that they'll have to share the family fortune with you. Ginger grasps at any excuse to go off the deep end and get attention. Benson Williams once again comes to the rescue, putting the proper spin on events.''

Logan couldn't help asking, ''Haywood—my father—seems very intelligent and forceful, yet he allows Benson Williams to call the shots. Why?''

''Who knows? Benson's been a family fixture for years. He's never married; instead he devoted his life to Haywood's political career. Some people say he has something on the senator. Other people claim he and Ginger are lovers. I don't know what's going on."

Kelly backed out the door, carrying a tray. Uma followed her, holding another tray laden with food. Logan's stomach grumbled like distant thunder. God willing, he'd eaten his last lizard. Pop described the shrimp in *caldillo* sauce with cactus, explaining *caldillo* was a gravy made from chilies. Shrimp was one of Logan's favorites.

Shrimp with cactus? Aw, hell. Cactus reminded him of survival missions. Nothing like being dropped in the desert and having to find food and water on your own. Eating a cactus was a necessity. Why pair it with shrimp?

"Help yourself," Pop told Logan, and he did, barely managing to thank Uma and tell her good night before plunging his fork into the mixture.

The cactus and shrimp in *caldillo* sauce was kick-ass good! Surviving in the desert would never seem the same. The shrimp and cactus dish was even better than Twinkies—his very favorite food.

He caught Kelly staring at him and realized he was gobbling as if he were starving—another legacy of life at The Last Chance Camp. Food was always scarce. You wolfed down your meal before someone snatched it away from you.

He winked at Kelly. That got her. She smiled, or tried to, then concentrated on her own food. Logan forced himself to slow down, which was still hard for him.

"How did your father treat you when you showed up after all this time?" Kelly asked him.

Logan put down his fork, having cleaned his plate, and told himself not to help himself to seconds until they were offered. "The family anticipated meeting 'little lost Logan.' No one expected to see a dead-ringer for Haywood Stanfield. All they cared about was the impact this would have on the senator's political career."

"How did you feel when you met your father face-to-face?" Kelly asked.

"It was a shock, but I'd had a couple of days to adjust to

the fact that the McCords weren't my natural parents.'' Logan vividly recalled the door opening and his father standing there. He'd wanted to kill the bastard, but he couldn't say that. "When I saw my old man, I knew what I would look like in twenty-five years.''

"What did you tell them about your past?'' Kelly said.

He shrugged as if it didn't matter, but he was still pissed big-time. The Stanfields hadn't given a damn about him. All they'd cared about was the impact his reappearance would have on their political fortunes. "Not much. They assumed someone had found me in the ravine and kept quiet about it. I told them a couple raised me until I enlisted.''

"That's all they asked?'' Kelly's surprise was echoed by Pop's angry expression.

"It was damage control time,'' Logan assured her. "I didn't matter.''

Logan noticed the way Pop's eyes narrowed and wondered if the older man suspected he wasn't telling the whole truth. Kelly seemed to accept his explanation. The next question came from her sexy lips without missing a beat.

"What are you going to say at the press conference tomorrow afternoon?''

"Not a damn thing. Let Benson give his version, which attempts to keep my father, in the good graces of the voting public. I told them I would pose with the family for one—just one—picture. Then I'm gone.''

"Son,'' Pop said, leaning toward him. "You'll have to outrun a media gauntlet. It'll be impossible to get away easily.''

Normally, anyone calling him "son'' would have pissed-off Logan, but concern etched Pop's lined face. There was no doubting his sincere interest in Logan's predicament. It was almost touching, but Logan steeled himself. No way should he get close to these two.

"There'll be movie and television offers,'' Kelly added. "Oprah will want you on her show. You won't be able to refuse.''

"Watch me.''

* * *

As soon as Kelly had served them warm apple tartan for dessert, she'd excused herself, saying she needed to write the story.

"You're coming with me to the press conference tomorrow," Logan said as she left the table.

"I wasn't invited. I—"

"I'm asking you. I know you'll want to see everything yourself."

"If I'm going to scoop everyone, I have to have my story in New York by the morning. Television instantly reports news, but magazines need lead time. *Exposé* is usually printed late Friday night and shipped Saturday so it can be on the stands across the country on Monday morning."

Logan nodded, and she couldn't help noticing the long sweep of his eyelashes. On another man, they might have been feminine, but the dense black lashes made Logan's eyes sexy. "If you're with me, no one will suspect that you've already filed your story. I'm not allowing anyone but you to interview me."

An exclusive, a golden opportunity, she thought, so why was she suspicious? Her past experience with an unreliable source had snuffed a very promising career. Worse, a woman had taken her life because Kelly had pushed and pushed to get the article printed.

Without verification.

Something in Logan's story didn't quite ring true. It was a plausible explanation, accounting for why he hadn't attended school and had no records of his past. But still . . . something was missing.

What if the Stanfields told a completely different story? The past would repeat itself.

"I can hardly wait to hear Benson Williams spin this." Kelly suddenly remembered Logan was here without a car, and she didn't have the time to take him back. "Pop, do you feel well enough to drive Logan into town?"

Before Pop could answer, Logan said, "Don't bother. I have

my things with me, I'll hike out into the country and make camp there.''

Kelly waved one hand toward the military-style backpack Logan had kept beside his chair throughout dinner. ''Do you have enough in there to camp?''

''Everything I own is in my pack.'' He patted the bulky canvas in a way that was oddly affectionate. ''People lug around far more than they really need.''

Kelly banked an astonished gasp as Pop said, ''Stay here tonight. We have two *casitas* on the property. Kelly's in one; you can use the other.''

Logan hesitated, and Kelly quickly added, ''It would be perfect. Then I won't have to find you for the press conference tomorrow.''

''All right . . . thanks,'' Logan said, but Kelly had the distinct impression he would rather camp under the stars and hone his survival skills.

Kelly kissed Pop good-night, then rushed out to her *casita* leaving the men to their coffee. Somewhere in the cottonwoods behind the main house, an owl hooted . . . once . . . twice.

She knew the owl was hunting, counting on the noise to make a rabbit nervous. As soon as the creature left the cover of the thicket of mountain mahogany, the owl would pounce. When she opened the door to her bungalow, the owl was still trying to lure out his prey.

She flicked on the light, thinking how much she loved her grandfather, and how much she owed him. Not only had he taken care of her financially, he'd given her a sense of values and an appreciation of nature. As a child, he taken her on hikes throughout the area, explaining the geologic formations that made Sedona unique and teaching her about all the creatures that shared the area.

Kelly rushed into the darkroom she'd set up in the closet when she'd first taken up photography in high school. The equipment had been purchased secondhand, but it worked nicely. Just last week, she'd developed two rolls of film she'd taken of Pop with Jasper.

She carefully developed the shots of Logan McCord, then

she studied the negatives with a magnifying cube. Using a red chinagraph, she circled seven shots. One of them showed a smiling Logan with Jasper.

She concentrated on that negative first and cropped some of the background. Saying a prayer, she slipped a sheet of bromide paper into the frame then clicked the print button. She removed it and kept her eyes on her watch's second hand. Fifty-nine seconds seemed like eternity. She carefully removed it. Next came the stopper, then the fixer.

As she pulled it out of its last chemical bath, she cried, "Oh my God!"

She hung it up to dry, then dashed into the central living area where a Santa Fe-style bed and *trastero* dominated the room. Struggling to contain her excitement, she rushed up to the open shelf cupboard where her books and pictures filled the shelves and picked up the telephone.

Chapter 7

Kelly couldn't keep the smile out of her voice when a very sleepy Matthew Jensen answered the telephone. "I have the story of the year."

"Kelly? Is that you? What story?"

"Senator Stanfield's adopted son, remember?"

"Oh, yeah." Matt sounded less than interested. "That story."

Didn't this scoop mean a lot to him? He'd come all the way out to see her with it.

"I've interviewed Logan McCord. I have pictures you won't believe."

"Really?" Matt perked up. "How'd you manage that?"

She couldn't very well say Logan had walked into her office. It wouldn't sound as if she'd done a first-rate job of investigative reporting. "It's a long story."

"Great! I knew you were the one to write this article."

"Matt, you aren't going to believe this. Who do you think Logan is?" She didn't wait for him to respond. "Haywood's illegitimate son. Logan looks exactly—exactly—like the senator."

"You're kidding. Do you know what this could do to Stanfield's chances of becoming president?"

Kelly sank down into the chair beside the *trastero*. "Lots of presidents have gotten away with worse especially in these last few years. Infidelity isn't an issue—"

"Unless you're an ultra-conservative like Stanfield who built his career hawking family values. His supporters won't be thrilled to learn about Logan."

"So it'll be a hot story. Add to that the interest the public will have in a child who disappears, then is found years later." Kelly's voice could not conceal her mounting excitement. "The pictures I have of Logan today are fantastic. He's not the guy in the passport photo you gave me. He's drop-dead good-looking with a killer smile. Put him on the cover and you'll have your best-selling issue of the year."

The silence from the other end of the line made her wonder if the connection had been broken. Finally, Matt spoke, his voice flat. "Kelly, is McCord another lost soul?"

"What do you mean?"

"Well . . ." The hitch in his voice upset her. "Daniel Taylor spent his youth in foster homes. He was a lost soul when you rescued him."

Kelly gazed at her favorite picture of Daniel, not knowing what to say. She had thought her future was with Matt until Daniel appeared, and she fell for him with all her heart. His death had taken the light out of her life, the song out of her heart.

If anyone was a lost soul, it was she.

"Matt, let me put the photos and the story I've written on the FedEX plane. Look at them and tell me this isn't the scoop of the year."

"Kelly, I didn't mean—"

"It's all right. I know you weren't crazy about Daniel. This isn't about Daniel or about us. This is about the son of a man who might be our next president. It's about a national nightmare—abducted children."

The long silence made her wonder what Matt was thinking.

Once they'd been inseparable, destined to marry and live their lives together. B.D.

Before Daniel.

"Kelly, if this is as good as you say, I'm going to put Logan on the cover."

"Wonderful!" Kelly said, relieved to be discussing the article again. "But I'm worried the press conference the Stanfields called tomorrow will scoop us."

"News conference? No one called *Exposé!*"

Kelly explained why the Stanfields hated Pop and the *Sedona Sun* which ran scathing editorials critical of Haywood Stanfield. Logan must have told Benson Williams that Kelly had mentioned *Exposé,* and he had taken the magazine off the A list.

"*Exposé* doesn't hit the stands until Monday. TV reporters will have the story Friday night on the late news. Then they'll broadcast it all day Saturday and Sunday," she said, hoping Matt would volunteer to do a special issue.

"Don't worry," Matt told her. "I'll wallop them with the power of the Internet. Our Website will publish some of the details and a photo, beating them to the punch and encouraging readers to rush out to buy the special edition of *Exposé.*"

"Perfect, Matt. Thank you." She didn't know what to say exactly. There was an undercurrent to their relationship that she didn't know how to handle. "This really means a lot to me."

He hesitated a moment, worrying her. "If I blast through cyberspace with this, are you positive it's the truth?"

Ordinarily, Kelly would have trusted her instincts and said, yes. But her horrible experience with an unreliable source had taught her a bitter lesson.

Verify every story.

She couldn't lie to Matt, the man who'd found her wandering the Yale campus, a homesick freshman from the Southwest thrown in with Eastern preppies. He'd encouraged her to join the *Yale Herald* staff, and he'd introduced her to all his friends.

Somewhere along the way—probably that first day—she had fallen for Matt. They'd been inseparable until Daniel Taylor appeared to eclipse the other men in her life. Still, Matt had remained her friend, being Daniel's best man, seeing her through Daniel's funeral, and understanding when she'd made a mess of her career and everyone else deserted her.

"Matt, I only have Logan's word that there is a press conference."

"Let me make a few calls, then I'll get back to you."

Kelly hung up and waited, going into the darkroom to check the print. Awesome, totally awesome. A picture *could* be worth a thousand words. A man and his dog, at least that's how it would appear. There was a connection between them, an emotional bond that the camera had captured. Not only was Logan handsome, he was the type of man that readers would want to *know*.

She even found herself wanting to know him, not just his story, but know what he thought about things like movies and books and the ozone layer. His compelling blue eyes gazed up at her from the photograph, seeming to speak to her alone. Get a grip, she told herself. It's just a picture. The reality is very different.

"Kidnapped!" she said out loud. "The perfect title. People will wonder just what it means when they see a grown man."

If only she could be positive Logan were telling the truth, she would be assured of a Pulitzer Prize caliber story.

If only.

Using the 45mx enlarger, she made the picture 8 x 10. That would leave room for the *Exposé* masthead.

Seven minutes later her telephone rang. Matt's clipped voice came over the line. "Your information is correct. The barbecue/news conference is set for tomorrow afternoon. Everyone who's anyone has been invited—except *Exposé*. People believe Haywood Stanfield is announcing his bid for the presidency. No one has a hint of a missing child. If we run with that story and it isn't true, I'm fried—big time."

The nervous tremor in Matt's voice surprised Kelly. She couldn't remember when he hadn't been cool even in a crisis. She wondered if her fall from grace for not substantiating a story had also taught him a lesson.

"Kelly, you need a corroborating source."

"Without announcing to the Stanfields that I'm a step ahead of them, there isn't anyway to verify this. You look at the pictures of Logan and tell me that he isn't Haywood's son." She'd saved her ace for last. "One other thing. This is an exclusive interview with Logan McCord. He's just taking one picture with the entire family. I have the only photos of him alone and the only interview."

"Christ, Kelly. That's awesome." He hesitated a moment, then his tone changed becoming disturbingly somber. "After the special edition is on the stands, I want to come out there and talk to you."

She said good-bye and hung up, convinced Matt was coming here to offer her a job. If this story was even half as big as she suspected it would be, she would be in a position to return to New York. How could she leave Pop? He needed her and listening to Logan describe his life made her feel even luckier that Pop had raised her.

Sedona was a beautiful town, the perfect place to bring up children. If Daniel had been alive, she would be happy to live here and run the paper for her grandfather. But Daniel was gone, and the children they'd put off having were never going to be born.

A weight settled on her chest that made it hard to breathe, and tears blurred her vision. She'd always counted on having a big family. Growing up as an only child had been lonely despite Pop's love. She'd promised herself when she married, she would have at least three children.

With Daniel gone, her biological clock had become a time bomb. But men didn't interest her. Actually, nothing had interested her until this story.

"Stop wasting time feeling sorry for yourself."

She returned to the darkroom and developed the remaining six prints. They were all winners, but none could compare with the shot of Logan with the dog. Now if she could just write the text and have it be as good.

A sharp knock startled her, and she opened the *casita* door to find Logan McCord. A thought flashed through her mind: no man could do for denim what Logan could do. He was handsome, yet he projected a rough masculine look that assured her no one ever considered him a pretty boy.

Behind a smile rife with charismatic charm that had garnered his father countless votes, Logan's eyes were sharp and assessing. Cold. For all his 14-karat smiles, and the striking appeal of his face, Logan McCord was a calculating, dangerous man.

A very strange man.

He kept all his worldly belongings in a backpack that would have been hard-pressed to hold her toiletries. Odd, very odd. He'd told them a bare outline of his life, the details he wanted them to have. Nothing more.

He walked into her bungalow without being invited, saying, "How'd the pictures turn out?"

His words stunned her, and surprise must have shown on her face. He chuckled, a rich masculine sound that escalated into a laugh.

"Sweetheart, no one gets the drop on me. Not even a pretty blonde. I knew you were shooting pictures through the kitchen window.

He's a gifted actor, she silently reflected. She would have sworn he was being completely natural. Be very careful of this man, warned an inner voice.

Leaning against the counter separating the bedroom area from the kitchenette, he said in the gravel-like voice she'd come to associate with him, "Pop told me you were an amateur photographer. He says you have a darkroom set up out here."

She silently cursed her grandfather for falling under this man's spell. No doubt, he'd told Logan a lot of things that she would rather he not know. She didn't have time to examine the reasons, but she felt threatened by him.

Logan had barged into her life, and in a matter of hours had won over her grandfather. All through dinner she'd been acutely aware of how taken Pop was with Logan. She wasn't jealous; she was concerned.

"Would you like to see the pictures?" she asked, more than a little uneasy to find herself alone with him, but she had intended to show him the pictures.

"Sure." He sounded as if it didn't matter, but she didn't necessarily believe it. He'd already proved how adept he was at concealing his feelings.

He followed her into the makeshift darkroom, and she showed him the six photos she'd selected. She couldn't tell what he thought; his face remained expressionless.

"Which one are you putting on the cover?"

"What makes you think this will be a cover story?"

He studied her for a moment, in that disturbing way of his, then said, "It's a kick-ass story. An American soap opera—a real one. Love, lust, infidelity, money, politics, and a kidnapped child. What more could you want? Murder?"

"It's up to Matthew Jensen," she informed him, suddenly aware of how close they had to stand in the small closet. She backed out the door. "I'm overnighting everything to him."

"Use the shot of me with Jasper. John Q. Public will lap it up with a flavor straw. They're suckers for cute dogs."

She didn't tell him that she'd reached the same conclusion. Coming from him in such a snide tone, it seemed to be the type of deliberate manipulation of public opinion that made people distrust the media.

A niggling suspicion returned. What wasn't Logan McCord telling her?

"I haven't written the story yet. It would help if I had more background. You know, stuff about your childhood, any career information that isn't classified."

His eyes drifted over her face, then moved downward, a dark glitter in his eyes as the pupils dilated. She crossed her arms over her breasts and stared him down—or tried to. She wondered if he mentally undressed women for the fun of it, or was he trying to distract her?

If so, it was working. An unexpected weightlessness filled her chest. She was acutely aware that they were alone together in a bedroom with a small sitting area and a kitchenette off to one side. If he thought she was some easy piece, he was dead wrong.

Daniel's position as the South American Director of the Universal News Syndicate meant he spent a lot of time in

Venezuela where the regional headquarters were located. Often he was gone for weeks at a time. She had plenty of opportunities, but she never had been unfaithful.

"I've said all I'm going to about my past," he said in his gruff voice. "You have an exclusive interview with me. That puts you way ahead of the pack."

With the back of his hand, he lifted the hair off her neck and peered at the scab below her ear. His thumb slid gently over the small cut, then down the side of her neck. He'd touched her before at the office, but she'd been too on edge to notice his touch had a delicacy she never expected. Beneath her bare feet, the floor seemed to shift.

He's trying to manipulate you, she warned herself. Be on guard. She moved away, asking, "What's wrong with your voice? You sound hoarse all the time."

"I haven't had any women complain about it."

Indeed it was a bedroom voice, but she refused to admit she found him attractive. No doubt women fell all over him. Well, she wasn't joining the ranks.

"Oh, then you deliberately try to sound as if you smoke ten packs of cigarettes a day," she said to provoke him.

"No, it's not deliberate," he responded. "A couple of terrorists poured battery acid down my throat. I'm lucky I can still talk."

"Oh, my God," she cried. "I'm sorry. I had no idea."

He merely shrugged as if it meant nothing, but he gazed into her eyes with such intensity that she battled the urge to run out of the room.

"Don't be sorry. What doesn't kill you makes you stronger."

Something in his eyes told her the terrorists had died a bloody, violent death. She heard herself whisper, "What happened to them?"

He moved closer, never breaking eye contact and she felt the heat emanating from his body. "Off the record?"

She nodded, unable to speak. There was something so compelling, so overpowering about Logan McCord. On one level, he frightened her, yet on another, she found him more exciting than anyone she'd ever met.

"I slit both their throats."

She didn't know what to say, but now she was convinced that she would have to write two articles on this man. She didn't have time to unravel his past, but when she did, she was positive she would discover a story just as fascinating as his link to the Stanfields.

"I need to write the article," she said, ashamed of the way she'd teased him about his voice. "I'll have to have everything at the airport at 2 A.M. when the last FedEx flight leaves. Do you want to read it before I send it in?"

A strange heat unfurled in her stomach as he leaned toward her with a caressing masculine glint to his eyes that usually preceded a kiss. She wanted to pull away, she honestly did, but she couldn't move. His warm palm circled the nape of her neck, sending chilling goose bumps across her breasts.

His gaze held hers as his fingers skimmed the back of her neck, barely stroking her, but his touch scorched her tender skin. Their lips were a scant inch apart now. His smoldering, brooding eyes mesmerized her.

She inhaled sharply, filling her lungs with the faint woodsy smell of his shaving lotion. Minute flutters of heat feathered through her body. What was she doing? Backing up, she groped for something to say.

Any second he was going to kiss her.

He whispered in a raspy undertone. "I don't have to read the article, but I'm going with you to the airport. Remember, a little boy was kidnapped not far from here. You never know who's out there or what they might do."

Chapter 8

Logan cursed himself as he walked down the path from Kelly's place to the bungalow where he'd put his things. What in hell was he doing coming onto her like that? Stupid ass! Did he want to blow everything?

Kelly was sexy as hell. But getting involved wasn't part of his agenda. Telling his story—his way—was the reason he'd sought out the blonde.

Yet something about her intrigued him besides her captivating lips. Part of her attraction was her quick mind. She was suspicious about his story, and he knew it. You're on, babe. He'd never been able to resist a challenge.

Kelly's grandfather had been a total surprise. Logan had never known a grandfather—or even a father. For damn sure, the men at the camp like his uncle Jake hadn't been interested in being a parent.

He could still hear Jake's booming voice. What doesn't kill you makes you stronger, and make it on your own or die trying. What kind of a man said that to a little kid? He couldn't imagine Trent Farley uttering those words.

Pop had a paternalistic attitude, but he also conveyed a willingness to accept people the way they were that seemed more like a friend to Logan. But what the hell did he know? His youth had been dominated by people who did not fit the mold of mainstream society.

He couldn't help liking Pop and respecting him for sticking to his beliefs. He was a burr under the Stanfields' saddle, which added to his appeal. Pop was down to earth while the Stanfields reeked of money and power.

And total arrogance.

His old man might have been willing to accept Logan, but the rest of the Stanfields would rather see him dead. They'd hated him on sight and had made no attempt to conceal their feelings, yet he'd stake his life that they'd be sweet as sugar for the reporters tomorrow.

What a crock! He didn't need the Stanfields. The last thing he wanted in his life was a father. A politician who was pussy-whipped by a neurotic wife and dominated by a pompous political advisor, was worse than no father at all.

"Forget them," he told himself as he came into the dark bungalow. He flicked on the light and saw his backpack in the corner. It was tilted at a certain angle, so he could make certain no one had touched it while he'd been gone.

He opened the canvas pack and took out the new computer that was much smaller than any laptop available to the general public. This prototype had been developed for military use. He could have attached a micro-antenna and contacted the surveillance satellite overhead, but he decided to save the battery for an emergency and use the telephone instead.

He plugged into the phone and booted up the computer. He typed in a message to his supervisor at the National Military Command Center.

Where do I stand?

Considering the time difference between Arizona and Washington, Logan didn't expect an answer from "the bunker" until morning. Someone could blow Washington off the face of the earth, but "the bunker" would still be operational. At least, in theory. He added his code name—Nine Lives—to the message and was ready to sign off when a response appeared on the screen.

> **Have conferred with the brass. You will be reassigned to the Pentagon. Your expertise is invaluable. We need you here. Meanwhile, watch your back.**

''Unfuckingbelievable.'' His voice ricocheted off the walls of the small bungalow.

He'd given the best years of his life to the Cobras. Why was he being assigned to a desk job? Tight-asses from the Pentagon would ride herd on him, monitoring his every move.

No way! He wanted to be out in the field—his own man. He slapped his hand, palm down, on the table. Life as he knew it—and loved it—was over.

> **Watch my back. Why?**

Logan waited a moment until the answer appeared on the small screen.

> **The Armed Services Committee requested your file. I took a lot of bull because it had been electronically deleted.**

''Haywood Stanfield was on that committee for years,'' Logan muttered to himself. ''The old man or one of his flunkies must have asked to see my file.''

> **I took care of my file before I left Argentina.**

Logan had never met his commander in person. All communications were conducted via computer or by ''bouncing'' messages off the intelligence satellite. But Logan trusted the man who went by the code name: Raptor. In Logan's experience, Raptor was professional, quickly and thoroughly doing his job. He was not an alarmist. Logan typed another line.

Do you know what is going on?

Raptor immediately replied:

No. Just remember, you're worth more to them dead than alive. If the Stanfields are asking questions, something's up.

"What in hell is going on?" Maybe his father had checked his records just to see what he'd been doing in the military. But his sixth sense kicked in and told him that he was in danger. He'd spent less than a day with the Stanfields, yet the undercurrent of hostility toward him had been unmistakable.

He didn't want their damn money and had said so. But maybe someone hadn't believed him.

The following afternoon, Kelly drove Logan out to the barbecue at the Stanfields'. They were twenty minutes late.

"Let them sweat," Logan told her. "They'll have egg on their faces if I don't show up."

His quirky attitude didn't surprise her. He was a complex man. After flirting with her last night, he'd been quiet and distant when he'd accompanied her to deliver the article and the pictures for the last FedEx shipment.

"Logan McCord and guest," he told the guard at the gate.

The man waved them on, then turned his attention to the next car. They gave her Toyota to the parking attendant and walked side-by-side into the estate. It was an ultra-modern structure that reminded Kelly of a museum. Vast sweeps of glass two stories high brought the magnificent landscape inside while soaring walls of white marble featured modern art.

Beyond the house, plush green meadows were enclosed by white picket fences. Prancing through the clover, manes flying behind them like banners, roamed a dozen prize-winning Arabian stallions.

The grass and horses trumpeted the Stanfields' fortune even more than their lavish home. Numerous wealthy people had built fabulous homes in Sedona, but no one kept this many show horses or had a golf-course-sized pasture for them. The expensive horses and the water it took to keep them in clover was impressive.

"This place looks more like Kentucky than Sedona," Logan remarked.

"The Stanfields brought in bulldozers and leveled several hills, ruining one red rock formation."

"I'm surprised the city let them get away with it."

"It couldn't happen today," she assured him. "Thanks to Pop. He used the editorial power of the *Sedona Sun* to rally the people. They started the ESLR—Environmentally Sensitive Lands Regulations to protect the natural attributes of Sedona."

"I'll bet my old man didn't appreciate the negative publicity. No politician wants a reputation for destroying the environment."

"Woody was not a happy camper, but that was just one of the many disagreements Pop's had with the Stanfields. The *Sun* is a small paper, but its articles often get picked up by UPI like that one did. Is it any wonder the family hates Pop?"

Logan was silent for a moment, then he said, "I've spent enough time in third-world countries to know the power of the press. It's the first thing dictators ax because they don't want their opposition to have a voice. For damn sure, the Stanfields would love to shut up your grandfather."

"Pop is saving one salvo for Woody in case he runs for president." She glanced up at Logan. His sunglasses reflected her own image. "Can you keep a secret?"

Logan nodded, guiding her through the mammoth great room out to the terrace where people were gathered.

"Most of your father's money doesn't come from gemstones," she informed him. "True, Arizona is the second largest producer of gems in this country, and the Stanfields own most of the mines, but they have several other businesses."

"Are they trafficking drugs?"

"No. They're not doing anything illegal. They're just snobs. Gems are far classier than cat box litter."

Logan stopped in his tracks and stared down at her.

"The family owns several large quarries. Most people thought Haywood had gotten taken on the deal. The stone was soft and crumbly. To give your father credit, he devised a process to crush the rock into small pebbles."

"And he was clever enough to know how to market it." Logan's voice had a faraway quality as if this information put his father in a new light.

"It's one of many Stanfield companies, but he never mentions his most successful venture. Pop plans to call him the Kitty Litter Candidate."

Logan chuckled, then said, "They broke the mold when they made Pop."

Benson Williams rushed up to them, and Logan took her hand, circling it with his, the pad of his thumb pressed against her palm. A tingle waltzed up her arm, reminding her of the way he'd touched her last night. What was he trying to prove? She attempted to pull her hand away without attracting attention, but he refused to release her.

"There you are." Benson's attention was focused on Logan. If he recognized Kelly, which was unlikely since they'd met only once, he didn't acknowledge her. "Keep on your hat and sunglasses until after the barbecue when the senator makes the announcement."

Logan nodded, but didn't say anything. He was wearing the same aviator sunglasses and Arizona Wildcats baseball cap that he had worn when he appeared in her office. It was a very effective disguise; no one would suspect he was Haywood's son.

"Introduce me to your friend," Benson said, turning his attention to Kelly.

She stuck out her hand, tempted to remind him that they'd met already. "I'm Kelly Taylor from the *Sedona Sun*."

If looks could have killed she would have been pushing up daisies. She was mentally banishing the man to the eternal fires of hell when she realized Logan's arm was around her.

"Meet my main squeeze," he said.

Benson's attempt to smile failed miserably. "Logan, I'll send for you when I need you."

He disappeared into the crowd, and Kelly couldn't help saying, "What a jerk."

Logan's expression was impossible to read because of the sunglasses, but his arm circling her shoulders felt tense. He wasn't a man accustomed to being ordered around. He had too much pride in himself, in all he'd achieved on his own to allow these people to humiliate him.

"If your father becomes president, Benson Williams will be the power in the White House."

"Can we trust the American voters to deliver us from evil? I doubt it." His grip on her shoulders tightened. "It's hot. Let's get something to drink."

He kept his arm around her while they walked toward the crowded area around the mountain lake pool where food stations had been installed. She saw an Asian chef stir-frying something in a wok while guests waited, plates in their hands. A pasta bar was serving a variety of pasta with interesting-looking sauces.

Across the grassy putting green off to the side, a chef in a Stetson was basting barbecue sauce on a steer being roasted Southwestern style over mesquite. Smoke billowed toward the flawless blue sky, bringing with it the scent of the wood and the spicy sauce.

No one paid any attention to them. It was clear that most of the people were movers and shakers from the East and knew each other. They formed tight circles, chatting among themselves.

Some of the guests might have recognized Kelly, but following Logan's instructions, she wore sunglasses and a scarlet cowboy hat. Her sassy red cowboy boots complemented the red leather concho belt at her waist and off-set the denim dress.

Logan leaned down and whispered in her ear, his breath rustling her hair. "Is this bullshit, or what?"

"Or what."

"You're a real clown. You hate these people as much as I do, don't you?"

Hate was a little strong, she decided, stepping out of the circle of his arm. She resented the Stanfields' money and their assumption that their wealth made them better than everyone else. But hate implied a venom and a lust for revenge that she didn't quite feel.

What she was positive she did feel was wariness—of Logan. She was dead certain he was trying to manipulate her on every level. What had he been trying to prove last night?

Disgust filled her as she recalled just standing there, letting him touch her. What on earth was wrong with her? Since Daniel's death the thought of a man touching her had been revolting. But last night, she hadn't been revolted until afterward when she had time to think about how she'd behaved.

She didn't answer his question, instead she asked, "Why lie to Benson and tell him that I am your main squeeze?"

"I wanted to see Benson squirm. Let him think I'm sleeping with the enemy and shooting my mouth off about family business."

"You despise him. Why? He's one smarmy character, I admit, but you hardly know him."

A waiter came by and offered to bring them a drink. Kelly requested a Cadillac margarita, preferring the mellow taste the Triple Sec and Grand Marnier gave the tequila. Logan ordered Herradura Anejo—straight. Like Pop, he could drink straight tequila. Kelly had to be careful or she'd be woozy after one slushy margarita.

"Williams is a bottom feeder," Logan told her as they waited for their drinks. "Lower even than a politician, he lives off the Stanfields. How would you like to return home, having just learned you'd been adopted, only to get another shock when you discovered you were a rich man's bastard? My father wanted to know what had happened to me. Had I suffered with the McCords? Could he do anything for me?"

Kelly looked around the crowd. It wasn't difficult to spot Logan's father; he was the only man as tall as Logan. Across the lawn Haywood Stanfield was holding court, talking to Peter Jennings and Tom Brokaw while Ginger stood beside him.

"Before I could say anything about myself, Benson Williams jumped in. He immediately panicked everyone. What would happen if the media learned about me? What about Ginger's feelings? That's when good old Ginger decided to faint and Benson had to carry her to her room.''

''By now the twins were thinking you were a threat on another level, right? You could inherit part of the Stanfield fortune.''

''Exactly. All they discussed was damage control and how to make this work for the family not against them. I told them to take their name and shove it. I was going back to the Cobras and use my own name.''

''I'll bet Benson applauded your decision.''

''Of course. I walked out, pissed big-time. No one had asked anything about me. You know more about me than any of them.''

Thankfully, the waiter arrived with their drinks. Not knowing what to say, Kelly sipped the ice-cold margarita, the first swallow bringing the tang of the salt on the rim. Logan's tone was so casual that they might have been discussing a ball game, but the underlying bitterness was unmistakable.

It seemed to be out of character for him to reveal something so personal about himself, but she couldn't imagine what motive he might have. He was an extraordinary man, complex . . . and unpredictable. She couldn't shake the feeling that her ''exclusive'' was just the tip of the iceberg.

''Logan, I would really like to hear the rest of your story. On the record or off the record, it's your call.''

He kicked back the double shot of straight tequila. ''Would you? Let's go over there and have a chat.''

His hand on the back of her waist, he guided her across the crowded lawn to the shade of an ancient sycamore whose gnarled branches spread outward, embracing the endless blue sky. A squirrel saw them approaching and scampered up the trunk near a blue jay who was scolding them for invading his privacy.

Logan turned his back to the people gathered for the party and pulled off his sunglasses. Then he reached toward her, his strong fingers brushing her cheek as he took off her sunglasses. For a moment they were brim to brim, the bill of his baseball cap nudging the curved rim of her cowboy hat.

"Kelly, if you want all the gory details of my life, all you have to do is trot over to my room tonight . . . and bring a box of condoms."

His deep blue eyes flashed in a way that was now becoming familiar. He smiled, a cunning grin that said he was deliberately baiting her and enjoying every second.

Last night he'd tipped his hand, revealing he knew about her relationship with Matthew Jensen. Logan must know how much she had loved Daniel, remaining loyal to his memory long after most women would have begun dating again.

"You know I wouldn't trade sex for a story. Can't you be serious?"

"Isn't that what reporters do? Aren't we in the era of checkbook journalism? Sex or money, what's the difference?"

She calmly took her sunglasses out of his hand and put them on again. "Reputable journalists don't pay for a story—in any type of currency. That's what sets us apart from tabloid journalists who feature stories about alien abductions and homeopathic cures for cancer."

"Too bad." His eyes widened with false shock as he put on his sunglasses. "I'm a lot of fun in bed."

In bed. The image that popped into Kelly's mind was definitely X-rated. She sipped her margarita and assured herself that she was never going to see Logan with all his clothes off. In her bed.

"Logan, Logan," called a seductive female voice.

Kelly looked up to see Alyx Stanfield coming their way. The beautiful blonde was over forty now, but looked Kelly's age. According to rumor, Alyx spent hours in the local spa where they soaked and steamed and purged and peeled her until her own mother wouldn't recognize her. That wasn't saying much. Ginger seemed zoned out most of the time.

Alyx had never married, which seemed odd. Supposedly she was active in the family business, but Kelly wondered. The times Kelly had seen Alyx and Tyler together, she'd noted the telepathic bond that seemed to link them. Like many twins, they silently communicated with each other.

"Hello, Alyx," Logan said in his gruff voice.

Alyx waved a half full champagne glass at him. "Introduce me to your friend."

Kelly cringed, resisting the urge to make a sarcastic remark. Benson Williams rarely came into Sedona, but Alyx flitted around town, spending money like a drunken sailor. How many times had she been introduced to Alyx Stanfield, yet the woman *never* remembered her?

Not recognizing Kelly was demeaning. *You're nobody and no matter how many times I meet you, it isn't worth my time to remember your name.*

"I'm sure you've met Kelly Taylor from the *Sedona Sun*." His tone dared the woman to contradict him, making Kelly want to kiss Logan. He was right; she despised these people.

"Kelly? Yes . . . of course." Alyx said, then she leveled her China blue eyes on Logan. "Woody is going to read the statement Benson drafted after the barbecue. Are you ready?"

"Yep," Logan said, his voice rougher than usual.

"Don't drink too much tequila, Logan. We don't want you soused for the news conference."

Soused? It was impossible for Kelly to imagine Logan inebriated. He was much too in control. Alyx had a lot of nerve to be so insulting. Evidently, she didn't know how dangerous Logan could be.

"I'm not saying anything, remember?" Logan told his half-sister. "I agreed to *one* family photograph. Then I'm outta here."

"Don't forget your promise," Alyx said in a smooth voice that implied she was accustomed to people following her orders. "Leave immediately after the photograph is taken."

As Alyx slinked away, hips swaying provocatively in her black sheath, Kelly whispered, "What a bitch."

Logan shrugged off Alyx's insulting attitude. "This is a toxic family. Dysfunctional does not describe it. I was damned lucky to be kidnapped."

No sooner had Alyx left than Tyler Stanfield emerged from the crowd. A natural politician, Kelly decided, noting Tyler's patronizing smile.

"Logan, I see you're finally here. I want you to know how

happy we are to have you back with the family. Let me be the first to say—"

"Can it, Tyler." Logan cut him off. "You're scared pissless what I might do to your senate bid. Worse, dear ole dad might not become president just because some damn computer decided I was your little brother."

Tyler kept smiling, and Kelly decided it must be a genetic defect. In the face of any problem, the Stanfields smiled and smiled and smiled.

Benson Williams joined them, his brow furrowed with worry. He seemed much younger than his late fifties, Kelly observed. He was a good-looking man, tall with dark hair that was barely showing gray at the temples. It was difficult to understand why he had been content to live his life in Haywood Stanfield's shadow.

"I want you to get your food and sit close to the podium." Benson gestured toward the area where a microphone had been placed on a dark oak podium emblazoned with brass lettering: Senator Haywood Stanfield. "I want you to be ready for the family photograph after Haywood makes his statement. Don't say one word to any of the reporters."

Next to Kelly, Logan's whole body became rigid. The tension emanating from his body told her he didn't like being ordered around. She waited, holding her breath, expecting Logan to deck the pompous creep.

Chapter 9

It took every ounce of self-control to prevent Logan from punching Benson Williams. Everything about the man pissed-off Logan.

Just wait. Williams would get his.

The older man strutted away, and Logan glanced down, suddenly aware of Kelly's soft hand on his arm. A swift shadow of anger swept across her face, then disappeared as she smiled up at him. Logan wasn't fooled; she was disappointed he'd just stood there, taking that crap.

He hadn't learned patience until he'd been selected for the Cobras. Outsmarting terrorists required more than just skill and intelligence. You had to know when not to tip your hand.

From the moment he'd met the Stanfields, Logan had deliberately concealed the anger that continued to fester. Fury choked him now, and he was afraid anything he said would reveal more about himself than he wanted Kelly to know. He'd already told her more about himself than he'd intended.

In the field, mistakes like that got you killed—if you were lucky. The most serious blunder he'd made had nearly left him unable to talk. As it was, his voice sounded like a bad bruise.

Watch your back.

Concentrate on the warning, he told himself. Not on Kelly Taylor.

"You don't feel like eating, do you?" Kelly asked when he made no move to join the barbecue line—or follow Williams's order to move closer to the podium.

"I'd rather eat a lizard without salt than take any of their food."

She laughed, a light mellow sound that caused several men nearby to turn and look at her in a way that spiked his anger. His irritation with the Stanfield clan must be getting to him. He couldn't be jealous.

"I say we wait until we get home and eat with Pop."

"Good idea." From behind his sunglasses, he gave her a slow once-over. Kelly had no idea how she looked in that soft denim dress. He turned away, uncomfortably aware of the subtle change in his body. He squeezed his eyes shut for a moment, so his usual willpower could reassert itself.

"In your article, what did you say about the Stanfields?" he asked, opening his eyes.

"I told the story from your point of view. It doesn't paint a flattering portrait of the family." She caught her bottom lip between her teeth for a moment, thinking. It wasn't a deliberately provocative gesture, but it made him aware of just how attractive her lips were. "If I'd known how badly they'd treated you, I would have been harder on them. Why did you wait until today to tell me?"

"I hate whiners. I wasn't raised to be a cry-baby." *Wasn't that the truth.*

She tilted her head slightly, a mannerism she shared with her grandfather, and he could feel her studying him from behind the dark glasses. "What aren't you telling me?"

He didn't bother to smile, knowing it wouldn't work on Kelly. She had a built-in bullshit detector and knew he was up to something, but she hadn't quite figured out what.

"Some of the info is classified. The rest . . . trust me, babe, you wouldn't want to know."

"Try me."

"The offer is still open. Come to my room tonight." He

knew Kelly wouldn't do it. The information he had on her revealed she had been faithful to her husband, and judging from what Pop had told him, she was still struggling to cope with Daniel Taylor's death.

What the hell? He was only teasing Kelly, getting perverse pleasure out of baiting her. But he had to admit the thought of her sharing his pillow, her blond hair tousled, her sweet lips breathlessly parted—was a real turn-on.

Benson Williams's voice came over the microphone, instructing everyone to help themselves to the food, then find a table. It took another few minutes for the guests to take their places.

While they did, reporters jockeyed for spots in front of the podium. All cameras had been banned because this was a ''family celebration'' and they didn't want to make the barbecue too much like a political event. One photographer had been hired to take the single family photograph, which would be released to the media.

What a crock! Didn't the media understand that Nazi prick, Benson Williams was manipulating them, putting his spin on the story?

''Shouldn't we move a little closer?'' Kelly suggested.

''Nope. They'll find me here.'' He was through being treated like shit and ordered around. As soon as this press conference was over, he was leaving the Stanfields behind forever.

Trouble was, he didn't have a clue where he was going or what he would do when he got there. For damn sure, he wasn't taking a desk job in the Pentagon.

Benson Williams began speaking again, thanking everyone for coming, and saying how much the Stanfield family appreciated their friends.

Kelly whispered, ''Do you actually think they have any friends here? Political cronies and media people are all I see. What would it be like not to have any real friends?''

He could tell Kelly wasn't being sarcastic. She was genuinely distressed at the thought. Little did she know that he was more like the Stanfields than she suspected.

Danger was his best friend. His only friend.

Okay, Brodie Adams could be considered a friend. The two of them had been on enough missions together. Logan could turn his back on Brodie, something he rarely did with anyone. It had been Brodie who'd broken the news about being the missing boy to Logan.

Kelly tuned out Benson Williams and checked her watch. It was almost five o'clock, which meant it was eight in New York. Information about her article on Logan McCord would be posted on the *Eposé* Website at eight. Word would spread quickly. She'd bet anything that by ten minutes after the post, someone in New York would contact one of the media honchos attending the barbecue. Most of them had cell phones or pagers, or both.

Haywood Stanfield would be asked some tough questions, she thought, trying not to smile. She glanced sideways at Logan and wondered how he would react to his father's speech. She tried to imagine what it would be like to suddenly discover you were part of a family like this.

A love child.

She couldn't conceive of what Logan must be feeling. His reception by the family had angered him, which was lucky for her. Now she had an exclusive interview, but she couldn't shake the impression that there was more to this story than what Logan had told her. If he'd lied to her, and she'd convinced Matthew to run the story, it could ruin Matt's career.

She shuddered inwardly at the thought. Matt did not deserve to have his life turned inside out because of her. She mentally crossed her fingers and prayed Logan hadn't lied to her.

Haywood Stanfield walked up to the podium, and Ginger stood beside him. The twins, Tyler and Alyx waited nearby. They were ten years older than Logan, and had their mother's Nordic blond looks while Logan could have been Woody Stanfield's younger brother.

Despite her beauty and her father's money, Alyx had never married and rarely dated. She was very active socially, never missing an A-list party, but she was usually with her brother or with Benson and Ginger.

Tyler had been married several years ago. His wife Suzanne's tragic death must have been a terrible blow because Tyler had never remarried. Even though Tyler seemed shallow, life having been far too easy for him, Kelly sympathized. She knew how achingly lonesome the world seemed after you lost someone you loved.

Haywood began by thanking everyone for coming. His expression was somber, his dark blue eyes—Logan's eyes—were troubled. Kelly sensed the crowd's anticipation. They were expecting him to announce his intention to run for president and were wondering why he wasn't more upbeat.

"I have something important to share with you all, my closest friends. That's why I asked you here today, so you would be the very first to know. Years ago our family suffered a tragic loss. The son we adopted vanished. His disappearance has haunted us ever since. Not a day went by that we didn't pray for our son."

Ginger sighed and dabbed her eyes with a lace-edged handkerchief. Haywood paused to put his arm around her. The guests murmured to each other, wondering what this was all about.

Kelly stole a glance at Logan. He had taken off the cap and was raking his fingers through his hair. He didn't appear to be nervous, even though in a few minutes he'd be the center of attention.

And controversy.

"Our prayers were finally answered."

Haywood let the words hang in the air, and Kelly decided he had a flair for drama. Or was this Benson Williams's idea? The political advisor was on the sidelines, his arms crossed in front of his chest, watching intently.

"You all may remember me sponsoring legislation that became the 1995 National Crime and Terrorism Prevention Act. As a result law enforcement agencies received funds to electronically store fingerprints and photo identification to check the tidal wave of crime sweeping this country."

Kelly heaved a sigh, detecting Benson Williams's attempt at rescuing Haywood's reputation.

"The FBI was able to update their files, adding information from across the country. The Cobra Force asked them to run a fingerprint check. They discovered our boy, now a grown man, was working for the government and using the name Logan McCord. Logan had no idea that his last name wasn't McCord. He had been kidnapped by a couple who never told him the truth."

The guests whispered excitedly. Kelly noticed a prominent newscaster pull out his cell phone. It had been exactly three minutes since *Exposé* had posted the information about her upcoming article on their Website.

Haywood continued, explaining how Logan had "suffered," never attending school and living in abject poverty. He made the McCords sound heartless, which was not the impression Logan had given her.

And it wasn't the way she'd portrayed the McCords in her article.

True, she condemned them for stealing the child, but she didn't say Logan had been miserable with them. Just today Logan had said: *I was lucky to have been kidnapped.* The more she thought about it, the odder his comment seemed.

"Naturally, Ginger was delighted to hear Logan was alive and well." Haywood's arm was still around his wife, the perfect image of a loving husband. "We invited Logan to come here and meet the family again. It was a shock to all of us when he arrived."

Kelly noticed several other guests had out their cell phones. She glanced at Logan and smiled. Earlier she'd told him about the Website post. He said the reporters at the barbecue would be furious with Benson and Haywood for allowing Kelly to scoop them.

"I had done something terribly wrong," Haywood admitted, a quaver in his voice. "I never told my family the truth. Logan wasn't just some child we happened to adopt. I'd had a fling with his mother, and she became pregnant. I should have told

Ginger before we adopted Logan, but I love her and didn't want to hurt her.''

A buzz rippled through the crowd. The twins remained stoic, but Ginger began to cry silently. Logan's mirrored sunglasses concealed his face, but he was leaning against the sycamore as if he weren't involved.

"In the end, I hurt my wife . . . and my entire family by not telling the truth. When Logan returned, it had been many years since we'd seen him. Logan had been five and had light hair and blue eyes. The man who knocked on our door looked exactly like me. You can imagine how shocked Ginger was . . . and how terribly devastated.''

Ginger had stopped crying, but tears glistened on her cheeks. She was one of the few women who could cry and still look beautiful. She'd aged well, Kelly observed. There was hardly a line on her face, and she was as slim now as she'd been in the photographs at the time Logan disappeared. Most men would find it difficult to imagine cheating on her.

Kelly wondered what Logan's mother had been like. She'd asked, but he didn't know anything about her. And he didn't seem to care.

"I can only thank God that I have been blessed with a wonderful, understanding wife. I explained what had happened and Ginger immediately welcomed Logan into the family.'' He looked over at the twins. "Tyler and Alyx were thrilled to have him home again.''

Thrilled was not how Kelly had described the family in her story. The Stanfields were portrayed as self-absorbed, interested in the political implications of Logan's return, not in the man himself.

"We begged Logan to stay with us, but he has his own life and a career combating terrorism. He's chosen to return to the Cobra Force and keep the name he's always believed was his own—McCord. Logan did agree to come today to meet all our friends.'' Although Haywood had never looked in their direction, he now motioned for Logan to join him.

People pivoted in their seats, craning their necks to get a glimpse of Logan. He handed Kelly his cap and sunglasses.

He strode forward, looking neither right nor left as he passed the tables and went to the podium.

Kelly couldn't help being proud of him. Despite his nonchalant attitude, this had to be difficult for him. He smiled too often, joked too much. There was something about him that suggested a bleak soul who had traveled the back roads of life and had seen unimaginable things, experienced things that would have destroyed a lesser person.

As sophisticated and urbane as most of the guests were, startled gasps and excited chatter filled the air as Logan stood beside his father. Haywood's revelation had stunned them, but seeing Logan, a clone of his father, shocked them even more. Kelly knew they were all assessing the effect of this on Haywood's political career.

A dozen reporters jumped to their feet, shouting questions. Kelly exhaled fully for the first time since Haywood had begun speaking. She had been worrying without a reason. Logan had told her the truth about what Haywood Stanfield would say.

Benson moved to take charge of what was quickly becoming bedlam as reporters shouted questions. "The senator has made his statement. Now Tyler Stanfield is going to explain about—"

"You said we were the first to hear this, right?" A reporter cut off Benson, directing his question to Haywood.

"Absolutely. That's the reason for this party," Benson assured him, but he seemed flustered, obviously sensing something was wrong.

"Then why is *Exposé* publishing a special issue featuring an exclusive interview with Logan?"

Logan stepped forward, answering the question in his distinctive voice with its husky catch. "I gave them an exclusive because one of their reporters was way ahead of the pack. Kelly Taylor tracked me down before any of you knew I existed."

Kelly suddenly became the focus of attention and she did her best to look every inch the sharp investigative reporter. Logan had given her more credit than she deserved; Matthew had dropped the story in her lap. There was a moment of astonished silence, then everyone began talking at once.

Except the Stanfields.

They closed ranks, the twins flanking their parents as Logan walked off. He shouldered his way past reporters shouting questions at him. When he reached Kelly, he took her arm.

"Take me to the airport," he said as he led her away.

She waited until they were out of hearing range before asking, "Do you really want to go to the airport? Your stuff is still at Pop's place."

"I don't want any of these jerks looking for me here. Let 'em think I've left town."

They were waiting for the parking valet to bring up Kelly's Toyota when Haywood rushed up to them.

"Are you satisfied? You just ruined my chances of becoming president."

Logan opened the door to Kelly's car and helped her inside saying to his father, "Did you ever think you ruined my mother's life?"

Chapter 10

Kelly tipped her champagne until the glass kissed the rim of Matthew Jensen's martini glass. She couldn't remember being happier.

Since before Daniel had died.

The record-breaking success of the *Exposé* issue with Logan Stanfield on the cover had been a major coup. Her reputation as a cutting-edge journalist had been restored even more quickly than it had been destroyed.

Thanks to Matthew Jensen.

He'd brought her the story, and now he'd come to Sedona to offer her a job in New York. She dreaded telling him that she couldn't leave until . . . She didn't want to think about the future when Pop would die and leave her alone. With luck it would be years from now.

"I should have printed twice as many issues," Matt told her with a smile. "We sold out overnight."

"All TV had was a still shot and a voice over from a reporter," she responded, resisting the urge to laugh.

The cover made the issue a blockbuster, she decided. A drop-dead gorgeous hunk and an adorable golden retriever with the headline:

KIDNAPPED!

What did it mean? people wondered. Inside they read the shocking tale of a potential presidential candidate's illegitimate son who had been abducted as a child.

Every time she thought about her success, Kelly blessed Matthew—and Logan—for making this happen. She had been sitting in the middle of nowhere, her career had nose-dived when Logan's story fell into her lap.

Matthew had flown into Sedona to celebrate, and he'd taken Kelly to Enchantment for dinner. Kelly was prepared, having rehearsed all the reasons she could think of to persuade Matt to employ her as a freelance reporter. As a FL, she would be able to work for him, yet keep her home base here with Pop. She already had a great idea.

Kelly waited until after they'd ordered to say, "There's more to this story than Logan or the Stanfields are telling. I want to nose around a bit and do a followup piece."

Matt's dark eyes narrowed slightly. "It'll be toast by Friday."

"I know it will be old news with all the media rehashing the story, but I'm positive there's something else going on. Logan hates the Stanfields. His reaction seems extreme, considering he just met them."

Kelly could have added that she was certain Logan had diabolically planned to disgrace Haywood Stanfield. He'd used her to do it, his comment about his mother still troubling her. There was much more to Logan's story, and she intended to uncover all the facts.

"We rarely run follow-up articles." Matt sounded distracted as if the last thing on his mind was this story.

"Logan claims not to know anything about his real mother, yet he was furious with Haywood for ruining her life. Doesn't that seem strange to you?"

"Yes," Matt agreed without enthusiasm.

"Let me see what I come up with, then you decide if you want to run the piece."

Matt nodded, the candlelight glinting off his dark hair, but he didn't encourage her. "Do you know where Logan McCord is? No one can find him."

"When he gave me an exclusive, he never intended to discuss his life with anyone else. Movie companies have called me, looking for him. The tabloids are willing to pay him megabucks. Oprah, Rosie—everyone wants him, but Logan doesn't care."

The waiter served their salads, and Matt took a bite before asking, "You didn't answer my question. Where is McCord?"

"Pop convinced him to stay with us. Reporters will never think to look for him there." She didn't add that she liked the idea. She didn't want to chance a crafty reporter getting to Logan.

"Staying with you?" Matt's voice conveyed more than a hint of disapproval.

"There are two *casitas* beyond the main house," she reminded him. One summer Matt had spent a week in Sedona, staying in a *casita*. "Pop told Logan to live with us until he decides what to do. He doesn't want the desk job they offered him."

Kelly could have told Matt how uncomfortable their relationship made her. Logan spent hours with Pop, hiking on Sedona's trails and training Jasper. Macho male stuff, but she felt left out in a way that she could never have verbalized.

Matt put down his fork. "Tell McCord to put an ad in *Soldier of Fortune*. That would be right up his alley."

Kelly took her time eating her salad, not knowing what to say. She recalled Matt's comment about Logan being another "lost soul" in need of rescue. It was apparent Matt did not like Logan hanging around.

"Matt," she said, deliberately changing the subject. "how can I thank you for giving me this chance?"

He gazed at her, his expression becoming even more serious. "You know you've always been special to me, don't you?"

"You're special to me, too," she replied, but she knew her feelings weren't as strong as his. The subject made her uneasy. She didn't want Matt to embarrass himself and regret it later. He was her friend and she wanted to keep it that way.

"I would never do anything to hurt you . . . if I could avoid it."

His voice had a disturbing undertone to it. The night he'd come to her apartment to tell her Daniel had been killed, Matt had the same tone to his voice, as if he was being forced to do something at gunpoint.

"What is it, Matt? What's wrong?"

He pulled something out of his pocket, and she saw it was a photograph that was worn around the edges. Hesitating for a second, he handed it to her.

It was a snapshot of a child. Big blue eyes. Wavy hair the color of rich chocolate. A distinctive cleft in his small chin.

"It's a picture of Daniel when he was a child," she cried. "Where did you get it?"

"That's not Daniel Taylor."

She tilted the photograph toward the dim candlelight and saw the date that showed when the picture had been taken. It was less than a year old. Baffled, she studied the child's face. "It looks exactly like him. Who is it?"

He studied her face for a moment, then said, "His son."

It can't be. Her lips formed the words but no sound came out. She stared at the candle on the table, overcome by a gamut of perplexing emotions. The little boy couldn't be more than three, four at the most, which indicated he'd been born while she had been married to Daniel.

She was hardly aware of the waiter removing the salad dishes, then serving the main course. Osso bucco was one of her favorite dishes. Prepared by a chef at a four-star resort like Enchantment, it was undoubtedly first rate, but the scent of the meat brought a rush of bile to her throat.

Rising, fighting back tears, she rushed away from the table. She streaked through the open French doors onto the patio. Enchantment was set on 70 acres of Red Rock country in Boynton Canyon. Nearby was Boynton Vortex, famous for its healing powers.

Kelly inhaled deeply, taking a gulp of piñon-scented air into her lungs and holding it. The positive energy from a vortex was supposed to calm your mind and heal your spirit.

"It's not working," she said to herself.

Tears trembled on her lashes as she let out her breath, and the cold vise of reality cinched her, cutting off her breath. Daniel had fathered a child, a love child. Her sense of betrayal was so overwhelming that it stopped the tears.

Theirs had been the perfect marriage, she'd told herself. They had juggled two careers—on two continents—and still had a wonderful relationship. But how happy could Daniel have been to engage in an affair that resulted in a child?

"The truth hurts," she whispered.

What she felt went beyond pain beyond tears. She'd loved Daniel and trusted him. She'd believed with all her heart that he loved her just as much as she loved him.

She had been living a lie.

Kelly gazed out at the moon-washed escarpments that were a deep rust color by day, but at night they were dark, mysterious silhouettes. Lonely. A fickle breeze riffled down from a mountain ridge, bringing with it the mournful sound of a night bird singing of lost love. Usually the natural beauty of the land soothed her.

Not tonight.

She staggered off the patio and dodged a saguaro cactus. She clutched her chest with both arms as grief tore through her, gouging deep inside over . . . and over . . . and over. She charged headlong toward the wilderness area surrounding the resort.

"Kelly! Kelly! Wait!"

She raced faster as if she could outrun her grief and leave it behind her. The wind billowed through her hair, whipping a strand across her eyes. She stumbled over one of the countless rocks that made the landscape unique. Suddenly she was on her knees, palms scraping across the dirt. She picked up a fistful of loose pebbles and flung them at a nearby boulder.

How could Daniel do this to her? How could he?

Matt dashed up to her, puffing like a race horse, and gently helped her to her feet. He pulled her into his arms, and she rested her head against his shoulder. He hugged her tight, whispering her name.

Tears poured from her eyes. They gushed out along with a keening cry of utter misery. The sob reverberated through her chest, ripping at her, but doing nothing to lessen the grief.

"Go ahead and cry," Matt whispered, stroking the back of her head. "Let it out."

She wanted to stop, but she couldn't. Tears flowed in a torrent, and with them, came gut-wrenching sobs that made her ribs ache. Matt anchored her to his chest, whispering words she couldn't hear because she was crying so loudly.

She had no idea how long she'd stood there, sheltered by his arms, until her chest shuddered, and she had to gulp for breath.

Matt dabbed at her eyes with his handkerchief. "Darling, it's all right."

His words sobered her in a way nothing else could have. She took the handkerchief from him, air filling her lungs in ragged gasps. Matt cared about her, she thought. He truly cared.

He'd always been at her side, ready to help. Seeing her profound grief for another man had to hurt him almost as much as Daniel's betrayal devastated her. Why couldn't she have fallen head over heels for Matthew Jensen?

Matt had warned her about Daniel. Don't marry him, Matt had told her, claiming Daniel would only hurt her. At the time she thought he was merely jealous, but now she wondered if he'd detected something in Daniel that she had not.

Life is not fair. Suddenly, her grandfather's sage comment took on real meaning. No, life was not fair, but you had to deal with it.

She stepped out of his arms and blew her nose. The snorting sound could have flushed out the white-tail deer that hide in the thickets of alligator juniper. But she was beyond being embarrassed.

This was her best friend, Matt. He'd seen her at her worst. First, when he'd brought her the news of Daniel's death, and now, when he'd told her about Daniel's love child.

"I'm sorry," she mumbled. "It's just that I had no idea."

His arm around her waist, he guided her over to a slab of

red rock. They sat down, and Kelly tried to stop shaking. Her breathing became more even, but the internal pain remained.

"What did I do wrong?" she asked.

He took her hand, gently squeezing it. "Nothing. You're a wonderful person. Loving. Giving. Intelligent." He kissed her forehead. "Beautiful."

"Matt, please, tell me the truth."

"The truth? No one knows what goes on in someone else's head." Bitterness underscored his words. "Daniel Taylor was damaged. Being bounced from foster home to foster home must have done something to him. He craved the spotlight and always wanted to be the center of attention."

"You're right. He was always the life of the party. He was fun to be with. He never seemed to be down. He was so happy that I never suspected—"

"When he was promoted to the South American Bureau and went to Venezuela, Daniel entered another world. He was lonely."

"I should have gone with him, but he said it was only temporary and I shouldn't give up my career for him. We saw each other as often as we could. It seemed to work."

At the time she questioned her decision to remain in New York. Now she knew she should have quit and started a family.

"Tell me about the boy. What is his name?"

"He's Rafael Zamora. At the orphanage the nuns call him Rafi."

"Orphanage? Where's his mother? Didn't she want him?" Kelly already hated the woman who was responsible for Daniel betraying her. How could she give up her child?

"Carmen Zamora was a secretary in Daniel's office." Matt paused to squeeze her hand again. "She was on the plane with him when it crashed. Her mother had Rafi, but she died. There was no one to take the child, so he was sent to an orphanage."

She remembered the photograph. The adorable little boy had Daniel's blue eyes and thick dark hair. He'd been staring at the camera with the same captivating intensity Daniel had, an endearingly familiar expression. This should have been her child—their child.

"How did you find out about the boy?"

He hesitated, then answered, "Daniel told me."

For a moment her mind refused to register his words. Finally she managed to respond. "Daniel discussed his affair with you? Why?"

Matt shrugged. "He knew how much I cared about you. I guess he thought I could help you."

"That doesn't make any sense. If you came to me and said Daniel was having an affair I would have been terribly hurt. How could that possibly help?"

When he didn't respond, strange and upsetting thoughts raced through her mind. Slowly she realized what he was trying to tell her. "Daniel was leaving me for that woman, wasn't he?"

"Yes, Kelly . . . he intended to file for a divorce."

"Why didn't you tell me before? Why wait two years?" She struggled to temper the shrill note in her voice. Matt was a good friend, and she could see this wasn't easy for him.

"I didn't want to hurt you. I didn't tell you because I believed Rafi's grandmother was going to raise him. Someone in Daniel's office down there called to tell me Rafi's an orphan now. I thought you would want to know." He pulled the photograph out of his pocket and handed it to her.

Even in the moonlight she could see how special the child was. So innocent, and yet she couldn't help resenting him, the living proof of Daniel's betrayal. A disturbing memory crept in from the past, and she recalled being a young child who had lost both parents. She'd accepted the news bravely because she didn't comprehend what this loss would mean until later.

All she knew was that she was alone. And she was terribly frightened. She'd been staying with friends of her parents when the news came. She hid under the bed, so no one bad could find her.

Then Pop arrived. There was no reason to be afraid, he assured her. She wasn't alone in the world because she had him and he loved her with all his heart.

Who would love Daniel's son?

"Of course, I want to know about Rafi." Hot tears stung her eyes, and she blinked them away. "I won't lie to you and say this hasn't crushed me. In a way, it's worse than hearing Daniel had been killed in a plane crash—much worse. But I can't blame the child, and I certainly can't allow him to spend his life in an orphanage. I'm going to get him.''

''I wish it were that simple.'' Matt looked away for a moment, and the lonely howl of a coyote pierced the night air. ''A single woman cannot adopt a child in Venezuela. Rafi is in an orphanage that requires a Catholic family adopt him.''

''I'm Catholic,'' Kelly responded, her voice barely above a whisper.

Matt scooted nearer, closing the small space between them. ''Kelly, I know this is a terrible shock to you. We've been close for almost fifteen years. It can't come as any surprise how I feel about you.''

Kelly looked down, not wanting to hear this. She knew Matt still cared for her. They had been destined to marry—then Daniel Taylor came along.

Her thoughts reeling, she couldn't concentrate on what Matt was saying. All she could think about was a young child—alone—in an orphanage. That could have been her, except Pop had been there ready to take her into his heart. Could she do that for Daniel's love child?

Would she resent the boy and blame him for an affair that wasn't his fault? Of course, not. She identified with the pain the child must be experiencing. All she wanted was a way to bring him here, so she could see that he received what every child deserved—love.

''Kelly, we've always been so close. I'm positive if you married me, you would come to love me the way you loved Daniel. We could adopt Rafi.''

Matt's words didn't come as a total surprise; Kelly had known he hadn't stopped caring about her just because Daniel had blazed into her life. Kelly almost said, yes, but stopped herself in time.

How self-centered could she be? Matthew Jensen had been her friend since the first day she'd set a foot on the Yale campus. He'd championed her even to this point when her career had been in the gutter.

Didn't Matt deserve someone who truly loved him?

Kelly chose her words carefully. "I have no idea how I am going to handle this situation. But I can't take advantage of you simply because I want Daniel's son. That wouldn't be fair to you. You must marry someone who truly loves you."

Chapter 11

Logan booted up his computer and saw his e-mail icon flashing. It could only be Raptor. About time. He'd been waiting for over a week to hear from his commander.

We have a new field assignment for you. In six months we'll relocate you in Africa. Until then you are on leave. Have some fun for a change.
Raptor

"Fun? Aw, crap," Logan stared at the message on the screen. It had been two weeks since the *Exposé* article had been published. He'd known the Cobras couldn't send him back to South America even though he was an expert in the area and spoke Spanish fluently.

"Why Africa?"

Terrorism was common in North Africa, especially in Egypt, but he knew Raptor well enough to realize that he would have specified North Africa if that was where he was being reassigned. He'd be out in bumfuck, rotting away in some country most Americans couldn't spell or find on a map, a country that changed its name with every coup.

"Don't jump to conclusions," he muttered as he shut off the machine.

He walked over to the open French doors and stood on the small patio. The lights in the main house were out. Pop was asleep earlier than usual. No doubt he was exhausted after their hike in Lockett Meadow high up in the San Francisco peaks. Pop insisted that they go there to see the aspens turn.

A small lake had reflected the craggy peaks with ribbons of blazing aspens flowing into the ridges between the rocks. It was nature at its best, but the lake reminded Logan of the pond behind the camp where he'd grown up.

"Forget it." He kept the past locked out of his thoughts— most of the time.

He looked toward the other *casita* to get his mind back on track. Kelly's lights were still on, and if the last week was typical, they'd be on most of the night. What was she doing? He'd expected her to continue to pry the details of his past out of him, the way she had just after the barbecue, but she hadn't.

After Matthew Jensen left town, Kelly had been strangely subdued. She always had dinner with them, but she didn't say very much. Pop probably knew what was wrong, but he hadn't told Logan.

It was just about the only thing about Kelly that Pop hadn't mentioned. Logan and Pop spent their days on the hiking trails around Sedona because it was the only place reporters weren't looking for him. Pop's health kept them off the steepest trails, but he enjoyed getting out.

Pop was someone special. He took great pride in two things. Nature and Kelly. He knew the name of every plant and animal they came across. With amazing detail he recalled Kelly's accomplishments from her first piano recital to her graduation from Yale.

Despite his willingness to share those stories, Pop never mentioned Kelly's wedding or anything about Daniel Taylor. Logan had asked and found out the wedding had been here in the Catholic church. The reception had been held at the Poco Diablo resort.

"Kelly was the most beautiful bride in the world," Pop had

assured him. Not that Logan had any doubts. Other women were prettier, but there was something special about Kelly. He could just imagine her coming down the aisle, eyes bright, face glowing with love.

"Marriage. What a crock!" he said out loud. He'd never attended a wedding. Hell, he'd never been in a church except the time when he and Brodie had hidden in some musty chapel in Colombia, one step ahead of hit men from a drug cartel.

He needed to hightail it out of here. He was becoming way too fond of Pop. And he was spending too much time thinking about Kelly. He hadn't been laid in three weeks, an all time record. That must be why Kelly was on his mind so much.

Leave tomorrow. But where would he go? Six months was a long time to "have fun" if every reporter on the planet was after you.

When were they going to give up?

A noise from the underbrush nearby distracted him. Probably just a javelina. Pop said they hunted at night. For the hell of it, he went inside and took his binoculars out of his pack. They were a military prototype, and like the miniature computer, not available to the public.

The binoculars fit in the palm of his hand, yet they were extraordinarily powerful and had a night-vision adapter. He checked the underbrush. Sure enough. It was a javelina.

For kicks he scanned the area and spotted a mountain lion on a ledge a quarter of a mile away. No, not a mountain lion, he decided, observing the creature more closely, noting the tufts of fur that made its ears pointed. A bobcat.

He swung around and accidentally picked up Kelly. He flicked off the night vision and looked at her for just a minute. Her expression made something tighten in his chest. She wasn't crying, but it might have been better if she were.

What was wrong?

He told himself to look away and not invade her privacy. There was something in her hand. His curiosity got the better of him. He took a closer look and discovered Kelly was staring at a photograph of a young boy.

Pop had never mentioned a child, he thought as he forced

himself to put down the binoculars. Kelly and Pop had no immediate family—just each other. So who was the little boy?

Why do you care?

The little voice in his brain kept him on course. He didn't give a damn. It was time to get the hell out of Dodge.

"I told you that we should have killed him."

How often was she going to remind him? Since Logan McCord's little stunt at the barbecue, she'd harped on this endlessly. Tonight they were in his room, stretched out across his bed, their clothes tossed on the floor.

"If I could find Logan McCord, I would kill the son of a bitch," he assured her.

"It's too late. The damage is already done."

"True, the Haywood Stanfield for president campaign is dead. Why not kill the bastard who's responsible?"

"You'll have to find him first. If the *National Reporter* can't find him, no one can."

His derisive snort told her what he thought of the nation's leading tabloid. Anyone who believed what they read in supermarket checkout lines were idiots, but he had to concede the tabloids usually found ways to get stories no one else could. So, why couldn't they locate the prick?

"Logan McCord may have gone to ground, but he'll resurface." He slid his hand up and cradled her full breast in his palm. The rosy nipple spiraled into a tight nubbin as he brushed it with his tongue. "Meanwhile let's not waste time talking about him."

At breakfast the next morning, Logan announced he was leaving. "I'm getting a new assignment in the field, but it doesn't start for quite a while."

"You don't have to leave," Pop told him, concern furrowing his grizzled brows. "You're welcome here. I enjoy having you."

The heartfelt emotion in Pop's voice stunned Logan. Sure,

he knew the older man liked him, but Logan wasn't prepared for the depth of Pop's emotion. Logan's eyes clouded with memories of the past, and he didn't know what to say.

No one had ever said they liked him—at least not a parental type. Women often said they loved him. In bed talk was cheap. Meaningless.

But this wasn't bedroom talk. They were on the terrace overlooking Oak Creek, eating Uma's fabulous breakfast burritos. A finch was warbling from the willow tree on the far bank. Jasper was at Logan's side, looking up at him with adoring eyes, silently begging to be petted.

Way, way past time to get out of Dodge.

"Did I hear you say you were leaving?"

Kelly came up to the table, a cup of coffee in her hand. The shadows under her eyes were deeper than he'd remembered. She appeared to be losing weight. No wonder. Lately she'd been living on coffee. Logan hadn't seen her eat much since the night Matthew Jensen arrived to take her to dinner.

They hadn't seen him, but Logan had watched them through his binoculars as the cocky jerk helped Kelly into the car. She'd been laughing and happy, at ease with Matthew in a way that she never was with Logan. She'd returned early that evening, and Logan could have sworn he heard her crying. But when he went to the patio door to listen, the only sound was the yipping of coyotes, foraging in the hills.

"I've got six months before I'm reassigned," he told her as she sat down. "I'm going to have some fun."

She nodded slowly, studying him intently. Had he done something wrong? Okay, he almost choked on the word "fun." He didn't know what in hell he was going to do or where he was going to go, but staying here wasn't an option.

"Where are you going?" she asked.

"Disneyland," he said without hesitation.

There was a second of stunned silence, then Pop and Kelly burst out laughing. What was so damned funny? His childhood had been one long course in survival training in preparation for a doomsday he now knew would never come. He'd never been to an amusement park of any kind.

He was curious that's all. He wasn't planning to go on any of the rides. Everywhere he traveled people talked about Disneyland as if it were heaven on earth. He wanted to see what the fuss was about.

"We're not making fun of you," Pop explained. "Haven't you noticed that when some sports figure wins a championship, they always say they're going to Disneyland? They get paid to do it, of course."

"Oh, yeah," he said as if he knew what Pop was talking about, but he didn't. Logan had grown up without a television or even a radio. The outside world had been a mystery until he'd enlisted.

Then his life had changed. He'd been busy playing catch-up on his education and training as a Cobra. He rarely watched television.

"Are you really going to Disneyland?" Kelly wanted to know.

He shrugged, a little embarrassed to admit that was his plan.

"How would you like to make some money instead?" she asked.

"Kelly—no!" Pop's voice was stern.

Logan could have told her that he was rich. Granted, he didn't have a fortune like his old man, the cat-litter king, but Logan had saved every penny he'd made since enlisting. Incentive pay for high-risk operations, combat pay, underwater demolition pay, joint-operation pay for special projects when the DEA had needed someone with counter-terrorism experience.

He'd invested wisely, avoiding Wall Street's more volatile stocks, placing his money in mutual funds. He had enough money to retire now. But what would he do with the rest of his life?

Being a Cobra *was* his life.

"What did you have in mind?" he asked, intrigued by the tension between them. It was obvious they had discussed this, and Pop did not approve. Weird. Pop usually acted as if Kelly walked on water.

Pop grimaced and Kelly hesitated, her hand clutching the

mug of coffee. Logan's pulse skittered. His sixth sense kicked in and told him this was no ordinary job.

Great! A challenge beat the hell out of Disneyland.

''My husband died in a plane crash,'' she began. ''I recently discovered he has a son who's in an orphanage in Venezuela.''

The boy in the picture, he realized. She was going to ask him to get the kid out of the orphanage. This wasn't much of a challenge, but it was a way to kill time.

''I'll go get him,'' he said. ''Where is he exactly?''

''Son, wait a minute,'' Pop said. ''You'd better listen to the whole story.''

Kelly stared into her coffee cup as if she were reading tea leaves. ''He's in a Catholic orphanage in Elorza.''

''You're kidding. I've never been there, but I spent months just over the border in Cravo Norte.''

''Colombia?'' Pop asked with a worried frown.

Logan shrugged it off. Sure, his activities in Colombia caused the drug cartel to put a bounty on his head. That's life.

Uh, oh. Logan had been so focused on the danger element that he'd missed the obvious. This wasn't a child from a previous marriage. This was a bastard son—left behind. Sound familiar?

Something inside him ripped, tearing open a wound he'd believed had been completely healed. He fired back without thinking. ''The boy's better off with the nuns than being here.''

They both stared at him in astonished silence. Finally, Pop spoke. ''How can you say that?''

''Kelly will resent the child. It's better to leave the boy for the nuns to raise him. He'll be all right.''

''That's ridiculous!'' Kelly cried. ''He's all I have left of Daniel. I don't care about his mother. I'll love him as if he were my own child.''

''You think you will, but you won't.''

''How can you be so sure?'' Pop asked.

Logan shrugged, thinking he had to be careful. Pop understood him in a way that no one else ever had. But Logan had experience being the bastard son. He knew what he was talking about.

"I don't want you to even consider it," Pop told him. "It's too dangerous for you to go to South America again."

Tempting, mighty tempting. He loved a challenge. The rush he felt when he took risks made him feel alive in a way that nothing else ever did. Give him any other reason to accept this job and he'd accept her offer, but he didn't want another child to suffer.

He glanced at Kelly and wondered if she would be cruel to a child. Nothing he'd seen indicated that she would. Still, he didn't want to take the chance.

"How much money do you want?" Kelly asked.

"It's not about the money." His voice was more harsh than usual. He was insulted that she thought he was angling to get more money.

"You're afraid to go. All the publicity has made you easily recognizable."

Now he was damn mad and struggled not to show it. "I don't think you'd be a good mother—that's all."

"Of course, she would," Pop insisted. "I'm just worried about you going down there again. I don't want anything to happen to you."

There it was again that heartfelt emotion in Pop's voice. The older man sincerely cared about Logan. He told himself not to be touched, to keep his guard up, but it was difficult.

"Find someone else," Pop told Kelly. "Don't ask Logan to take unnecessary risks."

Kelly stared at her computer screen. She'd lost what little interest she'd had in the upcoming Jazz on the Rocks. Writing articles like this one about the annual jazz festival usually interested her because Sedona drew high quality musicians, but today she was too distracted to write.

Where was she going to find someone to help her get Rafi? She'd thought Logan was the perfect choice. He'd worked in South America, and he spoke Spanish, which she did not. Oh, she knew a few words from living in the Southwest, but she didn't speak it well enough to convince the nuns to let her adopt Daniel's son.

Daniel's son.

The image of the adorable little boy instantly came to her. How could Logan possibly believe she would blame an innocent child for Daniel's betrayal? The ache in her chest returned, the way it did every time she thought about Daniel.

She wanted to be angry with him and told herself he wasn't worth her misery. But her heart wouldn't listen. She missed him terribly. There was nothing left of Daniel on this earth— except his son.

She loved Rafi already. Night after night, she thought about him and planned all the things they would do together. She'd always wanted children, and this child needed a home.

Pop had been dead set against asking Logan to help. She was being selfish, he'd told her, but she didn't believe that one short trip to Venezuela would endanger Logan's life. Granted, his work with the Cobras had involved several joint missions with the DEA, and he'd made powerful enemies. But how would they even know he was there?

It doesn't matter. Logan had not taken the bait when she'd mentioned danger. The "Haas Factor" hadn't prompted Logan to accept her offer. He was a very strange man. Evidently, he truly believed she would harm Rafi if she adopted him.

Where would he get such an idea? Undoubtedly, it had something to do with his own experience. Now she was totally convinced Logan was hiding things about himself. If she didn't have Rafi to worry about, she would have pursued the story.

She might not get another chance. By now Logan must have left, she decided glancing at the clock and seeing it was almost time to go home for dinner. Logan's leaving would hit Pop hard. Although she resented the way Logan had become so important to Pop so quickly, she had no choice but to accept it. She needed to spend more time with Pop to soften the blow of Logan's leaving.

Out of the corner of her eye, she detected a movement, and she turned, astonished to see Logan McCord walking into her office with Jasper at his heels.

He swung a chair around backward and straddled it, saying, "I'm in. Tell me when you want to go and get the kid."

Shock caused words to wedge in her throat, and it was a few seconds before she could speak. "What made you change your mind?"

His response was to lift his shoulders, hold them high for a moment before letting them drop. He could shrug if he wanted, but she knew the element of danger lured him. The "Haas Factor" had worked after all.

Could she use Logan like this? Did she have any choice? How else was she going to get Rafi?

"I don't want any money," he told her. "I'm doing this because Pop convinced me that he'll watch out for the boy."

But you don't trust me, she thought. Why not? Oh, well. It didn't matter to her what Logan believed. All he had to do was help her adopt the child.

"Great! I really appreciate this." She smiled for the first time since learning about Daniel's affair.

Logan returned her smile with an appealing grin. No wonder women found him so attractive. She had to admit he had an irresistible smile.

"The first thing we need to do," she told him, "is get married."

Chapter 12

Kelly watched Logan, assuming Pop had explained that they would have to get married in order to adopt Rafi. Logan's blue eyes narrowed and the hand near Jasper's golden head clenched into a fist.

"Didn't Pop tell you?"

He shook his head, two quick, impatient jerks. She noted his set expression, jaw clamped shut, eyes trained on her with lethal calmness. A cold knot formed in the pit of her stomach.

Please, don't let him change his mind.

"Single women aren't allowed to adopt children in Venezuela. Even if they were, the state of Arizona must certify the parents and their home before they are permitted to adopt any child."

Her words punctured what had become a thick silence. His unsettling eyes bored into her across the small space of the desk.

"All you have to do is marry me, pretend to be a loving husband when the social workers interview us. As soon as I have Rafi, we can get a quick divorce in Las Vegas."

"Marry you?" he said, sounding as if she were speaking in tongues.

"It's the only way." She came around from behind her desk and stood before him. The intensity in his eyes had faded, and they were now as flat as the winter sky, cold and bleak. "All you have to do is pretend . . . for a little while. Then you can leave."

"Find some other sucker," he said, rising to his feet. He turned to head out the door. She almost tripped over Jasper but managed to grab his arm.

"Logan, listen to me, please."

Their gazes locked, and they stared at each other. If possible the air became thicker and charged with what she guessed was his anger. Somehow—despite his better judgment—he'd volunteered to help her, not realizing marriage was part of the deal.

"I know you had a terrible childhood. It was so bad that you won't talk about it, and you don't want anyone to find out what really happened." The words came out in a breathless rush, a hitch of desperation in her voice. She had no idea how to reach a man who carried all his belongings in a backpack, a man whose past was a black hole.

"You think I'll be like the McCord woman who kidnapped you. I swear, I won't. You've spent time with Pop. You know what kind of person he is. Well, he raised me with those same values."

Logan had a knack for smiling with the devil's own charm, yet he could erase every readable emotion from his face, his eyes. She couldn't tell what he was thinking, but raw anger seemed to shimmer in the air. Why?

"Every child has the right to be loved. I want to give Rafi . . . the love you never had.'"

He yanked his arm from her grasp and was in the outer office in two long-legged strides, Jasper trotting after him.

"I'll love him. I promise," she called after Logan. "Think about it—please."

An hour later when she returned home for dinner, Kelly discover that Logan had dropped off Jasper, then left on foot.

He's a strange one. Kelly assured herself that she'd done the best she could.

"His pack is still here." Pop's voice was hopeful as Kelly helped Uma serve homemade flour tortillas and *Carne Adovada*.

Usually the pork and onions stewed in mild Chimayo red chili was one of Kelly's favorite dishes. Since Matt had told her about Daniel, her appetite had disappeared. She used her fork to rearrange her food, but doubted she'd fool Uma.

"Logan is trained in survival techniques," Kelly reminded Pop, who was worried because Logan hadn't returned for dinner. "He's probably out there honing his skills."

Sedona was surrounded by national park land, noted for its ruggedness and inaccessibility. A man who caught a lizard, then cooked it—to test his skills—had to love Red Rock country.

"I'm glad Logan changed his mind. It's better if he stays in this country."

"Pop, I contacted several sources in Washington. I don't think he would have been in terrible danger just by going to Venezuela for a few days."

"It would have made him an easy target."

She stalled an exasperated sigh. Pop truly cared about this strange man. Kelly tried not to be irritated, but it was difficult.

I must find someone else to help me, Kelly told herself. Who? Matthew Jensen would help her, but she couldn't let him. He deserved someone who would truly love him. Kelly had experienced that powerful all-consuming love with Daniel.

She never imagined Daniel didn't love her.

Her sense of betrayal was so profound that she wanted nothing to do with men. Most certainly, she would never again trust her heart to a man. She wouldn't even consider a marriage of convenience if it wasn't the only way she could bring Rafi home.

After dinner, Kelly said good night to Pop and went out to her *casita*. For the first time in over a week, she felt ready to sleep. A night's rest might give her brain a chance think of another man to help her.

She flicked on the light and went to the *trastero* where she'd left Rafi's picture propped up beside the telephone. Everything else was in its place on the cupboard, but the photograph was gone. Uma must have moved it, she decided.

She frantically looked around the room, but didn't see the photograph. The door to her patio was open a crack. A flicker of apprehension coursed through her. She was positive that she had left the door closed.

When she came near the French doors that opened onto the small flagstone patio, the light from the room revealed a tall man stretched out on the chaise. Logan, she realized, relief replacing the attack of nerves.

Earlier he'd been as volatile as a keg of powder. What mood was he in now? Why was he sitting in the dark on her patio?

"Looking for this?" He held up a photograph.

It was too dark on the patio to see it clearly, but she knew it was Rafi's picture. "What are you doing here?"

He swung his long legs to the ground and sat up, facing her. His T-shirt fit snug over a chest most women dreamed about. The light was dim but she could see a faint glint of humor in his eyes and noticed his grin. The devil's sidekick had vanished. The charming rascal had returned.

He put the photo on the small table between the chaises. "If I'm going to be a father, I might as well know what the kid looks like."

It was all she could do not to jump up and hug him. Instead she sat rigid on the other chaise. "You'll do it? You'll marry me?"

He set aside the picture, then dropped down to his knees. "Kelly, will you make me the happiest man on this earth by marrying me?"

The way his eyes crinkled at the corners made her suspect he was holding back a laugh. He reminded her of a naughty little boy, the kind who would pull your hair and run. A tease.

In this case, a dangerous tease.

"Logan, be serious. Are you willing to take the job?"

He rose then sat on the chaise beside her, and she had to battle the urge to scoot away. His nearness was overwhelming, but she pretended not to be affected. After all, she was going to be close to Logan a lot in the next few months.

Her pulse beat in double time and her heart clamored in her chest with loud pounding thuds. He was so unpredictable and mysterious that he frightened her, which was unusual. During her years in New York, she'd tracked down several dangerous men for articles about crime.

Get a grip, Kelly. Get a grip. You are going to have to live with this man.

He turned to her, his eyes now cold and sharp. The hint of humor had disappeared. "What I'm doing isn't a job. It's a mission. I'm not taking your money."

"Why are you doing it?" Oh, Lordy, did she have to blurt out such a stupid question? He might change his mind ... again.

"I'm accepting the mission to help Pop. He'll be one hell of a grandfather."

The inflection in his voice told her that nothing had changed his mind about her. He didn't trust her to love Rafi, but he put his faith in Pop. It was just an excuse, she decided. The element of risk in going to South America was responsible for Logan changing his mind.

She should have been ashamed of herself for allowing a psychological quirk like the Haas Factor to lure him into danger. But she was too desperate to turn away the only man who could help her. Logan McCord could take care of himself better than most men on this earth.

"Thank you," she said. Something made her add, "You won't be sorry."

He was looking down at her, his eyes resting on her lips for an uncomfortably long time. The minutes stretched into a taut stillness. Even the shrill howl from a coyote in the plum thicket nearby seemed muffled and faraway.

A charge of sexual current arched between them. She tried to stop it with a sarcastic remark, but the words lodged in her throat. His eyes narrowed, and in the dusky light, she marveled at how his vivid blue eyes were now, almost totally black with just a thin rim of blue.

He lowered his head and touched her neck with the tip of one finger, using the back of his hand to lift away her hair.

She realized he was just checking the scab from the knife cut. It was almost gone now and wouldn't leave a mark.

He cocked his head to one side, his face just an inch from hers, to inspect the damage. Even in the faint light, she could see the whiskers bristling across his square jaw. They were several shades darker than his hair, the kind of beard that grew quickly.

She imagined him waking in the morning, sleepy-eyed, badly in need of a razor. Wearing nothing but a smile. Stop it! But it was hard not to think of those things when she knew she was marrying Logan.

"It's healing nicely." His warm breath fanned across her cheek and into her hair, then seemed to ripple through her entire body. "That's good."

His fingers traced the arc of her throat, moving so slowly that at first she thought she imagined it. But the heat generated by his calloused fingertips was impossible to miss. She remembered the way he'd touched her the other night. Then he'd been trying to manipulate her. What was he doing tonight?

His compelling eyes riveted her to the chaise and he gazed at her, a slightly questioning expression as if she had the answer to some question. His nostrils flared a little above a mouth that appeared more sensual than she had first thought. But it was the touch of his fingers that escalated the nervous flutter in her chest.

"Don't," she whispered.

Above their heads a cat's paw of wind ruffled the cottonwood's leaves, bringing with it the fragrant scent of sage. From the banks of Oak Creek rumbled full-throated bullfrogs. Down the road a dog barked, the noise bouncing off the red rocks. Her harsh intake of breath seemed louder than any of these sounds.

Don't touch me screamed one inner voice. *I hate men.* Another, stronger voice told her not to move.

"Don't . . . what?" he asked.

"I-I hardly know you. I think we should take our time and let things . . . ah . . . happen naturally."

Naturally? The mere touch of his hand had caused a shiver

of warmth to course through her body. Why did Logan McCord have to be the only man around who could help her?

Instead of responding to her comment, his free arm encircled her, and half a second later, she found herself snug against him. His virile torso pressed into the soft contours of her breasts. She swallowed tightly, suddenly glad she was sitting down, and her fingers curled into the palms of her hands.

She held herself rigid like one of the stone pillars in Red Rock country, afraid of what might happen if she allowed herself the pleasure of putting her arms around Logan. He pulled his head back a fraction of an inch, looking down at her with a teasing smile.

"Darlin', there's nothing more natural than this."

His heavy-ridded eyes and parted lips told her that he was going to kiss her. The anticipation welling up inside her caused a sharp intake of breath, but the air didn't seem to reach her lungs. She still felt breathless and a little dizzy.

For the love of God, no . . . don't let him kiss me.

She braced herself, imagining how his firm lips would feel molding against hers. He'd aggressively part her lips and slide his tongue forward to mate with hers. The expectation sent a fluid heat from the tips of her fingers down to the soles of her feet.

The tip of his tongue moistened his lips, and his head slowly descended. She wanted to turn away, she truly did, yet something stopped her. It was the throbbing of her own blood that suddenly became a savage drumbeat in her ears.

She fought hard, but her eyelids fluttered, then dropped shut, and she felt her lips part as a small sigh escaped into the night air. She waited for his kiss, pleasure mounting even though her brain told her to push him away.

A second passed . . . and another.

She was about to open her eyes when his lips caressed her neck, the tip of his tongue flicking against the skin. His searing kiss sent a ripple of goose bumps across the back of her neck. The heady sensation intensified as his tongue traced the soft curve of her neck.

Her head dropped forward, fitting perfectly into the hollow

between his neck and sturdy shoulder. He pulled her closer, his lips now at her ear, his hands exploring the hollow of her back.

The strength of his body, with its barely leashed power, unexpectedly excited her. How easy it would be to lose herself in the moment, to forget the heartbreak of the past.

His lips explored the curve of her neck, the sensitive spot just beneath her ear, the tender edge of her earlobe. The tip of his tongue caressed every imaginable place, forcing her to press her lips together to stifle a moan of pleasure. The rough drag of his whiskers chafing her skin caused a rush of heated longing.

Her arms stole around his neck in spite of herself. Her reaction to the consuming heat of his kisses astonished—and confused—her. She wanted only one thing from this man, help bringing Rafi home.

She found herself wiggling, hoping to encourage him to kiss her on the lips. He pulled her so close that she felt the heavy thud of his heart against her breast. She furrowed her fingers through his hair, impressed by its rich, silky texture, its unexpected softness.

"Kelly, Kelly?" Pop's voice cut through the sensual haze. "Are you awake?"

She found the strength to push Logan away and stumble to her feet. "Logan is out here with me. We have exciting news."

It had been a command performance with the entire family and every ranch hand summoned to the corral to see Haywood Stanfield's newest acquisition, an Arabian colt with an impeccable lineage and an equally impressive price. Behind his sunglasses, the man rolled his eyes. It looked like just another long-legged colt.

The crowd murmured their approval, as Haywood Stanfield led the colt around the paddock by its halter. The man seized the opportunity to move closer to the woman at his side, taking a moment to inhale the fragrance of her custom-blended perfume.

"I've located Logan Stanfield," the man whispered.

She kept looking at the new colt as if fascinated, but he knew better. "Really?"

"This morning he took out a marriage license."

The sweet curve of her lower lip dropped. "Someone around here is going to marry him? Who?"

He pretended to watch the colt as it pranced by, playing the moment. "Kelly Taylor."

Color flamed her high cheekbones, then smoldered in her blue eyes. "That bitch! She's going to use the paper to destroy us."

"I'm not so sure. The presidential race is off—at least for now. McCord took care of that."

"They could be targeting the Tyler Stanfield for Senate campaign. It would be just like Trent Farley to use the *Sun* to defame another Stanfield."

The venom in her voice didn't surprise him. She was every inch a lady, beautiful, elegant. In another era should would have made the perfect queen. She believed in the power of the Stanfield dynasty, the way kings had believed in their divine right to rule. She saw the press, especially the *Sedona Sun,* not as a necessary evil—but as a plague, which should be eliminated.

"The first mistake was not doing away with Logan years ago."

"True," he conceded, "but we didn't, so now we have to deal with a man who's a lot more dangerous than a young child. Here's my plan. Disgrace him. We've got plenty of time to do it before the presidential primaries begin."

The glimmer in her eyes told him how badly she wanted Haywood Stanfield to be in the White House. As if he couldn't have guessed. She loved power, and the White House was the center of power in this country.

"I've used all my contacts in Washington to try to get the dope on McCord. No one knows anything."

"They know, but they're not talking."

"What does that tell you? McCord has something to hide. So, I contacted a P.I. firm in LA. They're all Israelis with impressive experience in surveillance as Moussad agents.

That's the Israeli equivalent of the Secret Service. They're going to bug McCord's place and find out what's going on.''

The group moved toward the paddock when the gate swung open. He looked down on his newest pair of Bruno Magli shoes. Christ! He hated getting dust on them, but everyone was expected to make a fuss over the new colt.

''I say discredit Logan, then kill him,'' she said as the group funneled through the gate.

''Not to worry. He's as good as dead.''

Chapter 13

Logan glared at the reflection in the mirror. Aw, hell, was that him in a suit and tie? Son of a bitch! What was he doing?

Why had he agreed to marry Kelly so she could adopt the boy? The stranger in the mirror didn't have an answer.

"Shit for brains," Logan told the reflection glaring back at him. Why hadn't he just walked away and left Kelly to fend for herself?

The wry smile reflected by the mirror mocked him. Okay, okay, Logan knew better than to get involved, but Kelly had managed to hit his hot button when she had accused him of letting his own past color his judgment. That was exactly what he had done.

"There's a kid down there who's a lot like me," he told Jasper.

The retriever had fallen into the habit of tagging around at Logan's heels when the dog wasn't with Pop. Jasper wagged his tail and gazed up at Logan as if he understood every word.

"Rafi. Cute name," Logan muttered. "I have to help that little boy."

For years he'd avoided thinking about the past, telling himself the present was his life. But Kelly—damn her sweet hide—

had forced him to open a door that he'd slammed shut when he'd enlisted. He'd taken a long, painful look at the past and analyzed his feelings like some armchair shrink armed with the latest self-help book.

Jasper nuzzled Logan's hand, a signal that the dog wanted to be petted. Logan was tempted, but resisted, reminding himself he was already too involved with this family. The last thing he needed was to become attached to a dog.

After Kelly and Logan told Pop that they were getting married, Pop insisted on driving Logan into Phoenix to purchase a suit for the wedding. So, here he was trying on the Brioni suit and tie that he'd bought—feeling like a horse's ass.

"You're one sorry son of a bitch," he said out loud.

Now he couldn't get everything he owned in his backpack. Without moving his head, he glanced sideways to make certain the pack was still in the corner. It was right where he'd put it, the strap set at an angle to tell him no one had touched it.

Not that he was really worried. If the barracudas from the tabloids hadn't tracked him down, no one else was likely to find him. Trouble was that he could feel himself slipping into civilian life and not being as alert as he should be.

"In six months I'll be worthless," he informed Jasper as he shrugged out of the jacket.

The retriever nuzzled him again, imploring Logan with soulful brown eyes to pet him. Logan gave in and ran his hand over the dog's soft fur and fondled his ears. He should have left instead of allowing himself to become involved in Kelly's personal problems, he reflected as he stroked Jasper.

Man, oh, man, he could still taste Kelly's soft skin beneath his lips and feel the erotic way her body molded against his. This was one part of the bargain he intended to enjoy. It had been weeks since he'd gone upstairs with that woman in Argentina. He was horny as hell.

Kelly wasn't the type of woman he usually selected. He preferred one night stands because you could walk away. This was a similar situation, he decided as he stepped out of his trousers and hung his wedding suit in the closet.

This time he was the one being used, and Kelly would have

paid him for it, if he would have allowed it. He wouldn't have to walk away when the mission was complete. Just the opposite. Kelly would kick his butt out the door.

All she wanted was the child. That was fine with Logan. He'd examined the past and decided this situation was nothing like his childhood. Kelly had been deeply wounded by her husband's betrayal, but she was a good person who would love the boy. A grandson would be good for Pop, and Logan couldn't help wanting the older man to be happy.

"What is it, Jasper?" he whispered as he turned and realized the retriever was facing the door, ears cocked.

A dog's hearing was far superior to a human's. Someone was coming toward the *casita*. He pulled on his jeans, but didn't bother with a shirt. Barefoot, he silently crossed the floor and angled his head so he could see out the window without being spotted.

It was just Pop coming up the flagstone path. He was walking much faster now than when Logan had first arrived. His gait was steadier, more purposeful, giving Logan a glimpse of how Trent Farley had been in his youth.

Logan swung open the door. "Looking for Jasper? He's right here."

"No." Pop gave Jasper an affectionate pat. "Woody's here. Your father wants to talk to you."

"How'd he know where to find me?"

"He's a politician. Lots of people around here owe him favors. He found out about the marriage license and guessed you would be here."

Logan reached for the T-shirt he'd slung over a chair and pulled it over his head. "Tell him to drop dead."

"There's nothing I'd like better, but let's be realistic. Woody Stanfield is a powerful man. You and Kelly will have to go through a battery of paperwork and an inspection of your home before you'll be certified for adoption under Arizona law. Woody could speed up the process with one call."

"I don't want anything from him. Not one damn thing."

Pop gazed down at Jasper for a moment, then looked straight at Logan with the earnest expression that Logan had come to associate with the older man. "You don't know what brought him here. Why don't you find out? It could be important."

Curiosity always had been a weakness. One of his earliest lessons had been at the camp just after his tenth birthday. He had picked the lock on the shed and had gone inside. It had been alarmed, of course, and Jake had caught him snooping around the storeroom where the camp's guns and ammunition were kept.

Even though he'd been just a child, his uncle gave him the same punishment that he did the adults. *The box.* Logan suffered through a week in the root cellar, shivering, rats hovering nearby ready to eat him.

For years after, he'd been afraid of rats. Then he'd joined the Cobras and turned the tables. Survival school had taught him that rats were everywhere, a good food source—if you were desperate. He craved Twinkies, but if it became necessary to survive, he'd eat a rat.

"I'll see him." Logan shoved his bare feet into shoes, then slung his pack over one shoulder.

Logan found Woody waiting at the edge of the terrace overlooking Oak Creek. The sun's rays slanted through the trees and glinted off the water as it rumbled over the stony creek bed. A raccoon darted through the cluster of palo verde trees downstream and vanished.

"You wanted to talk to me?"

Woody spun around, startled. Once again Logan was struck by how much he looked like his father. Sure, his old man's hair was gray and his face was lined, but it was the same face that gazed back at Logan each morning when he shaved. Looking closely, he could see the same dimples that appeared at the top of his cheekbones when he smiled. Woody's were masked by lines, now, but they were there.

Woody wasn't slightly stooped over the way many men his age were. He was an inch shorter than Logan's six feet four, but his erect stance and squared shoulders duplicated Logan's.

Woody walked toward him, confident but not smiling. "I've been thinking about what you said. We should talk especially now that you're marrying Kelly Taylor."

Logan choked back a cutting reply. No telling what Stanfield would do if he knew the truth. He might blab to the press and prevent Kelly from adopting the boy.

Woody gestured to one of the chairs with a view of Oak Creek. Logan turned the chair so he could see anyone who would come onto the patio from the house. He eased into the chair as if he was comfortable, but he wasn't.

The first rule Cobras learned to follow was watch your back. The second was never to stay out in the open where you were exposed on all sides. Sweat prickled across the back of his neck as he scanned the dense foliage along the banks of the creek.

What are you worrying about? This isn't some terrorist operation. No one is hiding in the brush, setting the sights of a high-powered rifle on you. He set his pack beside his chair, the compartment with the gun easily accessible.

"Apparently you think I was unfair to your mother." Was there a tinge of apology in his voice, or was he merely a politician playing the moment? "Amanda waited like a vulture until I finished my first term in the Senate, then announced I had a son. She threatened to take it to the press if I didn't adopt you and give her fifty thousand dollars."

"Where is she now?" Logan asked, a preemptive strike to make Woody think he didn't have a clue.

From the chair next to his, Woody's gaze sharpened. "I expected her to continue blackmailing me, but she was as good as her word. I never heard from her again. I assumed you knew where she is. You accused me of ruining her life."

Logan ran his palms over the smooth arms of the bent willow chair. He'd lashed out at his father, a rare loss of control, when he'd accused Woody of ruining his mother's life. It was true, of course, but the implications of his allegation could blow his cover.

And cause his mother more pain.

Not that he owed her one damn thing. If she wanted to spend her life at The Last Chance Camp, let her.

"How would you know her life was ruined if you haven't seen your mother?" Woody probed.

Logan shot him the *do-you-have-a-death-wish* look that would have made even the most hardened terrorist's knees shaky. Woody stared right back. Inwardly, Logan almost chuckled. Maybe his old man was stronger than he seemed.

"I was just making a wild guess." Logan faked a light tone. "A sixteen-year-old girl is never going to recover from the trauma of giving up a baby."

The color leached from Woody's face, leaving mottled splotches of pink behind. "Believe me, I never knew Amanda was so young. She told me she was eighteen. You know how some women are. She looked much older than she was."

"You were twice her age."

"How'd you find out? That's been a well-kept secret."

"You'd be surprised what a Cobra can learn," he hedged. "Amanda McCord was just seventeen when I was born. It doesn't take a calculator to figure out she was sixteen when she conceived."

Woody sank back in the chair, his gaze following a red-tailed hawk as it swooped low over the opposite bank of the creek. "She was one of the volunteers on my first campaign. Amanda was on her own, working The Bobcat Bite. I never suspected she was underage. I was so ambitious then. I would never have risked my career by having sex with a minor."

Logan tried to temper the caustic tone of his voice, but it was impossible. "You never told your family the truth until I showed up."

Woody stared at his expensive Italian loafers, seeming to search for words. "It's all out in the open now. They even know how young Amanda was. They know everything."

Not quite everything.

Awkwardly, he cleared his throat. "Logan, I'm sorry about what happened when you came home. I allowed myself to become caught up in the political ramifications of your reappearance. Politics has been my life for too long. I didn't take the opportunity to find out about you."

There was an oddly gentle quality to Woody's voice, but Logan shoved that impression aside. "There's not much to tell if you read the *Exposé* article. It covers my life."

''What happened when that couple kidnapped you? Did they treat you well?''

Nothing on earth could have made Logan tell this man the details of his youth. ''Do I look as if they mistreated me?''

His father's eyes darkened as they held Logan's gaze. ''It's impossible to tell just by looking. When I see you, I see myself, yet I don't know anything about you. The people who abducted you must have been desperate for a child. If they wanted you that much, they must have loved you.''

It was a natural assumption, so Logan allowed Woody to believe it. ''They made me a survivor. That's what counts.''

''You're so much like me.''

Woody's voice was embarrassingly sentimental now. Aw, hell. Was this supposed to be one of those heart-to-heart talks between a father and his son?

''I was a stone Oakie when I came to Arizona. I had nothing but a cardboard suitcase and dreams. I worked hard—manual labor—and saved every penny.''

There was such pride in Woody's voice that Logan almost admired him for what he'd accomplished. Almost.

''Someone suckered me into buying a rock quarry that was supposed to be granite.'' Woody chuckled, mocking himself. ''It turned out to be D-grade shale that crumbled so easily it was worthless.''

Logan had already heard about how his father had invented a machine that turned the shale into dustless cat box litter and made a fortune, but he let Woody ramble on and on.

''You married a beautiful woman,'' Logan finally cut him off. ''Why did you have to sleep with my mother?''

Woody almost flinched at the bitterness in Logan's voice. ''My marriage to Ginger hasn't been perfect. She's emotionally fragile. She would have been better off with a sensitive man like Benson instead of a roughneck like me.''

Woody thought a moment, a mocking bird's song lilted through the mid-morning air. ''Amanda McCord was as smart as a whip. That's why I first noticed her. She was pretty but not beautiful like Ginger. Yet Amanda was far more attractive. She had warmth and sparkle.''

Warmth and sparkle, huh? Those were two words he never associated with his mother. Never. Yet he supposed she must have been that way—once. Before Jake McCord and The Last Chance Camp.

If Amanda hadn't gotten pregnant, she would never have been forced to return home. She would have escaped her brother Jake's wild schemes. Crazy as it was, there were times when Logan blamed himself. For being born.

"Amanda was unique, the kind of woman a man is drawn to—in spite of his better judgment. Every time I see Kelly, I'm reminded of your mother. Of course, you don't have any better judgment issues. You're not married, and Kelly isn't underage."

Aw, hell. Just what he didn't want to hear. Was he trapped in an emotional Bermuda Triangle? He looked exactly like his old man, lived for his job the same way Woody had been devoted to politics. Now he was involved with a woman who attracted him—no denying it—the way his mother had attracted Woody.

In spite of Logan's better judgment.

"I'd hoped that Amanda took the money I gave her and enrolled in college. With an education and her looks, she could have done anything, been anything."

His old man would be shocked to learn what his mother did with the money. Part of it went to buy the backwoods acreage that became the Last Chance Camp. The rest was spent on weapons.

"I thought I might get a call from Amanda when you vanished. Your picture was everywhere, but I never heard from her."

Interesting. His disappearance must have made Woody sweat. The truth might have come out. It would have served him right.

"Why did you want to see me?" Logan asked.

"I was curious about your plans. Are you going to stay here?"

Logan couldn't admit this marriage was the only way for Kelly to adopt the child without risking Social Services finding out and refusing to certify them. "A lot will depend on Kelly. We haven't worked out the details."

"I hope you decide to stay. I'd like the chance to get to know you better."

The raw emotion in Woody's voice made Logan want to squirm in his chair, but he kept himself stock still as if he were hiding from the enemy and his life depended on it.

"Ginger and I would like you and Kelly to come to dinner tonight. That way we can get to know each other before you go off on your honeymoon."

Logan had enough experience with rats to spot one in a heartbeat. It wasn't the smell. Rats were actually quite clean, considering they had no qualms about what they ate or where they had to go to get it.

What gave them away was shiftiness. Rats moved in one direction—until they sensed trouble—then they changed course before you could blink. That was what was going on here. Last time he'd seen his old man, after the press conference, he'd been pissed big-time.

Now he was being friendly. Why?

Chapter 14

"That's Bell Rock," Kelly told Logan, pointing to an unusual dome-shaped rock the color of burnt cinnamon. "See the notch on top where you'd pick up a bell and ring it?"

"Yep. I like Court House Rock better. It's bigger, more impressive."

Kelly sped along the highway, driving them to the Stanfields' for dinner in Pop's late-model Cadillac. The sun was dropping quickly, firing the buttes and steep hills with the blazing hues of vermilion and gold that made Sedona's sunsets famous. But Kelly's mind wasn't on the spectacular light show. She kept wondering about Logan's unexpected change of mind about the Stanfields.

Logan had called her at the newspaper and asked her if she would accompany him to dinner at their estate. Considering his dislike of the entire family, Kelly found his request surprising. But then, Logan was as unpredictable as he was mysterious.

There was much, much more to his story than the tidbits he'd tossed her for the article in *Exposé*. She definitely planned on writing another story, but lately she'd been so consumed by worry about Rafi and devastated by Daniel's betrayal that she hadn't pursued what few leads she had.

Why not start now? They had a week to go until the wedding. God-only-knew how long the state would need to go through the red tape and certify them for adoption. Working on the story would take her mind off the past.

She glanced at Logan out of the corner of her eye, admitting to herself that she found him exciting. Her reaction disturbed her and caused her to question herself. Why had she let him kiss her neck? She'd stood there, enjoying the erotic feel of his lips and the rasp of his emerging beard on her skin.

Since learning about Daniel, the wall of pain imprisoning her heart had dulled to a gnawing ache that she was going to have to learn to live with for the rest of her life. Becoming emotionally involved with another man was unimaginable. What she was experiencing with Logan had to be a physical reaction.

She hadn't been with a man since Daniel died. It stood to reason that her body would remember . . . and crave. It was a perfectly normal response of a healthy woman to a handsome, virile man. She would have to control her reactions.

"Back of the Beyond Road. Now that's a fitting name," Logan commented as she turned down the narrow lane leading to the estate. "Nothing much is out here."

"Most of the land is the Coconino National Forest. The area that can be developed has building restrictions to protect Mother Nature. You'd be amazed how many people are like the Stanfields and think nothing of bulldozing acres of unique red rock to make pastures for their horses."

Kelly braked to avoid hitting a cottontail. The rabbit scampered across the road and disappeared into a clump of mesquite. "When the Stanfields built out here, it was truly the back of the beyond. Who could have foreseen how popular Sedona would become?"

Logan didn't respond, so Kelly kept quiet. Undoubtedly, he was anticipating this encounter with his family. She eyed him, trying not to notice how handsome he looked in khaki slacks and a long-sleeved blue chambray shirt, which was open at the neck and the cuffs rolled up to his elbows.

The only clothes he seemed to own besides what he was

wearing were Levis, two T-shirts, a navy polo shirt, and a well-worn leather belt. He must have socks and underwear as well as a sweater or jacket stashed in the backpack. Buying an expensive suit for their wedding next week must have been a sacrifice.

Not a financial sacrifice, she decided, recalling Logan telling her that he'd saved all the money he'd made. This had to be an adjustment in life-style. Along with the suit, he'd had to purchase a dress shirt, tie, belt and shoes. She couldn't imagine all of that in the backpack with whatever else he kept in there.

"Pull over," he ordered when the car came to a wide spot in the road.

She drove onto the soft shoulder, a little surprised when he motioned for her to shut off the engine. Following his line of vision, she spotted a bird, soaring just above the sage, primed for a kill.

"It's a golden eagle! Pop will be so excited! They used to be as common as deer or elk, but now we rarely see them."

The eagle arrowed into the brush, wings at its side. A second later, the bird shot heavenward, a ground squirrel dangling from its talons. She turned to Logan to see what he thought of the spectacular sight.

His eyes weren't on the eagle. Instead, he was studying her with a disturbing concentration that set off warning bells. This was a very remote area—truly the back of the beyond—a long way from Sedona and a mile or more from the Stanfields' home. There's nothing to be afraid of, she assured herself.

Still, she couldn't quell the apprehension tightening her throat. The aura of danger and mystery that Logan projected lured her in a way she'd never anticipated. It was what made him so much more intriguing than other men she'd known.

"Do you know how to hunt a terrorist?" he asked.

Some of her anxiety evaporated, leaving only confusion. Why would he ask such a question? She shook her head and resisted the urge to scoot away from him, realizing he would pick up on her nervousness—if he hadn't already.

"To hunt a terrorist and catch him, you must become one."

She recalled the first night they'd met and the deadly knife at her throat. "You're prepared to fight the way they fight even if you break the law."

He touched her arm, nothing more than a light brush of his fingertips, but a chill waltzed down her spine. He was a ruthless man, ready to do anything to get what he wanted. And she was going to marry him.

"Everyone breaks the law. If you cheat on your taxes or jaywalk, you're breaking the law. That's not what I'm talking about." His voice, even grittier than usual, sent a another tremor through her. "The Stanfields live only for themselves. I'm a threat, and by marrying me, you're a threat. After your article, I'm dead certain there is nothing they would like more than a way to discredit us both."

"Then why did you accept Woody's invitation to dinner?"

"Six months and I'm outta here. If we play this right, Woody will help us adopt Rafi as soon as possible," he replied. "Pop gave me the idea."

Ironic. Pop told Logan to use Woody's influence to help them. Pop had spent a lifetime blasting Haywood Stanfield for using his influence as a senator to help his rich cronies.

"Kelly," he said and she mustered the courage to look into his eyes, aware that whatever she was feeling for this man was intensifying. The gathering darkness had changed his eyes to a slate gray color, making them as unreadable as stone. "Do you seriously expect the Stanfields to believe we've fallen in love when you treat me like a cockroach that's too big to squash?"

She'd never even considered what they thought. Now she realized Logan was more aware of the problems than she. The only hope the Stanfields had of resurrecting Woody's presidential bid was to somehow disgrace Logan, or to prove her story wasn't true. It was also possible that Woody wanted to make amends so Benson could put the "happy family" spin on this story.

"I guess I shouldn't wear my wedding ring any longer." She held up her left hand, and in the amber light of the setting sun, her gold wedding band looked as shiny as it had the day

Daniel had slipped it on her finger. She pulled it off and tucked it into the side compartment of her purse.

Something shifted in the depths of Logan's eyes and Kelly wondered if he thought she was a little nutty for continuing to wear her ring even though her husband was dead. And he'd betrayed her.

After Matthew had told her about Daniel's son, she'd wanted to throw the ring in Oak Creek. She'd even taken it off, stood on the terrace cantilevered over the creek, set to toss the ring. Something had stopped her. She couldn't throw away the symbol of her love even if she knew Daniel had died loving another woman.

Logan turned and levered his hips off the seat, shoving his hand into his trouser pocket. She gazed at a yucca bush and told herself to concentrate on the future—not the past. She should have taken off her ring long ago.

I've been living a lie.

Her marriage hadn't been perfect. Far from it. Her relationship with Daniel had been so deeply flawed that he had intended to leave her for the mother of his son.

What was wrong with her, Kelly asked herself. Why hadn't she detected a problem?

Logan touched her shoulder, his strong hands grazing her bare shoulders, and she realized seconds had passed. She looked into his eyes and detected a hint of some indefinable emotion that vanished as quickly as it had appeared.

His fingers circled her left hand, and she looked down as he slipped a ring on her finger. Even in the duskiness of the car's interior, shards of blue-white light shot off the diamond.

"When a man's serious about a woman, he gives her an engagement ring."

Kelly lowered her head, not wanting him to detect the sheen of tears in her eyes. She and Daniel had been engaged—without a ring—for months. She'd secretly hoped he'd give her one, but he hadn't. Now, the stranger she'd asked to marry her had bought her a emerald-cut of breathtaking beauty.

"It's so big," she tried to joke. "It could put out someone's eye."

"An engagement ring should help convince the Stanfields we're in love." There seemed to be a husky caress in his rough voice, or perhaps she'd just imagined it.

Love? The word echoed through her car, heightening the wary feeling she'd had since Logan had agreed to her scheme. She had to pretend to be in love with this man, not just to fool the Stanfields. The social workers must be convinced they had a stable marriage and could provide a proper home for an adopted child.

What had she gotten herself into?

"Look," he said, his gravel-like voice more rough than usual. "I've never loved a woman, so I'm not much good at this. But being a Cobra taught me how to observe people— from across a room, not hearing a word—and interpret their body language. I've watched you a lot. You don't like me much, and you're afraid of me."

"Don't be . . ." The word "ridiculous" died on her lips. Why lie? She'd been living a lie all these years believing Daniel loved her. Logan was willing to help her. She owed him total cooperation—and the complete truth.

"It's not that I don't like you, exactly." She shrugged to hide her confusion. "I've never met anyone like you. Just as I think I have you figured out, you change. I don't understand you."

"You don't have to understand me. We're on a mission, remember? If you're afraid of me, you won't trust me. That could be very dangerous. It could cost you the boy."

She didn't understand this man, and she probably never would. But she *must* learn to trust him. He was doing his level best to help her, she decided as she admired the stunning ring on her hand.

"I appreciate all you're doing for me. I want to trust you, really I do."

He ran the tip of his index finger up her neck as he gazed into her eyes. He paused at the faint bump on her neck marking the spot where he'd nicked her with the knife. A perplexing weakness invaded her body, and she suddenly felt her muscles go rigid while her bones seemed to turn to molasses.

"People will be watching us from now on," he said. "We're going to have to become terrorists."

Terrorists? Wasn't this taking a marriage of convenience a bit too far? Maybe not. Considering the problems they'd caused the Stanfields, and their determination to resurrect Woody's presidential bid, she and Logan would have to convincingly act their parts.

Could she do it? When she'd asked him to marry her, the plan had seemed so simple. But the reality was quite different.

"One of my first assignments with the Cobras was to protect an ambassador from a guerrilla group. The agent training me warned me that I would have to guard the ambassador and his wife at a big embassy bash. He didn't mention the ambassador had a mistress, and she would be attending the party."

"How did you spot her?"

"People in love tend to stand a little too close, laugh a little too much, hold each other's gaze a little too long." Something kindled in the depths of his eyes, and he gazed at her until she had to look away. "And they can't keep their hands off each other."

She thought about it a moment, then said, "You're right."

"At the embassy party, I spotted the mistress right away. I also noticed the way she looked at one of the waiters. He turned out to be the guerrilla leader."

"What happened?"

"We took out the guerrillas before they got to the ambassador. It was one of those low-profile missions Cobras do best." He acted as if this were no big deal just another "mission," but she suspected he wasn't giving himself enough credit. "Tonight I want you to observe the Stanfields closely. Something strange is going on there."

Granted, the Stanfields were arrogant and obnoxious, but she wondered if Logan's homecoming hadn't been such an emotional experience that the entire family had been in a state of shock. Logan's acute perceptive skills would have been altered by the event, too, making him slightly paranoid.

"We can't stand six feet apart all night," he continued. "Stay close to me and I'll put my arm around you, or sometimes, you could hold my arm. Go for as much eye contact as possible and keep looking at me until you feel yourself blush.''

"All right," she agreed, but she couldn't imagine behaving like a lovesick teenager.

"Hey, sweetcakes, this isn't easy for me either," he said, and she realized her apprehension must show in her face. "I've never been in love. I've never even dated anyone. The first time I had sex was when I went out with a bunch of guys to celebrate making it through boot camp. In town we found some hookers. My experience has been with pros or one-night-stands. I don't do relationships.''

"Really?" She sounded like the village idiot, but it was impossible for her to believe such a handsome, virile man hadn't been snagged by some gorgeous woman—at least for a couple of months. Maybe he was never in one place long enough.

But that didn't account for his attitude. *"I don't do relationships.''*

Logan opened the car door saying, "Come on."

"We'll be late," she warned as he came around to her side and opened the door.

"You don't know much about power, do you?" he asked.

She swung her legs out and a light breeze riffling down from the hills sent a wave of goose bumps across her bare back. The days were still very warm, but the nip of fall was in the air. Perhaps the halter-top sundress that she'd chosen for this evening exposed too much bare skin.

She rose to her feet and nearly bumped into Logan. She lurched to one side and steadied herself, determined to avoid touching him if possible. His sharp glance told her that she was about as graceful as a hog on ice.

With the heel of his palm, Logan shoved the car door shut. The unexpected sound flushed a dozen quail out of the clumps of sage and mesquite flanking the road.

Logan slipped his arm around her bare shoulders. She told herself this was only part of the act. Kelly, don't you dare tremble. Just act as if this is perfectly natural.

"Like I said, you don't know much about power. If we're

on time, half the family will be late. Making us wait is their way of showing us that we aren't important.''

Kelly bobbed her head, uncomfortably aware of Logan's strong arm around her. Get a grip! If they were going to fool anyone, she couldn't get the jitters every time he touched her.

His thumb moved in lazy circles across the rise of her shoulder while his arm was nonchalantly draped around her back. There was nothing provocative in the way he was behaving, but Kelly had to concentrate to keep walking a straight line.

''See? This isn't so bad,'' he said when they'd progressed a few yards down the road, the mellow light of the waning sun disappearing behind the towering red rocks. ''It would be even easier if you leaned against me a little.''

Eyes on her shoes, she let her hip touch his, and her shoulder found a comfortable spot against the side of his chest. He matched his stride to hers, and they walked in silence along the deserted road, the last rays of the setting sun barely lighting the way.

He stopped abruptly and faced her. They were just inches apart, his arm still around her. He gazed down at her and something in the depths of his blue eyes forewarned her.

Oh, my God! He's going to kiss me, Kelly thought. The impending kiss shattered something deep inside her. She couldn't believe it, but she actually wanted him to kiss her.

''The key is being totally comfortable with each other.'' His grainy voice was hardly more than a whisper, yet it had a powerfully erotic affect on her.

He lowered his arm to her midriff, and despite the heat of his hand, a chill prickled across the back of her neck then whipped down her spine. His thumb explored the hollows of her back. She trained her eyes over his shoulder, unwilling to let him see how disturbing she found this.

He might be an expert counter-terrorist who could pick up on subtle clues like body language, but she was a one-man woman. Matt had been her first love; Daniel had been her true love. She simply wasn't comfortable letting any other man touch her.

What she was feeling now went beyond discomfort into

another realm she didn't wish to examine too closely. They were on a "mission"—nothing more. She couldn't afford to become emotionally involved—or attached—to a man like Logan.

"Now isn't this simple?" he said, his voice a shade shy of a whisper. "It's easy, isn't it?"

It took her a second to get out one word. "Easy? Oh, sure. That's what the IRS said when they simplified the tax form."

He chuckled, a deep, masculine sound that seemed to rumble through his chest into hers. His free arm circled her waist, and he slowly pulled her flush against him. His sense of purpose and strength was so, so . . . exhilarating. No man had the right to possess such masculine vitality, she told herself.

He cradled the back of her neck with his large hand, gently coaxing her to relax and place her head on his shoulder.

We're on a mission, she assured herself. A mission, a mission, a mission. The thought echoed through her brain as she lowered her head.

Her nostrils filled with the woodsy scent of his shaving lotion. It was a powerful aphrodisiac, she decided as his solid, steady heart thrummed against her breast. His arms tightened possessively and protectively around her.

A strange, completely new, almost erotic, sensation unfurled in the pit of her stomach. Slowly, totally against her will, a swell of pleasure hummed through her, and she let out her breath in a faint sigh.

"Touching each other has to be second nature to us," he said, stroking her hair in long, slow movements.

His fingers sifted through her hair, lifting as if he were testing its weight, its texture. There wasn't anything overtly sexy about what he was doing, yet she felt his touch everywhere. Bewildering emotions were streaking through her, unbelievable in their intensity.

"This is the first time I've had to train a female operative," he whispered, his breath warm against her ear.

It took a second for the word "operative" to register. He was right. This was a mission. Why was she acting like some love-starved old maid?

She tried to pull back, but his strong arms kept her anchored to his chest. She ventured a look into his eyes, but couldn't see much. The sun had taken its last bow. The rocks around them were no longer crimson. They were hulking black shadows that blended with the night sky.

Even though she couldn't see clearly, she had the distinct impression he was going to kiss her. She braced herself, silently reminding herself that they were on a mission. She had to become totally comfortable with this man.

She parted her lips and struggled not to sigh as his head came toward her. She couldn't keep her mouth from opening a little more in anticipation, but at the last second, Logan stopped.

With a cocky grin, he said, "You know, this mission might be more fun than I'd thought."

"I can't believe the great Haywood Stanfield invited Logan and Kelly to dinner. Woody must have lost his mind."

The man sprawled across her bed as she paraded around the room in the black panties and lacy bra he'd given her. Over the years, he'd watched her dress countless times. It was a game they played, pretending they didn't know how it would end.

Before dinner she'd take care of him. Then during the meal, he would conceal his boredom and anticipate ripping off the bra and panties that were no bigger than an eyepatch. She'd fight him, of course. She always did. She loved rough sex.

He loved her. He always had. He always would.

"I expected good ole Woody to contact Logan," he replied, his eyes on the dusky shadow at the crotch of the lace panties. Tonight, he'd pin her down and rip off that swatch of black lace with his teeth.

"Logan McCord ruined the presidential campaign." She pranced by with an exaggerated pout on her sexy lips, tits jiggling. "No one can believe the family values candidate kept an illegitimate son hidden from his family all these years. Why would he ask Logan here for dinner and expect a command performance from the family? I don't get it.''

"It's simple," he said, watching her rifle through the countless dresses in her closet. The ones she rejected, she flung to the floor to let the maid pick up. ''You read the *Exposé* article. A kidnapped child leads a life of hardship, yet rises above tremendous odds to become a success. Combine that story with a stud that women in America are drooling over and what do you have?''

She turned, yet another dress in her hands, and gazed at him. Poor baby. He loved her, but she wasn't bright enough to grasp the nuances of the human mind. She lived for three things: clothes, jewelry, and kinky sex.

''So? I still don't get it.'' She dropped the dress, then kicked it aside. Something about the way her slim leg stretched the lace panties made him harder than he already was.

''What you have, love, is the wanna-be president, Haywood Stanfield all over again, right? Right. Logan McCord is a mirror image of his father, a son to be proud of.''

She dropped a dress that she'd just pulled off the rack, then she stomped across the delicate black silk. ''Of course, why didn't I see it? What are we going to do?''

As usual, she was beautiful but clueless, yet she had the cunning instincts of a predatory animal. He checked his watch, resisting the urge to gloat. ''As we speak, the man I hired is bugging their place. We need to find out what's really going on before we can blow the bastard out of the water.''

''You said that before. All you do is threaten. I take action,'' she said as she sidled up to him.

''True,'' he admitted. ''Your *action* got my attention, love.''

She turned, deliberately giving him a provocative view of her sweet ass. ''Last time you took care of the problem. To this day no one knows Suzanne was murdered.''

He didn't need to remind her of the time when she'd royally botched things. She'd been young then, and he'd been much younger as well. He'd covered the mess and fallen in love with her.

''Suzanne's mother suspected. She blabbed it around—''

"Nobody believed her, did they?"

"True," she conceded. "I want to punish Logan even more than I wanted Suzanne to die. Much, much more."

Sitting on the bed beside him, she cradled his penis in the palm of her hand. Even through the fabric, he could feel the heat of her hand. Quicker than a snake, she unzipped his trousers.

"Angel," he whispered as she freed his turgid cock. "McCord deserves to die a slow, painful death."

Her head went down. "I'd love to see him suffer . . . really suffer this time."

Chapter 15

"You were right," Kelly whispered to Logan as a maid opened the Stanfields' door and invited them inside. Woody Stanfield was waiting for them, but the rest of the family wasn't around. "I don't know enough about power."

Logan greeted his father, not making any excuse for their late arrival while Kelly told herself that she knew less about men than she did about power plays. Why did she keep expecting Logan to kiss her? To him this was a job—a mission—and he was merely training an operative.

Woody turned to her. "Kelly, you look especially beautiful tonight. That shade of green suits you."

Logan's arm was around her waist, casual, yet possessive. He smiled down at her, and she reminded herself not to look away. Just gaze at him like a lovesick puppy.

"Kelly's more than pretty," he told his father. "She's got special appeal. Only a few women have that special something, right?"

For a second, Woody looked confused. "Ah-ah, you're correct. A few women are more than beautiful."

Kelly sensed this conversation wasn't about her looks. Something else was going on, some hidden agenda she didn't understand. Her training as a reporter told her to ask a probing question, but some inner voice warned her to keep quiet.

"Why don't we go out to the stud stable and see my new colt?" Woody suggested. "Ginger and Alyx are late, as usual. They're probably still trying on dresses. Like mother, like daughter. Tyler's on the telephone." He led them through the arched doorway onto the terrace. "Benson's around somewhere, too. He will be serving drinks by the time we get back."

They followed Woody down a flagstone walkway lit by tulip-shaped lights. The mare's stable was off to the left, he told them, gesturing toward a white building with a red tile roof. Dramatic spotlights illuminated the sign above the entrance: STANFIELD'S CHAMPION ARABIAN HORSES.

Ahead of them Woody took the left fork in the path, rambling on about how many prizes his Arabians had won and how carefully he bred his stock. Logan looked down at Kelly and rolled his eyes. Obviously, he wasn't impressed.

Inside the stud stable, a gust of arctic air blasted across Kelly's bare shoulders. As if sensing the goose bumps swelling upward, Logan put his arm around her shoulders. Her heart lurched, then pounded furiously, leaving her light-headed.

"The studs like it cool," explained Woody. "We have ceiling fans above each stall as well as air conditioning. The fans keep the flies away."

Greeting each stallion by name, Woody headed toward the rear of the stable. The pleasant smell of hay swirled through the air combining with the distinctive scent of horses and leather tack. The ceiling fans whirred overhead, creating a slight hum. The swish of horses tossing their manes and the thud of hooves told Kelly the stallions were very high strung.

"Does anyone ride these stallions?" Kelly asked.

"Yes. Most of them are show champions," Woody said, pointed to a gleaming white horse with wild eyes. "That's Outlaw. He's just used for breeding. He's too undisciplined to show."

The horse glared at Kelly, its nostrils flaring as it pawed the stable floor. He was awesomely beautiful, but he frightened her. She had been riding all her life, yet she couldn't imagine having the courage to put a halter on this Arabian.

Logan stepped forward, and Outlaw snorted furiously, his nostrils quivering, his eyes ablaze. With a quick, violent jerk of his powerful neck, the Arabian tossed his head, sending his mane into the air.

"Whoa, easy boy." Logan's voice was husky, yet pitched low in a manner meant to reassure the horse.

Outlaw regarded Logan with suspicion, but he stopped moving. Logan reached out his hand and stroked the Arabian's nose. Outlaw went stock still, his fiery eyes becoming less turbulent.

"Come here, darling. Let Outlaw know you're his friend."

Darling? She caught Woody staring at her intently. She quickly stepped up beside Logan, thankful for the steel gate separating them from the rebellious stallion. He put one arm around her, and with his other hand, he took hers.

Guided by his strong fingers, she petted Outlaw. His coat was as soft as a magnolia petal, and unexpectedly warm, considering the air circulating in the barn and the Casablanca fan whirring overhead.

"Outlaw's something, isn't he?" There was more than just a trace of awe in Logan's voice.

"H-m-m-m," Kelly responded, suddenly deciding the man and the horse had the same effect on her. They were both magnificent, yet they made her inhale sharply and remind herself not to be afraid.

"It's strange that Outlaw should take to you. Only my head trainer, Jim Cree can do anything with him." There was an odd note in Woody's voice, and Kelly pulled her hand away from the horse to look at him.

Woody moved closer to Logan. "Do you still like to ride?"

For a second, Kelly thought Logan wasn't going to answer. His arm was draped casually around her shoulder, but she could feel the extreme tension in his body like a honed blade.

The silence in the stable became awkward, magnified by the thrashing movements of the stallions, the gurgle of water as the stainless steel water troughs automatically filled, and the whir of the ceiling fans overhead.

Finally, Logan stopped petting Outlaw. "I didn't know I could ride. The only time I was on a horse—that I remember—was when I rode some nag out of a rebel camp in Ecuador. I was sore for a week."

Woody's brows drew together. "Too bad. Riding is a lot of fun especially in Red Rock country. You're welcome to ride my horses. It won't take long for you to catch on again."

"You'll love it," Kelly said, batting her eyelashes shamelessly at Logan. "I could teach you."

He managed to smile at her. "Maybe."

"The colt's over there," Woody said as he stepped away from Outlaw's stall.

Kelly sensed Woody sincerely would like to get to know his son better. A pang of guilt made her ashamed of herself. Logan was here because he was committed to helping her. Why give Woody false hope?

"This is Thunderbolt," Woody announced proudly.

The white colt was at the gangly stage where his legs seemed too long for his body. He had soulful brown eyes like a doe and long, jet-black lashes. His platinum mane and tail had been brushed until they glistened.

"He's precious, just precious," Kelly said.

An elderly man walked through the door at the stable entrance. Kelly might not have noticed him for some time, but Logan's head turned the second the door opened. Kelly recognized Jim Cree immediately.

The head trainer and shaman had mentioned a skinwalker at the old hogan. It was easy to understand why Jim thought Logan was a witch who could take any shape he chose. Logan looked exactly like his father had at the same age.

Jim ambled toward them, using a horseweed cane. The heavy stalk was gnarled slightly, but very sturdy. His inverted pear shape with a barrel chest and slim hips and skinny legs was typical of many Navajo men.

What set Jim apart, and always had, was his ability to command respect from his fellow Navajos for his work as a *yataalii,* shaman. He was equally respected by white men for his ability to train Arabian horses. For as long as Kelly could remember, people had flown into Sedona from around the country to consult with Jim Cree.

Woody was rattling on and on about Thunderbolt and hadn't noticed Jim come into the barn. Jim's hitching gait slowed even more as he spotted Logan. Jim had to be almost eighty now, Kelly decided. His eyesight wasn't as good as it once was, and he couldn't walk without the horseweed cane, but he spent hours in the saddle.

"Hosteen," she called, using the Navajo term for a respected elder, hoping to put Jim at ease. "*Yaa' eh t'eeh.* Woody's son has come home."

Unlike Uma, who rarely looked directly at people until she knew them well, Jim gazed right at Logan as he came closer. He was dressed in Levis and wore a red shirt with Western detailing. He'd taken off his black Stetson with the band of silver conches around the crown, but it had left a mark on his forehead.

He shuffled up to the stall and stopped in front of Logan. "You have come home. *Yei Yiaash.*"

"Arrival of the spirits," scoffed Woody from inside the stall where he was petting the colt. "Now, Jim, don't you pull a shaman routine on us. This is just Logan. You remember searching for him, don't you?"

Jim's weathered hand dropped to his leather belt. Hanging between the gleaming silver conches set with turquoise was a *jish.* Inside the leather pouch would be a vial of pollen, sacred feathers, at least two crystals and small mineral stones, the tools of a shaman's trade.

"I remember," Jim said, his hand on the *jish.* "I remember."

"Jim is the best trainer in the world," Woody told Logan. "When you were lost, he searched for you."

"I wanted to call the *belacani,*" Jim said, "but Benson did not want the sheriff. I rode out to search."

"When Benson finally reached me, I told him to call the sheriff," Woody said.

"A computer found me. Go figure." Logan's response

seemed casual, yet Kelly thought she detected a certain stiffness in his voice that went beyond its usual harsh intonation.

Jim hobbled into the stall, telling Woody, "Thunderbolt is not eating as he should. He does not yet know what happened to his mother. I am going to chant for him."

"Navajos chant to cure things," Kelly told Logan.

"We'll get out of your way," Woody said. "Let's go back to the house and have a drink."

Woody and Logan started to leave, and Kelly said, "Go on. I'll catch up. I might do an article on chants."

Jim carefully set his horseweed cane against the side of the stall and hung his Stetson on the hook with the curry comb. "What do you wish to know, Kelly Taylor?"

He's a very perceptive man, she decided. He knew she didn't want information about chants.

"I was wondering if you were in the stable the afternoon Logan went riding Hellion."

Jim took an eagle's pin feather out of his *jish* and placed it on Thunderbolt's forelock. "I was here."

She noted that he answered the question without adding any more information. Like Uma, he'd been taught to evade, but not to lie. "On the day Logan disappeared, did you see him leave on his pony with the twins?"

He made counter-clockwise circles in the air with his hand facing palm down above the feather. "No, I had a horse running on the treadmill."

Jim began to chant in Navajo, his voice barely above a whisper. She started to ask him another question, then stopped. Native Americans considered interrupting rude. Interrupting a chanting shaman was unthinkable. She certainly hoped this wasn't one of those chants that went on for days.

In a matter of minutes, Thunderbolt's fringe of eyelashes drooped over his chocolate-brown eyes. His long legs slowly folded under him, and he sank to the bed of straw. Jim leaned over and took the eagle's feather off the sleeping colt.

Jim took great care in putting the feather back into his *jish*.

Then he closed the leather pouch and secured it to his belt. He picked up his cane and hat. He pressed his finger to his lips and limped out of the stall.

Kelly had known Jim for years, since her grandfather had served on Sedona's Tribal Liaison Committee. He was usually more talkative than this. He wasn't going to lie to her, but he wasn't volunteering anything.

"When did you realize Logan was missing?" she whispered.

"Luz Tallchief came to get me."

"She'd been in her room sick, right?"

"Luz Tallchief is *ahnii*. This was not her fault."

Kelly had not realized that Luz had the status of a judge, being held in the highest esteem by her clan. She had never met the woman, but knew Luz had worked for the Stanfields from the time Ginger had discovered she was carrying twins. She served as nanny to the twins, then stayed on to help Ginger raise the children.

"Until the day Logan vanished, Luz had never missed work. She ate something bad the night before and became ill."

Interesting, Kelly thought. He's volunteering information about Luz to make certain I don't blame her. Why?

"You wanted to call the *belacani*," she said, using the Navajo term for white policeman. "The Coconino Sheriff back then was Tony Montoya, right?" Jim nodded. "Why didn't Benson call him?"

"Benson said the sheriff was *nakai*. A Mexican worth nothing. I could find the boy faster on horseback."

It was just like Benson to let prejudice over-ride his better judgment. Or was it really prejudice? Something strange had gone on that day.

"You searched and searched, but didn't find a trace of him, true?"

They had reached the exit, but Jim stopped, his world-weary eyes sought hers. For a moment he was silent, then he said, "I am born to the Silent Waters Clan, born for the River Bend People. Our history is as old as the red rocks of Sedona. I am *yataalii*. The great one has given his shamans the gift of diagnosing illnesses, identifying witches, and finding lost things.''

He spoke with the deep pride and firm sense of honor that Kelly often heard in her grandfather's voice. He also told her first about his clan—his family—which was more important to a Navajo than his own personal achievements. This was a man who would not lie, yet she suspected he was hiding something.

''I have seen much in my time,'' he continued. ''Cured many of my people. Found a lot of things that had been lost. If I had wanted to find Logan, I could have.''

She wavered, struggling to comprehend what he had told her. ''Wait!''

Jim hobbled out the door without another word. He disappeared into the night, leaving her baffled.

Why hadn't he wanted to find Logan? Why would he leave a little boy out in the wilderness at night? It made no sense.

Kelly walked down the path toward the house. Jim had given her a tip, but he had withheld much about the case. She supposed she couldn't blame him. He had a job he loved, and he must feel loyalty to Woody after working for him all these years.

Common sense said he would have done his best to find the boy. Unless he'd been told to do something different. Who would have been able to influence him?

Luz Tallchief, the nanny. It was obvious that he deeply respected her. She was an *ahnii,* a matriarch with as much power as a judge. Jim would have seen her as an equal and listened to her.

Unlike the male-dominated world of the white man, Navajo society was matriarchal. Upon meeting a stranger, they gave their born-to clan's name, their mother's clan. Then they told their born-for clan, their father's people.

In their world, the word of an *ahnii* would have been honored even by a man like Jim who was also a leader of his people. Most definitely he could have been influenced by Luz.

From what Kelly understood, Luz had taken Logan's disappearance hard. She'd quit her job and retreated to a cottage near Indian Gardens. She never ventured into town, so Kelly didn't know her.

Tomorrow she was going to find Luz Tallchief and try to discover the whole truth about what happened to Logan.

Chapter 16

Kelly returned to the main house, disturbed and confused by what Jim Cree had told her. She paused outside the open French doors, asking herself what had happened all those years ago. Why hadn't Jim tried to find Logan?

Inside, Logan and Woody were sitting at the bar, sipping drinks while Benson Williams stood behind the massive black granite counter, making a Martini for Ginger. Woody's wife sat back, her eyes tracking Benson's every move.

Still beautiful despite her age, Ginger wore a black silk sheath, a perfect complement for her shoulder-length, silver-blond hair dramatically swept behind one ear. Diamond studs that had to be four carats each adorned her ears.

Off to one side, stood Alyx, a glass of wine in her hand. She exuded a petulant arrogance that never failed to annoy Kelly. She giggled under her breath. Alyx couldn't forget her name now. They were going to be related.

Scary.

Alyx was not the kind of woman who inspired dumb blonde jokes. Instead, she reminded Kelly of the devil in drag. She couldn't help wishing she were home with Pop.

Away from these people.

"Kelly," called Logan. "Come in here, darling."

Everyone turned to look at her, and Kelly faltered a moment, then moved forward. Logan strode up to her, slid his arm around her in a way that said they'd been intimate for some time.

His seductive smile confirmed it. Boy, oh, boy. He was a good actor, Kelly thought. She hoped she was as adept at hiding her feelings. His touch elicited reactions she'd come to expect: heart beating out of sync and a hint of light-headedness.

Alyx glided over to them the moment they came close to the bar. "Look at Kelly's engagement ring. Wow!"

Alyx gushed over it, and Ginger walked up, carrying her martini, which was already half gone. Logan's arm was around Kelly's waist but there was a sinewy tension about him, a man constantly on the alert.

"Tyler, look at this stunning ring," Alyx said as she looked up.

Tyler was walking into the room, but Logan had spotted him even before Alyx had spoken. Kelly was learning to pick up on subtle clues from Logan, a slight tilt of the head or a shift of his eyes.

A blue-eyed blond like his twin sister, Tyler was an exceptionally handsome man. A fact that had not escaped his notice. Kelly sensed the elevation of tension emanating from Logan's body. Kelly was positive Logan did not like his half-brother.

Logan was casually dressed as was Kelly, but Tyler and Alyx wore fancy cocktail outfits. A sheer red silk slip dress emphasized the sensuous contours of Alyx's body while Tyler's lightweight navy jacket and white trousers with stiletto creases would have been more appropriate for a yacht in the Mediterranean rather than a dinner party in Sedona.

Kelly couldn't help wondering if the family had deliberately dressed up to make them feel uncomfortable. Benson was in a sports jacket with a tie—a rarity in Sedona—and Ginger appeared more formal than necessary. Only Woody was casually attired in Dockers and a short-sleeved shirt.

"Let's see the ring." Tyler took her hand and examined the diamond. "Is it real?"

"Of course, silly," responded Alyx, but her tone indicated she had her doubts.

Logan grinned at Kelly, then winked. He had a devastating effect on her body, but she doubted that was his intention. He had to be fighting the urge to tell off the obnoxious twins.

"It looks like a Tiffany setting to me," Ginger added, clearly astonished. "It'll have the store's name inside the band. Woody buys most of my jewelry at Tiffany's, don't you dear?"

Woody walked up to them. The corners of his mouth had dropped a notch. It was obvious that he didn't care for the way his family was behaving.

"It's a really beautiful ring," Woody said with a sharp look at the twins. "Let's go in to dinner."

Benson Williams, who had yet to say a word, took Ginger's glass. Tall and attractive with a patrician bearing made aristocratic by a touch of silver hair at his temples, Benson had about as much charm as Atilla the Hun. He guided Ginger to the far end of the great room where a massive table was set with crystal and silver.

Interesting. The twins walked across the room, side by side, speaking in such low voices that it was impossible to hear what they were saying. Woody trailed behind them, alone. Kelly speculated about the rumors she'd heard about Benson and Ginger engaging in an affair that had lasted for years.

The glass table was long enough to be a bowling alley, Kelly decided as Logan pulled out a chair with swan's wing forming the back for her. The mammoth table was supported by the spread wings of two preening swans. It was a bit much for her taste, and it certainly wasn't "Sedona."

"Having fun?" Logan whispered as sat down beside her. The intimate pitch to his voice and the way he smiled at her did shameless things to her pulse. She reminded herself to smile at him.

It was embarrassingly easy.

Benson prattled on about his golf game that afternoon at Poco Diablo Resort while a uniformed maid served something odd-looking that Kelly didn't recognize. Another maid offered them a choice of red or white wine.

Taking care to conceal her hand with her napkin, Kelly slipped off the ring. Tiffany & Co. was engraved on the inside of the band. Oh, my God! He really had bought the ring at Tiffany's.

Why? He could easily have gone to a less expensive jeweler. Had he done it to impress the Stanfields? If so, why hadn't he told them Ginger was right? The ring had come from Tiffany's.

As silly as it seemed, Kelly already adored the ring. Every time she moved her hand, a dazzle of light like a sparkler shot upward. The diamond had an inner fire that she'd never seen except in the windows of ultra-expensive jewelers. True, it was embarrassingly large, but the setting's simple lines made it elegant not gaudy.

When everyone had wine, Woody raised his glass, "To Logan, welcome to the family."

Kelly lifted her glass and smiled brightly, saying, "To Logan," but she couldn't help noticing the rest of the family was far less sincere-sounding than Woody. And Benson Williams had merely tipped his glass.

Logan turned to her, the searing blue of his eyes catching her off guard. She knew the Stanfields were watching and mustered a besotted smile. The look he gave her was as seductive as a caress.

Oh, my. How was she going to do this? A marriage of convenience to a man like Logan was more difficult than she could ever have imagined. She managed to smile adoringly at him.

"We wish you both a long and happy marriage," Woody continued.

"Isn't this rather sudden?" Ginger asked.

"You two just met," Benson added almost as if he were accustomed to finishing Ginger's sentences for her.

"It was love at first sight," Logan said.

The heart-rending tenderness of his gaze stunned her. He was a gifted actor. She was almost convinced he did love her.

"Th-there's no man on earth like Logan," Kelly stammered. Now, that was a fact.

"I'm so-o happy for you," Alyx gushed. "I've never been married."

"You're nuts, that's why." Tyler's comment was delivered with a teasing smile, and from Alyx's amused expression she was accustomed to her brother's jokes.

"I'm not nuts," Alyx replied. "Poor people are nuts. I'm eccentric."

Woody was watching Logan while Benson concentrated on something Ginger was saying in a low voice. The twins gazed at each other for a second, then chuckled as if sharing a private joke. The air had become dense, charged with emotion . . . and expectation.

Logan was the only one eating the suspicious looking brown mush that they'd been served. She had noticed that he had a tendency to eat too fast, and he hunched forward slightly as if expecting someone to take his food away from him.

"What is this brown stuff?" asked Woody, putting his fork down.

Ginger's gaze shifted to Benson, then she said, "It's *huitla-coche*.

"That's French for what?" Woody asked.

Ginger hesitated, then said, "It's an Aztec delicacy."

"It looks like something the chef scraped out of the bottom of the garbage disposal," Woody told her.

"It's supposed to taste like a cross between corn and truffles." Ginger's voice was barely above a whisper, and blotches of red mottled her face.

"I don't care what it tastes like. What is it?"

Ginger's lower lip quivered, and Benson answered for her. "It's a fungus that grows on corn cobs."

Alyx piped up, "It's all the rage in LA."

"Logan likes it," Tyler added.

Woody's brows drew together as he cast a glance at Logan's nearly clean plate. He picked up his fork again and began to eat. Kelly took a bite, finding the *huitlacoche* tasted much better than it looked.

She could resist saying, "It's yummy."

Under the table, Logan squeezed her knee. The ludicrous way Kelly smiled at him and batted her lashes would have made Pop laugh, but the Stanfields didn't know her that well. She kept eating, as did Woody.

Ginger must have felt silly not trying the dish she'd had the chef prepare. She jabbed at it with her fork, then forced a bite between her lips. Benson studied her a moment before forking down a bite or two. The twins had no choice but to sample the concoction as well.

Woody finished his *huitlacoche*, chatting about his Arabians, obviously trying to fill the awkward silence. Kelly wondered if he realized Ginger had deliberately ordered something repulsive to embarrass Logan. If he did, he gave no indication.

Ginger projected a fragile vulnerability that Kelly always associated with Southern belles—before the Civil War. Remembering all the rumors she had heard about Ginger's drug problems, Kelly wondered if that accounted for her slightly distracted air as if she existed on another plane. Benson's sidelong glances at Ginger silently indicated his concern.

"I guess you must have eaten some really interesting food doing your work in South America," Tyler said.

"You'd be surprised," Logan replied as the maid cleared their plates.

"Isn't that what you commando types do?" Alyx asked. "Smear your face with black tar and slip into the night to do God-only-knows-what and live off the land?"

"Alyx," Woody warned his daughter in a tight voice.

In the uncomfortable silence that followed, a depth charge of anger exploded deep inside Kelly. What a bitch! Kelly felt oddly concerned about Logan even though she was positive he could protect himself.

Didn't anyone but Woody care about Logan? Apparently not. They hadn't asked a single question about his past. They saw him as a threat.

"You know, Alyx," Kelly said, her voice saccharine sweet.

"It's a leap of faith to think you and Logan come from the same gene pool. You couldn't survive anywhere without your American Express card."

Ginger's face had been splotchy red before, but now every bit of color had drained from it. She nervously dabbed at her lips with her napkin.

"Ladies, please," Benson said. "You're upsetting Ginger."

What a tragedy.

"Actually, Cobras put soot on their face, not tar," Logan said without a lick of humor. "We take supplies, but if we run out, we usually can find a rat to eat." He looked right at Alyx. "Rats are everywhere."

"Why don't we try the wine?" Woody suggested in an obvious attempt to change the subject.

Benson launched into a dissertation about the relative merits of California wines versus French wines. Tyler added a few comments about the new Australian wines he'd tried.

Alyx held her crystal goblet up to her nose then inhaled so deeply that Kelly had expected the bitch to suck it up through her nose. Then she took a dainty sip. "Excellent. It's not one of those pretentious little wines produced by a small-time boutique vineyard. The flavor is subtle, very subtle."

There was something so condescending about the way Alyx spoke and the look she cast toward her brother. It seemed to Kelly that Alyx was implying that Logan couldn't tell the difference between a great wine and grape juice.

"I've always despised pretentious wines," Kelly told everyone with a smile. "I select wines with nifty-looking labels."

"Good idea," Benson said. "Rothchild has reproductions of Impressionist art on its labels. You can't go wrong."

"No, no. I meant cute labels and cute names like Frog's Leap."

"That's Stag's Leap," Tyler said. "It is one of the better California wines, although I prefer French wine."

Kelly shook her head. "Haven't you tasted Frog's Leap? It has an adorable green frog on the label. It's almost as precious as Rabbit Ridge with the gold bunny with the *huge* ears on its label."

For a moment, Kelly thought Alyx was going to laugh, but a stern look from Woody kept her quiet. Benson looked slightly baffled as if he didn't know whether or not to take Kelly seriously. Ginger merely gazed into her wine glass as if some message had been written there, and she was attempting to decipher it.

Kelly couldn't stop herself from adding, "I just bought a bottle called Marilyn. It has Marilyn Monroe on the label. I'll bet it's *really* good."

Woody remarked at what a great investment wine had become, and Benson agreed with him. Tyler explained which years he'd personally chosen for the estates wine cellar, which was in the basement.

"You're doing great," Logan whispered in her ear, his warm breath ruffling her hair.

She forced another sappy smile and lowered her lashes. Tyler was boldly staring at her, inspecting her cleavage. Her breasts were okay, but she wasn't expecting a call from *Playboy*. The halter top probably did reveal more than she normally did, but she'd selected it because she always got compliments when she wore it. But Tyler's scorching gaze made her feel like a two-bit hooker, who was cheap, not pretty.

Logan leveled Tyler with a glare that said only someone with a death wish would look at his fiancée like that. Tyler quickly turned to his sister and mumbled something Kelly didn't catch as the maids served the main course.

"Great! Steaks," Woody said a little too effusively. Clearly, the dinner was not working out the way he'd hoped.

Kelly looked at her plate and knew the slab of meat next to the polenta and French haricot beans was not from a cow. It was probably elk. They were common in the area, but if this was fresh, someone had shot the poor thing out of season.

"What in hell is this?" Woody's voice ricocheted off the two-storey ceiling as the maid served him.

Logan cut into his meat, then took a bite while Ginger stammered something about the newest craze. The twins weren't eating, but they didn't seem surprised at what had been served and neither did Benson. Kelly suspected they were all in on this together, thinking this would somehow humiliate Logan.

"It's bison," Ginger confessed. "It's fat content is lower than chicken."

"Bison?" Woody barked. "That's just a fancy word for buffalo. I told you to ask the chef to prepare a first-class meal, and you serve buffalo?"

"Well, I-I thought it would be something new and different," Ginger muttered, her blue eyes filling with tears.

Benson touched Ginger's shoulder. "It's served in many French restaurants."

"If the French serve it, bison must be the height of culinary ecstasy," Kelly told Logan.

Benson tried to smile and nearly succeeded, but instead his shrewd eyes narrowed as he glared at Kelly. She was convinced he had the disposition of a rottweiller—if he was that friendly.

Logan kept eating.

"It is interesting," Alyx commented even though she had yet to try the bison. "I believe they serve a lot of it in Montana."

"We're in Arizona," Kelly said, implying Alyx was either lost or stupid. Probably both.

Logan paused between bites, down to his last piece now. "It's mighty tasty and not one bit like anything I've ever eaten."

Ginger perked up a bit. Tears glistened on her lashes as she gazed at Benson for reassurance.

Tyler shoved his plate aside. "Logan, it looks like you can eat just about anything."

Logan finished chewing the last of his bison. "You'd be amazed at what I've eaten. I've learned how to survive—anywhere."

The air wasn't just thick any more. It shrouded the room like a poisonous gas. Woody kept staring at the twins as if he held them responsible for the fiasco. Benson put his arm around the back of Ginger's chair.

This whole food bit was childish, stupid. It made Kelly want to hurl her hunk of bison at Alyx's smug face. Instead she, grinned at Logan. This time she was the one to reach under the table for his knee. Her hand missed the mark as he shifted in his seat. She touched his firm thigh, dangerously close to the no-no zone. She gave him a quick pat, then jerked her hand away.

"We met at a barbecue, right, darling?"

Logan winked. "I'm a hell of a cook."

Alyx took the bait. "Really? What did you prepare?"

"Lizard. Slow-roasted on a mesquite branch."

That got her. It floored everyone, actually. Tyler went slack-jawed. Benson's lips crumpled inward. Woody's quick intake of breath startled Kelly. Ginger's tears disappeared with a flutter of her lashes.

"Logan's so talented. He knows how to gut a lizard, starting here." Kelly pointed to the underside of her chin and made a slashing motion downward. "You skin it while it's still alive, so you can drain the blood quicker. Many lizards have sacs of poison at the base of their neck. You have to squeeze them dry," she said, making this up as she went. "Of course, you remove the innards last. You can't believe the smell."

"Mercy, me!" Ginger's voice reached a decibel only achieved by opera singers. She gagged, her hand coming up to cover her mouth. She dashed from the table with Benson at her heels.

"You're not serious. This is a joke," Woody said.

"It's true," Kelly informed him. "That's exactly how we met. Logan had roasted a lizard."

Woody's eyes widened and he stared intently at his son. He seemed to want to say something, but was at a loss for words—a rarity for a politician.

Logan's large hand settled on her thigh in a way that was disturbingly familiar. She was becoming accustomed to him touching her. And she liked it more than she dared to admit. He gently squeezed, giving her the impression he found this as hilarious as she did.

"You learned all this training as a Cobra?" asked Tyler.

Logan shook his head. "Nope. I've been hungry most of my life. Long before I became a Cobra, I learned how to survive."

Kelly hoped this wasn't really true. Perhaps Logan said it to make them feel guilty about serving bison.

Tyler wouldn't let it go. "What's the most exotic thing you've eaten? Snakes? Cockroaches?"

Alyx had sense to glare at Tyler to warn him to shut up. Even Kelly was sorry she'd started this. She imagined Logan had seen more than his share of hell, and she didn't want these people making fun of him.

Benson returned to the table, saying, "Ginger's in her suite. She's not feeling well."

Woody nodded, and Kelly hoped this would end the discussion about eating to survive.

"You were going to tell us about the most exotic thing you've ever eaten," Tyler reminded Logan.

"If you're ever stuck in the Amazon," Logan said, "try the Orinoco tarantula. It's about the size of a grapefruit. Skinning it is tricky, but it's a whole meal."

The stupid grin on Kelly's face kept her from gasping, but Alyx stood up and excused herself. Woody summoned a maid and ordered an assortment of ice cream and toppings, so they could each make their own sundae.

"I'm not taking any chances with whatever Ginger ordered for dessert," Woody said, in a futile attempt to lighten the mood.

One maid took coffee orders while the other cleared the plates and removed the wineglasses. Such waste was a shame, Kelly reflected. Too many people in the world went to bed starving.

"It's going to take some adjusting, Logan, but I want you and Kelly to become part of this family," Woody said with a sharp look at Tyler.

"We'd really like to come to your wedding," Tyler announced.

"We're looking forward to it," added Benson.

Kelly's stomach roiled worse than it had when she'd thought about eating a tarantula. Wasn't it enough that Pop insisted on a reception following the civil ceremony? All her life, Pop had taught her to be honest. Living a lie was much harder than she'd anticipated.

"We're being married in Judge Hollister's chambers," Logan said. "There'll be a reception afterward for close friends at Kelly's home."

"I'd love to be included."

The stark emotion in Woody's tone touched Kelly. He truly cared about the son he'd lost so many years ago. He wanted to attend the wedding, to become part of his son's life. Evidently, he didn't blame Logan for costing him a chance to become president.

"We'd love to have you," Kelly heard herself say.

She didn't dare look at Logan. Having the Stanfields at the wedding had not been part of the plan. Heaven only knew if Pop would even allow them on his property. When Woody announced his retirement from the senate, Pop had written a scathing article, claiming Haywood Stanfield had done about as much for Arizona as Idi Amin had done for Africa. It took a vivid imagination to envision them in the same room together.

"There may be something you can do to help us." Logan's voice was flat as if he were speaking to a total stranger.

Tyler leaned forward slightly, and Kelly would bet Tyler was anticipating Logan was going to ask his father for money. She almost laughed, but this meant too much to her. Woody might be able to help.

"Kelly and I want to adopt a child. It's a paperwork jungle, then we'll have to go through miles of red tape, including visits from social workers. If you could help us speed up the process, we would appreciate it."

"Of course, I'll do anything I can," Woody said without hesitation.

Tyler had the nerve to say, "Shouldn't you at least try to have your own baby?"

"Good idea," Benson added. "It's too soon to give up hope."

"I never was exposed to childhood diseases, so I never had them. I was on a mission in Chile when I caught the mumps." Logan shrugged and gave Kelly an adorable grin. "They went south on me. I can't father a child."

Chapter 17

Logan walked out of his father's home with his arm around Kelly's waist. He led her down the flagstone path to where she had parked Pop's car. He waited until they were too far from the house for surveillance equipment to pick up their conversation.

He stopped and pulled her into his arms, whispering, "You were great tonight. Just great!"

She no longer tried to get away from him all the time, but he could feel the slight resistance in her body. She would have to get used to him because he intended to touch her often. He was more than a little amazed at how much he enjoyed just holding her.

The only female he'd ever gotten to know had been at the camp. Amy had been pathetically in need of affection, but Jake's rules, the rules everyone had to abide by, forbid touching. Make it on your own or die trying.

He'd never once touched Amy until she became hopelessly sick. Even then, he'd only put his hand on her forehead to check her fever. He'd tried for years to protect Amy, the best way he could, feeling like her big brother. But in the end, nothing mattered.

After he had enlisted, he'd never had a so-called "relationship.'' He hadn't had time for one, hadn't had a career that allowed for intimacy.

Things had changed.

Now he had time on his hands and one of the more interesting—and certainly the sexiest—partners that he'd ever been with on a mission.

Mission? What a crock! But Kelly had fallen for it. This was not like the missions that were assigned to Cobras. There was only the slimmest element of risk involved. It was possible the drug cartel leader, Manuel Orinda, would discover Logan was in Venezuela and order his men to kill him.

''Great?'' Kelly hissed into his ear. ''You think I was great. Are you kidding? What went on tonight was the most childish stunt I've ever seen. Doesn't Ginger have a brain in her head.''

''Don't underestimate her. I think she's a damn fine actress who knows how to manipulate Woody and the family''

Kelly tried to pull away, but he refused to let her wiggle out of his arms. He liked the way her breasts molded against his rib cage and the firmness of her thighs against his. Sexy as hell.

She had a depth and power to her that he hadn't expected. She was tender with Pop and treated Uma with respect, but she turned into a gutsy wiseass with the Stanfields. Amazing! She had been defending him. In his entire life, no one had ever defended him.

Hell. He didn't need her help. He didn't need anyone, but he had to admit he was strangely touched. Even more interesting, he reflected, was that working with Kelly had been fun.

''Don't be fooled. What went on tonight was just a smoke screen.''

''What do you mean?'' The moonlight caught her expressive brown eyes, deepening the color as she gazed up at him.

''I think someone put Ginger up to the food bit. They hate me and want me out of their lives, but they don't want me to be on guard. By doing something so silly, I'm supposed to think they're mean-spirited not dangerous.''

''Dangerous?'' Her eyes widened, then the dusky fringe of lashes dropped and she tried to squirm out of his arms.

"Pretend we're so hot for each other that we can't keep apart." His lips found his favorite spot, the soft dip behind her earlobe. He kissed her, savoring the sweet scent rising from her skin and the throb of her pulse beneath his lips. "They're watching us."

"Who?"

He hated to admit he wasn't positive. He'd thought coming here for dinner would accomplish two things: get his father to expedite the adoption certification and discover which of the Stanfields were after him.

Watch your back.

Since Raptor's initial warning, he had again cautioned Logan that more questions were being asked about Logan's activities in South America. Every reporter in the country wanted to find out more about him, but a person with contacts on the Armed Services Committee was also nosing around big-time. It had to be someone in the Stanfield camp.

"Trust me, babe. Ginger and Benson or Alyx and Tyler are out to get me. Hell, I don't know. Maybe all four of them are in on this together. They're watching right now with night vision binoculars to see what we're doing."

The moonlight flickered over her hair, glistened softly on her parted lips, and danced in her eyes. He imagined her hair fanned across a pillow. His pillow.

"What about your father? Do you think he's part of—of whatever is going on?"

That was a damn good question. "I don't know, possibly."

"Your father seems sincere, at least to me, he does."

There was so much evil in the world. She couldn't possibly imagine, and he didn't want her to know. Her jerkoff of a husband had hurt her enough. She didn't need any more heartache. This unexpected surge of protectiveness made him uneasy as hell.

Don't get involved.

That was damn near impossible. He was going to marry her—and sleep with her. Night after night.

"I hope you're not upset that I invited your father to the

wedding. He seems so genuinely interested in getting to know you,'' Kelly said.

"That's what he told me while you were talking to Jim Cree.'' Logan had pretended to be interested, but he knew better. The family was a powder keg primed to explode. He didn't want any part of it.

"It's going to be embarrassing to have them at the reception. Pop and Woody are like oil and water. I'm not sure Pop will even allow Benson Williams on his property. That's how much he hates him."

"I'll talk to Pop," Logan volunteered as he released her and began walking toward the Cadillac. "When we get into the car, we're going to get hot and heavy for a few minutes for their benefit. During the drive home, don't say anything that will tip them that we're not crazy about each other. Whatever you do, don't mention Venezuela or Rafi. The less they know about our plans the better."

As he guided her toward the car, his hand on her bare back, his fingertips testing the softness of her skin, she whispered, "Do you think they bugged the car?"

"It's doubtful since its your grandfather's car, but I can't rule it out. I'm certain they've bugged Pop's house and our *casitas*. I can check as soon as we get home, but I can't poke around this car with a flashlight while they're watching."

"You're right," she said, her voice pitched low as she moved closer to him. Her lips were dangerously close to his. She definitely had a kissable mouth. Very kissable.

He didn't want to kiss her, did he? No way. Kissing was not his thing.

"What do you see?" Her bare breasts pressed into his back, hot and hard against his skin. "What are they doing?"

"The same thing they were doing out front. Kissing. His hands are all over her."

"Let me look." She reached for the binoculars.

He moved aside, handing her the glasses. He caressed her silky smooth ass with his hand, running his fingers along the cleft. He'd come to her room after that farce of a dinner and with his teeth, ripped off the filmy black lingerie he'd given her. He'd taken her, standing up against the marble wall of the bathroom.

It had been raw, primitive—the way they both liked to start. Later, they would take their time and spend hours to accomplish what they'd just done in minutes.

"I can't see anything," she complained.

"Train the glasses on the dark shadow at the end of the drive. That's the car. Then press the button at the top," He reached over and put her finger on the button. "Night vision picks up all the ambient light. You should be seeing clear as day now."

She giggled, the throaty sound that always said she was up to something naughty. "If I had breasts like Kelly Taylor's, I'd get silicone."

"Has Logan pulled down her top?" So far the show had been only mildly interesting. He reached for the binoculars.

"No. The little prude is still dressed." She elbowed his hand away. "Why do you suppose he keeps kissing her neck and shoulders?"

"I noticed that too. Maybe he's a vampire." He saw the headlights flick on, cutting a blue-white swath across the emerald green lawn. "Show's over."

She handed him the binoculars. "Too bad you didn't have your man bug the car instead of just the house. I'd love to know what they think of the family."

"They despise the family. They're just using good old Woody to help them adopt a child."

"I couldn't believe it when you told me. I guess I left the table too soon." She giggled again, a little nastier this time. "Kelly's getting what she deserves, a man who can't give her children. Trent Farley won't have any grandchildren to call his own and brag about in that two-bit gossip sheet he likes to call a newspaper."

"There's something strange going on. I'm not sure I buy Logan's story."

''The bugs will tell us what's really happening so we can make our plans.''

''True, and the little scene tonight with the food should have convinced Logan we're nitwits not worth worrying about.''

She picked up what was left of her black panties and brushed the swatch of silk across his penis. ''Why would Logan be suspicious?''

''Since he's so mum about where he was all those years, I'm certain he knows more than he's telling.''

''He was barely five, for God's sake.''

He shrugged, anxious to finish the discussion and hop in bed. ''Someone found him. They might have seen something or . . . who knows?''

''I'm not worried,'' she assured him. ''It's Woody that I'm concerned about. He's taken with Logan, and mark my words, Logan doesn't just want help with an adoption. He'll hit Woody's wallet next. I say we murder Logan McCord, and frame Kelly Taylor.''

''If we kill him now, Logan will die a hero.''

She clamped her hand around his cock, stroking it through the silk. ''I can't help myself. Murder is the ultimate high especially when—like last time—everyone is too stupid to even suspect a crime has been committed.''

''You were right,'' Kelly told Logan. ''While we were having dinner with the Stanfields, someone bugged the house. Uma leaves right after supper, and Pop goes to his room. He never locks the doors unless he's going away on a vacation or something. This isn't LA. We don't expect people to sneak into our homes.''

''You followed directions perfectly. Whoever is listening will assume we're out making love under the stars. I've never gone in for screwing *al fresco* myself, but I could be talked into it.''

They were sitting on a flat boulder the size of a park bench beyond the main house and the *casitas*. Above them was an ebony sky emblazoned with stars, some mere pinpricks of light, others the size of a nickel. In the distance, Oak Creek rushed and rumbled over the river rocks. A symphony of crickets were courting in the underbrush accompanied by full-throated bullfrogs.

The gleam of desire in his eyes unsettled her. "*Al fresco?* How can you joke at a time like this?"

"Easy. Now we know what we're dealing with. We control the information they'll have about us."

She nodded, still a little stunned at the tiny chrome chips he'd discovered in every telephone receiver in Pop's home except for the one in his room. They assumed that Pop's room was clean because he was asleep inside.

"Whoever planted those bugs must have been very quiet," she said. "Jasper didn't bark. Not that he barks easily. Guide dogs are encouraged not to bark unless it's very serious. Constant barking would be frightening to someone who is blind."

Logan said, his voice low, "Whoever planted them knew exactly what he was doing. He wouldn't have made any noise."

"You're sure they can't hear us out here?"

"No. Infinity transmitters are electronically activated whenever there is noise in the room, but they don't have the range to pick up sounds this far away."

"Isn't a tape recorder hidden around the property somewhere?"

A gruff chuckle rumbled from his throat. He was not amused. "No. The old tape systems ran all the time often leaving miles of blank space when nothing was being recorded. Infinity transmitters record only when there is sound. Then the conversation is transmitted over the telephone lines to a laser disk-receiver. It could be anywhere."

He was sitting next to her on the flat rock, his hands, palms down on the rock. He looked at her when she spoke, but he'd made no attempt to touch her. Still, the sensuous undertone in his voice found its way into her body.

She was becoming more intrigued by him with each passing day. She had readily admitted the Stanfields would be perched like vultures eager to attack Logan the moment they had the opportunity. But she'd thought he was being a bit paranoid, expecting listening devices to be planted at Pop's house.

Typical CIA mentality, she'd privately decided, having done several articles on the agency. They'd turn over the White House to space aliens rather than let anyone peek at their files. Cobras, being a counter-terrorist unit under the CIA umbrella, indicated the same anal, secretive mentality where every activity was clandestine and every person suspect.

Boy, oh, boy, had she been mistaken.

She began to doubt her initial analysis of the situation just after she'd spoken to Jim Cree. Something was terribly wrong. The present must be linked to the past, to Logan's kidnapping as a child.

A niggling thought that had been with her all night demanded she review the file on the kidnapping, not just the articles but the original reporter's notes. They were Pop's notes, for he'd been the one who'd gathered the information for the article.

Luz Tallchief could be the key, Kelly reflected. The nanny who had raised the twins, then ten years later returned to raise Logan, might very well have the information Kelly needed. She had no intention of sharing any of this with Logan until she knew more.

"Did your work with the Cobras call for using sophisticated surveillance equipment like this?"

"Sophisticated?" He made it sound like a four-letter word. "This is high-end civilian stuff. The military has the truly cutting edge equipment. If this was a military operation we wouldn't be having this conversation. They have bugs that can pick up the sound of a hummingbird two miles away."

"Awesome. Our tax dollars at work."

He didn't respond to her lame joke. Instead he gazed at her mouth until her lower lip trembled and she had to clamp it between her teeth. Criminy! He was getting to her.

"Did you use a lot of that type of equipment?" she asked, eager to make him talk about himself.

"Sometimes. Counter-terrorist units are specialized. Agents specialize in an area of the world. I'm considered the ranking expert on South America. I'd be worthless in, say, Iran. I don't know the language or the customs or—''

"But you said you were in Bosnia. CNN was there to greet you,'' she reminded him.

"That was an emergency. So much sh—'' He smiled an adorable, little boy smile. ''So much was happening so quickly, they flew in a few of us to help. I was only there a short while.''

He was silent again and she was upset with herself for interrupting him. This was the first time he'd opened up and even given her more than a glimpse of his life.

"Counter-terrorist forces specialize in areas of the world and, ah, things like explosives or what?'' she prodded.

"I don't know what my new assignment will be. It probably won't be the same, so it won't matter if I tell you. I was a kidnapping expert.''

"I know it happens in South America once in a while, but you don't read about it very often.''

"If you read about it, I haven't done my job. The kidnapping of Americans is tricky to handle. We try to negotiate. If that doesn't work, we go in and get the person.''

"The Cobras must be very successful. If a kidnapped American died, it would make the news.''

"Not necessarily. Oil and timber companies in the Amazon have had employees kidnapped and killed. They persuade the families to keep quiet to ensure the safety of other workers.''

"How does that make the others safer?''

"It sends a message to terrorist groups. We're not playing your game.''

"Did you ever participate in a mission where the hostage was killed?''

"I've been lucky. My missions have been successful.''

There was a note of pride in his voice, faint but unmistakable. How odd, Kelly reflected, a man who had been kidnapped as a child now specialized in kidnappings.

Another thought occurred to her. ''You knew someone would ask you why we were adopting so quickly after being married, didn't you?'' Kelly was ashamed of herself for not having had a quick response to such an obvious question.

''Of course. It's something people instantly wonder about. Most of them won't be a jerk like Tyler and bluntly ask. But they'll be curious.''

''Can't you?'' She faltered, then rephrased the question. ''I mean are you . . .''

''Shooting blanks?''

''Well . . . yes.''

He leaned closer, and his eyes boldly raked over her, the meaning of his gaze obvious. ''There's only one way to tell.''

Chapter 18

There's only one way to find out.

Logan had laughed as if he'd been joking, but there had been
. . . something in the way he'd said it, Kelly thought the next
morning as she drove toward Indian Gardens. He was a perplexing man who sent conflicting messages. He insisted they
were on a mission and physical contact was necessary to convince everyone that love was the reason they were getting
married. Yet there were times when she was convinced that he
was attracted to her.

How did she feel about him, she asked herself as she guided
her car south toward Luz Tallchief's home. She didn't want
to become involved with him—emotionally or physically. Daniel's betrayal had severed a piece of her heart—with a hacksaw.

The knife edge of pain had dulled a little, eased by tears and
sleepless nights. It was a throbbing ache now accompanied by
a hollow, desolate sensation that went beyond tears. She did
not have the stamina for any more heartache.

And Logan McCord was heartbreak just waiting to happen.
She wished she could have found someone else to help her
adopt Rafi, but it was too late now.

"Ben," she slowed her car and called out her open window

to an elderly man who was opening his apple stand next to the highway that ran parallel to Oak Creek. "How's it going?"

"Danged if I haven't had the best harvest in years," Ben Hoyt told her with unmistakable pride. Above the baskets of apples hung bright crimson strands of dried chiles. Ben had strung the *ristas* himself, and they were immediately snapped up by the locals to be used in cooking during the winter.

Kelly congratulated him and drove on. Apples were ripening quickly in the orchards around town and needed to be sold or stored properly. When she'd left the house, Kelly had heard Logan and Pop making arrangements to pick the apples from the small grove near the house and store them in the root cellar for Uma.

Logan volunteering to pick apples. Pretty amazing. She didn't want to think about him doing things like an ordinary man. It was better to concentrate on his mysterious past. She tried to unravel the tale as she drove the short distance from Sedona to Indian Gardens.

"Hello, Tom," Kelly waved to the man who owned the old-fashioned gas station and General Store in Indian Gardens.

Across the street was the historical marker. It explained the canyon's early farmers, including Pop's grandparents, had arrived in the late 1800s and planted apple trees all along the Oak Creek Canyon. Although Sedona was better known world-wide for its scenery and vortexes, apple orchards still produced fruit that was shipped out of state or sold from roadside stands.

Kelly gazed up at the red sandstone ramparts towering over Indian Gardens, its vermilion color a sharp contrast to the radiant gold fall foliage skirting its base. She turned off the main road onto a gravel road marked Pendley Lane.

She braked hard, almost missing the battered metal mailbox on a wooden post. Behind it was an even smaller road and she drove more slowly down it. Aspens flanked the dirt lane, their fallen leaves scattered like golden doubloons on the red earth.

The road became dirt ruts, then stopped entirely at a semi-circular pad of dirt where a green pickup with a rusty dent in the rear fender was parked. She pulled her Toyota in beside it. The small wood-frame bungalow was almost concealed by overgrown apple trees heavy with fruit. A stone well with a new aluminum bucket stood off to one side. Nearby, a propane tank supplied fuel to the house.

Kelly knocked on the screen door and waited, but there was no answer. She peered through the screen into the dark living room. Beyond the house was a small patio where a young girl about sixteen was tossing apples into an apple press to make cider. Her gloss-black hair was coiled around her ears like the wings of a butterfly.

Luz Tallchief was Navajo, Kelly remembered. Her maternal clan, the "born to" clan was the Stone River Clan, but she had attended the Indian School in Santa Fe. There she'd met and married a Hopi man.

This young girl must be Luz's granddaughter, yet she wore her hair in the traditional Hopi fashion. Maternal clans dominated the Navajo culture. The first thing a person told you was his mother's clan, but obviously, this family valued their Hopi roots as well.

A waxy smell hit Kelly, and she craned her head to one side. On the stove was a huge vat of bubbling liquid. They were boiling yucca roots to make soap. Evidently they were very poor, but unless Kelly was mistaken, a priceless *yei* rug hung on the wall. The crisp red and white pattern made the gray vinyl sofa appear even more shabby.

"Yaa' eh t'eeh," she called, using the Navajo greeting.

The girl turned, saw Kelly and came into the house. "Yes," she said, but she didn't open the screen door.

"I'm looking for Luz Tallchief."

"She's not here."

"Will she be back soon? I'm Kelly Taylor. I—"

"I know who you are." There was a note of hostility in the girl's voice.

"Really?" Kelly couldn't recall having seen her around Sedona. The town was so small that the locals usually recognized each other even if they didn't know everyone by name.

"You wrote the article about Logan McCord."

"Yes, I did." That explained why the girl knew her name. Matthew Jensen had given her name prominent positioning in the *Exposé* article, and she had run the story again in the *Sedona Sun.* "May I come in?"

"My grandmother is not here. She is out chanting."

Just my luck, Kelly thought. Navajo chants could go on for days and days depending upon what type they were. "Do you know when she'll be back? It's important that I see her."

"Why?"

There it was again, a certain surliness to the girl's tone as if she didn't like Kelly. Why? They didn't know each other. The girl wouldn't have any reason to dislike her unless it was something her grandmother had said.

"It's about Logan McCord. Surely, your grandmother heard that Logan has been found after all these years. She must be very happy."

"Grandmother is very upset. She has gone all alone into the San Francisco Mountains to do an *Adant' ti* chant for Logan." The girl slammed the door shut in Kelly's face with such force that the screen door popped open.

On the way back to Sedona, Kelly tried to recall the Navajo chants that Uma had told her about when Kelly had been growing up. The Night Chant, Mountain Top Chant and the Blessing Way Chant immediately came to mind, but she couldn't remember an *Adant' ti* chant.

Interesting, she observed, no one seemed glad to have Logan McCord return. It was understandable why the Stanfields weren't thrilled, but even Jim Cree and Luz Tallchief were not happy campers. Their attitudes only reinforced Kelly's belief that the true story of his disappearance had never been told.

Back in her office, Kelly ignored the pink message sheets on the spike beside her telephone and called Uma.

The housekeeper answered on the seventh ring. Now was not a good time to be calling. Kelly knew Uma's favorite soap, "As The World Turns" was on.

"What's the haps?" Uma answered, using a greeting she must have heard on television.

"Uma, what can you tell me about the *Adant' ti* chant?"

"Get real! How'd you hear about that chant?"

Kelly was not about to give whoever had bugged the house

this bit of information. 'Someone mentioned it in passing. I don't remember you telling me about it, and I'm doing an article on chants." That should jive with the excuse she'd given Woody to speak to Jim Cree, assuming Woody was in on this.

"An *Adant' ti* is an evil person who has the power to change form or become invisible," Uma told her.

"I'm confused. I thought a skinwalker, a witch, had those powers."

"An *Adant' ti* is much, much more evil than a witch." Uma's voice had the reverent, hushed tone Navajos often used when speaking of witchcraft. They were terrified of the supernatural, yet it fascinated them.

"Why didn't you ever tell me about an *Adant' ti?*"

"Well"—Uma hesitated and Kelly didn't know if she was reluctant to discuss this or if there was a torrid love scene on the soap opera. "If you say a dead person's name out loud, you call their *chindi* to you."

Kelly waited through an even longer pause, vividly recalling Uma telling her that Navajos never spoke a dead person's name—or carved it in stone—fearing their *chindi* or ghost would appear.

As a child, Kelly had tried it, saying her parents' names over and over and over. But no ghost ever came. What she wouldn't have given to have seen her parents one last time.

She would have told them she loved them. When they'd left on their trip, she'd refused to kiss them good-bye because they wouldn't take her. The next thing she knew. They had been killed in an automobile crash.

"If you even think about an *adant' ti,* it pisses him off— big-time and he comes to get you," Uma whispered into the telephone.

Oh, brother. They broke the mold when they made Uma. See what happened when the Native American culture was exposed to too many soap operas?

"Okay," Kelly said, her voice indicating she was taking Uma very seriously. "Why would anyone go into the mountains and sing for an *Adant' ti?* Wouldn't that call him to you for certain?"

"No, no. It's a curing ritual to get rid of the evil person."
Uma was still whispering. "It's the season, you know. Curing
rituals can only be done when snakes are safely asleep."

Kelly thanked Uma, and hung up. The title of a popular book
popped into her mind—*Midnight in the Garden of Good and
Evil*. Like walking in a graveyard at midnight—alone—a chill
of fear tiptoed down Kelly's spine. In this case it was impossible
to tell who was good or evil.

She pored over the notes Pop had compiled to write his
articles about Logan's disappearance. Pop had been very thor-
ough, interviewing anyone who had ever come in contact with
the child.

"Perpetual motion," Kelly said, reading aloud one pre-
school teacher's comment and imagining Logan as a young
boy. Hell on wheels might have been a better description,
considering the man he had become.

"Interesting," Kelly muttered to herself. "Logan had to be
treated by the school nurse seven times, but the report didn't
say why."

The pediatrician listed his check-ups from the time he was
adopted. The immunization record was complete, but, of course,
there was no shot for mumps.

"Is he sterile?" Kelly asked herself. He seemed so masculine, so virile that it didn't seem possible. But with Logan you
never knew whether he was joking or telling the truth.

She directed her thoughts back to Pop's notes. The interview
with Logan's pediatrician indicated the little boy needed better
supervision. Too often he fell down the stairs or out of trees.

The folder with information from the Coconino Hospital
where Logan had been treated in the emergency room revealed
that when he was three years old, he had broken an arm falling
out of a tree. Later that same year he'd backed into the barbecue
and burned his shoulder. When he was four, Woody had brought
him in when Logan complained of a pain in his side.

A complete set of X-rays revealed three broken ribs and two
badly cracked ribs. The doctor taped his ribs and ordered his
father to make certain he stayed quiet for two weeks so the
ribs could heal.

Three days later, Logan had been readmitted after falling from the water slide into the pool and hitting his head on the decking. X-rays of his skull indicated a hairline fracture.

"My God!" Kelly cried when she looked at the date.

Less than a week would pass before Logan would ride off with the twins and disappear. They'd been fifteen, ten years older than Logan who had just turned five. Kelly leaned back in her chair, closed her eyes and tried to imagine the arrogant twins at that age. She'd bet anything that they hadn't liked having a tag-along little brother and often tried to ditch Logan.

Kelly wondered if they had run away from him the day he'd disappeared. Was that why they had so much trouble finding the exact spot where he'd fallen? Or was it something much more sinister?

"Kelly? Are you all right?"

She opened her eyes and saw Pop standing in front of her desk, Jasper at his side. She'd been so absorbed with the case that she hadn't heard him come in.

"I'm fine. I'm just thinking." She motioned for him to sit down.

He took the seat opposite her desk, and Jasper curled up at his feet.

"Did you talk with Logan this morning?" she asked, not afraid to discuss things with Pop because she had already checked her telephone and had not found a bug. She'd followed Logan's instructions and looked under her desk and behind the pictures for other listening devices. Whoever had planted the bugs at home hadn't gone to the trouble of breaking into a locked building.

"It's okay, honey. I can stand having Haywood Stanfield in my home—for a good cause. It's Benson Williams that I may shoot on sight."

Kelly laughed, thankful yet again for being blessed with such a wonderful grandfather. She couldn't help wondering what the people who had kidnapped Logan had been like.

"I see you have my notes on Logan's case. Are you planning another article?"

"Not now, maybe later," she said, then went on to tell him

about Jim Cree's strange remarks and Luz Tallchief doing an *Adanti' ti* chant for Logan.

"What do you make of all this?" she asked.

"It's odd, very odd, but then the entire case is strange."

"You have extensive notes on Logan, yet I can't find the interview with his nanny. Didn't you speak with Luz Tallchief after Logan vanished?"

Pop shook his head. "She packed her bags and was gone just hours after the sheriff was called to the ranch and interviewed her. I heard Luz was living outside Indian Gardens. I went to interview her, but she refused to talk. You know how stubborn the Stone River Clan can be."

Kelly wondered if she would have any better luck. Now that Logan had returned would Luz be willing to discuss the past?

Even though she was positive no one could overhear them, Kelly lowered her voice. "Did Logan tell you about the bugs?"

Pop nodded, his expression grim.

"It might just be that the Stanfields would like to discredit Logan after he embarrassed them so much that Woody isn't considering running for president, but I wonder if there isn't more going on here. I think the key is in the past."

"The key to the present is always in the past."

Pop's enigmatic answer startled Kelly. She hesitated a moment, then asked, "Did you ever consider the possibility that Logan was an abused child? I think he had too many "accidents." I wonder if . . ."

"If what?"

"If they found him too hard to handle and got too rough with him, or maybe Ginger couldn't control a wild little boy. Woody might have lost his temper—"

"Woody was out of town when the major incidents occurred."

"You checked and came to the same conclusion, didn't you?"

"Yes," Pop said, leaning down to pet Jasper. "Teachers and doctors weren't required to report suspicious injuries the way they are now. They tended to believe parents, especially rich parents like the Stanfields.

"Miss Halburton, one of the pre-school teachers told me off the record that she found some of his cuts and bruises suspicious. She mentioned it to Ginger, but she denied any problem and said Logan was just a little rascal who managed to get into everything."

"Pop, why didn't you tell me this before?"

"It was just a suspicion. It always bothered me, though. I wondered if someone hadn't gotten too rough disciplining Logan and accidentally killed him. They dumped the body in a remote spot where it would never be found, or if it was, wild animals would have mauled it so badly that determining the cause of death would be impossible. The story about falling into a ravine might have been fabricated. The twins conveniently couldn't remember where Logan supposedly fell."

Pop paused for a moment, leaned down and petted Jasper again. "Maybe they were only doing what they were told, covering up for someone."

"Benson and Ginger are the logical suspects."

"True. Benson is like an uncle to the twins. Maybe he's even closer than an uncle. After all, he's lived with the family for years."

Kelly mulled over the situation for a moment, then she jumped to her feet. "Pop, everyone was stunned when Logan reappeared, looking just like Woody. He couldn't deny Logan was his son, but back then, people thought it was an ordinary adoption. What if someone discovered the truth and wanted to get rid of Logan?"

Pop studied her a moment, his expression solemn. "I assume Benson Williams knew the score. He handled all of Woody's business, but I doubt Ginger was aware of it."

"Logan doesn't think Ginger is nearly as fragile as she appears. What if she uncovered the truth? She took it out on Logan, slapping him around, and deliberately allowing him to get into dangerous situations. One day she went too far . . ."

"It's possible," Pop said. "It happened on a Sunday when most of the servants weren't around. Ginger could have enlisted the twins help and concocted the story about a fall."

''I can hardly wait until Luz returns. I'll bet she knows the truth.''

''Good luck getting it out of her. She must have some reason she's refused to talk all these years.''

Chapter 19

Pop rose to leave Kelly's office, steadier on his feet than he had been in weeks. Jasper followed, his tail held high. Pop paused in the doorway and looked over his shoulder.

"You know, Kelly, when Tyler Stanfield's wife died, her parents insisted she had been murdered."

"Really?" Kelly had been away at college when Suzanne Stanfield had died. She remembered very little about the woman except she had been exceptionally beautiful, a statuesque blonde with china blue eyes. She looked a lot like Ginger and Alyx. At least that had been Kelly's impression when she'd seen her shopping at Tlaquepaque when Kelly had been home for Easter break.

"The coroner ruled her death was due to natural causes, but the Hartleys, her parents, put up a stink. A second autopsy was performed by the Phoenix coroner, who reached the same conclusion. Suzanne had died from a congenital heart problem."

"Why would Suzanne's parents think she'd been murdered?"

"I interviewed them myself. I thought their theory about murder was a result of profound grief over the loss of their only child. I doubted any of the Stanfields would kill Suzanne just because she was pregnant, but the Hartleys were convinced Woody planned to will his entire estate to this grandchild.''

"Leaving his wife as well as Tyler and Alyx out of the will?" Kelly asked. "Why would they think that?"

"I don't know. You might want to talk to Lydia Hartley, though. Her husband passed away, but she still lives out near the Enchantment Resort on Javelina Trail.''

Fifteen minutes later, Kelly turned right off the main road onto Javelina Trail. She hoped this wasn't another wild goose-chase like her search for Luz Tallchief. Lydia Hartley had an unlisted number, forcing Kelly to take the chance she was home.

Many of Sedona's residents had second homes elsewhere and weren't here full time. Most left in the fall and returned in the spring. Lydia's home was in one of the more affluent areas, indicating she might very well have a second home.

The address was near a hoodoo, a narrow stone pillar that vaulted heavenward. Against the indigo sky, the unusual red rock spire was breathtaking, but the curtains in the modest home were drawn, blocking the spectacular view.

Kelly revised her impression of the Hartley's economic status as she parked her car. The small home had been constructed using red rocks from the area, the way many of the original homes had been. None of the high-flying architects who designed Santa Fe-style structures or unusual contemporary homes had left their signature on this building.

Kelly remembered the Hartleys moving here when she'd been in high school. Suzanne had been off at college then, and Kelly had never gotten to know her. Since she'd returned to be with Pop, Kelly hadn't seen Lydia Hartley. Evidently she didn't spend much time in town.

A strikingly beautiful older woman with silver-blond hair and blue eyes answered the door. Although she was dressed casually in beige slacks and a cranberry colored turtleneck, she projected elegance. In a way, the woman reminded Kelly of Ginger except that this woman had something Ginger lacked—self-confidence.

"Lydia, I'm Kelly Taylor. I want to talk to you about the Stanfields."

"I don't have anything to say."

Bitterness was too mild a term for the tone Kelly detected in Lydia's voice. Venom fit perfectly. Kelly's experience in interviewing others told her that this woman would vent her hatred—if only Kelly could get her to talk.

"My grandfather sent me," Kelly told her. "He knew your late husband."

Lydia arched one regal eyebrow just slightly. Kelly scrambled for something else to say. "You thought someone might have killed your daughter—"

"One of the Stanfields murdered Suzanne."

A bead of perspiration marched down the back of Kelly's neck. The mid-day sun, even though it was autumn, seemed as hot as it did in the summer. "May I come in for a minute and discuss the case with you?"

She opened the screen door and stood aside as Kelly walked into the small living room. Lydia gestured toward a moss green sofa, and Kelly took a seat. Sitting at the other end, Lydia directed her gaze at Kelly as if she expected her to explain exactly why she'd come before Lydia changed her mind and decided to throw her out.

"Did you read about Logan McCord being found after all this time?" Kelly asked and Lydia nodded. "It's possible that someone tried to kill Logan when he was a little boy. Saying he accidentally fell into a ravine might have been an attempt to hide the truth."

"They're evil, the lot of them. They're not above murdering a small child. They killed my daughter, didn't they?"

There was so much hostility in Lydia's voice that Kelly was speechless for a moment. "Why would they kill Suzanne?"

"Money. They're all greedy parasites who live off Woody. The twins, Benson, Ginger—the whole bunch. They were afraid that Woody was planning to leave his fortune to the baby Suzanne was expecting." The minute she said her daughter's name, her expression softened and her voice dropped a notch. "The coroner told us it was a little boy."

"Why would the senator cut out his wife and his own children to leave everything to a grandchild? That seems farfetched."

Lydia's gaze shifted across the small room to where a large photograph of a bride stood on a bookshelf. The lovely woman must be Suzanne on her wedding day. She looked exactly like Lydia only younger and happier.

"If one of them killed your daughter, Logan might be in danger," Kelly said, hoping to prompt Lydia to say more. She seemed to be far too intelligent a woman to not have a better reason for believing her daughter had been murdered.

Lydia turned back to Kelly. "You bet Logan McCord is in danger. Mark my words, they'll kill him."

"Why? Logan has made it clear that he isn't interested in Woody's money."

"They won't chance it."

"They? Who do you mean?"

She sighed heavily, then replied in a voice raw with anguish. "I wish I knew. I suspect Alyx or Benson even Tyler and Ginger. I'm not sure if they all weren't in on it."

"What about Woody? Isn't it possible—"

"No, Woody would never have killed Suzanne." Lydia rose from the sofa and walked across the room. She picked up the picture of her daughter and studied it in a way that told Kelly that she had looked at it hundreds and hundreds of times, but still enjoyed gazing at the photograph.

"I'm marrying Logan," Kelly said, her voice low. She almost didn't want to disturb the older woman whose expression said she was reliving some fond memory of her only daughter. "If he's in danger, I must help him."

Lydia turned slowly and faced Kelly. "You're marrying him? Oh, my." She returned to the sofa and sat down as if she were suddenly very tired.

Kelly leaned over and touched her arm. "Tell me the whole story. I don't want to lose Logan the way you lost Suzanne."

Lydia scrutinized her a moment, silently assessing Kelly's sincerity. Kelly was afraid this shrewd woman would somehow detect that this was nothing more than a marriage of convenience.

Lydia looked at the magnificent diamond Logan had given Kelly, then she gazed into Kelly's eyes, saying, "What I'm going to tell has to remain confidential. What do you call it?"

"Off the record. I won't repeat anything you tell me."

"You'd better tell Logan. He needs to know."

The bitterness had vanished from Lydia's voice, replaced by the defeated tone of a person who has lost someone she loves dearly. Nothing, not even sweet revenge, will bring the person back. Kelly knew the feeling. She would have given anything she had, or ever hoped to have, to bring Daniel back. But there was nothing she could do.

"I'm not sure where to begin," Lydia said, and Kelly feared the older woman was wavering. Lydia was witholding something.

"Take your time. I'd like to know the whole story."

"Earl, that's my husband—was my husband—always wanted to live here. He took an early retirement from the post office in Chicago, and we bought this place even though we could barely afford it. Suzanne was in her last year at the University of Illinois. She was on a special scholarship."

"She must have been very intelligent as well as beautiful," Kelly said, and Lydia nodded, pride sparkling in her eyes. "How did she meet Tyler?"

"Suzanne was working as a hostess in the Yavapai Room at the Enchantment Resort during the summer. Tyler saw her and asked her out. They dated all summer and decided to marry."

"How did you feel about that?"

"I never liked Tyler. He's vain and arrogant, so full of himself it's sickening. But I kept my mouth shut."

"How did the Stanfields feel about the marriage?" Kelly asked.

"Woody was charming when we met just before the engagement party. Ginger didn't say much, and neither did Benson, although I had the feeling they would have preferred Tyler marry a daughter of one of their rich friends."

Lydia gazed at Suzanne's wedding picture again. Kelly waited for the older woman to collect her thoughts.

"Alyx didn't hesitate to let us know we were beneath her. Do you know what she said at the engagement party? We weren't supposed to hear, but of course, she made certain we did. She told a group of her friends that now she understood why postal workers were always shooting each other."

"She's a total bitch."

"If you ask me, she has an unhealthy attachment to her brother."

"Really?" Kelly had noticed the conspiratorial way the twins always whispered to each other. "What did Suzanne think?"

"She was blinded by the Stanfield life style. Spending time in Washington really appealed to her. Suzanne loved politics, and Woody found her a job with a lobbyist."

Kelly couldn't see where this was going. Suzanne had been seduced by money and power, a tale as old as time. How did this lead to murder?

"It was several years before Suzanne realized how shallow and self-centered Tyler was. He spent more time with his sister than he did with her."

"They must have been together a little. She was having his baby."

"No, Suzanne came to despise Tyler." The slight tremor in Lydia's voice told Kelly the woman was having difficulty keeping her emotions in check. Lydia stopped speaking, again gazing at her daughter's photograph.

"Was she considering divorce? Did the baby stop her?"

Lydia faced Kelly again, a sheen of tears brightening her eyes. "She wasn't carrying his child."

Kelly waited, only mildly surprised by the news. Affairs were commonplace in the Stanfields' circles, and Suzanne was a beautiful woman who would have had her pick of men.

"Was your daughter planning to marry the baby's father?"

"Yes," Lydia replied, softly. "They were getting married as soon as both divorces were final."

"Did you meet him?" Kelly prompted when Lydia again lapsed into silence.

"Oh, yes. I met him."

4 BESTSELLING HISTORICAL ROMANCES BY YOUR FAVORITE AUTHORS CAN BE YOURS, FREE!

Kensington Choice brings you historical romances by your favorite bestselling authors including Janelle Taylor, Shannon Drake, Rosanne Bittner, Jo Beverley, and Georgina Gentry, just to name a few! Each book is filled with passion, adventure and the excitement of bygone times!

To introduce you to this great club which is part of Zebra Home Subscription Service, we'd like to send you your first 4 bestselling historical romances, absolutely free! And once you get these 4 free books to savor at home, we'll rush you the next 4 brand-new books at the lowest prices available, as soon as they are published.

The way the club works is that after your initial FREE shipment, you will get our 4 newest bestselling historical romances delivered to your doorstep each month at the preferred subscriber's rate of only $4.20 per book, a savings of up to $8.16 per month (since these titles sell in bookstores for $4.99-$6.99)! All books are sent on a 10-day free examination basis and there is no minimum number of books to buy. (And no charge for shipping.) Plus as a regular subscriber, you'll receive our FREE monthly newsletter, *Zebra/Pinnacle Romance News*, which features author profiles, subscriber benefits, book previews and more!

---

*We have 4 FREE BOOKS for you
as your introduction to
KENSINGTON CHOICE!
To get your FREE BOOKS, worth
up to $24.96, mail the card below.*

FREE BOOK CERTIFICATE

Yes! Please send me 4 Kensington Choice (the best of Zebra and Pinnacle Books) Historical Romances without cost or obligation (worth up to $24.96). As a Kensington Choice subscriber, I will then receive 4 brand-new romances to preview each month for 10 days FREE. I can return any books I decide not to keep and owe nothing. The publisher's prices for Kensington Choice romances range from $4.99-$6.99, but as a preferred subscriber I will get these books for only $4.20 per book or $16.80 for all four titles. There is no minimum number of books to buy and I may cancel my subscription at any time, plus there is no additional charge for postage and handling. No matter what I decide to do, my first 4 books are mine to keep, absolutely FREE!

Name _____

Address _____ Apt. _____

City _____ State _____ Zip _____

Telephone ( ) _____

Signature _____

(If under 18, parent or guardian must sign)

Subscription subject to acceptance. Terms and prices subject to change.

KF0598

Something in her tone disturbed Kelly. "Who was the baby's father?"

The long silence made Kelly afraid that Lydia wasn't going to tell her, yet she couldn't imagine why not.

Finally, Lydia whispered, "Woody Stanfield was the baby's father."

"Oh my God," Kelly blurted out before she could stop herself. She wondered why Suzanne's mother hadn't mentioned this to the authorities. "Now I understand why Woody would have willed this baby a great deal of money, but that doesn't mean he would have cut out Ginger and the twins."

A wry but indulgent smile spread across Lydia's lips. "Woody is not the twins' father. It's a well-kept family secret. He raised them as if they were his, but Ginger had an affair with another man, and he is their real father."

Kelly took a quick breath of utter astonishment. "Are you sure? How do you know?"

"Tyler told my daughter shortly after they became engaged, when things were perfect between them. Woody confirmed this and claimed he had stayed with Ginger for political reasons."

Kelly slowly shook her head. Pop was right. Politics in America brought out the best in people, didn't it? "Do you know if Woody told Suzanne anything about Logan?"

"No, and I'm certain she would have mentioned it. She called us every week."

"When did Suzanne tell you about her affair with Woody?"

"She didn't say anything—at first. Then Woody and Suzanne came to us to explain about the baby. Woody planned to divorce Ginger and marry Suzanne as soon as they were both free."

"What about his political career?"

"He was tired of all the bickering and in-fighting." Yet again, Lydia gazed at her daughter's picture. "I believed him. They were so happy together."

"How did you and your husband feel about Suzanne marrying a man old enough to be her father?"

"We weren't thrilled, but we kept our disappointment to

ourselves. Suzanne was literally radiant. Woody was as excited about the baby as Suzanne—maybe more.''

Kelly wasn't quite sure she bought Woody's story. She'd seen him at work, too often, using the charisma and charm that Logan had inherited—in spades. Lydia Hartley had not been exposed to enough politicians to have developed a bullshit detector.

"When Suzanne died, Woody was beside himself with grief. Ask anyone who was at the funeral. I think someone discovered Woody's plan and killed my daughter to prevent him from rewriting his will.''

"Why didn't you tell the sheriff the entire story?''

"Earl and I discussed it, but we felt certain the autopsy would reveal the cause of death, then an investigation would surely prove who killed Suzanne. When the first report found nothing, we kicked ourselves for keeping quiet.''

Lydia rose and walked over to the picture. She cradled it against her bosom, as if it were a baby. "We asked ourselves what Suzanne would want us to do. We decided she truly loved Woody. We didn't want to tarnish her memory by revealing what others would have called an ugly affair. What good would that do? Instead we insisted the coroner from Phoenix examine the body.''

"He didn't find anything unusual either,'' Kelly said as gently as possible. "Do you have any other reason to believe Suzanne was murdered?''

"The day before she died, Suzanne called me. She sounded very upset. She said she couldn't talk long. She wanted to come home for a while. She sounded afraid.''

It wasn't much to go on, and it might well have just been Lydia's imagination, but Kelly had her doubts. Something was terribly wrong with the Stanfields.

"You can't believe how thrilled Woody was to be having his own child,'' Lydia added wistfully.

Kelly thought about the way Woody had ignored Logan and the numerous injuries Logan had suffered as a child. At first, she had suspected child abuse, but now she wondered if something even more sinister had happened. Had they diabolically planned to murder a defenseless little boy?

And where did Woody fit in?

Lydia returned her daughter's picture to the shelf, then looked at Kelly as if she'd sensed the direction of her thoughts. "Tell Logan to be very, very careful or he'll end up in a grave like my Suzanne."

Chapter 20

"It's all right to be nervous," Pop told Logan. "I was like a hummingbird on uppers just before I married Emma."

Even on the most dangerous mission, Logan never had an attack of the jitters. So, why now?

"Once the judge starts the ceremony, you'll be okay."

They were on the terrace of Pop's house, overlooking Oak Creek. Rows of folding chairs had been set up to accommodate the guests. Since the Stanfields had asked to be invited, what was supposed to be a simple civil ceremony in a judge's chamber had escalated into "an event." Uma had been in the kitchen around the clock for days, preparing food for the reception.

Logan had rarely seen Kelly. She managed to avoid him by working late, claiming she had to get things in order at the paper before the honeymoon. He'd spent his days in the orchard with Pop, picking apples of all things.

Christ! He'd had his fill of bringing in the harvest—what there was of it—when he'd lived at the camp. He never thought he'd be doing anything like that again, but it wasn't so bad. Pop never questioned Logan about his work as a Cobra. Or about the past.

Logan appreciated Pop's attitude. He genuinely liked the

older man and didn't want to lie to him. But he wouldn't discuss the past even with Pop.

Logan tugged at his shirt cuffs, then adjusted the knot in his tie. Son of a bitch! What was he doing getting married?

"I've never even been to a wedding," he confessed to Pop, keeping his voice low so the few guests who had arrived early couldn't hear him. "Is there anything I should know?"

Pop hitched one eyebrow, surprised. "Surely you've seen weddings in the movies."

"No. I haven't had much time for entertainment like that."

Pop nodded, obviously wanting to ask more, but restraining himself. "When Judge Hollister is ready, you and Kelly will stand facing him. The judge will ask you to repeat after him, so that's easy. Do you have the ring?"

Logan patted his pocket and felt the wedding band. It had been designed to match the engagement ring he'd given Kelly. He still didn't know what had gotten into him. Pop had subtlety reminded Logan that an engagement ring might help convince people that they were really in love, but it had been Logan's idea to go to Tiffany's.

Why hadn't he gone to some cut-rate jeweler? The best he could figure was that he'd once been on a mission that required a lot of waiting. He and Brodie Adams had been holed up in a flea-bag hotel in Peru. When they had electricity, they watched *Breakfast at Tiffany's* on the ancient video recorder. He'd lost track of how many times they had seen the damn movie, but the jewelry store had made a lasting impression.

Tiffany's in Scottsdale was small, nowhere near the size of the one in the movie. He'd looked at several rings with Pop silently standing at his side, then he'd seen the kick-ass diamond. *The perfect ring for Kelly.*

Aw, hell, if he didn't cut out the sentimental crap, he'd be worthless when the Cobra Force sent him to Africa. A Cobra had to be totally focused, his mind on the mission and nothing else. That's why only single men were selected for the most dangerous assignments.

"The Stanfield entourage has arrived," Pop informed him.

Logan looked across the terrace. Alyx and Tyler led the

group while Benson and Woody walked beside Ginger. The men were dressed in suits and the women wore floral print dresses and hats with the widest brims that Logan had ever seen.

Alyx and Tyler stopped to speak to a couple, but Woody guided Ginger and Benson over to where Logan was standing with Pop.

"Senator, Benson," Pop greeted the men, then turned to Ginger. "That's quite a hat."

"Thank you," Ginger said with a smile only a politician's wife could muster, but Logan wasn't sure Pop meant it as a compliment.

"We didn't bring a wedding gift," Benson explained, "because you two weren't registered anywhere, so we had no idea what to get."

Logan noticed that hadn't bothered the other guests. The gift table was filling fast. Not that he wanted a damn thing from the Stanfields.

"Could I have a word with you in private?" Woody asked Logan.

He followed his father to the side of the terrace. The older man gazed down at Oak Creek for a moment before turning to Logan.

"I wanted to get you something special," Woody said "but I have the feeling that you wouldn't accept an expensive gift from me."

"You're right. I can buy anything Kelly and I need."

"I know. I mean, well, Ginger called Tiffany's in Scottsdale. They told her you did buy a set of rings there."

"That's damn nosy." Logan scanned the crowded terrace for Ginger. She was huddled with Benson in the front row of chairs next to Alyx and Tyler.

"Ginger meant well. She wanted me to give you the money for a real diamond. I told her I thought Kelly's ring was real, so she called Tiffany's to check."

It was all Logan could do not to say exactly what he thought of Ginger. Didn't Woody realize the woman was a manipulator? She pretended to be weak and fragile, but Logan would bet anything the opposite was true. Hell, he wouldn't be surprised to discover she was the one behind those bugs.

"I wanted to tell you in private that I have contacted a friend in the social services. Next Wednesday they've scheduled a home visit. You'll be approved to adopt a child immediately."

"I don't think much of your private detective," she whispered. "What has the Israeli found out that can help us? Nothing. Those bugs haven't picked up anything except useless chatter."

They were seated, waiting for the wedding to begin. He checked to be certain no one was paying attention to them.

"I have a plan." He leaned closer, keeping his voice low. "According to the info picked up by the bugs, Kelly and Logan are going camping for two days. Then after they get the adoption approval, they are going to South America for a real honeymoon."

"I despise camping. Think of the dust and the bugs."

"Think of what could happen with them all alone out in the wilderness."

The brim of her hat cast a shadow across her beautiful face, but he was close enough to see the gleam of excitement in her eyes.

"What if they fell off a cliff or something?" she whispered. "Imagine how devastated Woody will be."

"It would be a shame especially since Woody has an appointment with his attorney next week."

"He's changing the will."

Out of the corner of his eye, he saw Woody talking with Logan. His only son. "Yes, Woody contacted his lawyer in Phoenix."

"Remember how thrilled Woody was when Suzanne was going to have his baby? He kept grinning all the time. Disgusting."

"It's a natural reaction. Woody has spent his life building an empire. He wants to leave it to his own flesh and blood. Now he has a national hero to leave his fortune to."

Her mouth crimped into a grim line. "Be certain something dreadful happens to Logan while they're camping. If he's dead, Woody won't have any reason to change his will."

"Be still my heart!" Uma thumped her chest with one hand and rolled her eyes heavenward. "Wait until you see Logan. What a hunk!"

Normally Kelly would have laughed at Uma, but Kelly was too nervous to smile. Uma had come to tell her that Judge Hollister had arrived. It was time to leave her *casita* and go down to the terrace.

She dreaded deceiving all the people who'd come to the wedding. A marriage of convenience should have been called a marriage of inconvenience. It meant telling one lie after another until she despised herself.

She glanced at the *testero* where Rafi's picture was propped up against a vase and reminded herself that there wasn't any other way she could bring Daniel's son home. She had no choice but to go through with this sham marriage.

She checked herself in the full-length mirror, asking Uma, "Do I look all right?"

She was wearing a lavender silk sheath with a scoop neck. It was simple yet the dress had a touch of elegance thanks to the string of pearls Pop had given her when she'd graduated from Yale. She'd taken extra time with her hair and managed to smooth out some of the curl. It hung to her shoulders in soft blond waves that made her brown eyes seem darker than usual.

"You're drop-dead gorgeous," Uma assured her.

It wasn't true, of course, but Kelly knew she looked as good as she could. The only thing missing, her reflection told her, was the happy glow she'd had when she'd married Daniel. At least this time she was going into a marriage knowing it was going to end.

What would happen before it did? Even though Logan had yet to kiss her on the lips, she had the distinct impression that he intended to have sex with her. True, he was a hunk just as Uma had said, and Kelly was physically attracted to him. But she knew herself well enough to realize that a physical relationship would lead to an emotional commitment.

She refused to take the chance.

Daniel had loved her—at least in the beginning—and she'd lost him. She had asked Logan to marry her, but he didn't love her. In six months his new assignment would begin, and he would leave.

She would never love Logan the way she'd loved Daniel. Yet if she weren't very careful, she might grow fond of him. And miss him terribly when he left.

"Baby-cakes, they're waiting."

Kelly realized she had been staring at her reflection for some time. "I'm coming." She closed the door behind her. "Uma, you're a guest today. Stay out of the kitchen."

"Get real," Uma said with a derisive snort. "Tillie Habenny and those relatives of hers don't know squat about serving. They're Talking Waters Clan. That means they'll be in the kitchen gossiping. They'll mess up everything."

"Uma, I mean it. Let Tillie handle things."

Uma grunted her consent, and they walked in silence through the main house. Kelly froze in the doorway to the terrace, her mind and body suddenly numb. Could she go through with this in front of all Pop's friends who honestly believed this was a match made in heaven?

She glanced over her shoulder to the front yard where the security guards were patrolling. When news of the wedding leaked out, reporters stationed themselves outside the house, reminding Kelly of the pagan hordes camped outside Rome's gates. Stalkarazzi.

Uma nudged her. Kelly managed a tremulous smile as Uma left her to take a seat in the front row next to Pop. She waited for Uma to sit, then walked out onto the terrace. Everyone else was seated, and heads turned in her direction.

She mustered a smile that she prayed looked appropriate for a bride in love and looked directly at Logan. He was standing in front of Judge Hollister, waiting for her to join him. Be still my heart did not cover it, Kelly thought.

An electrifying shiver reverberated through her, and it was

all she could do to keep the silly grin plastered on her face and walk at the same time. Was she really marrying this 'hunk?'

She'd never seen him dressed up, so she wasn't quite prepared for how heart-stoppingly handsome he looked in the navy suit. The color deepened his eyes to cobalt blue. The cut of the suit emphasized his height and the breadth of his shoulders. For a man who acted as if he never put on anything but jeans, Logan wore the suit with an air of self-assurance that bordered on arrogance.

But the smile he gave her wasn't the least bit haughty. He broke into a wide, open grin that revealed dazzling white teeth. There wasn't a woman on earth who could resist his captivating smile. She was extremely aware of his virile appeal. Each time she was near him, the pull became stronger and stronger.

His gaze dropped from her face to her shoulders, then rapidly slid downward. His pleased expression would have convinced the devil himself that Logan believed she was truly beautiful.

It would be easy to misinterpret the way he looked at her. No question about it. He was a skilled actor with undeniable sex appeal. A very dangerous combination. She was out of her league with this man.

And in a few minutes she would be his wife.

Unbelievable.

She managed to stand beside Logan, a ridiculous smile on her lips. This close, he seemed taller, even more powerfully built. She gazed into his eyes and her heart lurched, then pounded furiously. The smoldering look caught her off-guard, and she quickly glanced away.

Kelly gazed at her grandfather and was astonished to see how happy—no, thrilled—he looked. Oh, Lordy. Pop adored Logan. The expression on his face made her suspect Pop was secretly praying this marriage would work out despite everything.

Judge Hollister cleared his throat. "Are you ready?"

Kelly and Logan turned to face him. Kelly heaved a sigh of relief; at least her back was to the group. Out of the corner of her eye, she'd seen the Stanfields. She didn't mind lying in front of them, but she wished she didn't have to lie in front of the others.

"Kelly ... Logan, we are gathered here on this fine day to join your lives together as man and wife," Judge Hollister began.

Like a parrot, Kelly repeated the vows, hardly hearing the judge's words, kept her mind focused on Rafi. The little boy needed her, and since she wasn't going to have children of her own, she needed him, too.

The next thing Kelly knew, Logan's warm hand clasped hers, and an involuntary chill swept through her. He slipped a ring on her trembling hand. Oh, my God! It wasn't an ordinary gold band at all. This ring had channel-set diamonds designed to fit around the stunning engagement ring. Together the two rings were spectacular.

As their eyes met, she detected a certain apprehension in his expression as if he was concerned that she might not like the ring. She squeezed his hand and smiled, silently trying to reassure him.

"Repeat after me," the judge told Logan.

Kelly listened as Logan responded to the questions she'd just answered. Was it her imagination, or did his voice sound huskier than usual?

It suddenly struck her that in a moment the judge was going to tell him to kiss the bride. It would be a quick peck, she assured herself, nothing more. They were standing in front of about fifty people. Don't worry about it.

The judge said, "By the power invested in me by the state of Arizona, I now pronounce you man and wife." He smiled at Logan. "You may kiss the bride."

Kelly looked up at Logan, telling herself that it was only a kiss. It would be over in a second. His expression didn't change, but he became rigid, every muscle tensed as if he were staring down the barrel of a submachine gun.

Time halted, seconds fractured and became an excruciatingly long minute. The guests waited, dead silent while a meadowlark, bobbing on a cottonwood branch sang scales. Heat inched up Kelly's neck as she felt every eye riveted on them.

Waiting. Wondering.

He was not going to kiss her.

If he didn't, what good were the magnificent rings and this reception? People would know their marriage was a sham and ask why. Couldn't he just peck her cheek or something?

She recalled the other times she had expected him to kiss her, yet he never had. He must have some hang-up about kissing. Why else would such a devastatingly handsome man avoid kissing?

The moment lengthened, and Judge Hollister cleared his throat. Kelly decided she had to take action. Even though she was in heels, she had to draw herself up to the tips of her toes in order to throw her arms around Logan's neck. She smacked her lips against his.

It wasn't graceful, it wasn't sexy, but it got the job done. His lips were clamped together and as rigid as his body.

At least put your arms around me, she silently screamed. Make it look good. But she might as well have been embracing one of Sedona's red rocks for all the response she got.

She moved her lips, encouraging him. Nothing. Poor guy. He really did have a serious problem with kissing. As good an actor as he was when he wanted to be, Logan was having real trouble with this.

Kelly tried to pull back only to discover Logan's arms were suddenly locked around her. His lips parted hesitantly, and the tension left his body slowly like a wave retreating from the shore. His lips were warm and sweet on hers—for a moment.

Then he angled his head to one side and hesitantly brushed her lips with the tip of his tongue. His kiss was unsophisticated, hardly the kiss of a man who knew what he was doing. Instead it seemed as if her kiss had breached some emotional barrier, and he was allowing himself to kiss her—against his will.

Yet there was no mistaking the hunger in his kiss, the unbridled passion. The force of his body bent her backward. Clinging to his shoulders, she realized there was something almost desolate and needy about his kiss.

She recalled his expression when he'd slipped the astonishing wedding band on her finger. For a fraction of a second, his insecurity had been reflected in his deep blue eyes. Now, she sensed that same uncertainty, which was usually concealed beneath his brash veneer.

Encouraging him, she parted her lips. Big mistake! His tongue thrust between her lips and mated with hers in a shockingly primitive way that reminded her of a much more intimate mating.

Pleasure shuddered through her even though a warning bell rang in some distant part of her head. They were in front of all the guests—for God's sake.

In another second the bell stopped ringing. She was kissing him back, loving the feel of his mouth on hers, loving the strength of his embrace. It had been so long since she'd been kissed with such passion. She hadn't missed it until now.

Until Logan.

She didn't know how long they stood there, kissing each other, but Logan finally pulled away. Kelly felt him release her and she let go of him reluctantly. That's when she realized all the guests were clapping.

And Pop was grinning from ear to ear.

Chapter 21

It was dark by the time Pop drove around Sedona long enough to elude the paparazzi. He dropped off Kelly and Logan at the Sterling Pass trailhead. Logan used the powerful military flashlight that she had seen in the hogan to guide them up the trail. The path was steep, bounded on one side by boulders that jutted upward. The other side was a sheer drop into a dry creek bed.

They concentrated on the path, neither of them saying anything, which was just as well. He had her totally confused after that scorching kiss in front of everyone. Given the mixed signals Logan sent, it was difficult to tell what he was thinking.

She was worried about what would happen tonight. She was tempted to give him a lecture on this being a mission, and sex was not part of the plan.

What if she were mistaken? He might behave in a totally professional manner and not touch her.

She stumbled over a loose rock on the trail, and Logan stopped and turned to check on her.

"Are you all right?"

The concern in his voice changed her mind. She mumbled something about being tired and decided not to make a fool out of herself with a no-sex lecture. If he tried anything, then she could set him straight.

Overhead lurked unusual rock formations, awesome in their size. The darkness and their surrealistic shapes made the area seem almost as if she'd been transported to another world. Despite the low level of light, she spotted tenacious clumps of mesquite that had found footholds among the boulders. Its aromatic scent perfumed the cool night air.

"Are you sure they can't find us here?" she asked when they reached their destination.

"No one is going to find us." He slid his backpack off his shoulders, his eyes scanning the area in that hyper-alert way of his.

His instinctive responses to the world around him amazed her. Logan seemed to have an ingrained ability to scan his surroundings in a way that might seem casual to most people. She knew better. No detail escaped his notice.

Here was a man who accepted danger, expected it. His life was in grave danger. Maybe he wasn't at risk immediately, but she was convinced danger lurked around him.

Waiting for a chance to strike.

"You saw me check everything we have with us for micro-transmitters to prevent anyone following us."

Logan had explained to Kelly and Pop that a micro-transmitter the size of a peanut could have been planted in their things. It would send out a silent, electronic signal, telling someone exactly where they were.

She shrugged her pack off her shoulders and dropped it on the ground. Logan didn't seem the least bit tired, but she wondered if she could have made it much farther. She massaged her shoulders where the pack had chafed against her skin.

Logan was busy lashing the food Uma had packed into a satchel and hoisting it up into a tree, so animals wouldn't be lured into their camp, enticed by the smell. Kelly concentrated on taking out what little she'd brought in her pack.

They were only going to be gone two days. Logan had suggested camping because people expected newlyweds to go somewhere after their wedding. It seemed like a good idea at the time, but now Kelly wasn't so sure. This place seemed terribly isolated.

If anything happened, they were miles from help. Logan was accustomed to danger, she knew as she watched him, fascinated. What a way to live, yet he seemed to thrive on it.

There was no moon, and the usually bright stars were haloed by brush-stroke clouds. A trio of bats hovered near a night-blooming cactus at the perimeter of their camp, sipping nectar from its blossoms. From a distant ridge, a coyote howled, a distinct, shrill sound that was immediately answered by yips from the rest of the pack. The only light in the small clearing came from Logan's Krypton flashlight.

She felt more than a little useless. Not only had he carried most of their gear, he'd evidently been here before on one of his hikes. He hauled an armful of mesquite from a stash behind a boulder, and built a fire more quickly than she could imagine. He must have built dozens and dozens of fires.

Then he draped both bedrolls over a rock, letting the bottom part of each trail on the ground. This is about as close as we're going to get to a comfortable seat.'' He sat down, his back against the rock and patted the spot next to him. ''Come on. You're tired.''

The prickle of uneasiness that had been with her all day kicked up a notch as she dropped down beside him. ''This is heaven.'' She rested against the rock, the bedroll cushioning her back. 'This is the first time ''I've sat down all day.''

Logan didn't reply. He turned down the flashlight until it was little more than an eerie glow in the darkness.

''I want to talk to you about something.'' She hadn't told him about her visit to Suzanne's mother or about Jim Cree's strange comments. Now she was glad. It gave her something to talk about.

''I'm listening.'' Logan turned toward her, his head cocked slightly to one side in a way that indicated conversation was *not* uppermost in his mind.

They had changed into jeans and sweaters for the camp-out. Logan was wearing a navy blue pullover that Pop had worn for years. The color and the lack of light had turned his eyes almost black with just a thin band of slate blue rimming the pupils. He had been heart-stoppingly handsome in his suit, but now there was something rugged and outdoorsy about him that she found even more appealing.

He waved his hand in front of her face. "Earth to Kelly."

"Sorry, I was thinking."

"I was afraid of that."

She ignored his joke, asking, "Did you know Tyler had been married and his wife died?"

"Yes. I used Cobra sources to check on the entire family."

Kelly wasn't surprised, considering his occupation. "Did your sources say there was anything unusual about her death?"

"There were two autopsies. That's highly unusual, but both coroners agreed that she'd had a heart condition."

"Suzanne was three months pregnant when she died." She stared straight ahead, suddenly reluctant to tell him. "Do you know who the father was?"

"Obviously it wasn't Tyler." A beat of silence. "It must have been my old man."

How had he guessed so quickly? It had taken her a long conversation with Suzanne's mother before Kelly had begun to suspect the truth. "That's right. Suzanne's mother says Woody planned to divorce Ginger and marry Suzanne as soon as she divorced Tyler. What do you think?"

"I don't give a damn about any of them." He scooted closer, his gaze riveted on her lips. "Why don't you kiss me again? I can do better this time."

Now she had her answer. Logan did intend to make love to her. She was going to have to set him straight, and it probably wouldn't be easy. He was accustomed to getting his own way.

"Logan, be serious. This is important."

"I'm dead serious. Kiss me again."

His gaze was so seductive that it sent a tremor of anticipation through her, but she managed to calmly ask, "Do you realize Tyler and Alyx aren't Woody's children?"

"You're kidding. Is Benson their father?"

"I don't know. Do you think Woody would have allowed

Benson to live with them and be his right-hand man all these years, if he'd had an affair with Ginger?''

''They're all so screwed up. Anything's possible. How many fathers get their son's wife pregnant?''

''Tyler isn't really his son,'' Kelly pointed out.

''He raised him. If nothing else, Tyler is like an adopted son.'' He leaned closer and whispered into her ear, his warm breath ruffling her hair. ''Let's forget about them. Go ahead. Kiss me again. I like women who take charge.''

Take charge?

He was teasing her, and she knew it. True, she'd kissed him, but he had been the one who had taken charge.

Her head would fit perfectly into the hollow between his shoulder and neck, she realized, then mentally gave herself a hard shake. Stop it! She edged away and chastised him with her go-to-hell glare. It didn't faze him. His smirk said he'd read her mind.

''You need to hear this, Logan. Suzanne's parents believed Woody was going to rewrite his will and leave his fortune to his child, cutting out the twins as well as Ginger. That's why Suzanne was killed.''

''Do you honestly believe they murdered her?''

''Suzanne's mother was very convincing. I took a close look at both autopsy reports, and I brought them with me.

He threw up his hands and rolled his eyes. ''Aw, hell! I've married a woman who brings autopsy reports along on her honeymoon.''

''Suzanne's mother is concerned that they'll try to kill you. We know someone bugged the house. At the reception you kept saying we were camping out near Devil's Bridge. You took every precaution not to let anyone know where we were going. True, we wanted to ditch the stalkerazzi reporters, but don't tell me it isn't possible that your life is in danger.''

He shrugged, seemingly not concerned ''It doesn't surprise me. It would be easier to deal with, if I knew who was behind it. Tyler? Alyx? Ginger and Benson? All of them?''

''When we were at the stables, I talked to Jim Cree alone. He said something that made me very suspicious.'' She recounted her conversation with the shaman in detail. Logan listened intently, his brow furrowing into a slight frown. "I tried to talk to Luz Tallchief but she's out doing an *Adant' ti* chant for you."

"What in hell is that?"

"Navajos go to a sacred place and chant. Sometimes they do sand paintings as they're chanting. Some chants can go on for days. The *Adanti' ti* is supposed to rid you of an evil person. Luz and Jim think you're in danger now because you were in danger as a child. I've studied reports that indicate you might have been abused.

"I'll bet someone discovered you were Woody's own son, and wanted to get rid of you. I suspect that you never accidentally fell into a ravine. I think they dumped you in some isolated spot and left you to die. Luckily someone found you."

"Lucky me," he responded with a touch of irony. Once she wouldn't have detected the subtle change in his raspy voice, but now she knew him better. "I have an idea. Let's take a look at those autopsy reports."

She pulled the sheets of paper from the side pocket of her pack, then sat with her back against the rock and watched him read the reports, which were only a few pages long.

Logan's reaction wasn't totally unexpected. He didn't seem surprised that someone might have tried to kill him when he had been little more than a toddler. He was utterly self-reliant. He couldn't be shocked the way most people could.

Lucky me. He might have escaped death, but he had no love for the people who had raised him. She imagined that he had survived something so terrible that nothing life threw at him now could hurt him. She knew that she was going to have to find out about those missing years.

"It looks to me as if the Phoenix coroner used more sophisticated equipment than the coroner here," Logan said. "He picked up a trace of a strange substance that he's identified as an alkaloid."

"The coroner claims Suzanne died of a congenital heart

defect, but subaortic stenosis causes chest pains. It's treatable. Few people die from it. Plus, Suzanne never reported having chest pains.''

Logan reached over and pulled his pack closer to where they were sitting. He opened it and took out a black box that was slightly larger than a paperback book. He winked at her and flashed the adorable smile that she'd come to realize meant he was up to something.

''Your tax dollars at work.'' He attached a small antenna with a tip like a mushroom to the back of the box, then pressed a button. The lid flipped up and a fan-shaped keyboard slid out of the bottom. ''It's a prototype of the next generation of military computers.''

''It's so small.''

''They have to be,'' he told her as he booted up the machine. ''If computers are going to be useful in the field, they have to be compact and lightweight.''

''It's amazing, but how can it help us?''

He checked his watch, then pointed to the sky. ''See the Little Dipper? Right now the Department of Defense satellite's orbit is taking it alongside the Little Dipper. I'm going to contact the DDS's computer by using the antenna on the back of my computer.''

''It's powerful enough to do that?''

''You bet. Anti-terrorist units and the DEA often need info from the satellites. Sometimes we need the 'eye in the sky' to help us locate a person using the satellite's high-powered cameras. They can do a meter by meter search of an area and tell us where to find someone.''

''Great! Big Brother is spying.''

''Actually, there are more television and telephone satellites up there than anything else,'' he said.

''Is it all right if I watch?'' she asked and he nodded.

She looked over his shoulder as the screen came on and a huge menu appeared, but it was too small for Kelly to read from where she was. Logan clicked on an icon in the lower corner of the screen. Bold black letters appeared: **DEPART-**

MENT OF DEFENSE. Below it was: **Name and Military Branch.**

"Branch?"

"The satellite is a joint venture with all the services," he said without looking up from the screen as he typed in his name and Marines/Cobra Unit. "The Joint Chiefs of Staff control its use. For those of you paranoid about Big Brother, the honchos—that's the Joint Chiefs—review every request to use the high-powered telescopes to watch people."

"That's how they know what's going on in Bosnia and places like that."

He nodded as the next question appeared on the screen: **ID Number?**

He typed in a number that Kelly attempted to memorize, but caught only the first three digits 641 before the next question flashed on the screen: **Code Name?**

Nine Lives.

That was Logan's code name? Strange.

"Yep." He leaned forward as a box appeared in the middle of the screen. He placed his index finger on the screen, then turned to her. "It'll scan my fingerprint and compare it with the access authorization file."

"Couldn't some terrorist torture you, get the codes, then cut off your finger and use it to obtain vital info from the Department of Defense?"

"You know, Kelly, you're smart. You think like a terrorist. I like that in a woman." He chuckled, still holding his finger to the screen. "It's possible, but they would have to use the finger within minutes of killing me. Once the skin dehydrates, it shrivels more and more as time passes, which alters the print. They're using a high-definition computer. That's why this is taking so long. If the computer detects any change in my print, it'll reject my entry request."

The computer beeped, and he turned back, removing his finger. On the screen appeared a single word: **Approved.**

"Impressive," she said as he typed something on the computer, using his index fingers. It wasn't the equipment that impressed her. It was Logan himself. What she was seeing now was a glimpse of his world, the way he worked and lived each day.

"I'm instructing DDS to link us to the mainframe at the Centers for Disease Control. Let's see what they say about traces of unknown alkaloids."

For the next few minutes, he was silent, tapping on the computer, totally absorbed by the task. She'd never met anyone like him, she reflected. He might be a dead ringer for his father, but Logan was so much more intriguing and complex.

He accepted his good looks. but didn't depend on them, or preen the way Tyler did. Logan had his own brand of inner strength and power. He couldn't be manipulated by money or status, the way most men were.

Other than his work, what did Logan care passionately about? As far as she could tell, nothing. He wasn't into sports or hobbies. He'd made it clear that he'd never had a relationship with a woman. All he cared about was his clandestine life as a counter-terrorist.

Too bad. He was missing out on so much. Seeing him with Pop, it was obvious Logan had a lot to give. But he wasn't accustomed to caring about people, nor was he comfortable with people showing him that they were fond of him.

"Interesting." He tapped on the keyboard. "Alkaloids indicate a toxin. Disease Control suggests we contact the National Clearing House for Poison Control Centers."

"They poisoned her," Kelly cried, positive she was right. She'd liked Lydia and had been convinced the woman wasn't imagining her daughter had been murdered.

"Let's see what Poison Control says about alkaloids." He poked at the keyboard, amazingly fast considering his two-fingered style. "Okay, here it comes."

Over his shoulder she read the message as it emerged on the small screen. Alkaloids were associated with classic poisons such as arsenic, cyanide, or strychnine. Arsenic had a toxicity rating of 5, which meant it took less than a tablespoon to be a lethal dose.

Cyanide or strychnine had a rating of 6, meaning they were

among the most poisonous substances on earth. Less than seven drops killed a person—very quickly. They all shared a very bitter taste that often alerted people who accidentally ingested them.

Logan scrolled down. "See what it says here? Alkaloids were one of the first poisons to be detected in tissue samples."

"Scientists have been able to spot them in tissue samples since 1851," Kelly added reading the rest of the message "I guess there wasn't enough in Suzanne's tissues to alert either coroner the way you would expect."

"Let's check related poisons." He clicked on the appropriate icon and waited. Logan turned to her, shaking his head. "Alkaloid is a trace element left by brucine."

"What is brucine?"

"Let's find out." He clicked on: **More Information.** The screen that appeared was long and detailed. Logan scrolled through it faster than she could read. "Brucine has a toxicity level of 6 and kills quickly. It's almost impossible to detect. The victim suffers a lot of pain. That's helped save them—if they get to a hospital in time."

Kelly sucked in her breath, imagining Suzanne in pain. "The Stanfield mansion had been filled with people on the night Suzanne died. Why didn't she ask someone to call an ambulance?"

Logan's face was expressionless, but she thought she detected a slight hardening of his jaw. "Maybe she did and that person failed to summon help."

"Oh, my God," she whispered, imagining Suzanne writhing in pain, begging someone she trusted to call a doctor. Had he promised to get help? Or had he—maybe they—just stood there and watched her suffer? Until she was beyond pain at last.

"Does it say anything about how to confirm brucine killed Suzanne?" Kelly asked.

"What we're going to need to do is see if the coroner in Phoenix has more detailed notes," he said as she shut down the computer. "Hopefully he saved them."

He pulled her into his arms without a word. The warmth of

his embrace was so male, so comforting. She rested her head against the crook of his neck. As she'd predicted, it fit perfectly.

"I'm frightened," she confessed. "I'm so worried about you, Logan. These people are ruthless and as sneaky as the devil. No telling what they might do."

Chapter 22

I'm worried about you.

It was all Logan could do not to groan out loud. Kelly's head was nestled against his shoulder. For one totally illogical moment, being married to Kelly, having her worry about him, felt right—so right.

Christ! This couldn't be happening to him. Not now. Not after all the precautions he'd taken to avoid caring about anyone.

"I'm terribly concerned about you, Logan. I'm afraid you'll be murdered."

He wasn't worried about someone killing him. He could protect himself. He didn't need anyone. He never had; he never would.

"Forget about it," he said, his lips grazing her hair. "I can outsmart them."

She lifted her head and looked into his eyes. "Is that why your code name is Nine Lives? You've managed to elude killers like the terrorists who ruined your vocal cords with acid."

"No. I chose Nine Lives for a different reason. On each anti-terrorist assignment, I've had to take on a new identity—"

"And put your own life at risk."

"Sweetheart, that's all part of being a Cobra." He was

disturbed by how seriously she took his work. Hell, he'd never minded the danger. It was all part of the game, and that's what his job was to him, a challenge he thrived on, high-stakes entertainment.

"Logan, how many lives have you gone through?"

"Eight unless someone tried to kill me when I was a kid. Then it would be nine. This would be it—my last life."

"Oh, Logan, no," Kelly cried, her beautiful face etched with emotion.

"Hey, Kelly. It's just a superstition, right?"

He pulled her closer, tightening the arm circling her shoulders. Lowering his head to kiss her made Kelly turn toward the fire.

"Why do you want to kiss me now? You certainly didn't want to before."

"Hey, give me a break. There were dozens of people around. I'm not into group sex." His attempt at a joke didn't even prompt a suggestion of a smile. She wanted an explanation, and he couldn't blame her.

"You were supposed to kiss me, but I had to kiss you. It was terribly embarrassing."

Her heartfelt confession and the distressed look on her face caused an unexpected pang of guilt. Man, oh, man. Don't let her look at me like that. Kelly had a way of getting to him that he'd never experienced before. He decided to tell her part of the truth.

"Look, I did not have a normal childhood. I never saw television, and rarely listened to the radio. I—"

"Your parents were afraid you'd find out they kidnapped you."

He didn't answer her directly, not wanting to lie more than absolutely necessary. "I never attended a wedding. When the Marines sent me to "charm school—""

"Charm School? You're kidding."

"The initial test for joining the Cobra Force is passing Survival Training. The next step is Tech College. That's where they monitor your ability to use sophisticated equipment. If you fail at any phase, you're out. No second chances.

"Those who pass are sent to what the Cobra Force calls Cultural Enrichment Classes, but the guys call it Charm School. The Army's Rangers are also antiterrorist experts, but the Cobra Force is trained by the Marines. That means we're often assigned to embassies because their protection is a Marine Corps responsibility, and embassies are often targeted by terrorists.

"Cobras must learn embassy protocols—what to say and do with dignitaries from around the world. Charm School takes the rough edges off men who are tough enough to pass the other tests, but wouldn't know which fork to use at an embassy dinner."

"They teach you manners."

"Yes, and things I never knew existed like how to select an unpretentious wine." Kelly gave him an encouraging smile. "They didn't cover weddings. I guess they thought everyone knew what to do. I wasn't prepared for the judge telling me to kiss you."

He detected a hint of suspicion in her eyes that wasn't just a reflection of the flickering light of the fire.

"It wasn't the first time you've avoided kissing me. Other times you kissed my neck, but never my lips."

He suppressed a smile. When it came to ad lib, he couldn't be outdone—thanks to Zoe and her "drama" classes. Even so, it was damn hard to fool Kelly.

"Trust me, the women I've know aren't the type to exchange body fluids with. Kissing hasn't been my thing, but I'm willing to let you change my mind."

She hesitated a moment, and he thought she was going to ask him another question. What he'd told her had been the truth, but it wasn't the whole story. His aversion to kissing women on the lips went back to his childhood when he'd been expected to kiss Zoe every day after class.

Zoe. Even now, years later, his gut clenched thinking about the old hag. She claimed to have been a teacher before coming to the camp. She was supposed to teach them, and she had done a fair job. But not without making their lives miserable.

No matter how cruel Zoe had been, she expected a kiss—on the lips—at the end of each day.

"Logan, I think you need to get something straight. I was willing to pay you to marry me so I could adopt Rafi, but you refused to take any money. Sex isn't part of this arrangement."

He swore under his breath, told himself to count to ten, but got only to three. "Wanna bet?"

They stared each other for a moment, a silent test of wills. The challenging glint in her amber eyes was backed by the stubborn line of her lips. Her hair had hung to her shoulders in a slight wave at the wedding. The trip up the mountain had tousled her hair, making her sexy as hell.

He reached forward, giving into an urge he'd had countless times. His fingertips touched her hair, and she didn't pull back. He thrust both hands into the loose curls, and lowered his head until his mouth hovered over hers.

"Kiss me, Kelly."

Her response was a tight frown that wrinkled her cute nose. Her lips parted as if she was about to tell him to go to hell. Her mouth fascinated him, he decided as he waited for her to say something.

That first night in the hogan, he noticed her lips even though he shouldn't have. They were slightly tilted upward, which gave him the impression she often smiled. But it was the slight fullness of her lower lip that had an erotic effect on him. Even that night, when he'd thought she'd been sent to kill him, there had been tension in his groin.

Suddenly, he couldn't wait for her to kiss him. A burning need to have those soft lips on his undermined his desire to have her kiss him. Holding her head in place with his hands, he covered her mouth with such savage intensity that he felt her entire body stiffen, but he couldn't stop himself.

He explored the lush fullness of her lips with the tip of his tongue. Her mouth gradually softened, parting by degrees as he twined his fingers through her hair. Holding her and kissing her, aroused Logan more than making love to any other woman had. He edged his tongue between her lips and brushed the tip of her tongue. Hard heat surged into his loins.

He pulled away, trying to catch his breath, realizing he didn't kiss like an expert, but what he lacked in experience, he figured he made up for with enthusiasm. Otherwise her breathing wouldn't have altered the way it had. Her resigned sigh made him smile.

"For someone who never kisses, you managed to learn how to French kiss in a hurry." Her voice was just a little too breathy, a little too quivery to carry off the sarcasm.

"Darlin, I'm a fast learner. Teach me how to kiss, then I'll teach you a few tricks."

"I meant what I said I'd rather pay you than become involved with you." She didn't sound nearly as convincing as before.

"Don't worry. You're not involved with me. You're married to me."

"Can't you be serious for once?"

"Sweetheart, I'm dead serious. You're sexy as hell. I'm not traipsing around with a hard-on. We're married. Let's have some fun."

"Think of it as a mission."

"Mission impossible, believe me. Stop trying to fool yourself by living in the past. Your jerk of a husband is dead. If you'd had any real sex life at all, you wouldn't act like this."

She scrambled away from him, then attempted to stand. He lunged for her and they toppled sideways onto the ground. She brought her knee up, aiming for his groin, but his superior strength made it ridiculously easy for him to shove her leg down. He angled himself across her body, his hips rubbing against hers.

"Stop it," she moaned, her eyes wide and dazed as she realized he was fully erect.

"Hey, it's our wedding night. I have a responsibility to men around the world to perform so well that you wake up smiling."

"Chauvinist pig."

"I don't give a damn if I'm politically correct. Never have. Never will." To emphasize his point, he ground against her.

Damnit all! That only made him harder—if possible—and closer to losing it. The way he had the very first time he'd had sex.

Even through the heavy fabric of the sweater he was wearing, Logan felt her nails biting into his shoulders. Desire, pure and elemental assaulted him with unanticipated urgency. He told himself to take his time, not to lose control.

He speared his fingers into the clusters of golden curls around her face. He'd never, ever wanted to kiss a woman. Because of Zoe, he'd had an aversion to kissing that bordered on a phobia. Until Kelly.

His lips reclaimed hers, and he found her tongue waiting for him. With a dainty flick of her velvety tongue, a shaft of pure pleasure arrowed through him, fueling the hard heat mounting like a flood tide between his legs.

He kissed her, barely hearing the low moan rumbling from his throat. Her arms circled his shoulders, welding her body to his. Great, she was with the program now.

He nudged her knees apart and resettled himself between her legs, his sex riding hard against the cleft of her thighs. They were both in jeans, but the denim couldn't conceal her moist heat.

Knowing she wanted him excited him even more. He told himself to take things nice and easy, but his erection strained against the back of his fly. His cock was so friggin' hard that he ached when he moved.

No other man had ever kissed Kelly with such wild passion. It was almost as if Logan had been holding himself in check for so long that now he was finally allowing himself to enjoy kissing. Well, this was more than just a kiss, she admitted, his weight pinning her to the ground, his hips rocking against hers, the iron heat of his shaft ramming against her.

How could she have forgotten the exquisite pressure of a man's body? Her skin tingled and white-hot heat flooded every pore. She clung to him, digging her nails into his powerful shoulders.

Loving the way he kissed her.

His aggressive mouth ravaged hers with wild, scorching kisses. His eager lips pressed against hers while his tongue constantly thrust and chased hers as if he couldn't get enough of her, stealing her breath until she saw stars.

He slid both hands under her sweater, then yanked it upward. Pulling it off, he whispered, "Are you ready to become my wife, Kelly?"

He gazed down at her, his smile insolent, saying he'd wait until hell froze over or he got his way—whichever came first.

Kelly wanted to say she was *not* ready, she truly did, but something stopped her. She knew this was his way of telling her that he wasn't going to force her. If she didn't speak up now, there would be no turning back.

She didn't utter a single word.

In a second, his mouth recaptured hers in a fierce, reckless kiss. His lips captured hers again, hot and greedy. But it was the way his tongue mated with hers, stroking and caressing, each movement eliciting an erotic thrill in her lower body that made her moan out loud.

For the love of God! Logan had a devastating effect on her body. She had to be careful or he'd take advantage over and over and over.

"Now I know what people see in kissing." The rasp of his voice was deeper than usual, and there was a hint of amazement in his words.

She was as stunned as he was at the way passion had detonated between them like an explosion. She'd never experienced anything like this. She'd denied herself the pleasure of being with a man for too long. That had to be the explanation for her intense reaction.

A rush of cool air chilled her heated skin. Kelly realized he had stripped off her blouse. Logan caught a breast in his palm, stroking the taut nipple through her bra. He drew the tight bud into his mouth, wetting the lacy fabric with his tongue.

She whimpered softly as he rolled onto his side, taking his weight off her. His free hand roved downward and found the delta of her thighs while he continued to torture her, rolling his tongue over her nipple. Through the damp fabric she could feel the sweet suction of his mouth. She arched her back, filling the palm of his hand with her softness.

He lifted his head from her breast. "Aw, hell. I can't hold out much longer."

"We're just getting started," she complained even though she wanted nothing more than to have him inside her. Now.

"Don't be a smartass."

He unzipped her jeans, then slid his hand inside. Expert fingers purled over her stomach, stroking, kneading. Inching lower and lower. Kelly's breath stalled in her throat as he cupped the crotch of her bikinis. She knew he could feel the warmth seeping through the silky fabric.

His mouth found hers again, his lips gently caressing hers. The kiss that had been savage a few minutes ago was now sweet, measured, his lips closed even though hers were parted, inviting him in. Suddenly, she couldn't concentrate on the way he was kissing her.

His hand had slipped under the waistband of her panties.

The next instant he was touching her *there,* testing the slick, moist skin and teasing the taut bud. His technique was like a potent narcotic. She could not get enough. She moved beneath him, lifting her hips slightly. Anticipating.

He eased one strong finger inside her just as his tongue invaded her mouth. He boldly stroked her with his finger while his tongue performed a seductive parody, moving in sync with his finger.

"Logan," she cried, the unexpectedly sharp reaction of her body, forcing the words from her lips along with a moan of pure pleasure. "Hurry, hurry."

"Make up your mind. A minute ago you were complaining that I was rushing things. That's a woman for you."

He removed his hand, and it was all she could do not to scream for him to keep touching her. But she didn't want him to know how easily he'd aroused her to a frenzy.

His hand slid under the waistband of her jeans. He took a second to fondle her buttocks, then he hooked his thumbs over the waistband and shoved her jeans downward, taking her panties with them. She wiggled her feet, kicking the bunched denim aside while he unhooked her bra.

"No fair, Logan. You still have your clothes on."

He sat up and slowly pulled his T-shirt over his head. As he unbuttoned his jeans and pulled them off, she told herself to look away—but didn't. He stood before her, naked. Her lips parted helplessly, but she managed to keep a sigh locked in her throat.

A lean, mean, fighting machine.

The corny saying popped into her head. It described him perfectly except there was so much more to Logan than just a magnificent body.

Sheened by the low-burning fire, his body appeared more stunningly virile than ever. He was whipcord lean without a gram of fat anywhere, yet his muscles were clearly defined across his chest and shoulders. His biceps were much more powerful than she had realized.

Oh, my, he was a stud, too.

She tried not to conspicuously stare at his awesome erection. But it was aimed right at her. His sex jutted out from a tuft of dark curly hair flanked by muscular thighs.

Every woman's dream, she thought. And her worst nightmare. What would happen after they made love? Would her heart be lost forever?

Logan towered over her, wearing nothing but a smile that would have tested a nun's vows. "See something you like?"

She realized she had been staring slack-jawed at him. "I was just checking to see if you were circumcised. I never make love to men who aren't circumcised."

"Men?" His smirk told her that he was not buying that bridge. "Yeah, right."

"You're all show and no go."

"You're asking for it," he told her with a wink. "And you're going to get it."

He yanked one of the sleeping bags off the rock and threw it down beside her. He stretched out on it and pulled her into his arms, saying, "I've waited too long for this. I've wanted you since that first night in the hogan."

His words startled her, but she didn't have a chance to respond. Kissing her with the same fierceness he had earlier, he guided his erection between her thighs. He burrowed it into the cleft, stroking her intimately.

The flared tip of his penis nudged into her body, rubbing against her in a way that told her this man knew *exactly* how to please a woman in bed.

"Go on, go on," she heard herself cry.

"I just want to feel you for a minute."

It slowly dawned on Kelly what he meant. Undoubtedly Logan had a stash of condoms in his pack. He wasn't the type of man to be unprepared. Given his own past, she was convinced he would never father a child, then abandon it.

His comment about mumps "going south" on him could mean he was infertile. If it were true. She believed Logan had made it up to give them a plausible reason for immediately adopting a child.

She was feverish with desire, desperate to have him inside her. A thought hurled out of nowhere and didn't seem as wild as it might have under different circumstances.

She was right in the middle of her cycle.

"Go ahead. It's all okay," she whispered. "I don't have anything. I've been tested."

With a sharp intake of breath, he hesitated, but she rolled onto her back, pulling him with her. She arched her hips upward. A moan rumbled from his throat, a sound so intense that it might have been mistaken for pain.

"Kelly, are you taking—"

She cut off his question with a kiss while she lifted her hips, forcing him inside her. Grabbing his buttocks, she scored his skin with her nails in a vain attempt to relieve tension building by the second.

"You're so tight," he muttered.

She was tempted to tell him that he was too big, but the intense pressure of him thrusting forward made her moan instead.

"I don't want to hurt you."

"You're not, you're not."

He drew slowly back, back until he'd almost withdrawn entirely. Then with one swift, sure motion, he surged forward.

There was a flash of pain, then her body stretched to accommodate him. Imbedded to the hilt, he gazed into her eyes.

There was something shockingly primitive about the way he was looking at her. He was a talented actor, but she knew this was no act. His eyes were narrow, smoldering, the pupils completely dilated. He wanted to make love to her with an intensity she'd never imagined existed.

What would it be like if Logan were in love, not merely in lust?

She didn't have a second to dwell on the possibilities. He rocked his hips and she was utterly lost. Her body arched upward, contracting with an explosion of pleasure so profound that she screamed.

Chapter 23

He slipped into her bedroom through the terrace door, the way he always did. There were no lights on in the mansion's other suites, but lights were blaring down in the stallions' stable. No doubt, Woody was out there with the stupid Indian, Jim Cree, fussing over the expensive colt who refused to eat.

A smoldering fire cast a warm glow on the marble hearth and filled her suite with the scent of piñon wood. It was the only light on in the room, but it was enough for him to see her stretched out on the white silk chaise near the fireplace. She was wearing the ice-blue nightgown he'd given her that morning.

Her nipples jutted outward, stretching the lacy top. The slit on one side of the gown exposed a slim leg from the ankle to her upper thigh. Just the sight of her, gave him a full-blown erection and made the miserable hours he'd spent tromping around the Devil's Arch worthwhile.

"Did you kill them?" she asked.

"No. They weren't at Devil's Arch." He sat on the foot of the chaise, facing her.

"You heard Logan. That's where he said they were going."

"I looked everywhere." He pointed to his Ferragamo loafers.

They were coated with red dust and scarred by rocks along the trail. "Ruined. For what?"

"Poor baby," she cooed as she leaned toward him. One strap slipped off her shoulder, and the lacy top crumpled, unable to remain in place without support. A plump breast sprang free, its pert nipple beckoning him.

He reached for her, but she pulled back, deliberately teasing him the way she often did when she was interested in kinky sex.

"I'll bet I know what happened," she said. "You saw the forever kiss. A crowbar couldn't have pried Logan and Kelly apart. It's a wonder they stayed around for the reception. I'm sure they gave up the camping idea and checked into a hotel, then humped each other like wild animals."

"Probably. It may work out better this way. While I was searching for them, I came up with a brilliant plan."

She listened, her blue eyes glittering with anticipation as he explained what he had in store for the newlyweds. The original plan had been to find them at Devil's Arch and shoot them from a distance with a high-powered rifle. But an obvious murder would have caused a sticky investigation.

"This way, it'll be like Suzanne's death. There won't be any indication we were responsible," he told her.

With a sexy pout, she said, "It's a fabulous idea, but there is one problem. Woody plans to change his will before you get rid of them."

"I'll buy a little time. Woody's lawyer is going to have an accident."

"Perfect! I want to shoot him."

Why had he ever taught her to shoot? She had wanted to go after Logan and Kelly herself. "A car accident is better. We don't want to be implicated."

He pulled off his Ferragamos and tossed them into the fire. A spray of sparks showered the hearth, then flames engulfed his shoes.

"What if someone sees you going back to your room without shoes?"

"I'll think of something," he said. They'd kept their relationship secret—for years—knowing it would outrage Woody. If he discovered them together, they could forget about the will entirely.

Grabbing her other shoulder strap, he yanked it down, baring her to the waist. She crossed her arms over her chest and pretended to be shocked. Her wide-eyed innocent expression might have worked years ago, but now he knew better.

She whispered, "I have a headache."

He slid his hand inside the slit in her nightgown. The silk parted even more to reveal a satin smooth leg. A half inch at a time, his hand roved along her leg, starting at the ankle. He stopped at the soft curve of her upper thigh, savoring the texture of her skin.

"Does this make you feel better?" he asked.

"Much, much better."

Teasing her now, the way she'd teased him, he took his time, strumming his fingers along her thigh, moving dangerously close to the juncture, but not actually touching her.

"I have a surprise for you."

"I love surprises." He stroked her for one excruciatingly long minute, then finally gave in and touched her mound. What happened to the tight, springy curls? She was as smooth as the finest crystal, yet warm and baby-soft. "You shaved?"

"Ever since you told me that the high-priced call girls in Washington shave their pussys, I've wanted to do it. But I couldn't stand shaving every day. Now they can permanently remove hair with a laser."

"Is that why you spent so much time this week in that fancy spa?"

"Yes. It took hours, but it was worth it, don't you think?" She pulled up her gown and proudly exposed her crotch.

It was rounded and creamy white, the lips slightly parted to reveal a glistening pink that deepened into a dusky mauve. It reminded him of the subtle shadings of an exotic orchid. He lowered his head and caught a whiff of her favorite perfume. She parted her legs, and he repositioned himself between her thighs. He nibbled along the warm, smooth mound, flicking his tongue over her delicious skin.

* * *

Logan watched Kelly as she slept cuddled against him, her lips curved into a suggestion of a smile. He'd like to think he'd put the smile on her lips after making love to her all night, but it wasn't true. From the first, her lips had intrigued him because they always seemed to be on the verge of a smile.

She sighed in her sleep and burrowed closer—if possible. His cock responded with a surge of heat, and it took all his self-control not to start kissing her again. The way he'd gone at her, riding her hard all night, reflected some primal urge. He didn't know what in hell had come over him.

He'd been without a woman too long, he decided, but it was more than that. His job kept him in remote places where you could find a one-night stand in the local bar. He had never developed a relationship with any of them because he worked under cover and couldn't afford to let anyone get close to him.

Kelly was different. He'd wanted to make love to her from the very first night he'd seen her. Living with Kelly and Pop had drawn him into her life. She came with a lot of emotional baggage thanks to the creep she'd married, but Kelly was smart and funny. He still chuckled when he thought about the way she'd gone after the Stanfields at that stupid dinner.

He started to kiss the top of her head, then stopped himself. Shit! What was he thinking? He never woke up without checking to make certain his surroundings were secure.

First thing.

Easing away from Kelly, not wanting to awaken her, he levered himself up on his elbows and scanned the small clearing. Nothing. He hadn't expected anything, but caution had saved his life more than once. He had no business cuddling a woman and letting his thoughts drift.

Letting down his guard would get him killed.

Beside him, Kelly shifted in her sleep, her body seeking his. At some point last night, he'd zipped the two sleeping bags together and they'd crawled inside to make love again. By moving, he'd allowed the cool morning air to seep into the bag. But he knew it was more than a chill that made Kelly snuggle against him.

No question about it. They were dynamite together. He couldn't imagine a more giving, passionate woman. And he had scratches on his back to prove it. She'd tried to persuade him to leave her alone, but when it got right down to it, she wanted him as much as he wanted her.

Her bare breasts were nestled against his chest, and for a moment, he allowed himself the pleasure of feeling their softness. He steeled himself, not permitting his hand to touch her. Kissing her was totally out of the question.

He unzipped his side of the sleeping bag and slipped out as quietly as possible. He gently tucked the down-filled bag around her, then pulled on his jeans. Instead of putting on a shirt, his field training sent him straight for his hiking boots.

Always be prepared to run.

Son of a bitch! What had gotten into him? His socks weren't stuffed inside of them. He picked up one lightweight boot and shook it hard, half-expecting a scorpion to fall out. Nothing. The other boot was empty as well. He checked Kelly's boots before putting his on.

He took the computer out of his backpack and found a rock to use as a desk. The rising sun made the rocks seem to catch fire, a sharp contrast to the brilliant blue sky. There was a sense of mystery and isolation to Sedona that intrigued Logan. It filled him with a feeling he'd never had before, a sense of peace and tranquility, a result of being in constant awe of Mother Nature.

His computer beeped, bringing his attention back to the screen. He wasn't surprised to see his e-mail icon flashing. No doubt, Raptor had heard about the wedding and was wondering what was happening. A quick glance at his Brietling told Logan that Raptor would be at the command center.

He clicked on the e-mail icon and the message instantly appeared on his screen.

You're married. Does that mean you want a desk job?
Raptor

Using his index fingers, Logan pecked out his response.

Fuck the desk job.
Nine Lives

He sat back and waited, knowing Raptor's e-mail icon would flash on his screen.

You know we don't like to send married men into the field. I've got a spot for you here.

It took Logan a few minutes to explain the situation. He could tell Raptor didn't approve, but there wasn't anything he could do about it.

Let me provide you with a new ID. Miguel Orinda is still hunting for you. He has connections in Venezuela. I don't want him to find out you're there. Remember, he has a price on your head.

Logan thought it unlikely that the cartel boss would discover he was in Venezuela. From all reports the adoption would take just a few days. Quick in and quick out. Like a Cobra strike.

It'll screw-up the adoption papers unless I use my own name. I'll get out of there fast.

Logan heard Kelly stirring in the sleeping bag and looked over his shoulder. Tousled blonde hair was all that was visible now. She'd burrowed deeper into the sleeping blanket. He turned back and read the response on the screen.

How long does it take for an adoption to become final in Arizona? I don't think you can get a divorce before its final without risking Social Services revoking the adoption.

R.

**It's six months for adoptions of children born out of
the country. I'll be ready to return to action then.
N.L.**

Logan signed off and shut down his computer. The rustling
sound of autumn leaves being crushed alerted him. He reached
for his pack and pulled out his gun. Stepping back into the
shadow of the rocks, he saw it was a kit fox, foraging for a
meal.

He watched the small fox who was the size of a house cat,
thinking he was lucky to spot one. They were nocturnal animals
and used their large ears—about twice the size of other foxes—
to radiate heat during the hot summer months. By the way the
fox was nosing around the rocks, Logan assumed he had the
scent of a jackrabbit. With a whoosh of its bushy, black-tipped
tail, the fox disappeared into the rocks.

Logan put away his gun and the computer. As he stowed
his pack, another sound filled the small clearing. He turned and
found Kelly was sitting up, the sleeping blanket gathered around
her like a shield.

Aw, hell. She didn't regret last night, did she? He wasn't
any good at sweet-talking women. He hadn't a clue what to
say.

You can handle this. You can handle this. You can handle
this.

Like a mantra, Kelly silently chanted the words over and
over and over as she emerged from the sleeping bag. If she
repeated the words enough times, surely it would come true.

Across the small clearing, Logan was hovering over his
backpack. Dark stubble bristled across his jaw, making him
look more rugged than usual. He wasn't wearing a shirt, so the
blazing sun emphasized his tan and the dark hair on his chest.
It narrowed to a strip at his waist and disappeared behind the
unbuttoned top button of his jeans.

Last night had been . . . awesome. No word could describe her
experience accurately, but awesome covered it. The chemistry

between them defied all her closely held beliefs about love and sex. She had never believed it would be possible to have more arousing, satisfying sex than she'd had with Daniel, the love of her life.

Until Logan.

He was a magnificent specimen of a man, not a Hollywood hunk *de jour,* in style today and toast tomorrow. Logan was the real thing, a man's man who knew a lot about sex even if he didn't have much experience kissing.

Logan was looking at her now, a slight frown creasing his brow. She had no idea what to say. Had she made a fool of herself last night by moaning and crying out with pleasure? She decided to play it light and pretend this hadn't been such a soul-shattering experience. Her instinct for emotional self-preservation told her not to let him know how deeply shaken she was.

"Good morning," she called, mustering a smile.

He returned her greeting, his tight expression transforming into an adorable smile that triggered the unique dimples up high on his cheekbones. "Mornin', Kelly."

His easy drawl was low-pitched and husky. Her instinctive response to him was unbelievably powerful. Her body suddenly felt too warm, her heartbeat jarring her chest.

"I guess my clothes are around hear somewhere," she said to hide her reaction.

If she thought he was going to help her gather her clothes, she was dead wrong. He watched with an amused grin as she unzipped the sleeping bag and stood up, one of the bags wound around her. She hobbled barefoot across the rocky ground and retrieved her jeans. Getting into them while still keeping the sleeping bag around her was a trick that called for a contortionist in a circus.

"You know, Kelly, I've seen every inch of you—close up."

Given they'd made love so many times, her behavior seemed silly, yet to her he was still a stranger. She didn't feel comfortable parading around in front of him in the buff. But she had to pee in the worst way, so she dropped the sleeping bag and pulled on her jeans. Thankfully her panties were inside, which made it faster.

She looked around for her bra and blouse. Then she remembered Logan had ripped the blouse off her. It was worthless now. She glanced around the small clearing, but didn't see her sweater.

The fall air was a bit nippy even though the sun was out. She told herself to be sophisticated. *Do not—repeat—do not cover your breasts with your arms.* She peered around several large rocks, looking for her sweater, extremely conscious of Logan tracking every move.

Goose bumps pebbled her skin, and her breasts were drawn into tight buds. He seemed to be enjoying the view. Out of the corner of her eye, she noticed the amused expression on his face that reminded her of a naughty little boy.

"Looking for this?" He held up her sweater.

She marched over to him and snatched the sweater out of his hands. She pulled it over her head, silently conceding she couldn't be angry with him. His playful smile told her that their relationship had transformed. They were on a different level now.

Before she threw herself into his arms, she turned away and found her boots. Without bothering to put on socks, she shoved her feet into them. She headed for the cluster of thick, bushy palo verde trees, calling over her shoulder as casually as she could manage, "See if you can find my bra. I'll be right back."

Relieving herself gave her time to think. Making love to Logan had been raw, primitive, yet a searing, all-consuming experience. This act threatened to cost her more than she'd anticipated. She'd never given herself with such reckless abandon to any man, even Daniel.

Alarmed, she realized she hadn't been thinking about Daniel as much lately. The pain, the anger, the raw ache of betrayal had been dulled a bit. A chapter of her life had closed, she decided, and she had to let it go.

The future loomed ahead of her, misty and out of focus like a half-remembered dream. Last night, she'd done the unthinkable. She'd lied to Logan about birth control. Well, she hadn't exactly lied, but she had deliberately misled him. An impulse from out of the blue compelled her to see if she could conceive a child.

It seemed like a good idea at the time.

How many people had thought the very same thing only to find themselves regretting their actions? Her entire life, she'd missed not have brothers and sisters. If she had a baby, Rafi would have one sibling. It wasn't the big family she had dreamed about, but it was the best she could do.

She would never regret having a baby, but she did regret misleading Logan. It had taken some persuading to convince him to marry her so she could adopt Rafi. Apparently, Logan's childhood had been so traumatic that he didn't trust a woman to raise a child that wasn't hers.

How would he feel if he knew she was having his baby? He wouldn't like it one bit. He might insist upon an abortion, or he might think this was her way of trapping him, of keeping him in a marriage of convenience that was supposed to end in six months.

"What on earth have you done?"

She had made a stupid, impulsive decision. She had no choice now but to live with the consequences. While it was unfair to deceive Logan, there was no way she would get rid of the baby.

Of course, it was premature to assume she was pregnant. It was entirely possible Logan's "mumps" story was true, and he couldn't father a child. With Logan, it was impossible to tell whether he was acting or telling the truth.

Assuming she did conceive while they were together, could she keep it a secret for six months? Obviously not. Send him away just as soon as Rafi is home. Perfect, she thought as she made her way back to the camp.

Logan had taken the bundle of food that Uma had sent with them and had spread it out on a flat rock. He'd put on Pop's sweater, but it was inside out. He was entirely unaware of the captivating picture he made.

"Did you happen across my bra?" she asked as she came up beside him.

"Bras are only good for one thing—tourniquets."

"Are you saying bras are only good for stopping blood flow? That's a man for you."

"Trust me, that's the only use for a bra." He thought a moment, mischief flickering in the depths of his eyes. "Maybe a bra has another use. If I were into bondage, I could tie you up with it."

"Don't even think about it." Despite her words, for a second she did think about it. It seemed scary but tempting.

He put both his hands on her hips, then slipped up under her sweater. The air was cool against her bare skin, his palms warm. The seductive gleam in his eye said they'd be back in the sleeping bag in a second, if she wasn't careful.

"You don't need a bra, Kelly." His hands cradled her breasts, his thumbs massaging her nipples. "You're perfect just like this."

There was nothing she'd rather do than make love to him. Again. But an inner voice insisted she exert *some* of her usual will power.

"I was wondering," she began.

He shook his head and grinned. "Gimme a break."

"What would you like broken?"

He chuckled as she tried to squirm out of his grasp, but her efforts were futile. He merely spun her around and backed her up against a boulder, trapping her between his huge body and the rock.

"Seriously, we should discuss theories of raising children and decide what we'll tell the social workers. I downloaded information from America Online. Those parents told me what questions to expect."

"Okay, so tell me what to say and I won't let you down." He lowered his head to kiss her.

"Logan, wait. We've never had an intellectual discussion. I don't know what you think about anything."

He threw back his head and looked heavenward. She was pretty sure he wasn't praying. Given his burgeoning erection shoved up against her, now was probably not the time for an intellectual discussion. But she had a burning desire to know something more about him other than the tidbits he chose to tell her.

He looked down at her again, the sensuous light still in his eyes. "You're better educated than I am. Explain Einstein's theory of Relativity to me."

"Well, uh . . ." She found herself staring at his emerging beard and remembering how those whiskers felt against her tender skin in very private places. "The theory of relativity is about . . Well, I don't really understand it either."

"See?" He smirked at her, a trace of arrogance in his voice. "Neither of us is very intellectual. Let's skip the b.s. I waited for you longer than I've ever waited for a woman, but it was worth it. I promised myself two full days with you—in the horizontal."

Chapter 24

"Logan's some studmuffin," Uma told Kelly.

"A studmuffin is like a bimbo, all looks and no brains. Logan is smarter than any man I know."

"Then he's a stud, right?"

A stud. Now that was an understatement. "I guess," Kelly hedged, wondering if two days of uninhibited sex was tattooed on her forehead.

Kelly and Uma were in the kitchen, preparing lunch while Logan and Pop were out on the terrace working with Jasper. That morning Pop had picked them up at the trailhead and brought them home. Uma insisted on cooking an elaborate meal, saying she wanted to make something special for them. Kelly had come inside even though Uma rarely let anyone do much in "her" kitchen.

"Uma, I realize you don't know Luz Tallchief, but surely, someone in your clan must know something about her."

"Not really," Uma said, stirring a pot of black beans with one hand and dribbling flakes of Chimayo red chili into it with the other. "She never comes to town. They say that she took Logan's disappearance to heart. She blamed herself for being ill when he needed her."

"Yet when Logan reappeared, she didn't come to see him. Instead she trekked into the mountains and stayed there for days doing an *Adanti' ti* Chant for him."

Uma turned to face her, waving a wooden spoon. "Get real! Can't you see Luz is worried about him?"

"You're right. Do you think she'll want to talk to me?"

"Take Logan. She'll talk to him."

Kelly shook her head slowly. "Why didn't I think of that?"

"Marrying a man like Logan is bound to make a woman spacey."

Kelly opened her mouth to protest, then snapped it shut. Spacey did not cover it. She had forgotten all about the bugs. No doubt the one in the wall telephone near the refrigerator had picked up their conversation.

She kept her next thoughts to herself. After lunch, she and Logan would drive out to Luz's home. His former nanny should have returned. With luck, Logan could persuade her to tell them exactly what happened the day he disappeared.

Behind her, the kitchen door opened, and Pop walked in. Jasper at his heels.

She wanted to remind him—this was a marriage of convenience—nothing more. Pop thought Logan hung the moon, and she knew he was going to be acutely disappointed when he left.

"Uma, do we have a minute to play with Jasper down by the creek?" she asked, and Uma told them to be back in fifteen minutes.

"What's going on?" Pop asked after they'd made their way down the trail from the house to Oak Creek and were out of the range of the listening devices.

"Logan and I are driving out to visit Luz Tallchief later. What do you think?"

"Good idea. Maybe she can help." He looked at the sky where clouds were sulking on the horizon. "Take the Jeep in case of a gully-gusher."

Pop snapped a dead mesquite branch off a bush and hurled it into the stream. Tail wagging, Jasper looked up at Pop, waiting for the fetch signal. Pop clicked his fingers and pointed to the stick that was floating over the river rocks lining the bottom of the creek. Jasper bounded into the water, splashing noisily.

Kelly put her hand on Pop's shoulder. "Please don't count on Logan being around forever, Pop. It's entirely possible he may leave before six months."

"No way. Logan gave his word. He'll stay that long."

Kelly didn't dare tell her grandfather that she was hoping to get pregnant. If she had her wish, she would have to send Logan away before he knew about it.

"Any fool can see how right you two are made for each other."

"Pop, please, don't do this to yourself. It's an arrangement that's all. He'll be off on another assignment, and we'll never hear from him again."

He smiled at her with the indulgent expression she remembered from when she had been a child and had made a mistake. "You're wrong. Logan just wants an excuse to stay here. He's crazy about you."

Crazy about her body, maybe. "Pop all he talked about these last two days was how to survive in various types of terrain. Now I'm prepared to be dropped into the jungle or a desert or the Arctic with nothing but my clothes and come out smiling, ready to sell my story to television."

"It's the life Logan knows that's why he talks about it. Get him to open up and talk about himself."

"How?"

Pop reached down to take the stick Jasper had retrieved. The dog let him have it, then shook hard, blasting them with water. Pop hurled the stick again, saying, "Talk about yourself. Let him see you're willing to share your past with him. He needs you, Kelly. Only you can give him back a real life and the love he needs."

Logan would rather be taking a nap with Kelly than going to see Luz Tallchief. Two days alone with her had not been enough.

"At least let me drive." Logan took the keys from Kelly. "You can give me directions."

Kelly had been almost silent and distracted through lunch. Logan decided to keep quiet until she wanted to talk, but it was hard. What he really wanted to do was feel her lips part beneath his and hear the almost inaudible sigh that came when he kissed her.

They were on the road, heading toward Indian Gardens before Kelly spoke. "I never wanted to leave Sedona. I love it here. I went east to Yale to please Pop. I majored in journalism because he expected me to come home and help him run the paper."

He had absolutely no idea where this was going, but he didn't interrupt. He wanted to know more about her. Every little detail. He told himself he was crazy. When you knew a lot about a person, you were . . . involved.

Involvement required some level of commitment, something he was nuts to encourage.

Aw, hell, he could look at this another way. He was taking a risk by going to Venezuela. The more he knew about Kelly, the easier it would be to predict how she would behave should they run into trouble.

"Things happened," Kelly continued, gazing at him, her expression earnest. "I met Matthew Jensen and he introduced me to his friends. I worked on the paper with him, and slowly, day by day, I gave up my dream of coming home.

"Pop saw me slipping away. That's when he began preparing guide dogs for their formal training. I knew he was proud of his work, yet I never took the time to attend a graduation."

"Graduation?" Logan slowed to let a pickup loaded with sacks of apples pull out from a side road.

"It's a ceremony when the dogs are given official guide dog status and are handed over to their new owners. Pop says that seeing how happy a blind person is with a dog makes it all worth while. Pop was always there for me. He never missed a soccer game, a piano recital—anything. I let him down by not coming to at least one graduation to share his success with him."

Her heartfelt regret touched him in a way that he'd never experienced. Kelly and Pop shared a special bond of love and trust. For years he'd believed trusting someone made you weaker. Now he wondered if it didn't give you strength instead.

He had no one to trust, so it didn't matter to him. But for people like Kelly and Pop, good people with normal pasts, love and trust was essential. It made them stronger, but Logan knew without a doubt it wouldn't work for him.

"Don't be too hard on yourself," he told her. "I'm sure Pop understood. Just be certain you go to Jasper's graduation."

"Oh, I definitely plan to be in the front row," Kelly assured him. "I've made up my mind to stay here in Sedona. I could take a job back East, but this is the perfect place to raise a family."

"You're right," he said, wondering why she'd told him all this. It was more personal than anything they'd discussed.

"This is Indian Gardens," Kelly said when he slowed, approaching a cluster of buildings along the road. "The first settlers in the Sedona area lived here. They planted the apple trees and supported themselves by selling their crops."

If Logan used the word "quaint," which he never did, it would have described the gas station and country store. The red rock formation towering over what could best be called a wide spot in the road, was impressive.

"Turn here." Kelly pointed to a narrow side road.

Through the golden leaves on the branches of the cotton-woods and the slender aspens, Logan noticed storm clouds snarling in the distance. He heard thunder grumbling and saw lightning stabbing at the mountains.

"Monsoon season usually ends by October," Kelly said. "This is late to be getting rain."

"How much snow does Sedona get?"

"Not a lot. Around a foot a year except high up on the mountains. Why?"

He hesitated, then said, "I've heard the best place to be during a snow storm is under a blanket in front of a roaring fire with someone special."

He almost hadn't told her this. It might reveal more about

himself than he wanted her to know. The only fire he'd had experience with was the miserable fire in the pit at the camp. Too often it had been his job to chop the wood to keep the fire going so the women could cook. Later, when he joined the Cobras, there were other camps with fires.

Nothing romantic about any of those fires either.

Kelly's willingness to disclose something personal had compelled him to respond. He hadn't confessed anything too intimate, he assured himself. Be careful, cautioned an inner voice, she's damn smart.

"You've got the blanket and the special person right," she said in a tone that indicated she was teasing. "Hot cocoa or a glass of wine doesn't hurt either, and, of course, soft music on the stereo."

Too clearly he saw himself in front of a fireplace—under a blanket with Kelly, music crooning from a fancy stereo like the ones embassies had. Stereos, fireplaces. He was beginning to think in terms of 'things,' creature comforts that didn't fit into his backpack.

Okay, okay, he admitted it. He was also thinking about physical comfort and how good it felt to be with Kelly. He was on dangerous ground, quicksand, actually. It was sucking him under.

He slammed on the brakes, put the car in park, then quickly checked around them. Nothing but trees and dense underbrush. He leaned across the center console and kissed her. His mouth covered hers, his arms circled her, pulling her as close as he could with the damn console between them. He could have predicted the way her lips parted so sweetly and the low sigh of pleasure that came when his tongue brushed hers.

She pulled away, breathless. "Sh-shouldn't we get going?"

"No," he said, his lips touching hers. "I need to kiss you."

"I need you to kiss me, too."

They kissed, her tongue seeking his. Heat lanced through his groin as he thought about what she'd said. This was the first time she'd admitted how much she enjoyed making love to him. He'd known she liked it, but he'd wanted her to say it. Now that she had, he discovered her words were very arousing.

Thunder rumbled, closer now, and they broke the kiss. Kelly grinned at him, rummaged in her purse and pulled out a Kleenex. She dabbed at her eyes like a drama queen, then said, "Normally, I wouldn't go near a mouse, but since you have one in your pocket, do you mind if I pet it?"

Before he could think of a smart come-back, she dropped the Kleenex into her lap and covered his fly with her hand then squeezed. A tremor jolted his cock, forcing him to suck in his breath and hold it. She released him and he groaned as he tried to breathe again. She gripped him again, harder this time.

"You're asking for trouble."

She unhooked the top button of his jeans. "Trouble is my middle name."

She shoved her hand into the nonexistent space between his penis and the back of the zipper. "Don't you own any underwear?"

"Sure. I had a pair, but I lost them playing strip poker."

She shook her head, a mock look of disgust on her face, but the way her pupils had dilated and the rapid rhythm of her breathing told him how aroused she really was. Slowly moving her hand up and down, she leaned forward and kissed him. Her tongue darted in and out of his mouth, the tempo matching the movement of her hand.

Man, oh, man! He could kiss her forever and ever.

He heard the rasp of the zipper and knew she'd used her other hand to unzip his jeans. She freed his fully erect shaft.

"Uhh-ooh," she whispered, "you are in trouble. I'd better help you out."

She leaned over the console and pressed her lips to the flared tip of his penis. Continuing to kiss him, her tongue swept across his engorged flesh, circling, circling, circling. He was so hard now that he was actually in pain, aching to have the intense pressure released.

Taking him deep into her mouth, she sucked hard with one hand, gripping the base of his shaft, stroking up and down. Other women had done this to him, but they hadn't made his whole body shudder with each agonizingly sweet brush of the tongue.

This was pure torture, but he wanted it to last forever. He held out a few minutes, then he knew he was going to explode. Through clenched teeth, he warned her, "Kel . . . ly!"

He shot upward, ramming his head against the Jeep's roof, and his whole body vibrated as release hit him like a sucker punch. He was vaguely aware of her covering him with the Kleenex, then cleaning him up. He finally opened his eyes, not recalling just when he'd squeezed them shut. Kelly was smiling at him like a cat who'd just bagged a canary.

"Thanks," he managed to say. His breath was still coming in short spurts. "I needed that."

She dropped the wad of Kleenex on the floor. "Are we having fun yet?"

"I've had all the fun I can have—for now."

She giggled, a soft, throaty sound, but something inside him went cold and still. Obviously, she had experience at this. He didn't want to think about her being with another man. That's crap, the voice of reason countered. She'd been married, totally in love with another man.

He managed—God knows how—to get his cock back where it belonged. Climaxing brought physical relief, but he hadn't returned to normal size yet. Zipping up his jeans *was* all the fun he could have.

She winked at him. "Next time, I want to be on top . . . for a change."

Kelly rolled down the window as Logan started the car. Criminy! What had gotten into her? She had never been one for oral sex even with Daniel, but she'd actually enjoyed doing it to Logan.

It must be a control issue, she decided. The other times they'd made love, he'd been on top, the one in charge. She liked the way he'd surrendered to her even if it had been only for a few minutes.

The Jeep lurched over the dry creek bed near Luz Tallchief's home. The rain-scented breeze herded clouds against the mountains. Any minute the heavens would open and drench the red earth.

Sad, she thought, gazing at the aspens lining the dirt road. Their golden leaves were scattered across the red soil, but many shimmering leaves still quaked on the trees. Too bad, a storm would strip the branches bare.

They parked the car in the small clearing near Luz's cottage. The pickup was there near a battered Volkswagen bug held together with Bondo and bailing wire.

She stepped out of the car and stood beside Logan. "They're inside and they can see us. Luz must be a very traditional Navajo or she wouldn't have gone to do an *Adanti' ti* chant. It's customary to let them invite us in."

They waited while storm clouds with leaden underbellies roiled overhead. The first droplet of rain plopped on Kelly's cheek just as Luz's granddaughter came to the door and motioned for them to come in, but she didn't look happy about it.

Kelly whispered, "Don't call Luz by her name or even Mrs. Tallchief. To say someone's name while they are present diminishes their power. You only use a name when that person is gone, and people wouldn't know who you were talking about otherwise. Even then they say 'your son' or 'your husband,' anything to avoid using a name."

As they entered the home, Kelly noticed the clothesline strung back and forth across the kitchen. Evidently, they'd hastily brought in the rabbit jerky that had been drying in the sun. From what she'd seen the previous visit, the family lived off the land as much as possible.

An older woman, dressed in the traditional Navajo way with a velvet skirt and well-worn blouse, was sitting on a rocking chair in front of the fire. The only other light was a kerosene lamp on the table near the sofa where a gray-haired man was reading a magazine, ignoring their presence. The granddaughter disappeared into another room.

Luz Tallchief had a presence about her, an aura. Even before she said one word Kelly knew why she was an *ahnii*, the matriarch of her clan, someone everyone respected and came to for advice.

It began to rain, a steady but soft tap, tap, tap on the roof that reminded Kelly of Navajo pot drums beating a steady tattoo. It was dark outside, charcoal-black clouds shutting off the natural light.

"I knew you would come." Luz Tallchief's voice was low, yet world-weary as if she'd seen too much of life's hardships. "You are a windwalker, a man who will always find his way home."

Logan came up to her, then squatted down on his haunches and looked directly into her eyes. Inwardly, Kelly groaned. She'd forgotten to tell him many Navajos regarded direct eye contact with strangers to be rude, even confrontational.

"I wanted to see you again."

His words were simple, sounding so sincere that no one would have known Kelly had to coerce him into coming here. Didn't he want to know who was after him, Kelly wondered. Perhaps he already knew and hadn't told her.

With Logan anything was possible.

"Your voice. Are you ill?" Luz asked, concern in her voice.

Apparently, she hadn't read the article. Kelly had little to tell about Logan's Cobra activities but she did mention the incident that scarred his vocal cords.

"I had a run-in with some men who poured acid down my throat to kill me. I managed to swallow enough mud to save my voice."

The older man had tuned them out. He didn't look up from his paper, but it was all Kelly could do not to gasp, imagining Logan forcing mud down his throat.

Luz nodded, then unexpectedly smiled, revealing small, white teeth. "This is good, very good. Too many white men do not appreciate the power of the earth to heal. Some bathe in mud at those expensive places the white man calls spas, but that is all." She gestured toward the kitchen. "If you please, bring over a chair and we will talk."

Kelly wasn't sure if this included her or not. Logan took two chairs from the dinette and put them facing Luz. He held out Kelly's chair for her and she sat, careful not to make eye contact with Luz, showing her respect for the older woman.

"I wish I could remember you better," Logan began. "I don't recall much about those years. I was too young."

"It is just as well you do not."

"Why?" Kelly blurted out before she could stop herself.

Luz gazed into the fire and Kelly realized cataracts had formed across her eyes, making the pupils cloudy. How could she have possibly stayed for days in the mountains—alone—doing a chant for Logan?

A strobe of violet-white lightning lanced down from the sky and seared through the small living room, blinding Kelly for a second. An eerie silence followed . . . then a blast of thunder roared from the heavens with such intensity that the ground shook.

"That was a powerful lightning bolt," Logan said after the thunder died down.

"*Yei,* the holy ones are angry about something," Luz said, matter-of-factly. "They make thunder and lightning to punish us."

Luz's husband never looked up from his magazine. His body hadn't flinched or reacted in any way to the loud sound. Then Kelly spotted the peyote buttons in the ashtray near the lamp. Chewing the seeds from the peyote cactus caused an altered state of mind and hallucinations. He was zoned-out, in another world and didn't know they were there.

Kelly realized Logan was in a typical male macho mode. He wasn't going to admit his life was in danger. "If you could tell us what really happened the day Logan disappeared, it would really help. We have reason to believe someone wants him dead."

"I have no doubt this is so." She bent down and reached under the rocker and brought out a *paho.* The Navajo prayer stick was made of horseweed—like Jim Cree's cane—except this thick stalk had been sanded smooth, the tip adorned with eagle feathers. "I did a chant to ward off the evil ones. Now, we will see if it worked."

"It might help if I know what happened the last day you saw me."

Chapter 25

Logan thought Luz seemed very nice, but her husband was weird. Obviously, he was on something. He was staring at a magazine as if he were reading, but had yet to turn a page.

"The last time I saw you was the night before you disappeared. I tucked you in, the way I always did, then read you a story."

A fond smile touched the old woman's lips, softening her stern expression. He wished he remembered her, but he didn't. His earliest memories were of playing in the dirt with the chickens at the camp.

"The next morning I could not leave my room. I must have eaten something that made me ill. I told one of the maids to take care of you."

There was a long silence, broken only by the steady drumbeat of rain on the roof, then Kelly asked, "Why didn't Ginger take care of Logan?"

"She loved only *todilhil*—whiskey. Children did not interest Ginger, not even her own."

"Did the maid let Logan go riding?" asked Kelly.

Luz shrugged as if to say: who knows? "What happened that day began the moment the senator brought you home. I had worked there when the twins were young. The senator called me and asked me to take care of the baby they were adopting.''

"Were you surprised by the adoption?" Kelly asked.

Luz nodded with a wave of the gnarled stick capped by eagle feathers. "I was shocked. Ginger despised children. I raised the twins until the family went to Washington. The senator had just finished his first term when he called to tell me they were adopting. I could not imagine why he would want another child. He was interested only in his career.''

Logan knew his father had been blackmailed into it. Protecting his reputation had been upper most in Haywood Stanfield's mind. But how had he persuaded Ginger to accept another child?

"Did he give any explanation?" Kelly asked.

"No. I did not want to take the job." Luz gaze shifted toward the fire, and Logan's sixth sense kicked in, telling him that she was holding back something. "The senator offered me much, much money. I agreed to work there again.''

"Why didn't you want to take the job?" Logan asked.

Luz glared at her husband as he took something out of the dish near the kerosene lamp. It looked like a black pumpkin seed. A peyote button, Logan realized. The man popped it in to his mouth and sucked, noisily on the seed that would make him high.

From military bulletins, Logan knew peyote had been approved for use in Native American church services on military bases with the consent of the commanding officer. It could not be used on ships or planes because it induced hallucinations. Peyote had religious importance and wasn't supposed to be addicting, but unless Logan missed his guess, Luz's husband used the drug too frequently to escape the real world. And put an added burden on Luz.

"I did not want to be responsible for the twins," Luz said as she turned to Logan and ignored her husband's slurping. "They were born as evil as the north wind.''

"Navajos believe that all evil comes from the North," Kelly explained.

"The twins did bad things, terrible things."

"Like what?" Kelly gently prodded.

"Yes. The only animals that were safe from Tyler were the horses. He knew his father would never forgive him if anything happened to one of them. He was always sacrificing rabbits, catching them and then crippling them so he and Alyx could watch the coyotes tear them apart."

"Couldn't you stop them?" asked Kelly, her concerned frown reflecting her love for animals.

"I went to his parents, but Tyler called me a liar. Alyx protected her brother every time, telling lie after lie. I wanted to quit, but my husband was not working. We had four small children. I needed the money."

Logan watched Kelly react to Luz's pained expression and the emotion in her voice. "I can understand how difficult it must have been. Didn't Woody see what was happening?"

"He was rarely around. I went to him, and he said he would talk to the twins. Nothing changed. Things became much worse when Benson gave Tyler a rifle for his seventh birthday."

"What an idiot," Kelly cried, "giving a gun to a child."

"The senator is terrible with guns, but Benson is an expert marksman. He taught the boy to shoot just the way he taught Ginger. Later he taught Alyx. They're all excellent shots— except Woody.

"Tyler was not content to shoot rabbits and squirrels. He brought down a great blue heron. It was a very, very sad day. Killing for no reason angers the gods. Thunder and lightning ravaged the area, washing out the road to their home." Luz shook the stick as if she wanted to hit something.

"When the senator was elected, the family moved to Washington for most of the year. I found another job. I did not make as much money, but I was happier. The gods were happy, the sun shined every day."

"Did you need money? Is that why you returned?" Logan asked, realizing the rain had almost stopped. It pattered softly on the roof and pecked now and then against the window.

"My son needed an operation to correct his limp. The tribal clinic would do the surgery, but months of physical therapy would be required.'' Luz put the stick in her lap and stroked the feather. ''I took the money, but told the senator that I would not be responsible for the twins.''

''Who took care of them?'' Kelly asked, leaning forward slightly.

''The senator assured me that the twins would only be home during breaks. When they were home, Ginger and Benson would be responsible for them. They would live in Washington most of the time.''

''Wouldn't the baby go to Washington, too?''

Luz shook her head slowly. ''The senator told me the baby would stay here until he was old enough to go to boarding school.''

So what if his old man hadn't cared enough about him to want him around. He didn't give a damn. But it made him uncomfortable to know that Luz had cared about him, yet he had no memory of it.

''Didn't you find it odd that he would adopt a baby, then leave it here while he was in Washington?'' Logan asked.

''Yes. I thought it was very strange and told my husband so.'' Luz glanced at her husband who was in la-la land. ''He told me to mind my own business. A year later, I understood.''

''What happened?'' Kelly wanted to know.

''The family was home from Washington, but the senator was away buying another stallion. Ginger had been drinking more than usual that evening. Benson told her something and she began screaming and cursing.''

He struggled to imagine Ginger pitching a fit. She seemed semi-catatonic like Luz's husband. In another world. Or was it just an act?

''Everyone could hear what they were saying. It was a Sunday, and most of the servants had the day off, but I was there. The twins were watching television nearby, so they did not miss their mother screaming: 'Logan is Woody's son! He did it to pay me back, didn't he?' That is when I knew why the senator had adopted you.''

''What did adopting me have to do with paying back Ginger?'' Logan asked.

"The senator is not the twins' father," Luz revealed in a hushed voice. "Ginger kept screaming over and over that Woody was going to leave his money to his real son and cut her children out of the will. This was the only time Ginger ever seemed to care about the twins."

"Did she say who the twins' father is?" Kelly asked. "Is it Benson?"

Luz shook her head, gripping the feathered stick in one hand. "No, Benson was not the father. He said something about telling her to stay away from that gambler."

Logan asked, "Did the twins hear all this?"

"Yes. I tried to get them to go to their room, but it was impossible."

"Did they seem upset by the news?" Kelly asked.

"No. I think they knew that Woody wasn't their father. They always called him Woody, never father. That night Alyx kept saying, 'Little bastard Logan isn't going to get all Woody's money.' Tyler also seemed more concerned about the money than not being Woody's own son."

Luz's eyes narrowed slightly as she directed her next words to him. "Ginger grabbed a butcher knife in the kitchen. She threatened to slit your throat. I ran to the nursery and locked myself in with you. She pounded on the door, cursing me and saying I was fired. Benson finally dragged her away."

"Oh, my God," Kelly cried, a frantic look in her expressive eyes.

Logan felt . . . nothing. The nickname, Nine Lives, sure as hell fit. He had eluded death several times as a Cobra. It didn't surprise him that as a young child his life had been threatened. Nothing surprised him.

Except Kelly.

He shifted his thoughts—easily—to the way she'd behaved in the car. He was looking forward to tonight, to the next six months. Hell, at the way things were going, he wouldn't want to leave her to take the next Cobra assignment.

"I do not know what Benson said to Ginger, but the next morning, she was herself again. She ignored Logan and the twins. The senator returned but the scene I expected never occurred. Things seemed normal.''

"I'll bet Ginger threatened to tell the world about his illegitimate son, if he divorced her," Kelly said.

"He was going to divorce her and marry Suzanne," Logan reminded Kelly.

"You are talking about the woman who was foolish enough to marry Tyler." Luz pointed at the fire with the feathered stick. "They killed her."

"How do you know?" Logan asked.

"I am an *ahnii*, my clan's wisest person. I know these things. I recognize *adant' ti*—evil—when I see it. I am also a *yataa-lii*—a shaman who identifies witches. They are all witches, Benson, Ginger, Alyx, and Tyler. The minute I heard Suzanne had died, I knew they had murdered her."

Logan didn't buy any of the witchcraft b.s. He'd talked to Uma enough to realize Navajos saw *Anti 'll*—witchcraft—in many things. What he needed was hard facts, a chance to discover who was after him.

Kelly asked, "Who do you think killed Suzanne?"

"Does it matter?" Luz countered with a shrug. "Suzanne is dead. The evil ones are still among us."

Logan could see the woman harbored a deep mistrust of all of the Stansfields mixed with a little fear that Navajos had of all "witches." The feeling she was withholding something persisted, even stronger now.

"What happened after Ginger and the twins discovered that I was Woody's son?" Logan asked, deciding to close the discussion of Suzanne's death. All Luz had to go on was her instincts. She was probably right, but it didn't tell them who was out of to get him.

"Nothing"—she reached down and stowed the feathered stick under her rocker—"life went on."

Kelly had warned Logan that many Native Americans were reluctant to lie or discuss things with strangers. You had to ease the truth out of them a bit at a time.

"I was looking at Logan's medical records," Kelly said. "He certainly had a lot of accidents. Was he hard to handle?"

"He was no worse than other boys his age. My sons were terribly difficult."

"All of Logan's injuries occured when the family was home during the senate breaks, right?"

Logan knew Kelly was guessing here, but he gave her credit for thinking of a way to get the truth out of Luz.

"Yes. That is when he had problems."

"Was Ginger or Benson abusing him?" Kelly asked gently.

Her brows drew together in an agonized expression as she turned away from them and gazed into the fire. "They all were—all except the senator."

Logan tried to imagine himself as a child, living with the Stansfields but he couldn't. Life before the camp was just a black hole. If he'd been physically abused, it had been nothing more than an introduction to life in the camp.

"What do you mean?" Kelly asked when it was clear that Luz wasn't going to elaborate without prodding.

"Ginger and Benson would leave him alone at times when a child should be watched. That is how his back was burned when he fell against the barbecue. He fell out of the sycamore and broke his arm. Tyler was with him. I am certain Tyler purposely broke the branch."

"If he had, wouldn't I have told you?" he asked.

"I asked, but you didn't see it. You were very young. Tyler is sneaky."

"What about Woody? Did you tell him?" Kelly asked.

"I tried, but he said I was overly protective. These were accidents nothing more. I could not prove him wrong. I never actually *saw* anything. They are evil, devious people. All I could do was make certain I never took a day off while they were home."

"Thank you for helping me." His words didn't express his gratitude. All his life, he'd been on his own, responsible for himself. It had never occurred to him that anyone had cared this much about him.

It was hard to imagine this old woman, protecting him against the ruthless Stanfields. He thought he was brave, but this woman was truly courageous. Hardships had marked her life, he decided, judging from the small cabin without any modern conveniences. He doubted her zoned-out husband had ever been much help. She had been forced to work for the Stanfields to support her family.

Luz Tallchief had been the only one to protect him at a time when he'd been too young to guard his back. Was there any way to thank someone who had done this? He had never needed to thank anyone. He honestly didn't know where to start, but he felt the need to say something.

"What can I do for you?"

She leaned toward him, her clouded ebony eyes, narrowing. "Leave—now. This time they may succeed in killing you."

"Don't worry about me. Let me help you . . . somehow." He hated owing anyone anything, especially a kind old lady who'd protected him as a child. He wanted to give her money, but knew she would find it insulting.

"There is nothing you can do for me. Save yourself."

"Perhaps he can, if you tell us the whole story of what happened the day he disappeared," Kelly said.

Luz gripped the arms of the rocker and levered herself to her feet. She lumbered over to the window and gazed out. Logan glanced at Kelly, wondering why Luz wouldn't discuss this with them. Kelly arched one eyebrow and pointed at him, indicating he should speak up.

"Please talk to me. You're the only person who can help me."

Luz stared out at the clearing sky for a moment, then turned to face them. "I believe someone put something in my food to make me ill that day. I think they saw how I watched you all the time and wanted me out of the way."

"He was lucky to have you," Kelly said with an encouraging smile.

Luz returned to her rocker and sat down again, looking directly at Logan. "There had been too many 'accidents.' I feared one of them would kill you. You did not return that day, but I did not discover this until you had been missing for hours."

"Did he actually go riding with the twins?" Kelly asked.

"Yes, they all stopped to look at something and got off the horses. One of them pushed him from behind into a steep ravine."

"Oh, my God!" Kelly cried, grasping his arm.

"Who pushed me?" Logan asked, not in the least surprised by the news. There was something about the twins that had alerted him the very first day he returned home.

"You didn't see if Tyler did it or Alyx. When Jim Cree and I found you, it was dark, and you were sobbing your heart out. A moutain lion was hovering nearby."

"He wouldn't have lived until morning." Kelly's stricken look made him take her hand. She was too sweet, too trusting to imagine anyone wanting to hurt a child.

Logan knew he should feel something, but he didn't. Luz thought she'd done him a favor, and maybe she had. Life in the camp had been hell. Still, it was better than dying.

What doesn't kill you makes you stronger. So true.

"The twins went home and didn't tell anyone, hoping Logan would die," Kelly said, bitterness underscoring every word. "They deliberately led the searchers in the wrong direction. Do you have any idea if they acted on their own or did Ginger and Benson help them?"

"I do not know," Luz responded. "The twins were fifteen. They were capable of anything."

During his training as a Cobra, Logan had studied fear and knew there was an exact spot in the brain where receptors triggering fear were located. His immediate response to the twins had been hate. He wondered if in some primitive way his brain had retained the past he could no longer recall, activating his instant aversion to them.

"What did you and Jim do with Logan after you found him?" Kelly asked.

"I had overheard Benson telling Ginger that Logan's mother was Amanda McCord. She was living in Scottsdale. I thought it best that she take back her son before they killed him."

Kelly measured him with a cool, appraising look. He knew she was astonished to learn that he had been with good old

Amanda. He had deliberately deceived Kelly, leading her to believe a couple had kidnapped him.

"You never told anyone about this?" Logan asked.

"No. An *ahnii* must earn the trust of her clan. Lying, taking a child. These are evil things that skinwalkers—witches—do, not an *ahnii*. I believe I had done the best thing for you, but I never wanted anyone to know. Please, do not tell a soul."

Chapter 26

Kelly left Luz Tallchief's house, walking beside Logan. His eyes scanned the area, the way he always did. He tilted his head a fraction of an inch as he checked, reminding Kelly of a wolf picking up a scent. A lone wolf.

The storm had climbed higher up the mountains to where they'd camped. The runoff from the rain had spawned furrows in the red soil, producing a melodious sound like a brook. The air was still so laden with moisture that she could almost wade through it.

"What's that?" Logan asked as they reached her car.

From the house a singsong chant rose above nature's music. Kelly immediately recognized the chant Uma often used, but Kelly was so upset with Logan that she could hardly speak. "It's a *hozonji*—a good luck chant. Luz is asking the holy ones to bring you luck."

Without responding, he opened the car door for her and she climbed in. He got behind the wheel and started the engine. He'd lied to her about his mother, deliberately leading her to believe that a couple had found him.

Worse, she had reported the story that way in the *Exposé* article. Her earlier mistake had caused a woman's death. If anyone discovered she had again printed unverified information, her career was truly finished.

This time forever.

She planned to stay in Sedona, but who knew what might happen in the future? After her article on Logan's return, her career possibilities had seemed limitless. If the truth were uncovered, she might not be able to work even in a bi-weekly newspaper like her grandfather's.

Logan could have told her the truth, but he had mislead her on purpose. Had he deliberately sabotaged her career? Why? she wondered.

If she expected an explanation, she could forget it. Logan's attention was focused on starting the car. He didn't give a hoot about her.

"Luz saved your life, but you certainly didn't seem very grateful." She tried to temper the bitterness in her voice, but it was impossible. "She risked her reputation as an *ahnii* and the respect of her clan, not to mention the legal charges she could face. There's no statute of limitation for kidnapping."

Logan backed the car around and headed down the road, chuckling.

"What's so damn funny?"

He turned to her with a smile that could have melted both polar caps, his father's charismatic smile. This time, it didn't faze Kelly.

"See how great we are together? We're like an old married couple—fighting."

"I fail to see any humor in this. Alyx or Tyler tried to kill you once. They're going to try again, or they wouldn't have bugged the house."

"What makes you think Ginger and Benson weren't in on it?" He slowed the car to take a curve in the road. "One of the twins pushed me, but Ginger and Benson took their sweet time getting help."

"True, I'll bet they all hoped you wouldn't survive the night, but I think Tyler pushed you. He's the one who tortured animals at an early age. He enjoys killing."

"Tyler may enjoy killing but Luz has him pegged right. He's

devious, sneaky. If he used brucine to kill his wife, it was because it's hard to detect. He bugged the house so he'll know what we're doing. He's going to pull something when we least expect it.''

"Try to think like him, right?'' The anger had gone out of her voice, but it was still seething inside her, burning like acid.

"Yes. I expected him to have pulled something by now. Tyler is not the type to be very patient. Everything has been handed to him on a silver platter. He hasn't a clue about how to wait. There are snakes in the Amazon who can stay for days without moving a muscle, then—wham—they strike. That's not Tyler.''

"But is it Alyx? She could be the one who pushed you.''

"No, she's just as spoiled. If I were them, I would strike when we are in South America. An accident. A run-in with roadside bandits. The possibilities are limitless. That's why I don't want anyone to know where we're going. As soon as we have the adoption certification, I'll order airline tickets to Quito. Tell everyone we're taking a smaller plane from there out to the Galapagos Islands.''

"Oh, my God,'' she cried as they rounded the turn, then came to bone-jarring halt. The low spot on the road was now a rising creek. "Around here, we call these gully-gushers. You might as well turn off the engine. It'll be at least fifteen minutes, maybe longer, before the water level drops enough to safely cross.''

Logan shut off the engine and turned to her. "Okay, Kelly, you're dying to let me have it with both barrels. Go for it,'' he said with as much enthusiasm as a man about to hear the Last Rites.

The urge to smack his handsome face was almost impossible to resist. "Don't you have any feelings? That wonderful woman saved you. Now she's stuck way out here supporting a husband who's high on peyote. A quick 'thank you' and a half-hearted offer to help just isn't good enough.''

His smile vanished, replaced by a frown and the amusement left his eyes. "I don't have much in the way of feelings, so I'm not good at expressing them. I'm grateful for what Luz did. I was planning on asking you what I could do to help her. I think offering her money would be crass—"

"She has too much pride to take it. By saving you, she forfeited her honor. Nothing will give that back to her."

"I thought I might be able to help her granddaughter. Since she's living with them, something must have happened to her parents."

"That's a good idea. Let's have Uma find out what the situation is," Kelly said, her eyes on the water flowing across the road.

"Why did you lie to me about your mother? The whole world assumes a couple kidnapped you. My reputation as a journalist is shaky because I printed something I couldn't verify. Now, thanks to you, I've done it again."

"Everyone assumed someone abducted me. I just rolled with the idea. If you keep quiet, no one will ever know. Sure as hell, Luz won't talk."

Kelly lost it, yelling, "That's it! That's all you have to say? Don't you think you owe me an explanation? Where were you all those years? Where's your mother now?"

His expression changed, anger transforming his features into something resembling a death mask, yet when he spoke, his voice was low, controlled. "I don't owe anyone an explanation, not even you."

Logan had inherited his father's ability to turn on the charm, but beneath that veneer was a man with a heart buried so deep, she'd have to go to hell to find it. She tried to find a logical explanation for why Logan wouldn't discuss his past with her. It must have to do with something illegal, she decided.

All sorts of scenarios paraded through her mind. A child pornography ring. Dealing drugs. Perhaps his mother worked as a prostitute.

"What if they visit Luz Tallchief? I told you we should have gotten rid of that worthless Indian long ago."

"Never kill unnecessarily. The old bat doesn't know anything."

It was after midnight, and they were in the huge marble tub in her bathroom. Candles flickered in crystal votives lining the tub, giving off the aromatic scent of sage.

"Luz is smarter than she looks. You just don't like Indians, so you're prejudiced. Remember how she guarded precious little Logan? She knew we were going to kill him."

He shook his head, holding one hand up to the flickering light. Oh, shit. His skin looked like a prune. She loved to soak in the tub for hours, then do it doggie style. The dog bit, he liked, soaking sucked the big one.

"Forget Luz," he told her. "If she knew anything, she would have blabbed when they were searching for Logan, or later when Woody offered the reward."

"What about the couple who picked up Logan? He might not remember what happened now, but then being pushed would have been fresh in his mind. Undoubtedly he told them."

"They are not going to resurface and admit to kidnapping a child, are they?"

"No, I guess not."

She smiled at him, then took his hand and put it between her legs. She was so smooth, so sexy. Best of all, she'd done it for him. His dick was already rigid, begging for action.

"The agent I hired reported something I don't like," he said as he fondled the smooth folds between her thighs. "Suzanne's mother was at Hair and Now, getting a cut. She told everyone in the shop Kelly had visited her."

"Kelly's a real bitch. Why is she stirring up trouble? She must suspect something."

"She can't prove anything. That's why we used brucine."

She giggled, more a crackle really, then said, "I like your new plan. I won't be happy until Kelly gets what she deserves along with Logan."

Pop took Kelly and Logan to Cilantro's in the Tlaquepaque center to celebrate receiving their adoption certification. They were seated around a table, and Jasper was lying next to Pop.

"How do you pronounce it again?" Logan asked Kelly as

he pointed to Tlaquepaque on the menu. He'd been coaxing her to talk to him again. Not that she hadn't been talking, she had, but there was an unmistakable coolness since Kelly discovered he had lied to her.

"It's pronounced Too-locky-pocky," Kelly informed him without sparing a glance in his direction.

"Tlaquepaque is a suburb of Guadalajara. This center was built to look just like it," Pop added in an awkward attempt to mask Kelly's chilly attitude.

"Bring me the bill," Logan told the waiter as he handed them menus. "Do you have a 1984 bottle of Opus 1?"

"Yes, sir," the waiter said, impressed by his choice. "I'll bring it right away."

"Let me pay. This was my idea," Pop protested. "I made the reservation."

"Giving me a place to stay where the media wouldn't find me was a big help," Logan said. "I want to do something for you."

"Thanks," Pop replied. "In that case I'll have the most expensive thing on the menu."

"I think you should order filet mignon for Jasper, too," Kelly said.

"Jasper wants a rib-eye. He told me so," Logan teased her back. He would have bet his life that Kelly couldn't stay angry long. It wasn't in her nature. By morning, after he'd made love to her all night, she would be herself again.

Logan leaned over to pet the retriever whose ears where perked up at the sound of his name. He pulled his hand back before he touched the dog. He was getting too attached to these people and this dog. He had to be able to walk out without a backward glance.

The way he'd left his mother and the camp.

"Sedona has some of the best art galleries in the Southwest," Pop said while the waiter uncorked the cabernet and Logan sampled it. "The ones in Tlaquepaque are excellent. After dinner—"

Kelly interrupted with, "Don't look now, but guess who walked in?"

Haywood Stanfield led Ginger and Benson into the restaurant. Following them were Alyx and Tyler. Did they always hang around his old man like rock band groupies? Didn't any of them have lives of their own?

Undisguised hatred flared in Kelly's brown eyes. He fought back a smile. She was more pissed than he was about one of them trying to kill him. She honestly cared about him, Logan thought with stunned surprise. Aw, hell.

His mother had never told him that anyone had tried to kill him. She'd informed him in that cutting way of hers that the family who had adopted him did not want him. She had been forced to take him back, but he shouldn't get any wild ideas about her giving a damn about him.

The older he grew, the more he looked like his father. Of course, he hadn't known that. But he should have guessed by the way his mother glared at him. Her hatred increasing each day. He avoided her—when he could—not wanting the whack that would surely come if he gave her the slightest reason.

Sometimes she didn't need a reason.

Nobody had cared about him. The message had been etched into his brain at an impressionable age. He must have been hurt by it at first, but he'd gotten over feeling sorry for himself.

What doesn't kill you makes you stronger.

He did not need a woman trying to protect him. Especially not Kelly.

"Logan," Pop whispered, cutting off his thoughts. "I used the phone to make the reservations. I'll bet that's how the Stanfields happened to decide to come here to dinner."

"I'm sure you're right," Kelly said. "They'll ask when we're leaving for South America and where we're going."

"Be certain you don't give anyone a clue about where we're really going," Logan cautioned Pop. Kelly's grandfather was the only weak link that Logan could think of. He trusted him, but you never knew what little slip could give you away.

"Even if I have another heart attack, I'm not—"

Kelly cut him off. "Yes, in that case have the doctor call us."

What could Logan say? Shit happened. If Pop was hospitalized, the doctor would have to locate Kelly. He raised his wineglass for a toast. "Here's to our trip and adopting Rafi."

The clicked glasses, then sipped the wine. Out of the corner of his eye, he noticed the waiter guiding the Stanfields in their direction.

Woody stopped beside Logan. "I understand you two passed the home visit with flying colors."

"Yes. Thanks for the help." Logan mustered a smile. He hated asking anyone to do him a favor, especially this man.

Tyler examined the wine bottle and gave a low whistle. "Hey, Gus," he said to the waiter. "You picked out a great wine for them."

"Mr. McCord selected the Opus," Gus replied.

"Really?" Tyler looked at Logan as if he were a bug that should be squashed before it scuttled away and multiplied.

The look on Kelley's face almost made Logan laugh. Unless he missed his guess, it was all Kelly could do to stop herself from hurling the expensive cabernet in Tyler's face. Logan almost wished he could hate Tyler as much as she did, but he'd seen enough evil in the world to classify Tyler Stanfield as a rank amateur.

Even so, amateurs could be dangerous. Deadly.

"How was Devil's Arch?" Alyx asked.

"We didn't go there," Kelly said with a smile that was a shade too bright. "We were sidetracked."

"Devil's Arch?" Ginger asked as if they were discussing a planet in another galaxy instead of one of Sedona's most famous red rock formations. The woman had an I.Q. in the minus column. Either that or she was one hell of an actress.

Benson said to her, "That's where they were going on their honeymoon, remember? The red rock arch outside of town."

"Oh, yes," Ginger replied in a breathy voice.

Logan doubted she remembered a damn thing. Benson had prompted Ginger so many times that she automatically responded. A very strange relationship. Benson was about as friendly as a pit bull, but he treated Ginger with unexpected patience and tenderness while his old man looked the other way.

"I see you've brought your dog," Woody said to Pop.

"To a restaurant?" Alyx's soft coral lips uttered a gasp worthy of a phone sex call.

"In France, they are allowed to bring dogs into restaurants," Kelly said, her tone much too sweet. "They're so cultured, don't you think?"

Bingo! Alyx managed a faint nod. At dinner the woman had made no secret her admiration for all things French. She wasn't about to admit she found this disgusting. As far as Logan could see, people tacked French onto things when they wanted to overcharge you.

"Jasper is training to become a guide dog." Pop pointed to the orange vest with Guide Dog Trainee stenciled in black. "He's allowed to go anywhere."

"I've always admired your work with guide dogs," Woody said. "I wish I could do as well with my horses. I've got this new colt that refuses to eat much."

"Try putting him in the stable with the mares," Kelly suggested. "All that testosterone in the barn is frightening him."

For a split second Woody looked confused, not knowing if she was serious or not. Then he flashed a politician's smile.

"Where are you going on your honeymoon?" Tyler asked.

Logan knew Kelly had been anticipating the question. "Well, first we're off to the Galapagos Islands. Then we're leaving ourselves open."

"Honeymoon? Honeymoon? I thought they already . . ." Ginger gazed at Benson.

Logan watched Woody who was smiling as if everyone had a wife as dumb as a bag of dirt. Okay, she was still a looker even at her age, but nobody was home upstairs.

"They took a short honeymoon here," Pop explained, his tone kind. It was obvious to Logan that he felt sorry for the woman. "Then they're going on a longer honeymoon in South America."

"Do you fly directly to the Galapagos Islands?" Alyx asked Kelly.

"There are no direct flights. The islands are about six hundred miles from Equador's coast. We'll fly into Quito, then catch a smaller plane.''

''I've always wanted to go there,'' Alyx said.

The way she looked at Kelly sent a prickle of alarm through Logan. He was never concerned for himself. He knew how to watch his back, and trusted his own survival skills that had been honed at a very early age. But Kelly didn't have the same abilities, making her vulnerable.

For the first time in his life, Logan realized he was begining to care about a person who wasn't just an assignment in his anti-terrorist work. How in the hell had he let that happen?

Chapter 27

"What do you mean they're not dead?"

Her tone irritated him a bit. He had to rein her in. She wanted Logan and Kelly out of the way so badly that he was afraid she might do something that would expose them.

"The agent I hired accessed the American Express database and saw Logan had charged two first-class American Airlines tickets to Quito, Ecuador. He flew down the day ahead of them and met the flight. They weren't on it or any other flight that came in for the next two days."

"Maybe they took another airline, and he missed them. Did he check the hotels? Did he see if they were on a flight to the Galapagos Islands?"

They were in his suite, buck naked in his in his favorite spot for sex, on the polar bear rug in front of the fireplace. It wasn't even noon yet, but everyone else had gone to Phoenix, so they'd taken advantage of being alone. She'd brought a bottle of Cristal, believing they would have good news to celebrate. He'd waited until they were sipping the expensive champagne to tell her what had happened.

"The Israeli checked everywhere. They're not in Ecuador."

"That bitch! You saw the way Kelly acted at Cilantro's. She—"

"Let's keep cool and use our heads. Obviously, they suspect someone is after them."

She sipped her champagne for a moment, then said, "I have an idea."

She was sexy, the only woman for him, but she wasn't the brightest bulb in the chandelier. Not wanting to hurt her feelings, he listened politely.

"We torture Kelly's grandfather until we get it out of him."

He waited a moment, pretending to seriously consider her plan. "Trent Farley will die before divulging their secret."

"It's worth a try. It'll be fun." She topped off her champagne, then returned the half-full bottle into the silver urn beside the tub. "If we threatened to kill that dog he drags everywhere, then cut off its ears or something, I'll bet he'd tell."

She was getting bloodthirsty. That had the potential to be really dangerous. If someone needed to die like Suzanne, he preferred to use something untraceable like brucine.

He had to steer her back in his direction. "There is one thing we might try. Kelly is very friendly with *Exposés* publisher, Matthew Jensen. I wonder if she told him where she's going."

Her lip drooped into the familiar pout she used when she didn't get her way. "We can't very well just call him up and ask."

"No, but what if I posed as someone from Social Services doing a background check for adoption certification?"

"Great idea! Let me call him. He's more likely to tell a woman than a man."

She had a point. It took a few minutes to go over what to say, then phone Matthew Jensen. Standing beside her, they shared the receiver.

He kept a pad of paper and his Mont Blanc pen in his hand in case he needed to jot down instructions. She didn't have the finesse this might take, or he would have gone in the other room and listened on the extension.

"Mr. Jensen," she said when he came on the line, "this is Muriel Ames from the Arizona State Department of Social

Services. I'm reviewing an application filed by Mr. and Mrs. Logan McCord to be certified to adopt. Kelly McCord listed you as a personal reference."

"I'll be happy to give her a reference." Jensen didn't seem surprised.

"I've known Kelly since we were at Yale together. She's a fabulous person. She'll make a great mother." Jensen went on and on, about Saint Kelly's career and boring them.

"Do you know Mr. McCord?" she interrupted.

"I've never met him."

There was a hint of curtness to his voice, a certain finality. Jensen was about to hang up. He scribbled the next question on the pad as she stalled, asking him if he knew Trent Farley, a fair question considering the newlyweds were planning to live with him for a time.

She glanced down, read what he'd written, then asked, "Do you know of any reason the McCords should be denied an adoption certificate? Anything at all?"

"No . . . not really."

"If it's a minor problem, we can provide excellent counseling." He gave her credit for picking up on the slight hitch in Jensen's voice.

"It's not a problem exactly. It's the whole situation. Logan McCord was an illegitimate child. Now he's married Kelly and is going to Venezuela to adopt her late husband's illegitimate son. I'm not certain about how Logan McCord will deal with this, considering his own troubled past. I suggest allowing them to go to the Elorza orphanage and adopt Rafael Zamora, but I would counsel them for a time to see if McCord is adjusting properly."

"I'll be handling the case myself." she assured him. "I'll see they get what help they may need. I know you're a busy man, Mr. Jensen. Thank you for your time."

She slammed the receiver down with a delighted shriek. "Hot damn! I did it! I did it!"

"You were great."

"This calls for a celebration." She poured the last of the

champagne into her glass. "I have a new toy. It's a really big vibrator. It's called a Joystick."

"I'm scared," Kelly admitted.

Logan pushed his sunglasses to the top of his head, dragging back a hank of chestnut-brown hair. "Of what?"

"A hundred things maybe more."

They were sitting under an elm in Elorza's only sidewalk café. After three days in Caracas, taking the initial steps in the international adoption process, they had finally been granted the necessary papers. Traveling south in their rental car, they'd driven across the *llanos*, a vast plain like the pampas.

It was spring and lagoons filled with small crocodiles called *babas* dotted the plains. Clouds of colorful birds in dazzling colors from brilliant crimson to iridescent green would unexpectedly erupt from the ponds. There would be so many of them that they would block the sun like a giant cloud.

The awesome landscape had distracted Kelly, but it was ungodly hot. The air conditioning in the car had wheezed to nothing more than a whisper of warm air a few hours out of Caracas. Wet heat had surfed across the blacktop road in visible waves. What would it be like in the dead of summer?

The *llanos* was cattle country, Venezuela's wild frontier. Caracas had been modern like New York City with most people living in skyscrapers, but this area was isolated. Hours passed before they'd met another car.

It was an interesting country, like none other she had ever visited. She tried to learn as about it and absorb as many local terms as possible, so she could help Rafi remember his native land.

One road linked the villages and Texas-sized ranches called *hatos*. Elorza was the largest town along the route. There wasn't much choice in accommodations, so they checked into the Vista de Nada which was a *posada,* a very small hotel.

View of Nothing. It fit the hotel where the red floral carpet was worn thin in numerous places and filled with the dust of countless soles. The pungent air was stagnant, heavy with humidity and the loamy smell of the tropics.

"I'm not sure we have time to discuss over one hundred fears," Logan said. "How about prioritizing and start with what you fear the most."

He leaned across the small table and covered her hand with his. She'd left the stunning diamond rings behind at Logan's suggestion. He'd bought her a slim gold band that wouldn't be as noticeable in a third-world country. She watched as his thumb slid over the band while his fingers encircled her hand.

It was an oddly affectionate gesture. In the days immediately following their wedding, Logan rarely touched her unless he wanted to have sex. Then day by day he began to touch her more and more frequently.

At first, he touched her in a way that could be considered casual. A hand on her waist to guide her into a restaurant. Taking her hand to help her out of the car.

She remembered exactly when he'd first touched her in a truly affectionate way. They'd been having coffee on the terrace the morning the social worker was coming to certify them. Her anxiety must have been etched across her forehead. Logan had reached over and taken her hand in his, the way he had just now.

"Kelly? Talk to me. Tell me what you're worried about."

It flashed through her mind that she was always confiding in him, revealing her innermost feelings, yet he never shared his thoughts with her. She doubted he ever would. At first she'd been angry that he'd lied about his mother, but she'd forgiven him. How long could she be angry with a man who was being so incredibly helpful?

"What am I afraid of? You know, parent stuff. Will I be a good enough mother? What if I do something that messes Rafi up for life? What if—"

"Kelly, don't torment yourself. You'll do the best you can. Just be sure to give him plenty of what's important—love."

Love. Something you never had, she thought as she gazed into his blue eyes. Again, she wondered about his youth. She wasn't sure why—certainly he hadn't confided in her—but she was convinced his childhood hadn't been happy.

What had his mother done to him? Where had she taken him? Kelly wondered again and again. And why did he refuse to discuss it?

"I've always wanted children. I love Rafi already."

"I know you do." He squeezed her hand for a moment, then reached in his pocket. He tossed a few *bolivars* on the table.

They'd just had coffee and *arepas*, tasty corn rolls, but Logan had left a generous tip. One thing she'd learned about him was his sensitivity to the poverty around them. He was never rude to people that Tyler and Alyx would have relegated to ranks of the untouchables, and he always over-tipped.

"We better get going." He slung his backpack over one shoulder.

They crossed the small plaza, hand in hand. Vendors were setting up their stalls in the town square that was the heart of Elorza. Normally Kelly would have been interested in their wares, but today her mind was on Rafi.

At last she was going to be a mother.

Of two children. She was almost positive she was pregnant. Her period was rarely late, and she was overdue by several days. She wasn't surprised. They'd had nonstop sex since their wedding night.

Not that she minded. She discovered that she thoroughly enjoyed it. Being with Logan had released something shamefully wanton in her, a lustful side of herself she didn't wish to examine too closely.

Her only decision was whether or not to tell Logan. Even though she'd been so angry with him that she'd felt justified in blowing him off when they returned to Sedona by keeping the baby a secret, she'd reversed her decision. When she'd confirmed she was pregnant, she would tell Logan and make it clear she expected nothing from him.

Logan slowed down as they rounded the corner and approached a blind man sitting at a card table with a telephone on it and a cigar box of coins.

"What's he doing?" she asked.

"Making a living the only way he can. If you're disabled in South America, you aren't going to get any help from the state. That man lives in the building behind him. See the phone cord coming out of the window? He has telephone service, while many others do not. His neighbors pay him to use his."

"Aren't there any telephone booths?"

"Big cities have a few. This is how blind people support themselves in South America. The curbside division of Ma Bell." He walked toward the man. "Let's call Caracas and check on our airline reservations."

"But we don't know if we'll get Rafi today or—"

The light dawned, and she couldn't help smiling. Logan wanted to have an excuse to give this man money. Undoubtedly, a call to Caracas was much more expensive than local calls his neighbors usually made.

"*Buenos Días,*" Logan greeted the him.

Their fast-paced conversation was difficult to follow, but Kelly did catch a word or two. He handed the man a few coins, then picked up the telephone. The blind man couldn't see, but Kelly didn't miss Logan's finger depressing the button. The call would never appear on the man's bill.

As he rattled on and on to incur an overtime charge, Kelly couldn't help comparing Logan to Daniel. Her husband had suffered through a miserable childhood, being tossed from foster home to foster home. When they'd met, Daniel's need for love had appealed to her.

He'd soaked up all the love she could give, and the attention of anyone who came into his orbit. A man who loved to be the center of attention, Daniel would never have noticed a blind person. Or taken the time to concern himself with his plight.

Daniel's grip on her heart was slowly easing. Time and his betrayal had eroded her love for him. She still cared, but not as much as she once had.

"*Muchas gracias*," Kelly told the man as Logan paid him for the overtime. She was certain his disability had heightened his other senses. The blind man must have detected her presence. It would be rude not to thank him the way she would anyone else.

Logan put his arm around her as they walked to the spot where they had parked the rental car. Vista de Nada was not the type of hotel that had a parking garage or even a dirt lot. They'd parked around the corner from the plaza on a side street.

They drove along the elevated road toward the Sister of the Holy Trinity Orphanage. Riding horses with crude looking saddles with wooden stirrups, *llaneros* were herding cattle nearby, waving their straw cowboy hats to direct the cattle.

"The herd is going to market," Logan explained. "In another month this whole area will be one giant lake. That's why the road is elevated. In a heavy rain, it, too, will be underwater."

"Have you been here before?"

"No, but I downloaded the latest Cobra data on the area. The only time I was in Venezuela was when an oil executive was kidnapped. The oil fields don't look anything like this. That mission was a close call, but we managed to save the guy."

This was as much as he'd ever said about any of his missions. She waited, hoping he would tell her more, but he didn't. She had learned not to press. Pop was right, slowly, a scant inch at a time, Logan was responding to her openness.

"Stop!" she cried, spotting an animal sunning itself in the middle of the road. Whatever it was had fur and ears like a squirrel, but it's tail was more like a rat's. The creature appeared to be in the squirrel family, but it was much larger, the size of a cocker spaniel.

Logan braked, saying, "It's a *capybara*. The largest rodent in the world." He tooted the horn. The *capybara* stood up, shook itself, and blinked myopically at them.

"Amazing! It has webbed feet."

The creature ambled across the road and down the embankment. At the bottom was a small pond. The *capybara* slid into the water and gracefully swam to the other side.

"They're delicious," Logan informed her as he accelerated. "You find them in several countries down here."

"Yuck! It doesn't look like a rat, but all you have to do is say rodent, and I'm not interested in eating it."

"They were almost hunted to extinction. The Pope ruled

that since they have webbed feet and swim, *capybaras* could be classified as fish even though they tasted more like red meat. People who didn't like fish ate them every Friday. Later they were reclassified, but people still eat them. Rafi probably has *capybara* several times a week.''

Kelly gazed out across the vast savanna that stretched endlessly toward the horizon and tried to imagine what Rafi had experienced since the death of his grandmother. He'd lost his mother, too, but he'd been very young. He might not remember her.

''Be ready to pull a cheap bottle of Scotch out of your tote.'' Logan told her as they drove up to the *alcabala*. ''Just in case.''

She had a tote with Scotch and men's Levis for bribes as well as a few things for Rafi. Her hand on the cheap Scotch, she waited to see what would happen at the checkpoint. They'd used two bottles of twenty-year-old Glenlivet in Caracas to smooth along the adoption process. They had two bottles remaining.

Half a dozen soldiers were drinking what had to be warm Polar beer. *Alcabalas* were common in South America, Logan had told her. But she would never become accustomed to having soldiers brandishing machineguns, constantly checking her identification.

Logan greeted them in Spanish and the soldiers waved them through the checkpoint, obviously more interested in beer than examining their passports. She left the bottle in her tote, then pulled out the adoption folder. They rounded a bend in the road and spotted a gray bunker of a building ahead.

''Oh, my God,'' she cried. ''It looks like a prison.''

''It might have been a jail once. Those windows look too small for a normal building.''

They left the rental car on a pad of cracked concrete and went inside. With a sinking sensation, she looked around. Forbidding gray walls and dark hallways without a single light bulb.

''Look at the up side,'' Logan told her. ''It's clean and it's cool considering how hot it is today.''

She couldn't muster a response.

Logan stopped and put his arm around her. ''Look, I'm going

to tell them that we want to adopt Rafael Zamora. I'll claim that he's your cousin's son. That way we won't be shown every kid here, and we'll have an excuse for knowing about Rafi.''

Sister Maria Consuelo was in charge of adoptions. She was unexpectedly young, not looking a day over twenty, and she was obviously taken with Logan from the moment they were shown into her office.

"*Buenos Días*,'' Logan said.

The nun actually blushed. So much for sacred vows. Sister Maria Consuelo was going to have to say a zillion Hail Marys to atone for what she was thinking right now.

Logan introduced Kelly and she managed a cheery, "*Buenos Días*.''

Kelly listened silently, barely able to understand a few words of the conversation, as Logan—all smiles—explained the situation. He handed the nun their adoption file. She pored over it, examining every document.

Kelly decided the young nun merely enjoyed talking to Logan. Unless Kelly missed her bet, the girl came from a poverty-stricken family who had forced her to join the order. One less mouth to feed.

The minutes seemed like eons as the nun discussed each line in the file. Finally, Sister Maria Consuelo closed the folder, beaming at Logan. She said something as she rose, but the only words Kelly grasped were: Rafael Zamora.

Logan turned to Kelly, "She's taking us to see Rafael now. Along the way, she'll give us a tour.''

Kelly lagged back while Sister Maria Consuelo showed Logan the kitchen, which was straight out of the last century, right down to wood-burning ovens, but it was clean. From there they went to the play area where inner tubes hung from trees being used by older children as swings. Off to one side was a sandbox for the younger children.

How sad, Kelly thought, recalling her yard when she'd been a child. Pop had built a mini-amusement park. Some children had too much while other children had nothing.

Sister Maria Consuelo came as close to outright flirting as a nun could without relinquishing her vows, but at last she ran out of things to show them. She guided them down yet another long, dark hall to the dormitory where Rafi was napping with the younger children.

They peeked into the cavernous room. Cots lined the interior like cigars in a box. At the foot of each bed was a small wooden bin. Kelly assumed the children kept their clothes and whatever few things they possessed in the bin.

"It's going great," Logan whispered as Sister Maria Consuelo spoke to the nun in charge of the dormitory.

"They want us to meet Rafi out here in the hall," Logan explained. "That way we won't wake up the other children."

They waited and waited until Kelly began to pace. At last a little boy appeared at the door, holding Sister Maria Consuelo's hand. With one balled up fist, he rubbed his sleepy eyes, then blinked.

He looked so much like Daniel that Kelly inhaled sharply. True blue eyes and jet black hair. A vertical dimple in his chin. As he matured it would be a masculine cleft. He should have been their child, should have had a happy life and never had been in this miserable place.

He was smaller than she expected, and much thinner. Uncertainty masked his young face as he stood there bewildered. She could almost hear him asking himself why the nuns had brought him out. Too well, she remembered being orphaned and feeling lost and vulnerable.

Pop had rescued her, restoring the security that had been so suddenly snatched from her. Rafi had languished here without anyone to reassure him. And love him.

She realized she was concealed by the shadows and Logan's body. Stepping forward, she called, "Rafi."

The child's blue eyes widened, and he gazed at her for a moment as if he'd been struck dumb by a bolt of lightning. Then he sprinted across the corridor full speed, arms flailing. A gap-toothed smile lit his precious face.

In her entire life no one had ever looked at her like that. Rafi wasn't just happy to see her, the darling little boy was thrilled beyond belief.

He hurled himself into her skirt, grabbing her legs with his little arms. "Mommy! Mommy! Mommy!"

Mommy? Obviously the nuns had told him about his new mother.

Rafi jabbered in Spanish, but the only word she understood was "Mommy."

She dropped to her knees to be on eye level with him. Rafi catapulted himself into her arms and smacked her on the cheek. Gripping her neck with all his might, his little fingers tangled in her hair.

"Mommy, Mommy," He kept holding onto her as if he would never let go.

She'd always wanted her own children, but in this moment she knew this little boy was incredibly special. She'd told Logan that she already loved Rafi, and she thought she had, but now she knew what it felt like to love a child with all her heart.

Rafi kept talking to her, his little head tilting slightly to one side as if he expected an answer, but she didn't understand what he was saying.

"What is Rafi trying to tell me?"

"He thinks you're his mother. He's asking why you went away and left him here. Why didn't you come back for him when his *abuela*—grandmother—was called to heaven?" Logan stroked Rafi's head affectionately, but gazed into her eyes with a look she had never seen. For a second she thought she detected the sheen of tears. "He was terrified you'd never come back for him."

Chapter 28

Logan studied Kelly as she reacted to his words. Her brown eyes widened, a puzzled expression on her face.

"Why on earth would Rafi think I'm his mother?"

"I have no idea."

Logan didn't understand what was going on. The word Rafi had used was *"mami"* a Spanish abbreviation of *madre,* which meant mother. *Mami* sounded almost exactly like mommy. But why would the boy say *mami?*

"Señor McCord," called Sister Maria Consuelo.

He turned and listened to her tell him that Rafi might want to take his things with him. Logan seriously doubted the child would need anything he now had once he was with Kelly. She'd been unsure of his size, so she hadn't bought him any clothes. But he had no doubt the minute they returned to Elorza, Kelly would buy the kid a dozen outfits.

"Rafi, *está bien,*" crooned Kelly as Logan walked away. It's all right, she told the child. It was too bad she didn't speak better Spanish. The little boy desperately needed reassurance.

Logan followed the nun into the dormitory, walking as quietly as possible, his pack slung over his shoulder. Several of the children were stirring, and they stared at him as he walked by. It was all he could do not to shudder. They were still young, but in another year or two, these innocent children would know the truth.

They were going to spend their youth in prison.

Not that they had committed any crime other than being born to a mother who died or couldn't keep them. Or didn't want them. But the orphanage was off the beaten path in a country that already had more children than it could handle. Most of these orphans never would find homes.

They would live here until they were old enough to earn a living. Prison by any other name is still a prison, he thought, recalling some similar quote about a rose. The nuns would be kind to these children, but they were too overworked to give them any individual attention.

Love was out-of-the-question.

He thought about the camp where he'd grown up. It, too, had been a prison, but he'd rather have been here, taking his chances with the nuns than spend a week under Zoe's supervision.

''Señor,'' the other nun whispered as she handed him a brown bag that had been used countless times.

He took it and mouthed a *gracias* to her, then he followed Sister Maria Consuelo back to the area where Kelly and Rafi were waiting. The light in the dormitory was very dim, but when he reached the doorway where the light was better, he looked into the bag.

Instantly, he understood why Rafi had mistaken Kelly for his mother.

Ahead of him, Sister Maria Consuelo stopped in her tracks. Logan nearly plowed into her, but dodged the nun in time. They stood silently watching Kelly with Rafi.

Kelly was sitting on the floor, Rafi in her arms. The little boy was beaming up at her as she said something to him. Then Rafi giggled, the happy, totally uninhibited sound only a young child can make. Kelly smiled back at Rafi, but Logan noticed tears in her eyes.

Tears of joy.

The love in her eyes and on her face was impossible to miss.

For a heartbeat, Logan wished he were the little boy. Wished he could remember someone gazing at him with such love and total devotion.

But he wasn't a small child at the mercy of adults any longer. He was his own man. He didn't need anyone to look at him like that, even if some small part of him wanted it.

Another hour passed while they filled out the papers that released Rafi to their custody. The formal adoption procedures would take place when they returned to Arizona. By then Rafi was asleep in Kelly's arms, his thumb in his mouth.

The minute they opened the car door and tried to put the child in the car seat, the boy woke up and bawled so loudly that he could have been heard over the border in Colombia.

"No, *mami,* no," he wailed over and over, gripping Kelly's neck so hard that Logan was concerned. "No, *mami,* no!"

Logan tried to take Rafi, but that only agitated the child more. He flailed at Logan with his skinny, little legs and squalled so hard his face turned crimson.

"Kelly, get in the car and hold Rafi on your lap. There's hardly anyone on the road. It won't hurt to drive back to Elorza, not using the car seat. Obviously, he's terrified that if he lets go, you'll disappear again."

Only when they were settled in the car with Rafi securely planted on Kelly's lap, did the little boy stop crying. By then, he was hiccuping, close to hyperventilating. Logan drove off, wondering if he had cried hysterically when he'd been taken from his mother and given to the Stanfields. He'd been a year old, but given Amanda McCord's coldness and hostility toward him, Logan doubted that he'd pitched a fit like this.

Luz Tallchief had been different from his own mother. Even though he couldn't remember being with Luz now, Logan wondered if he'd cried when they'd been separated. Probably. She'd cared for him, read him stories, and protected him when he'd been terribly vulnerable, unaware danger existed.

The thought depressed him. He wanted to remember Luz; he wanted to think about her cuddling him the way Kelly was cuddling Rafi now. It touched a sweet spot in him, a hidden well spring of inner emotion that almost brought tears to his eyes.

Rafi's hiccups subsided, becoming snuffling sounds. Then, like a candle that had been snuffed, he stopped making noise. The little boy was sound asleep in Kelly's arms, his head resting on her breast, his thumb in his mouth.

"Uma told me to expect this," Kelly told him, whispering. "The papoose drop, she called it. That's when young children exhaust themselves, then fall asleep instantly."

Out of the corner of his eye, he saw Kelly stroking the sleeping boy's head in an instinctive, maternal way. He wondered if Rafi would ever realize how lucky he was.

"I'm shocked Rafi thinks I'm his mother," Kelly said, her voice pitched low.

"It's understandable." He slowed the car and reached over his shoulder to where his backpack was resting on the back seat. The top compartment was open; the brown bag was inside. He located the photograph and handed it to Kelly.

"Oh, my God," she said, probably a little louder than she intended. "This is a picture of me. What—"

"See the holes around it? Someone tacked it to the wall. At the orphanage, I noticed photographs tacked to the wall above some of the beds. I'll bet this photograph was above Rafi's bed the entire time he's been here."

"This is a picture of me with Daniel on the beach of a friend's home in the Hamptons. I remember the exact moment it was taken. How did it find its way to an orphanage in South America?"

The heartfelt anguish in her voice reached him in a disturbing way. He actually felt her frustration. her grief.

"It's pretty obvious what happened," he told Kelly as he stepped on the accelerator. "The grandmother was taking care of Rafi when Daniel and her daughter were killed.

"At some point she went through their things and came across the photograph. She kept it. Maybe she was already ill and expected to die. There must have been some link, some connection between Daniel and his friends in New York."

"Matthew Jensen," Kelly said. "Daniel told Matt all about his affair."

A prickle of alarm waltzed down Logan's spine. A base uncovered. He assured himself the chances of a leak were slim. But a slim chance had killed more than its share of men.

"That must be the explanation. The grandmother was shrewd. She told Rafi that you and Daniel were his parents." He glanced at Kelly and saw she was still cradling the sleeping boy. "Rafi was too young to have a mental image of his mother. She substituted your picture."

"But why?"

"She must have arranged for Jensen to find out about her death. She counted on you coming for Rafi. This it made it easier."

"I guess, but I'll have to tell him the truth."

"Not right away. You'll only confuse him."

"Thank heavens, you made up the story about being related to Rafi. Otherwise the nuns might have been shocked to see how much I look like the woman in the picture."

"We got lucky with that one," he agreed as he stopped the car to let a farmer lead a donkey loaded with firewood across the road.

Kelly gazed at Rafi, admiring his long, gloss-black eye lashes. He was still sleeping in her arms, exhausted from crying. But he was still clutching her, even in sleep terrified she might leave him.

What was she going to tell him? He believed she had deserted him. Not being able to speak the language was a tremendous handicap, she thought as she stroked his head. He shifted, his soft breath fanning her neck.

He was so incredibly precious. She hoped the months he'd spent alone at the orphanage, convinced she'd left him, had not scarred him emotionally. She made up her mind to take him to a child psychiatrist in Phoenix as soon as they returned home.

She was going to have to take a crash course in Spanish.

Being able to communicate with Rafi while he learned English was extremely important to her. Granted, he couldn't have an extensive vocabulary at three, but it would make him much more secure if she spoke his language.

They parked on the side street near the blind man with the telephone. Rafi lifted his head when the car came to a stop. He looked confused for a moment, gazing around him. Then he turned to face Kelly.

"Mommy, Mommy," he cried with a smile that broke her heart. He smacked her on the cheek, then peppered her face with little kisses.

She hugged him, saying, *"Mi Rafi,"* and wishing she knew other more reassuring words.

Logan helped them out of the car. "There's a small shop over there. It looks like it has clothes. Maybe you can get Rafi—"

He stopped speaking abruptly, and she followed his gaze. He was looking at the plaza where vendors were selling reed bird cages and split bamboo baskets from wooden stalls with woven raffia roofs to protect them from the blistering sun.

A gray plume of smoke rose from one stall, filling the hot, humid air with the smell of *arepas,* a tasty fried fish treat. Nearby four *llaneros,* were strumming *cuatros,* a four-stringed instrument that Kelly hadn't heard until she'd come to Venezuela. An old woman hunched over a large stone mortar, grinding cutter ants to make Amazonas hot sauce that many claimed was an aphrodisiac.

She didn't notice anything unusual. The plaza didn't seem much different than it had when they'd arrived yesterday afternoon and explored it while also looking for a place to stay. But the sudden tension in Logan's body alerted her.

"Logan, what's wrong?"

Rafi squirmed in her arms and she set him down. He clung to her legs, unwilling to let her go. She put her hand on his shoulder to give him confidence.

"See the policemen in front of the entrance to our hotel? Two others are directly across the street, leaning against the big tree."

"So?"

"That's too many cops in one place for a small place like this. Something is going on at the hotel. I'm going to ask the man with the telephone if he has a friend or relative who works at the hotel. I want to find out what's happening before I go in there."

A prickle of alarm unsettled her for a moment. Logan was just being cautious, she reminded herself, doing his job. "Is it all right for me to take Rafi into the shop?"

"Yes. Stay inside until I come for you."

The terseness of his voice unnerved her. He really believed something was wrong.

"Mommy, Mommy." Rafi tugged at her skirt, then he said something in Spanish that she didn't understand.

"He has to go to the bathroom," Logan said. "Ask in the shop."

La Tienda del Sol turned out to be a clothing store that catered to the entire family. The children's section didn't look particularly promising, but the rubber sandals Rafi was wearing had to be replaced immediately. He needed a couple of outfits to wear until she brought him home.

The one restroom that served both sexes was in the alley behind the store. It wasn't very clean and didn't have any soap, but she wasn't sure if Rafi could make it until they returned to the hotel. She realized that she had no idea about what to do with a little boy in a situation like this.

Evidently, Rafi had been on his own long enough. As soon as she shut the door and tugged on the chain that turned on the light bulb dangling from the ceiling, he pulled down his pants. His aim wasn't very good, but he did manage to hit the bowl most of the time. She held him up to wash his hands. She was drying them with her skirt when she heard Logan knock and call her name.

She opened the door, and he stepped inside. He didn't have to say a word. She knew they were in trouble.

"The police have found a stash of cocaine in our room. They're waiting to arrest us."

The air exploded from her lungs in a dizzying gasp, and she gripped Rafi's little hand. "It's a setup."

He brushed her cheek with his fingertips, a gesture meant to calm her, but the cold glint in his eyes frightened her even more. "Kelly, if they arrest us, we'll never come out of the police station alive."

"Mommy," Rafi clung to her leg with one arm. There was a frightened tone to his voice. Even though he couldn't possibly understand what they were saying, he was alarmed.

"Está bien," she told him. It's good; it's okay. But everything wasn't okay. If they arrested her, Rafi would be taken away. He'd be devastated if she deserted him again.

"Here's what I want you to do," Logan said. "Go back into the shop. Buy yourself sturdy shorts, a shirt, and hiking boots if they have them. If not, get the best tennis shoes you can find. Do it as fast as you can. I'll wait here with Rafi."

"What are we—"

"Hurry up. We don't have a second to lose."

The minute she tried to leave, Rafi began to sob. Logan pried Rafi's little fingers from the death grip they had on her skirt. He was wailing when she closed the door.

She managed to steady herself as she walked into the shop. It took her a few minutes to find what she wanted. She selected tan shorts and a polo shirt without trying them on. Hiking boots weren't available, so she bought tennis shoes and socks.

A mother with a gaggle of young children distracted the clerk just after Kelly had paid. She took advantage of the situation to slip out the back door. She rushed toward the restroom, expecting to hear Rafi crying.

Logan was singing in his raspy voice. *"Oh, mi chiquito bonito, mi chiquito bonito. Como está, mi chiquito bonito?"*

She opened the door and found Logan standing there, Rafi in his arms. The little boy was playing with the flashlight that Logan must have taken out of his pack.

"Mommy *está aquí.*" Mommy is here. At least that's what she hoped she'd said in a very primitive way. She kissed Rafi's cheek, but he was utterly absorbed by the beam of light.

Logan handed her the child. "Get the flashlight away from

him. We need to save its batteries. Wait outside while I change
my clothes. Then you put on the things you bought. We have
a chance—if we get out of Elorza.''

''Where are we going?''

''Over the border into Colombia.''

''No,'' she cried. ''You can't do that. There's a bounty on
you in Colombia. They'll kill you.''

He shrugged off the danger with a half-hearted smile. ''We're
only a few miles from the Colombian border. It's our only
chance.''

Chapter 29

He checked his Rolex and smiled. "By now Logan and Kelly are under arrest for drug trafficking."

She clinked her champagne glass against his. "Are you sure?"

"The agent I hired planted the stuff, then the Israeli alerted the local authorities. He bribed the police to shoot Logan and say he was trying to escape."

"What about Kelly?" she asked, keeping her voice low.

They were on the terrace, attending Woody's reception for the Arabian Horse Breeders Association, which was about as interesting as the flagstones they were standing on. Bullshit horse talk.

"Kelly is in for a special treat. The guards are going to take turns with her, then she'll be killed, but it will look like she committed suicide."

"I love the idea of her being raped over and over by those brutes, but won't that make people suspicious about her death?"

He could tell from the way the pulse throbbed at the base of her neck and the slightly breathy quality to her voice that the thought of Kelly being tortured, then killed, aroused her.

With luck they could slip away from these bores and have some kinky sex.

"I guess you don't read the Amnesty International newsletters," he told her, knowing full well she got all her news from the tabloids in the drugstore check-out lines. "In many third-world countries, women who are arrested are raped at the police station. Most are prostitutes, a few may have committed a crime, but the macho perception is that they have crossed over the line and are getting what they deserve."

"I hope dozens of brutes rape her until she's glad when they finally shoot her."

The venom in her voice disturbed him a little. He could understand why she hated Logan. He'd ruined her plans to live in the White House. But why did she hate Kelly so much?

At first he'd attributed her attitude to the fact that Kelly was younger and successful in her own right. Kelly had never been perceived as a woman who rode someone else's coattails. But now, he wondered.

"Kelly has something," he said to test the woman he loved. "If things were different, I might . . ."

She turned and walked over to the waiter who was passing champagne. After exchanging her empty glass for another flute of Cristal, she walked back to him. She angled her body so none of the horsy set could see.

"You're mine, and don't you dare forget it." Her hand circled his cock and squeezed.

He was hard the next second and immensely pleased with himself. She was jealous of Kelly. He loved it. Too bad Kelly was as good as dead. It might have been fun to flirt with Kelly a little, then see what she would do.

"Careful," he said, "Someone might see you."

She was becoming a little too bold, taking too many risks. He'd had to fight with her to convince her Woody's attorney needed to have an automobile accident that would prevent him from coming to Sedona to change the will. She had reluctantly agreed.

"When Woody discovers his son is nothing but a drug pusher—a dead one, I'll bet he changes his mind and decides to run for president," he said. "What else is he going to do with the rest of his life?"

She released his cock and took one step back. "Woody says he's devoting himself to his horses."

He glanced across the patio to where Woody was holding court. "He'll change his mind when he hears Logan is dead. Sweetheart, if we play this right, we will be in the White House."

Logan led Kelly through a warren of side streets to the outskirts of Elorza. When they were close enough to the town's only gas station to see it, Logan turned to Kelly.

"You stay here with Rafi while I find us a ride to Colombia."

She started to protest, but Logan left too quickly. Not that he would have listened. He was in the commando mode. They were going to Colombia—no matter what she said.

Kelly sank to the ground, Rafi sleeping in her arms. The late afternoon shadows concealed them, and from her position she could see Logan signal for them to join him. Rafi was a dead weight in her arms, and her back was aching from carrying him as well as her tote and purse, but she was afraid to set him down. What if he woke up and began crying?

A few minutes later, Logan held up his hand. She rose to her feet, pain searing up her back, taking care not to awaken Rafi. She walked quickly from the alley, across the street to the battered farm truck. The flatbed section was enclosed by chicken wire and covered with a tarp to protect the load from the brutal tropical sun.

"Get in quick," Logan told Kelly.

He took Rafi from her and she boosted herself into the truck. It was hot inside, the air so thick she could have sliced it. Evidently, the farmer had been transporting pigs. The truck's bed was littered with straw that was soggy and gave off an odor that could have knocked over an elephant.

Logan handed Rafi to her, then climbed in and pulled down the tarp. It was black as hell and just as hot, but Kelly didn't complain. She cradled Rafi, thankful he hadn't awakened.

The truck's engine rumbled to life and the vehicle lurched forward. She leaned against the side of truck, the chicken wire jabbing her back. Light seeped in from overhead, leaking through a gap in the tarp near the cab.

She could make out Logan's profile. He was sitting beside her, his back against the side of the truck, staring straight ahead. It was too dark to read his expression, but she couldn't help wondering if he blamed her for bringing him here. Would he have been any safer back home?

She doubted it. One of the Stanfields wanted him dead. She suspected they were behind this. It was an easy way to get rid of Logan, yet never be blamed. A coward's way.

"Is the driver heading to Colombia?" she whispered.

"Yes," Logan answered, rummaging through his pack. "We're getting off before the border checkpoint. Once the police realize we've fled, they'll alert the border patrol."

"We'll be in the rain forest then. How will we find our way?" Already she had visions of holding Rafi on one hip while hacking away at the dense foliage with a machete with her free arm.

"The Arauco Indians never bother with the border crossing. They hate the government. We'll follow one of their trails." He pulled out his tiny computer. "There's a special program in here courtesy of the EPA satellite."

"The Environmental Protection Agency has its own satellite?"

"You bet. A state-of-the-art satellite. It can spot a raindrop on an orchid and send a digitized, color-enhanced photograph to the White House in under one minute. They have detailed maps of the rain forest. It's their hot button."

She watched Logan click on Venezuela, then click again on Elorza. A map appeared, showing the city, the orphanage. And the road to Colombia.

"How do you know where we are? The truck keeps moving."

"The Breitling knows. They've always provided the military with specialized watches for pilots and astronauts. Mine is a

Cobra Force special. It's a Chronomat Blackbird with a Titanium band.'' He consulted the glowing dials, unmistakable pride in his voice. ''It will give me exact latitude and longitude information.''

He pointed to the computer screen. ''I compare it to the lat-lon information on the map. Judging by how fast this truck is going, we should be approaching one of the trails in about an hour.''

Rafi stirred and Kelly decided to let him sleep on the straw. It was beastly hot inside the truck, and holding him was only making each of them warmer. He mumbled something as she put him down, then went right to sleep again. She took off her blouse and put it under his head.

Even though she was just in her bra and the new shorts that she had bought, it wasn't much cooler. She stretched out beside Rafi and told herself to get some sleep. She rested her head near Rafi's; the rank smell of the straw caused her stomach to rebel with a swift, sickening lurch.

She should have been panic stricken, but a bone-deep calm had replaced her earlier state of near hysteria. She didn't know why she felt so . . . composed. It took her a minute to realize how much she trusted Logan. She knew that if anyone could lead them to safety, it was Logan.

Trusting anyone with her life—and Rafi's—was a startling revelation. Early on, Pop had given her a precious gift—self-confidence. Over the years, she'd learned to rely on herself and take charge. If she'd been in this situation with Daniel, she would have been ordering him around.

And he would have allowed it. Daniel's unhappy childhood had scarred him emotionally. He appeared to be out-going and assured, but he wasn't.

Logan must have had a very traumatic childhood like Daniel, perhaps even worse, yet he inspired confidence and had true leadership abilities. She didn't question him, instead she trusted him in a way that she had never trusted any man.

She listened to the chuff of Rafi's rhythmic breathing. He was a gift, a priceless gift. She'd expected to gradually grow to love him even though he was the living proof of Daniel's betrayal. But the moment he'd called her "Mommy," her heart had opened and a new type of love had surged through her with bittersweet intensity.

Already she was fiercely protective of Rafi. She would do anything to save him, even if it meant being killed. Somehow she had to get him home where he would be safe and loved.

She tried to sleep, but couldn't keep her eyes closed. Logan wasn't seizing the opportunity to rest. He was loading the Glock that he had checked at the airport, then picked up when the plane had landed. When he finished, he placed it in the side compartment of his pack where he could easily get it.

"What's that for?" she whispered to Logan when he took out a small knife.

"It's a special switchblade. I want you to keep it in your pocket."

She sat up, and listened closely as he explained how to use it. Just as she put the knife in her purse, she heard a siren. It wasn't like sirens in America. This was a keening wail, like sirens in Hitler's Germany.

Logan peered through the tarp at the road behind them. "Son of a bitch! It's the police."

For the first time since he was a child, Logan was afraid, not for himself, but for Kelly and the boy. Sweat peppered his upper lip, and he swiped at it with the back of his hand, trying to think what to do. It was dusk and the light was tricky, making it hard to see.

"There's only one car, but it looks like two men are inside," he told Kelly as the truck slowed and gradually came to a stop.

Two men and rural policemen at that. Normally, he wouldn't have been concerned. He'd taken on six trained guerrillas on one botched mission in Guatemala. But this was different. Two innocent people were now depending on him.

"I've got the knife," Kelly said gamely. "You've got a gun."

For a moment, he almost loved her. She had more courage

and spirit than anyone he'd ever met. But he refused to let her take a chance with her life.

He put his finger to his lips and listened while the cops went up to the driver's door and began questioning the man. He denied picking up any *norte Americanos*. Just goes to show you what one hundred bucks US would do. Of course, the cops insisted on searching the back of the truck.

Logan figured he could blow them both away when they pulled back the tarp, but he couldn't risk them having drawn guns and shooting. Kelly or Rafi could be seriously wounded or killed.

He jumped out of the truck just as the cops came around to the back. They were sauntering, almost swaggering, like so many South American policemen on a power trip. No wonder the people hated them. The driver probably would have lied even if Logan hadn't given him so much money.

The first man had his gun drawn, and he fired the second he spotted Logan's Glock aimed at him. The wild shot didn't come anywhere near Logan. It went wide and shattered the windshield on the patrol car.

Logan missed his chance to kill him with a single shot. He was afraid the bullet would rip through the cop and kill the driver who was standing right behind him.

"Cuidado!" He yelled for the driver to look out.

The driver ducked, but by now the second cop had drawn his gun. Logan instinctively hit the blacktop, the back of the shoulder first, the way Cobras were taught and quickly rolled to the side. Both policemen fired at the spot where he had been.

Logan's first shot brought down one cop, hitting him squarely in the heart. The other cop dove under the truck, and began firing in Logan's direction. Shit! Logan couldn't gamble that one of his bullets might go astray into the back of the truck where Kelly and Rafi were. The cop had more ammo than he did, and could keep him pinned down until help arrived.

Above the burst of gunfire, Logan heard Rafi's frantic cries, *"No! Mami, no!"*

What in hell was Kelly doing? Her head popped out through

a gap in the tarp just behind the cab. She climbed out and scrambled onto the top of the cab.

He realized what she was up to, but the cop under the truck couldn't see her. He kept firing at Logan. The truck kicked into gear and rabbit-hopped forward, giving Logan a clear shot at the man.

On the second hop, Rafi lifted the back tarp and jumped out. Logan didn't have a split second to think. His training took over and he reacted, firing at the man as he dashed across the road.

Rafi was standing there, frantically looking around for Kelly. Logan blocked the child with his body, cursing when he saw the man had jumped to his feet and was reloading his gun. Logan aimed, more carefully this time, knowing he only had one more bullet in the chamber.

His last chance.

The cop trained his gun at an angle so the bullet would hit Rafi. Logan threw himself over the child, and the bullet seared through his arm, splintering the bone.

The kick of his gun and the zinging sound of the bullet told Logan that he had fired, but he didn't realize he'd squeezed the trigger. A split second later, the man crumpled in slow motion, sagging to his knees, his head canted to one side.

The cop fired and fired, his bent trigger finger frozen on the gun. The slugs peppered the blacktop. The last bullet left the chamber just as the man hunched forward and hit the ground, faceup. A thin ribbon of blood oozed from the bullet hole between his eyes.

"Oh, my God," cried Kelly as she leaped from the cab and sprinted toward them.

"*Mami, Mami,*" wailed Rafi, sobbing, but unhurt.

Logan couldn't move. He instructed his mind to override the pain, to shut it out. *What doesn't kill you makes you stronger,* he told himself. But he kept wondering how in hell was he going to get them to safety with a bum arm.

Dazed, he barely heard Kelly cooing to Rafi to calm him. She took off her bra and used it as a tourniquet. She was naked from the waist up, her soft breasts pillowed against his arm as she worked on him.

His body failed to react as it normally would have. That's when he realized blood was gushing from the wound on his upper arm. No wonder he was light-headed, on the verge of passing out.

Chapter 30

Logan blinked hard, trying to get his bearings. Where in hell was he? A stench filled the dark, hot air, yet he felt chilled and clammy.

His brain struggled to process the information he was getting. He must be in the truck again. Nothing else on earth could smell quite as gross.

Then he remembered seeing Kelly half-naked. His arm! He lifted his left arm, and a white-hot blade of pain seared through him. He tried not to groan, but some sound escaped his lips.

"Logan, darling. Are you awake?"

It was too dark to see Kelly. but there was no mistaking the tears in her voice. Darling. She'd never called him that even when they were making love. Oh, Christ. He must be dying.

"How did you get me in here?" he asked, his head more clear now.

"The driver helped me. We dragged the men into the under-brush. Luckily, we were beyond the *llanos* and in the rain forest. I drove their car into the underbrush to buy us some time. I want to get over the border before their bodies are discovered."

"Good thinking," he said, and he meant every word. She

had an amazing sixth sense that was invaluable in anti-terrorist work. She'd noticed the opening in the tarp and had later used it to get into the truck. When he'd been unconscious, she hadn't panicked. She'd taken all the right steps.

"Can you pull the flashlight out of my pack? It's in the side pocket."

She flicked on the flashlight. "I took it out already. I reloaded your gun, and I've been checking on you. It was off to conserve the battery."

He inhaled sharply, aware of a new, deeper pain. Seeing Kelly with blood—his blood—on her hands, staining her face—made his heart heavy. Her red-rimmed eyes and wet lashes told him she'd been crying. For him.

No one had ever cried for him.

"We're about half an hour from the border," she said, her voice low. Rafi's head rested on her lap, his little fist clutching the hem of her shorts.

He checked his watch. The lat-lon indicator said they had just past the trail the Indians used. "Stop the truck. Have him let us out here. We can walk back to the trailhead."

"You can't be serious. You'll die in the jungle, and we'll die with you. Our only chance is to hope they don't search the truck at the border."

"They'll search it. Someone must have seen us in the gas station and reported it to the police. Why else would they have come after us so quickly? Believe me, they've phoned ahead."

"We're just going to traipse off into the jungle?"

"I have a plan. Trust me."

She gently moved Rafi aside and scooted over to the back side of the cab. Her banging on the wall made the driver stop. It also awakened Rafi.

"*Mami, Mami,*" he called, stretching his little arms out to her.

The driver came around to the back to see what was wrong. It didn't take much talking to persuade him to drive them back a quarter of a mile. The driver was a good man, but he had a family and didn't want any trouble at the border.

As soon as the driver returned to the cab, Kelly asked, "What is the plan?"

"The map shows the trail leads to a clearing about a quarter of a mile in. The EPA info says timber was illegally stripped from that part of the rain forest before it was stopped. We can spend the night there."

"Can you make it that far? You've lost a lot of blood."

"No problem." He had to make it. "I'll contact the DEA unit operating out of Colombia and have them send a helicopter for us."

She nodded, then turned off the flashlight. "We're going to need this. No use wasting its battery."

"Turn it on again. Painkillers are in the bottom of my pack in the yellow kit."

"I had to go through your pack. I found the pills. They're in my pocket, but there are only two of them. Do you want one now?"

The concern in her voice touched him, and for a moment, it overshadowed his admiration of her. She handled a crisis better than most men would have.

"I'll take one of those pills now. Don't bother to turn on the light. Just put it in my hand."

He figured it would take everything he had to find the trail and reach the clearing. He'd lost more blood than he realized. His body was incredibly limp, hot in places yet chilled in others.

But he didn't tell Kelly. Instead he tried to focus on the problems they might encounter. Finding the trail wouldn't be too hard, but the clearing had him worried. Plants grew incredibly fast in the rain forest. The EPA data in his computer was nearly a year old. By now the clearing might be too small for a helicopter to land.

Kelly placed the pill in the palm of his hand. He put it in his mouth and swallowed, but his tongue was so dry that it lodged in the back of his throat. Swallowing harder, it grudgingly went down.

Rafi was singing to himself, and Logan had to smile. Despite what he'd just been through, the little boy didn't seem traumatized. He was just happy to be with Kelly.

That made two of them.

"I can't thank you enough for saving Rafi," Kelly told him, the threat of tears in her voice. "I never thought he would jump out of the truck."

"He's terrified you'll disappear again." He winced, pain overcoming him for a moment. He took a deep breath, then, continued, "Rafi needs you, Kelly. He needs . . . love, a mother's love."

Kelly shifted Rafi from one hip to the other, almost stumbling over an exposed root along the trail. Sweat drenched her clothes plastering them to her body. The mossy scent of lichen and moldering leaves hung in the hot air, so thick and heavy with moisture that she wondered if a machete could cut it.

Around them, the trees and snake-like vines encroached on the trail seeming to grow as they passed. In places the rain forest had reclaimed the land, and they almost lost the path several times. The canopy of foliage was so dense that not a single star could be seen in the clear night sky. The only light was the blast of blue-white light from Logan's special flashlight.

From the secret world concealed by the jungle around them came mysterious sounds. Unseen and possibly dangerous creatures lurked in the moist thickets flanking the trail. Night creatures scuttled in the underbrush, foraging. A larger animal was moving along beside them just out of sight. But Logan didn't seem disturbed by the noises, so Kelly forged ahead.

The driver had left them off, and Logan had quickly found the trail the Araucos Indians had trod through the underbrush. God alone knew how Logan mustered the strength to sling his pack over his good arm and trudge down the path.

Kelly was ready to tell Logan that she had to rest when he stopped. She'd dumped what she didn't need in the back of the truck, keeping the Scotch and jeans in her tote. Her passport and the adoption papers were in the moneybelt around her waist. A quarter of a mile didn't sound far, but carrying Rafi and the tote in the stifling heat and humidity was a real endurance test.

"Is this it?" Kelly asked as Logan flashed the light around the small clearing just off the trail.

"Yes. Let's make camp over there."

He ground out the words, his voice grittier than usual. She knew that he had barely made it here. He walked over to a tree stump, dropped his backpack and sat down on it.

"Are you okay?" she asked as she came up to him.

For a moment he didn't answer. He gazed up at the lopsided moon peering down at them. It was obvious to her that this clearing was far too small for a helicopter, but she didn't mention it. Taking care of him was her first priority.

"There's a sheet of Kevlar rolled up in my pack. Put it on the ground and let Rafi sleep on it."

She did as she was told. Obviously, Logan was in far worse shape than he wanted to admit. It wasn't like him to sit there and let her go through his things.

"Buenas noches, mi chiquito bonito," she repeated what she'd heard Logan saying when she'd left him with Rafi to buy clothes. Then she kissed the little boy and said a silent prayer for his safety.

"Buenas noches, Mami."

He closed his eyes, and she couldn't resist giving him another quick peck. Then she turned to Logan, saying, "I think Rafi sleeps a lot, don't you?"

"I'm no expert on kids, but it seems that way. Have a doctor look at him."

"I will." She moved to examine the bandage she'd put on after she'd stopped the flow of blood with her bra. "Let me check your bandage." Blood had soaked through the gauze she'd found in the first aid kit in his pack. It had dried now, and had formed a thick crust on the bandage.

"You're going to have to take out the bullet, or I'll have blood poisoning."

For a second, she closed her eyes and said a silent prayer. God, please give me strength to do this. Too clearly she remembered blood gushing from the wound and her struggle to stem the flow with her bra.

Then he'd collapsed in her arms.

She'd dumped the contents of his pack on the ground in a frantic attempt to find his first aid kit. She'd managed to dress the wound, but she couldn't imagine prying out a bullet.

"You can do it, Kelly. Think of Rafi. We have to get him to safety."

"It's you I'm thinking about," she cried. "I got you into this mess. If it weren't for me . . ."

"Come here," he said and he patted the spot beside him on the huge stump.

She sat beside him, wanting to tell him how much she cared about him. When he'd thrown himself over Rafi, she'd been stunned that he would sacrifice himself. Daniel never would have done the same thing—even for his own son.

He slipped his good arm around her, saying, "You were brilliant back there. You knew exactly what to do."

Kelly gazed into his eyes and saw he meant every word. She hadn't done anything special. She'd merely done what was necessary. That's all.

"If I were the kind of man who got married and settled down, you'd be the woman I would want at my side."

For a moment she thought about telling him that she might be pregnant, but decided against it. This wasn't the time to place an added burden on him. Getting a little boy to safety was their priority.

"Thank you," she retorted with a light-heartedness she certainly didn't feel. "I just want you to know that if I ever had any intention of letting a man into my life again, it would be you."

He chuckled—or tried to, then said, "You have to take out the bullet now while Rafi is sleeping. He's seen enough blood for one day."

She reluctantly nodded. "Tell me what to do."

"Take off your panties. I need you to catch a tree frog." He trained the flashlight's beam on a nearby tree. "See the frog with the red spots on his back? Shake the tree until one falls to the ground, then bag him with your panties."

"Are we going to eat him?" she asked, recalling his story

about eating rats and tarantulas to survive. A frog wasn't so bad.

"No, those frogs secrete a deadly poison. That's why you need to put on the latex gloves from the first-aid kit. It's very important that you don't touch the frog. Your fingers will be too numb to remove the bullet."

"Is this what they teach Cobras?" She took off her blood-stained shorts, then pulled down her panties as he continued to explain what they were going to do with the frog.

"I want you to skin the frog's back where the red spots are. The poison he secretes from them acts like an anesthetic. He catches his prey by letting them touch him, then secreting the poison. It puts them to sleep, then he eats them. We're going to use just enough to deaden the pain in my arm so you can remove the bullet."

Logan aimed the flashlight at the tree while Kelly shook the lowest branch. Half a dozen frogs fell out, two of them landing on her head. They leaped out of sight in a heartbeat.

Standing on tiptoe, she grabbed the next branch and came nose-to-nose with two rather smug-looking frogs. Then she realized what they were doing.

"I hate to break up this party, but I need you both." She snagged them with her panties and returned to Logan.

"Great! That was fast."

"It doesn't seem quite fair to interrupt mating frogs to kill them, but that's life in the big city." It was a really lame attempt at a joke, but she needed to keep her mind off the task ahead. "Have you ever used a frog like this before?"

"No. It's in the survival manual. Harvard University and other medical colleges are studying the secretions. It may be developed as an alternative for people with severe reactions to anesthetics."

"How do we know how much to use? Maybe I had better skin both frogs in case one isn't enough."

"Good thinking," he said. "Don't throw away the frogs after you've skinned them. Hang them from a branch in your panties. We're going to need them."

She knew better than to ask why. "Shouldn't I put them out of their misery before I skin them?"

"Slit them from just underneath their throats to their legs, then gut them the way I did the lizard. That way they die instantly." He sucked in a deep breath and held it, pain evident in his eyes. "You'd better take the flashlight and do it away from here. You don't want to wake up in the morning and find Rafi playing with frog guts."

Chapter 31

Logan waited in the dark while Kelly skinned the frogs. Determination alone had propelled him down the trail. Determination and knowing Kelly and Rafi were depending on him had spurred him forward.

He'd plowed along the path with relentless tenacity. At each bend, at each point where vines shrouded the trail, he had told himself they'd reached their destination. Over and over and over, he'd been wrong, then finally.

THE CLEARING.

His watch had told him this was the space on the EPA map, but the reality was very different from what his computer had shown. The clearing was too small. No doubt the new growth would be on the EPA's updated disk, which Cobra Force members would receive in their intelligence packets next month.

But that wouldn't do him any good now.

He didn't have the strength to take out his computer and boot it up to check the map for another spot. He relied on his memory, which was pretty damn good. They were miles from anywhere a chopper could land except for the highway.

"Forget it," he muttered to himself. "They'll be constantly patrolling that road."

He studied the night sky visible through the opening in the canopy of the rain forest. A hunter's moon, he thought, automatically using a term that he had learned at the camp. Bright enough to hunt at night.

That meant Miguel Orinda's men would be moving drugs, taking advantage of the moonlight. The DEA helicopters would be tracking them. No one would notice if one chopper nipped over the border and picked them up.

Silver Bullets were manufactured specially for the military by Bell Helicopters. They had been designed for tight spaces. The chopper was small enough to dip down into the clearing, but there wasn't a place for it to land.

"They raped the forest," Logan murmured out loud, recalling the clearing when he'd scanned it with his high-powered flashlight. They had left tree stumps that were two feet high above discarded trees that had no value for lumber. The clearing was so littered with debris that even a Silver Bullet couldn't land.

They could lower a rope ladder. Rafi would have to be strapped to Kelly's back so she would have both hands free to climb the ladder. It would be scary. He'd done it himself a couple of times. The ladder tended to swing and gyrated wildly in a wind.

It was their only option even if it had one huge drawback. He hesitated a second, realizing the consequences. Go for it. Kelly was counting on him.

A jagged flash of light distracted him. Kelly appeared, the flashlight braced under her arm. In one hand were the frog skins while her panties dangled from the other hand. The grim set of her mouth eradicated any hint of the usual upward tilt of her lips that he liked to see.

"Are you okay?" he asked as she placed the skins beside him on the stump.

"I've just about had all the fun I can have."

She walked over to a discarded tree nearby and hung the panties from a lifeless branch. The remains of the frogs sagged to the bottom, blood oozing from the sheer fabric. With the heat and the humidity, they would be crawling with maggots by morning.

"Did you have any trouble?" he asked. It wasn't the neatest skinning he'd ever seen, but then, Kelly had never skinned anything. He'd started skinning rabbits in the camp's makeshift kitchen when he'd been a little older than Rafi.

She sat beside him, gazing down at the bloody Latex gloves covering her hands. "They were so cute. I've never killed anything before. I didn't think I could do it, but I thought about you dying and knew I had no choice."

She had a depth and power to her that he admired, but she was also tremendously sensitive. All heart. How lucky could he get? He'd spent his life alone, never having experienced a special woman. Until Kelly.

"I threw up afterward," she confessed in a sheepish voice and he felt her revulsion, her heartfelt anguish.

He reached out and touched her cheek with his good hand. Even that small movement caused a blistering arc of pain through his body. The painkiller was wearing off fast.

"Kelly, why don't you rest a bit? The skins—"

"No. I can't chance you getting blood poisoning." Her throat worked up and down, then she attempted to shrug. "Tell me what to do next."

"There's a hollowed-out log over there. I'll bet rainwater has collected in it. Use some of it to wash the blood off the gloves." Gritting his teeth, he reached into his pack and found the collapsible cup and handed it to her.

She walked quickly over to the log, leaving him in darkness. He stood up and the whirlpool of stars overhead made him dizzy and slightly nauseated. Before he collapsed, he quickly sank to the ground. It took all his strength to lift his injured arm onto the stump by the frog skins so Kelly could remove the bullet, using the stump as a table.

He figured the slug had ripped through tissue, severing his triceps and lodging in the bone. Getting it out was going to be a son of a bitch.

"I'll hold the light," he told Kelly when she returned. "That way both your hands will be free."

"No you won't. You might pass out. I'll prop it up with my tote."

Logan watched as she set things up, then pulled the Cobra Force knife out of her pocket. "I should sterilize this. You must have matches somewhere."

"Don't worry about sterilizing anything. In the tropics, a wound like this will become infected no matter what you do."

She started to argue, but changed her mind. Sitting opposite him, she worked carefully, cutting the bandage off his upper arm without reopening the wound. Her eyes were wide, a little fearful, but determined. "When do I apply the frog skin?"

"Make a tourniquet first so I won't bleed too much and make it even harder for you to locate the bullet, then apply the skin. Let's see if one will numb me enough. We don't want too much in my bloodstream."

She picked up one skin. "What happens if too much gets into your system?"

"It numbs the heart the way it numbs my skin. Too much causes cardiac arrest."

For a second, he thought she was going to be sick again, but she steadied herself. She took off her blouse and used it as a tourniquet. Her breasts were bare, but he didn't bother to stare at her the way he would have once. He studied her face, knowing that soon they would be forced to part.

He might never see her again.

He wanted to remember this moment, when the chips were down, and he had to put his life in her hands. It was something he'd never done, never contemplated doing. Yet here he was, allowing a woman to take control.

No denying it. Kelly had changed him, bless her sweet heart. He wanted to savor the memory of Kelly saving his life. Logan needed to be able to recall how Kelly looked at various times. He'd already memorized her laugh, her smile, the way she cried out when they were making love.

"Do you feel anything?" Kelly asked as she gently pressed the frog's skin against the wound.

"It hurts like hell," he said through clenched teeth. "It's supposed to take a minute before it kicks in."

They waited in silence; the only sounds came from the night world around them. A chorus of crickets trilled a mournful dirge, and a night bird called to its mate. In the distance a troop of howler monkeys screeched at each other. He watched Kelly concentrate, clamping down on her lower lip with her teeth.

"It feels better' " he said to encourage her. "The stuff must be working. Give it another minute."

"There's something I want to tell you." She kept pressing the skin against his wound, but her serious brown eyes sought his. "I've never met anyone like you."

"With luck you never will again."

"Be serious." Tears welled up in her eyes.

Man, oh, man, was she going to cry? Don't do this to me. You mean the world to me. I can't handle tears right now.

"I'm trying to tell you how special you are. If anything happens to you, I don't know what I'll do."

The heartfelt emotion in her voice, ripped through him like a serrated knife. Hell! He didn't want to be "special." He wanted her to love him.

Love?

The word love, a word he rarely thought about and had never said to anyone, released a juggernaut of raw emotion. Why would he want Kelly to love him? He had his life—a life he *loved*—on the Cobra Force. He'd lived this long without love. He didn't need it now, did he?

"Logan, at first you fooled me. I was afraid of you. I thought you were tough and mean, a talented actor who could turn on a smile in a heartbeat. I see through all that now."

"What do you see?"

"A wonderful man. I'm very lucky to have known you." She stifled a sob, then managed to gather herself. "You know how terribly sorry I am to see you in this mess."

"Darling, don't be sorry. I have absolutely no regrets. I would do it all over again."

He shocked himself by calling her darling. Obviously, the loss of blood and the wound were getting to him. But he had to admit Kelly was special. There had never been a woman in his life that he'd truly cared about.

Not ever.

His mother had ignored him. To this day she probably hadn't noticed he wasn't around the camp. Zoe had been a cruel, heartless bitch who lived to torture children. The other women he'd met after leaving the camp had one use—sex.

Kelly was different, special. She had an unusually close relationship with Pop. Rafi was going to benefit from that unique type of devotion and caring. Looking back, Logan realized that he had been part of it, for a short while.

Stunned by his sudden, totally unexpected self-awareness, he tried to steer his thoughts to his life as a Cobra. One hell of a thrill ride, sure, but . . . if he were brutally honest with himself, something had been missing. Those years were filled with desolate loneliness compared to the time he'd spent with Kelly.

"Feel anything yet?" Kelly asked.

Damn straight he was feeling something. A sense of loss, maybe, or perhaps nostalgia. It was a strange sensation, one he'd never had.

He missed Kelly already.

She had a heart as big as Texas and was as courageous as the most highly trained Cobra. Something inside him shattered when he realized they did not have much more time together.

"Logan? Do you feel numb at all? Is this working?"

"Yes, a little. Maybe the tourniquet has cut off the circulation. Poke me with the knife, then I'll know."

She hesitated, sucked in her breath, and finally picked up the knife with her free hand. Sparks of light danced off the razor-sharp blade. Fascinated, a little woozy, he watched as the tip of the knife disappeared into his skin.

"Son of a bitch! The friggin' frogs work, Kelly. Go for it."

She set the frog skin aside and studied the wound intently. He could see her reluctance etched across her beautiful face. It was difficult to slice someone open. He'd skinned enough rabbits and butchered deer for food at the camp. It would never be a problem for him, but Kelly's background was different.

Thank God. He didn't want to imagine Kelly suffering the

way he had. He wanted to think about her with Pop. He desperately needed to know Rafi was with them. Yes, that would make him happier than anything he could imagine.

"You'll feel the slug before you see it. Get it out. Don't worry about me."

He watched the knife slash though his skin as if it were butter. Kelly grimaced, a soft cry escaping her pursed lips. Logan watched, detached almost as if this were happening to someone else.

"I can feel it!" she cried.

The knife had cleaved open the wound. Despite the tourniquet, blood dripped from his skin. Absently, he wondered how much more blood he could afford to lose.

"It's stuck in the bone." The anguish in her voice alarmed him.

"Pry it out, Kelly. I can't feel a damn thing."

He watched her work, blood now pouring from the wound. It could have taken seconds, minutes or hours. Logan lost track of time. Finally the bullet popped out, hit his chin and landed on the stump beside the unused frog skin.

"You're fantastic, Kelly."

She shrugged, reaching for the roll of gauze. Logan watched her bandage him, no sensation in his arm, but his head seemed light, ready to float away. The last of the tape in place, Kelly untied the tourniquet.

A rushing sound like the water in Oak Creek whirred in his ears, and Kelly's beautiful face blurred. He blinked hard to banish the pinpricks of blackness obscuring his vision. He battled the engulfing shadows, but they tugged at him relentlessly until he was dragged into a dark whirlpool.

The last thing he remembered was collapsing into Kelly's arms.

The second Kelly noticed Logan's head tilting to one side at an odd angle, she leaped over the stump to his side. In slow motion he toppled sideways into her arms.

"You lost a lot of blood, but you're going to be all right," she told him as if saying it out loud would somehow make it come true.

Bracing her back against the stump for support, she managed to angle Logan's body so his head was against her breasts. The rasp of stubble along his jaw grazed her bare skin.

Cradling him, she gently laid his injured arm across his chest. Blood stained the gauze in an ever widening circle.

"Don't you dare bleed to death on me," she whispered to him. "Don't you dare."

She pressed her lips against his clammy forehead, remembering the first time he'd kissed her, really kissed her. In front of a hundred people on their wedding day. The experience had rattled her, embarrassing her in front of Pop's friends.

Who cared? Could she live with herself if Logan died?

She had used him. An ugly thought, but it was the unvarnished truth. She had been too fond of Matt to allow him to marry her so she could adopt Rafi. But Logan had not received similar consideration. Pop had warned her, but she dismissed the danger to Logan.

No denying it. She was selfish beyond belief. She was the one who deserved to bleed to death, not Logan.

Jazz on the Rocks each fall brought hundreds of tourists into Sedona. Naturally, Woody expected his family and friends to accompany him. Jazz was a total bore, but they went along anyway.

It wasn't until the concert was over that he had a chance to get her alone and tell her the news. They managed to ride in a limousine together and have the driver roar into the night before anyone else joined them.

"Something's happened," he said the second the driver rolled up the glass partition, allowing them to speak privately.

He leaned forward and shut the blackout drape, anticipating some real fun. "Logan and Kelly never returned to the hotel. They haven't been arrested."

In the shadowy darkness, her blue eyes gleamed with an intensity that was almost feral. If he didn't love her, he would have been afraid of her.

"What happened?"

"It's hard to say. When they didn't return, the police put out what amounts to an all-points bulletin. Someone reported seeing a blond woman with a small child getting into the back of a farm truck."

"So? What did they do?" Her words crackled in the small space.

"They've sent a patrol car out after the truck. That's all I know. The time difference makes communicating a bit difficult—"

"If you ask me, the Israeli agent you hired botched things."

His cell phone saved him from having to argue with her about the Israeli. Avram came highly recommended, but Logan was a whole lot cagier than they had anticipated.

"Hello," he said while she reached for the chilled champagne in the corner bar and poured herself a glass.

It was Avram. Squawks and static filled the line. It took several tries before the agent he'd hired explained the situation.

He punched the "end" button, then hit "power off." Getting another phone call in the next half hour was not part of his plan. He'd told her to forget underwear tonight. Bare pussy in the back of a limo was going to be his treat to himself for sitting through the jazz concert.

"Avram has an updated report. The two policemen who were sent after Logan and Kelly have been killed."

"Did Logan do it?"

He reached under the hem of her dress where it grazed her knees. "Yes. Now the police have put out an all-points, country-wide alert, and they've sealed the borders. They are instructed to shoot Logan on sight."

"What about his civil rights?"

"Civil rights? Honey," he said, inching his hand upward,

"we're talking about South America. Corrupt cops. Military juntas every six months. Who needs civil rights?"

"I love it. I wish we lived in a country like that."

His hand zeroed in on the target, and the sweet spot was ready, hot and melting for him. "The driver of the truck they used was stopped at the Colombian border. They beat the truth out of him."

She spread her legs for him, and he unzipped his trousers with his free hand. He gave himself a mental pat on the back for hiring a Flagstaff limo service instead of the service in Phoenix that Woody usually used to ferry his guests around Sedona. This man didn't know them from Adam. He wasn't going to blab even if he could see what was going on behind the blackout drape.

He stroked her, finding the moist, lush smoothness like warm cream. He wanted to ram into her so badly that he could hardly retain a coherent thought.

She whispered to him, "What about Kelly?"

"Avram promised the cops they could do whatever they wanted with her, as long as they shot her for trying to escape after they were done with her."

"What I wouldn't give to be there to watch them with Kelly."

He cocked his hips and pummeled into her. Her startled gasp fueled his aroused state and he drove harder and harder, the way he often did.

She opened her thighs, screeching his name. He slammed his hand over her sweet lips, his other hand on her throat. Pulling backward, a fraction of an inch at a time, he withdrew his penis from her sweet body.

Then he reared his head, arching his neck backward like one of Woody's magnificent stallions and rammed into her full-force. She gasped, trembling beneath him. She cried out, a mixture of pleasure and pain.

Shrieking with pleasure, she bucked upward. He seized the opportunity and clasped her buttocks, deliberately digging his nails into her tender skin. She moaned, writhing beneath him.

He jacknifed his hips, separating his body from hers. She rose upward slightly, reluctant to release his rigid dick. He smiled to himself, then cocked his hips. He slammed into her, harder this time.

She cried out, but before the sound reached his ears, he covered her mouth with his. Yet he kept ramming into her with all his might, over and over and over.

Chapter 32

Logan thought he heard Kelly saying his name and telling him how much she cared about him, how wonderful he was. He struggled to open his eyes to see if he was dreaming. That didn't work, so he tried drawing a deep breath.

Hot, wet air seeped into his lungs, clearing his head a little. Where in hell was he? Just above him came a pecking sound. Rain.

His head was resting on something warm and soft. Not a pillow, he decided. Kelly. He knew the feel of her skin, its sweet scent. She was talking to him in an anguished voice.

In a dizzying rush, flashes of images bombarded his groggy brain. The truck being stopped. Rafi jumping out of the back. Taking a bone-crushing shot in the upper arm.

Kelly's beautiful face taut with fear as she removed the bullet.

He tried to lift his good arm, but it was a dead weight. His whole body tingled, yet it felt heavy, lifeless. Maybe the friggin' frogs had mummified him forever. The only thing that seemed to be working were his ears, and they weren't doing too good.

"Come on, Logan. You're a fighter. Don't die on me, please, darling," Kelly was saying.

He couldn't open his eyes, so he tried to tell her that he was awake, but his hot, thick tongue refused to budge. Panic gripped him, then tightened like a steel vise.

He despised being powerless, not the one in control. It was an achingly familiar feeling, one he hadn't had in years. Not since The Last Chance Camp. He'd been young then, vulnerable—at their mercy.

Come on! Get a grip.

That was then, and this is now. His muzzy brain managed to focus on the present. They were in deep shit. He had to wake up and get on the computer. It was his responsibility—his mission—to get Kelly and Rafi to safety.

Battling hard for what seemed like minutes, he finally managed to crack one eye open enough so a slit of light blinded him.

"Logan? Logan? Are you awake?"

She tenderly kissed his forehead, brushing back his hair. The other eye popped open, and he gazed up at her, amazed. Kelly's lashes were beaded with tears, and her lower lip trembled. She cared so much that it frightened him.

"Thank God. I've been so worried about you."

He forced himself to concentrate on her face. She'd been out in the rain, and her hair was plastered in damp hanks around her head. Her luminous brown eyes usually appeared to be glazed by candlelight, making them almost amber in color and full of life.

Now Kelly's eyes were flat brown and bleak, a testament to the hours she'd spent nursing him, worrying about him. Something warm unfurled deep in his chest. Sensation was returning to his body, he thought.

Wrong. What he was experiencing existed solely in his head. A wild yearning to make Kelly care even more deeply about him.

Once his carefully honed, tough edge would have told him Kelly's concern was for her own safety. But the bullet or the damn frogs must have altered his perceptions, stripping away his emotional barrier.

Unusual thoughts jammed his foggy brain, and he tried to

sort them out, to understand himself. He needed Kelly. Not just to help him now, but he need her in a way that he'd never needed another woman.

He expected admitting this to weaken him in some way, diminish his power, but it didn't. Instead, he felt stronger—at least emotionally.

"Logan can you understand what I'm saying?"

His tongue wouldn't move, so he fluttered his eyelids to let her know he was coming to, but slowly.

"You can't talk yet, can you?" When he blinked again, she continued, "I think when I untied the tourniquet the blood started circulating, it took the poison through your entire system. I was terrified you would go into cardiac arrest and die."

That makes two of us. He seemed to be sprawled across her lap, his head propped up against what? Rolling his eyes to the side, he recognized his spare T-shirt on Kelly.

"You've been out for hours. I had to feed Rafi. I couldn't get him to eat the freeze-dried stuff, so I gave him the Twinkie. I wasn't sure about taking it. Everything in your pack is so lightweight and has a special purpose. Don't tell me Twinkies are used for burns or something."

Or something. Let the kid have it, anything to make this ordeal easier on Kelly. If he lived to get his sorry hide out of this jungle, he would never forget her strength and courage.

His concentration was returning, and he automatically shifted his gaze to take in his surroundings.

Sharp as always, she answered his unspoken question. "I made a shelter with the Kevlar that Rafi was sleeping on. It started to rain not long after you passed out. I had to drag you over to the rise where the loggers had left a pile of wood chips. I didn't want you to be in water."

He tried to ask her the time. His lips parted, but his bloated tongue refused to cooperate. All that came out was, "Ti—"

Kelly misunderstood. "Rafi's right here." She scooted aside so he could see the boy playing with her checkbook. He was drawing on a blank check with her lipstick.

Aw, hell. Logan's fine-tuned skills kicked in. How much

more time did they have before the powerful flashlight drained its battery?

"*Papi*," Rafi said to him with a heart-melting smile. "*Mi nuevo papi.*"

New Papa? What in hell was going on?

"Obviously, you're not the man in the picture Rafi has. He doesn't seem to really remember Daniel or his mother. He just knows what he's been told. Now he thinks you are his new father."

Great! Just exactly what he needed, the cutest kid on the planet, believing he was his father. And Kelly. His Kelly.

Since when had she become 'his'? Thinking back he'd wanted her since the very first night in the hogan, but he hadn't felt a fierce sense of possessiveness until they'd had dinner with the Stanfields. When Tyler had dared to strip Kelly with his eyes, Logan had experienced his first surge of jealousy.

From then on, the feeling had gradually escalated. He cared about her, and more than anything, he wanted to protect her. So why was he flat on his back, letting her cradle him like some damn baby when he should be getting Kelly and Rafi to safety?

"Time." The word shot out of his mouth, taking him by surprise.

"It's almost midnight. You've been out for almost twenty-four hours."

Shit! They'd be hot on their trail by now. He thought a moment, his normally acute reasoning powers still not up to speed. Rain turned roads to rivers. The police would wait until the rain stopped.

The thought bolstered him, then let him down the next second with a crash. Choppers wouldn't come into the rain forest during a storm either.

"Light . . . out."

"It's only been on a few minutes. I've been saving the battery." She turned to Rafi and reached out her arm. "*Aquí.*"

With a smile, the little boy catapulted himself into Kelly's embrace. She took her hand away from Logan's head and turned off the light. In the darkness, the patter of rain on the Kevlar,

Logan rested in Kelly's lap. She was singing some damn song about an ittsy bittsy spider who didn't have the smarts to know it couldn't crawl up the waterspout.

Judging from Rafi's delighted giggles and the motions he sensed in the air around him, Kelly had sung that song dozens of times. Rafi even managed to say "up the waterspout" in passable English.

Yes, sir. He'd made the right choice. No matter what happened to him, Kelly and Rafi belonged together.

He drifted off, not quite asleep, yet not fully awake. Kelly continued to sing, encouraging Rafi to sing along with her. By degrees Logan's body regained sensations, raw aches and jabbing pains replacing the tingling.

The last area to return to normal was his injured arm. When it did, his arm was an inferno. He had to look down to make certain flames weren't leaping from his upper arm.

"Kelly, what did you do with the frogs' remains?"

"They're stilling hanging from that bush. Why?"

"Please go get them. I need them."

"Logan, you're delirious—"

"No, I'm not—at least not yet. Trust me."

Without a word, she clicked on the light. A quick kiss for Rafi and she dove under the edge of the tarp.

"Mami! Mami!" wailed Rafi.

"Rafi," Logan called. *"Aquí."*

The child scrambled toward the sound of his voice. Logan grabbed his little hand and managed to maneuver him to his uninjured side. He spoke slowly to him in Spanish, telling him to be a good boy and do exactly what he was told. He wanted to prepare the child for the skyward climb on the ladder from hell.

Light stabbed into the lair Kelly had made. She returned, head first.

"You look like a drowned rat." He tried to joke, but it sounded stupid, considering their plight.

A spark of humor lit her eyes. "And to think an hour ago I was praying to hear the sound of your voice again."

Down on all fours to avoid the low hanging Kevlar, she held

her panties in one hand. They sagged at the bottom, telling him the remains were still there, but blood no longer dripped from the cloth. The rain had washed it away, leaving nothing more than a pinkish tint to the silky fabric.

"My arm's infected. I need you to change the bandage. When you do, I want you to put as many maggots as you can on my wound."

Silence filled the makeshift tent, magnified by the incessant spike of rain on the Kevlar. She tried to smile, but he wasn't fooled. "I read about this somewhere. Maggots consume the infected flesh, but not the good tissue, right?"

"Yes. Think you can stand to touch maggots?"

"After butchering two frogs who were in love, it'll be a piece of cake." She sounded like his Kelly, but the look on her face told a different story.

He kept his arm around Rafi and told him in Spanish to hold the flashlight steady while his mother cut away the old bandage. The incision she'd made had closed, but his livid crimson skin was swollen and puffy.

"I saw antibiotics in your backpack. I think—"

"I'll take them, but they won't be enough with this severe a wound. Slather as many maggots as you can against the incision. They'll eat their way inside and consume the deadly bacteria. At least that's how it's supposed to work."

"*Papi,*" Rafi whispered, then jabbered something. It took a second before Logan understood what he was saying in baby talk.

"He's asking why you talk so funny."

Kelly was preparing the last of the gauze for the new bandage. He was dead certain she was working up courage to take a handful of maggots. Smiling to assure Rafi that talking funny was a good thing, he explained to the little boy.

"*Bueno,*" Rafi said, but the flashlight wavered and Logan understood the reappearance of his "mother" and a new father and a new language was a lot to throw at a kid all at once.

"I told him that you learned another language, and you'll be teaching it to him."

"Thanks," Kelly muttered.

She picked up the panties and gingerly opened them. He heard a sharp intake of breath, then she clamped down hard with her teeth, trapping her lower lip. Suppressing a cry of disgust. Gingerly, she dipped her fingers into the bag she'd made of her panties and withdrew dozens of squirming maggots.

"Gusanos," cried Rafi.

Worms? Okay, close enough for government work. Maggots would look like worms to a young child. *"Gusanos blancos,"* Logan said to reassure him. White worms.

He lifted his arm, a piercing blade of pain arcing through him as he brought his arm up to a level position so as many maggots as possible could be heaped on his skin.

Kelly patted the maggots across the incision. "What does it feel like?"

"It tickles. That's all." Actually, it hurt like hell. Just holding his arm up took all the strength he could muster.

She applied another handful of maggots, her lower lip still firmly anchored in place by her teeth. Already several maggots had writhed their way into his wound, eating the dead flesh along the incision—just the way the survival manual described.

"Gusanos? Gusanos?" asked Rafi when Kelly began bandaging his arm, trapping the maggots against his skin.

"Sí mi chiquito." Logan knew "worms" on a person's arm was beyond anything this child had experienced. Rafi had to be confused, so Logan kissed his cheek.

In the backwash of the flashlight, Logan saw the little boy's thrilled smile. Rafi leaned into Logan, letting the weight of his young body rest against his. It was a trusting, lovable gesture that sent a surge of something Logan could never have described through him, easing the pain for a moment.

Kelly secured the bandage with tape. Her relieved sigh filled the tent, and her eyes met his. They shared a smile that became more intimate with each passing second. Logan felt as if he'd crossed some invisible bridge.

As if he'd become one with her, he felt her sense of accomplishment, a certain pride that empowers a person, taking them beyond themselves into another world that once might have frightened them. But the challenge had been met—conquered.

"Mice, spiders, maggots," Kelly said with a laugh. "Somehow they're scarier than a submachine gun."

Wanna bet?

"It must be a girl thing."

"You did great," Logan assured her. He released Rafi, his whole body suddenly weak from pain, and rested his head against Kelly's tote. "Give me the antibiotics and a pain pill, please."

"It's the last pain pill."

Logan didn't tell her how much he needed it. White lightning. He'd been wounded several times. Twice in the highlands of Peru and once in Chile in the dead of winter. He'd never experienced White Lightning until now.

Others in the Cobra Force had been wounded in the tropics and suffered virulent infections. Deadly bacteria multiplied at an astonishing rate in this type of climate. The pain from such infections radiated out from the wound with the white-hot, blinding intensity of lightning.

"*Papi.*" Rafi dropped down beside him and snuggled up, making Logan smile despite the pain.

He took the capsules and washed them down with the nutrient enriched solution developed for Desert Storm. A modern version of the canteen, the lightweight plastic cylinder contained not just water, but additives to restore vital fluids to his body. He took two swigs, knowing he needed to conserve for later.

"Could you get out my computer?" he asked Kelly.

It took a minute for her to get it out of the pack. By then Rafi was asleep, his head resting against Logan's chest. For a moment, Logan forgot his pain, forgot the mess they were in.

Since he'd been Rafi's age, he'd been trained to prepare for the worst, for a time when civilization—what there was left of it—would disintegrate. He would be left alone with no one to depend upon but himself.

Make it on your own or die trying.

Life in the camp had been harsh, cruel. It focused solely on surviving the coming upheaval. As he became older he understood The Last Chance Camp thrived on anti-government paranoia. By then Logan's personality had been formed, and he had developed an emotional shield.

He was selected for the Cobra Force because of his unique ability to fend for himself, a skill the Marines had to teach other enlistees who had lived a more normal life. At the time, he regarded the others as pampered wimps, but now he wondered if something irreplaceable had been stolen from him. The ability to care.

He had never been taught to care about those around him. Amy didn't count, he assured himself. She was weak, defenseless. Someone had to protect her. That was not the same as caring. Or was it?

He glanced at Kelly, thinking he didn't have an emotional compass. Life at the camp had not prepared him for a situation like this.

Something inside him clicked, remembered. Maybe, somewhere in the dark corners of his mind, he recalled Luz Tallchief caring about him when he was a young child like Rafi.

It must be that part of him, a secret window to his soul, that identified with the little boy. After all, he had been in similar circumstances when he'd been about the same age. Yeah, that must be it.

But nothing could begin to explain why he cared so much about Kelly.

He reminded himself that emotions only got in the way. If he thought too much about her, he might try to find another way out of this mess. And get them all killed.

Chapter 33

Kelly paused before handing the tiny computer to Logan. All the color had been leached from his skin, yet he had a fever that made his eyes burn like the blue-white core of a flame. At least he was conscious, she attempted to assure herself. For the last twenty-four hours, she'd alternately prayed and cried, frustrated because there was nothing she could do to help him.

Over and over, one image kept replaying in her mind: Logan hurling himself between Rafi and the bullet that might have killed the child.

Where had he gotten such tremendous courage?

She seriously doubted anyone had been there for Logan when he'd needed it the most as a child. A thousand fond memories of Pop whirled through her mind like a kaleidoscope, fractured, ever changing, but the feeling of love and security remained.

"Are you all right?' she asked.

A stupid question. His eyes weren't quite focused, and the corner of his mouth drooped a fraction of an inch, something others wouldn't have noticed. But she had catalogued every inch of his face as well as his myriad expressions.

He tried to lift his head off her tote, but couldn't quite

muster the strength. "Follow my directions, Kelly. This is very important."

Kelly glanced at Rafi, thankful he was nodding off. She followed Logan's instructions and contacted the Cobra Force command center.

"Raptor won't be at his station," he told her, his gritty voice pitched low. "Someone in the bunker will have to call him at home. That will take a priority clearance. You'll need to move the computer close to my hand, then press my right finger against the box on the screen. Do you remember how I did it?"

"Yes. The rain has stopped," she told him. Only a somnolent plop . . . plop. . . plop could be heard from the sheet of Kevlar above them.

He cocked his head and listened, frowning. It was all she could do not to gather him into her arms again. In her mind's eye, she kept seeing a lonely little boy betrayed by those who should have protected him.

On the screen the word **PRIORITY** blinked on, then off. "Logan, what do I do?"

"Type in Code 7, then wait. They'll ask for the print next."

The print box appeared on the screen. Kelly took Logan's hand, noticing how hot and clammy it was and pressed the tip of his index finger against the screen. It took a few seconds for the scan to be completed and the computer to compare the print with their records. Finally, two words appeared in bold type: **STAND BY.**

Logan closed his eyes, saying, "It'll be a few minutes. Raptor will need to get to his PC before we can communicate with him."

She waited, clicking off the flashlight and relied on the glow from the small screen. Rafi was sleeping in the crook of Logan's uninjured arm, looking for all the world that this was exactly where he belonged. Already Rafi was the image of Daniel, but she wanted him to grow up and become more like Logan.

She gazed at them, her heart filled with bittersweetness. What she wouldn't give to have Rafi be her own son. Logan would be his father, not Daniel. It was a silly thought, she decided.

They were in terrible trouble. She was distracting herself by wishing for what could never be.

A message flashed across the screen.

Nine Lives is there a problem?
Raptor

"Logan, he's responded and wants to know the problem."

"Pretend you're me. Tell Raptor that Miguel Orinda's men discovered we were in Venezuela—"

"Why? The Stanfields did this."

"Raptor won't send a chopper for us if he thinks this is a personal problem."

"I see." She listened carefully and typed in Logan's message.

When she looked at Logan again, his eyes were closed and his jaw was set at an odd angle as if he were biting down hard. Obviously, he was in terrible pain.

"Can you feel the maggots?" she asked while they waited for Raptor to respond.

"A little. It feels as if I'm being tickled."

She read him the message. "Raptor says he needs a minute to check the WeatherFax and to see if a Silver Bullet from the Anti-Heroin Task Force stationed in Cravo Norte can be sent to evacuate us."

Logan nodded, but didn't open his eyes. "Cross your fingers that the weather clears enough for the chopper to land before dawn."

"Why dawn?"

"The rain has stopped. Now the police will call in the military to help find us. Once it's light, they'll be down this trail in no time."

Before she could respond, a message appeared on the small screen.

You are cleared for a 0400 pick up by a Silver Bullet out of Cravo Norte. Weight limit 250 pounds.
R.

"Oh-400, that's 4:00 A.M." Relief swept through Kelly and she sagged forward, her shoulders hunched with the weariness that she'd been holding back for hours. Soon, they would all be safe.

Then the comment about the weight limited hit her like a karate chop. All three of them could not go on the helicopter. "You're not coming with us, are you?"

"I'm doing what I promised, getting you and Rafi to safety."

She shut down Logan's computer, struggling to control her mounting panic. Logan was in no condition to get out of the jungle on his own. If she didn't have Rafi, she would take her chances and stay with him, but she did have the little boy to consider.

"There must be some way that all three of us can escape together."

"The only other option is to hack our way to Rio Arayca. Loggers float bundles of logs that they've poached from the rain forest down the river. Swimming out to them is tricky. If the crocodiles don't get you the piranhas will. Do you want to risk Rafi's life?"

It was dark in the tent again, so she couldn't see the expression on his face, but his voice had a hollow, lifeless sound that frightened her even more. She switched on the flashlight. She had to see him; she couldn't carry on this conversation in the dark.

"Of course, I don't want to put Rafi at risk," she said. "But I don't want to leave you all alone when you're injured, barely able to sit up let alone out run the men on your trail. You'll—" She couldn't bring herself to finish the sentence.

"I might not die. If any of us has a prayer of making it out on foot, it's me."

"It's the Haas Factor at work You love taking risks. The—"

"Sure, Kelly, I really want to troop through the jungle, half dead. Then ride a log on the river from hell."

"I think that somewhere your brain has stored the memory of what happened that day you disappeared. You were very young, but you knew one of the twins had pushed you down the cliff, attempting to kill you. Surviving that fall, then waiting—

helpless—as a mountain lion lurked nearby made an indelible impression on you. Danger became a thrill to you, a challenge.''

His wry smile caught her off-guard. ''Danger is my best friend.''

''Oh, Logan, surely you don't mean that.'' But in her heart she knew he did. She wanted to be his best friend. Even more she wanted to give him all her love.

The thought stole the air from her lungs. She had hazy watercolor memories of Daniel, but those feelings weren't the deep, heartfelt emotion that gripped her now. Something in Logan's touch, his unique personality ignited a passion in her that Daniel never had.

Love just doesn't die a sudden death the way a person does. Instead, love slips away by degrees, not overnight. Daniel would always have a place in her heart, but she now realized that Logan was the only man she could ever truly love.

''Maybe danger drove me once.'' He tried to shrug, then winced. ''Not now. This clearing is too small to get in a big chopper. The Silver Bullet has a pilot and a man who literally rides shotgun with an AKC47. I weigh too much to come with you.''

She knew he was right, but she couldn't bear to leave him. This was nothing short of a death sentence. And she'd done it to him. How was she going to live with herself?

''Kelly, we have only a few hours left together. Come here.'' He patted the space on his good side.

''I'm going to take the tarp down and give us some fresh air.''

She yanked the Kevlar free. The air was laced with moisture and only slightly less hot than under the tarp. Overhead beams of moonlight lanced through tattered clouds, illuminating the small clearing.

Kelly switched off the flashlight and lowered herself down near Logan. Rafi whimpered as she settled him beside her on the ground littered with twigs and wood chips. She rested her head on the mounded tarp and gazed at Logan. He smiled, the unique smile that never failed to make her pulse kick-up a notch.

"It's going to be all right, Kelly. You'll see." He put his arm around her, taking great care not to move his other arm. "I wouldn't have done anything differently, if I had to do this all over again."

"Logan, I swear, I'm going to fix the Stanfields. I—"

"Promise me that no matter what happens to me that you won't go after them. Don't get yourself into trouble. You have Rafi to consider."

"I'll remember that," she hedged, secretly promising herself that she would pay back the coward behind this. And she had a good idea just where to start.

"Kiss me," he whispered. "'I like it when you kiss me."

She leaned closer, her hand tracing the strong line of his jaw. The rasp of his emerging beard beneath her fingertips brought the sting of tears to her eyes. She remembered the first time she'd discovered how erotic his beard could be. That time he had kissed her neck. Her reaction had been as intense as it had been unexpected.

Tenderness swelled inside her chest until her ribs seemed far too small for her body. Oh, please, don't let this be the last time I ever touch his beard like this. I'll do anything, anything . . . just let him live. He saved a little boy. He doesn't deserve to die—because of me.

Her thumb brushed his mouth, tracing the fullness of his lower lip. She savored the moment, the sparkle in his eyes, the way his dark hair fell across his forehead. His unique, high-dimpled smile.

Please, God, keep him safe, please. It hurt so much to think that she might have nothing more than this memory to treasure in years to come.

"What are you doing?" he asked, his lips so close to hers that they brushed her mouth as he spoke.

"Feeling your beard."

She kissed him, her lips gently meeting his. Soft and tender, her mouth caressed his. Taking her time, she explored the sensual curve of his lips. Then she angled her head to the side and nudged at his mouth with the tip of her tongue.

He uttered a low, throaty sound that made her want to hug him—tight. But she was afraid of hurting him, so she edged closer, setting her breasts against the sturdy wall of his chest. Her tongue found his and teased it in a light, playful way.

They'd never shared a kiss that was so sweet, so tender. Usually, his fierce eagerness fired them both. Passion underscored their other kisses, but now, he let her tell him with her lips how very much she cared about him.

"You're the only woman that I've ever wanted to kiss," he whispered when their lips parted. "Be certain you spend a lot of time touching Rafi. Touch is very important to a young child. No one ever touched me except to hit me," Logan said, his voice low and as coarse as sandpaper.

"Who?"

"My mother. Luz Tallchief probably thought Amanda McCord was a loving mother who would be thrilled to have her child returned."

Kelly couldn't imagine not wanting a child—even one who wasn't your own. She ran her hand over Rafi's head, and he burrowed closer.

"My mother claimed my father had sent me back to her because he didn't want me. She didn't want me either, but she had no choice except to take me with her to the camp."

"She didn't mention anything about them trying to kill you?"

"No. I didn't see much of her. She spent most of her time with Jake McCord, her brother. They'd been raised by my grandfather who headed an antigovernment militia in Arizona.

"When he died, Jake took over. My mother wanted out. She went to Phoenix. That's where she met Woody. She became pregnant, and had nowhere to turn, so she went home."

"She must have loved you. She kept you a year before she gave you up."

"No. Amanda and Jake had only one use for me—to get money out of Woody to buy a plot of land in the woods of northern California. They set up a bunch of tents for the band of misfits that came with them and called it The Last Chance Camp."

She gasped, unable to imagine a mother who would trade her child for a parcel of land. It was heartless, yet Logan seemed to accept it, which made her even sadder.

Evidently, he had lived with this for so long the pain this must have once caused him no longer registered. From the psychology classes she'd taken, Kelly knew this was the ultimate rejection. A mother turning her back on her child. Yet Logan continued his story as if it had never mattered to him.

"The land is owned by a dummy corporation. They pay the taxes. Believe me, the group at Last Chance knows every way conceivable to elude the government. They have an arsenal of weapons that are better than most police departments."

"Are they planning on attacking government facilities or something?"

"No. They're relatively harmless. They're dead certain that the people will see the light and rise up against the government. They want to be ready."

She tried to imagine growing up in a place like that, but couldn't. Her youth had been filled with memories of Pop and his friends. Granted, some of them were a touch weird, but that was to be expected in Sedona. It was a spiritual center which attracted New Agers.

Then there was the Native American influence. Uma and her Navajo traditions had colored Kelly's early years, leaving a lasting appreciation for nature. Pop, of course, brought a whole new dimension to her life.

These diverse elements converged, and ideas were freely exchanged. Kelly knew without being told that this was not the case at the camp. Logan had not been allowed to express himself.

"How many other children were there?"

"Five at one time. Three of them left with their parents before I was ten. Jake insisted people at the camp not have children. They would be a burden when it came time to fight."

In some ways Jake was right, she decided. If she were alone with Logan, she would never leave him. Having Rafi changed things. Yet she could never think of him as a burden, and she was positive Logan didn't either.

Rafi was a gift, a precious gift. She touched his cheek as he slept, not quite believing her good luck in having him come into her life. She would do anything, make any sacrifice to give him a happy childhood.

"There was only two of you for all those years until you left?"

"Yes. Amy was three years older and a little slow. She was too sweet for the hard life in the camp." There was a certain edge to his voice that it didn't normally have.

"Do you know if Amy is still there?"

In the silence that followed, a breath of air ruffled a nearby vine. Droplets of water splattered their faces.

At last he said, "Amy died the year before I left the camp. We both came down with mumps. Amy's fever spiked, and nothing anyone did could bring it down. Jake flat refused to take her to a doctor. 'Make it on your own, or die trying.' That's what he always told us."

Another short silence followed, then he added. "Amy died trying."

"Oh, Logan, I'm so sorry. I—"

"Don't be." He cut her off, his voice more brusque than usual, the way it became when he shutdown an emotional reaction. "The day they buried Amy, I made up my mind to leave. On my eighteenth birthday, I walked out."

She wanted to say something to comfort him, but knew he didn't want sympathy. "I'm amazed that you knew how to create an identity for yourself."

"You wouldn't be if you saw the library at the camp. It's just a shed, but it's filled with antigovernment literature that gave instructions on everything from evading taxes to making bombs. I had no trouble coming up with identification. I used an abandoned lot about five miles from the camp as an address. I often hunted rabbits near there."

"Now I understand why you didn't want me to include this in the article."

"My mother hated me and turned me over to Zoe." He groaned, but she couldn't tell if it was the pain from his arm or a painful memory. "She was worse than you can possibly imagine. But at the end of the day, Amanda McCord is still my mother. She wouldn't fit in anywhere else. I can't throw her to the wolves."

Chapter 34

"I understand," Kelly told Logan.

But what she meant was that she appreciated his loyalty to his mother and his sensitivity to her inability to fit in elsewhere after so many years in the camp. She'd seen hints of his sensitivity with Pop and Uma and the blind man in Elorza. It was another facet of his personality that she admired.

For the life of her, Kelly could not understand the way his mother had behaved. How could any woman literally sell her own baby? Granted, she'd heard numerous horror stories about the way some children were mistreated, but she never comprehended what made some mothers abuse their children. Why had Amanda McCord turned Logan over to Zoe?

"Tell me about Zoe."

"What's to tell?" he responded with more than just a trace of irony. "I remember her walking down the dirt lane into camp one hot summer day with nothing but a tattered, Christmas shopping bag with the word MACY'S on it. At that point the camp was full. Since we raised our own food, Jake insisted every person—no matter how young—worked after they finished their daily military drills."

Kelly stifled a gasp, unable to imagine forcing young children to drill or to work. "What did you do?"

"Fed the chickens, cleaned up after them, gathered eggs. Most of the easy jobs like that were taken by the children or the women who couldn't work the fields or hunt. There was nothing for Zoe to do, so she volunteered to teach the children. There were only five of us then, but Jake let Zoe stay."

Logan stopped abruptly and gazed up at the stars overhead, then back at her. Oh, please, Kelly prayed. Don't let him clam up now.

"Zoe hated kids. She taught us the basics, but not without slapping us around for any little thing."

"Obviously, she had a psychological problem."

Logan's brittle laugh took her by surprise. "You don't know the half of it. When class was over she would make us kiss her good-bye. A peck on the cheek wouldn't do. Zoe insisted on a kiss right on the lips."

"That's perverted."

She tried to imagine a little boy never feeling loved or wanted by the adults around him, then being subjected to this disgusting woman. Now she understood his aversion to kissing. It was nothing short of a miracle that he wasn't totally screwed-up.

"Perverted? Absolutely," he replied. "The older I got, the worse she became . . ."

She was almost afraid to ask, "What do you mean?"

He looked away. She could tell he didn't want to talk about this, but she had to know. Understanding him was terribly important to her even though they would soon be parted.

"The old bat would grab my butt when I kissed her. One day when Amy was gone, Zoe touched my penis. I told her I would kill her if she ever did it again."

Oh, God. This was worse than she had imagined. "How old were you?"

"Thirteen. I would never have gone back to class, but I couldn't leave Amy alone with Zoe. She always tormented Amy, ridiculing her because she was so slow. Zoe never touched me again, but the way she would look at me made me sick."

His concern for another at such an early age touched Kelly,

and she had to open her eyes very wide to keep back the tears. The last thing Logan wanted was pity, but it deeply disturbed her that Logan could care so much for another person when no one there gave a hoot about him.

"I thought about running away, but Amy was afraid. Her father was at the camp, and she adored him. I suspect Amy may have been slightly retarded. She didn't realize her father lived to clean the arsenal of guns. If he'd been any kind of a father, he would have stopped Zoe from tormenting Amy."

"Didn't your uncle do anything?"

"Not one damn thing. Jake ran the camp like the military, with a chain of command. Zoe was in charge of the classroom. No one questioned her, probably because she didn't seriously injure any of us."

He turned, his eyes on Rafi. The boy was snuggled against Kelly's side, dozing. "Always remember, psychological abuse is as devastating as physical abuse—sometimes even more so. The body heals more quickly than the mind."

She held her breath for a second to keep from bursting into tears. Logan was physically strong, but he'd been psychologically damaged. Time and love could heal the scars left on his psyche by life at the camp. She would help him heal—if only she could have the chance.

"Pop was wonderful with me," she told him in a shaky voice. "He corrected me when I needed it, but he made me feel special. Loved. That's how I'm going to raise Rafi."

"You'll be great. His life won't be like mine." He sucked in a deep breath, and she knew the bullet wound was eroding his strength.

"Did you ever say anything to your mother?"

"It wouldn't have done any good. She belted me whenever I came near her. It didn't matter. I could take Zoe, but Amy couldn't. Once Zoe screamed so much at her that Amy wet her pants. Zoe made her stand outside in the snow until her wet clothes froze. It's a wonder she didn't get pneumonia or freeze to death."

"Oh, Logan, I'm sorry. I can't imagine—"

"Don't feel sorry for me. What doesn't kill you makes you

stronger. That's what Jake always told everyone. I came through it like tempered steel. Feel sorry for Amy. She wasn't a fighter, so she paid the price with her life.''

Even though he had told her earlier about Amy's death, Kelly's throat thickened with an upwelling of emotion, and hot, salty tears pricked at her eyes. Logan didn't fool her, not for a second. He'd survived the old biddy's abuse, but it had scarred him in ways she saw, and in many ways she did not yet see.

"Did you have *any* fun when you were growing up?'' She desperately wanted to think of him, laughing and happy, at least some of the time.

"It was mostly hard work. We didn't buy anything we could make. Jake rejected creature comforts like mirrors and hot water. He refused to allow radios or television. We entertained each other by putting on plays at night.''

This is why Logan had the ability to switch roles with amazing speed. She'd noticed the morning when he'd appeared in her office. She hesitated, afraid he would be unwilling to answer, then asked, ''Zoe is the reason you never kissed women, isn't she?''

"Yes, but I didn't know you well enough to tell you about her until now.''

"I understand,'' she whispered. His tragic childhood had turned him into an insular man. Sharing as much as he had with her had been difficult. And she loved him all the more for it.

"We should rest,'' he said. ''I want to hold you until they come for you.''

She knew he didn't want to discuss the past any longer. His good arm was outstretched, waiting for her. She snuggled against his chest and hoped he didn't hear her troubled sigh.

"I need to explain a few things about the rescue operation,'' he said, his breath warm against her cheek. He explained about the rope ladder she would have to climb to reach the helicopter. It sounded easy, but she knew better.

"Is your passport and the adoption papers still in your money belt?'' he asked and she nodded. ''You won't be able to carry your bag and Rafi, too. Is there anything in it you *must* have?''

She thought a moment, then said, ''No.''

''Give me that gold wedding band. I'm likely to run into Indians who will want to trade. Let's see what else you have.''

They sorted through her tote, and he took several small items like the comb with a mirror on one side and the sterling silver key ring that Pop had given her last Christmas as well as the Scotch and Levis.

''I guess that's it,'' he said, placing her bag under his head like a pillow.

She wanted to enjoy her final hour with him. The few weeks that they'd been together might be all she would ever have, when there should have been so much . . . more.

These last precious minutes would have to last a lifetime. In her mind, the years stretched ahead, brightened by Rafi's sweet smile, but she would always miss Logan. The knowledge brought a raw ache just beneath her breastbone.

She placed one hand on his chest and was reassured by a solid, steady heartbeat beneath her palm. Under her breath, she prayed this brave heart wouldn't be silenced forever by another bullet. Realistically, she knew his chances were next to nil. If a bullet didn't kill him, something in the jungle would.

''Don't feel sorry for me,'' he whispered.

Where would he get such an idea? The light dawned. His tremendous pride had somehow been threatened by telling her about his youth.

''I'm missing you already. That's what I'm thinking.'' The truth out, her throat tightened, making it difficult to breathe. She blinked hard to keep the tears at bay.

She wanted to tell him how much she loved him. Her whole life she'd been waiting for him—yet she hadn't known it. Well, she probably suspected the first night they were married. By the time they flew to Venezuela, she'd known. But she hadn't wanted to admit it to herself.

No matter how much she loved him, he wouldn't want to hear about it. Danger was his best friend. If some miracle occurred and he made it out of this mess, Logan would go right back to the Cobras.

And risk his life all over again.

The glowing hands on his Brietling moved faster and faster, the minutes they had left together, silently ticking away. Chances were she would never see him again. What did she have to lose by telling him what was in her heart?

"I know how you feel about being a Cobra," she began, "but I want you to know how much I love you. I'll—we'll be waiting for you, should you want us."

"Kelly, I'm no good with words. I don't know what to say."

Say you love me, too.

"I want to spend a snowy night in front of the fire, the way we discussed . . . sipping wine and making love," she continued, anxious for him to understand how much she loved him. "I want to walk with you next fall when the aspens turn bright gold. We'll have a picnic beside a mountain creek. We'll . . ."

Do all the things you've never done.

"Aw, Kelly . . . Jesus."

"I love you. Nothing you've done, nothing about your past will change my mind. I want you at my side always. Nothing would make me happier than to have you with me, holding my hand, telling me not to cry when I send Rafi off to school."

"Kelly, please—"

"We could go to his Little League games together and yell like all the other parents. It would be such fun. I can't imagine doing it alone. You're the best thing that ever happened to me. It just took me a while to realize it. If you don't love me, I'll understand, but you can't make me stop loving you."

The arm around her waist squeezed tight. "Don't do this to me."

She ran her hand up his chest to the curve of his neck. Her fingertips brushed his jaw, and his whiskers prickled at her touch. "Is it so hard to have someone tell you that they love you?"

He heaved a sigh, his chest shuddering with pain or emotion she couldn't tell which. "I've never been comfortable with women. At the camp, they hated me. Later, it was just sex. You're different . . . special.''

He'd stopped short of saying he loved her, but "special" was a very good start, considering.

"We have to face the truth. There's a damn good chance that I won't make it back."

His statement set off a chain reaction of emotion. She had been frightened before, knowing his chances were slim, but now panic seized her. If Logan, who thrived on danger, believed he wasn't going to survive—it must be a lost cause.

He was putting up a brave front because his entire life he had been forced to face the world alone. Dying didn't terrify him the way it did most people. He had already accepted his fate.

Logan pulled her closer and gazed into her eyes. "You're the only woman I've ever known who was worth dying for."

Oh, my God. Suddenly everything crystallized and she damned herself for being such a fool. Logan had risked his life to save Rafi, and now he was ready to die to help her. She had been too willing to psychoanalyze him and say the Haas Factor compelled him to risk his life, but that wasn't true.

Despite the hell he'd endured, Logan had a noble side to him, a willingness to protect and help those who needed it. He cared about Rafi, about her. He didn't know how to express it in any other way except to make the ultimate sacrifice.

She opened her mouth to tell him that he had to make it back to her, but the alarm on his watch rang. He struggled to his feet, nearly doubled over with pain. How could she leave him when he was in this condition?

"Mami," Rafi cried, then muttered something she couldn't understand.

Logan was all business now, instructing Kelly to slash the Kevlar into strips with his knife. Following directions, she knotted the pieces together like a rope.

"Rafi," Logan said in a no-nonsense tone that silenced the child. Speaking in Spanish he gave the boy instructions then Kelly kneeled down. Rafi swung his arms and legs around her piggy-back style. Grimacing with pain, Logan secured the little boy with the rope.

"Will the Kevlar hold him?" she asked.

"Don't worry. Not only is it waterproof, it's bulletproof. It's the strongest material around." Logan stepped aside and pulled a long antenna out of a hidden compartment in his watch. "This is an emergency positioning beacon. The chopper will zero in on it."

In the distance, she heard the helicopter approach, it's wings beating the air like some prehistoric bird. "I loaded the Glock for you, and put the extra ammunition with it. I tried to put everything back just as I found it—in case you need it in a hurry."

Why, oh, why were they talking about such trivial things when there was so much to be said?

And so little time to say it.

"I love—"

"Kelly, kiss me one last time." In his eyes she saw that he truly believed this was their last kiss, their final good-bye.

Their lips met as he crushed her against his chest in a one-armed bear hug. His mouth opened and his tongue brushed hers. How many times had they kissed—and she'd taken it for granted? Now, in this dismal jungle, she kissed him good-bye, every beat of her heart praying for his safety.

Even if she never saw him again, she could live with it—if she knew he was alive somewhere on earth. She wanted to be able to look up at a harvest moon in Sedona and know that somewhere, anywhere Logan was alive and gazing at the same moon. During the day, she would be comforted, knowing the sun warming Red Rock country was blazing down on Logan . . . somewhere.

It wouldn't matter if he returned to the Cobras, not her. Logan had suffered so much. He deserved to live, to enjoy life.

Like a tornado, wind created by the chopper whipped through the small clearing, slinging her hair across their faces. Logan pulled back, and said something to Rafi. His tone calmed the boy as the rope ladder dangled from the sky coming closer and closer.

Too soon it was directly in front of her nose. Logan grabbed it with his good arm. She put her foot in the first rung and it wobbled. She hung on with both hands and climbed.

"I love you, Logan. Come back to me. I swear, I'll make you happy."

His hand was on the small of her back, steadying her as the ladder swayed. "I meant what I said. You're the only woman I've ever known worth dying for."

"Don't say that—please," she cried to be heard above the noise of the helicopter. "You're going to make it. You have to. You have to."

She was above his head now, out of his reach. The ladder gyrated wildly, swinging from side to side, driven by the air turbulence from the helicopter. She blinked hard to clear her tear-blurred vision.

"Hang on," she told herself "Don't fall."

The ladder pirouetted and Rafi grabbed her throat, clinging, obviously terrified. She could hardly draw a breath, but she couldn't spare a hand to remove Rafi's little fingers from her windpipe.

Somehow she made it to the next rung. Above her, half hanging out the side door of the helicopter was a soldier, extending his arms. The rope ladder lurched and she lost her grip. But he had both his hands on her shoulders.

He hoisted her upward with incredible strength and managed to pull her torso into the helicopter. Gasping for air, she lunged forward, kicking madly with her legs to propel herself through the opening.

Face on the floor, she peered downward, trying to catch a last glance of Logan. He was below, seeming terribly small from such a height, but she could see his hand in the air, thumb up. He yelled something, but the helicopter was making too much noise for her to hear.

"Good-bye, darling," she screamed as the soldier tugged on the door to shut it. "I'll always love you." From here until eternity.

The door was almost shut when she heard the noise below. Tat-tat, tat-tat, tat-tat. Machinegun fire.

"Help him," she yelled at the man, hardly noticing he'd cut Rafi free and the child was huddled nearby. "All he has is a Glock, and he's injured."

The soldier hurled a small canister out the door. It hit the ground with a flash of blinding light, then a deafening noise rocked the helicopter. Slamming the door shut, the soldier screamed something in Spanish to the pilot.

The helicopter vaulted skyward out of the range of fire from the men on the ground. Bullets zinged off its underbelly, but it whipped away from the clearing in less than a second.

"Ma'am, we are under orders not to fire. All we are allowed to do is pick up passengers and create a diversion."

It was no use arguing. Through the bubble-dome of the jet helicopter all she could see was the tops of trees. They were too far from the clearing to help—even if they had been permitted.

Sitting on the floor, she gathered Rafi into her arms, knowing he needed comforting. She kissed the top of his head and whispered, "Please, God, help Logan. He deserves a chance . . . a life. Someone to truly love him."

Chapter 35

Dawn edged upward, stealing its way between the crevices in the red rocks, backlighting the formidable bluffs and sugar-loaf mesas with the pale amber glow of dawn in the fall. He peered out her bedroom door, knowing he should leave before the servants began bustling through the house.

"Why is your hot-shot Israeli agent having so much trouble finding Logan and Kelly?" she asked from the bed.

They'd been over this once already last evening before she did a provocative striptease for him, so she could flaunt her smooth, bare skin. It had been some of the hottest sex he could remember in all the years they'd been sneaking around together. He shouldn't be irritated with her for questioning him again, but his inability to eliminate the problem was becoming a sore subject.

"Avram hired some Venezuelan ex-military men with extensive experience in the jungle to hunt down Logan and Kelly. They're out there now, searching for them."

She sat up in bed, pulling the sheet demurely up under her arms to hide her breasts. "You don't suppose they escaped?"

"No. It's been raining. It may take a while to find them. That's all."

"If Kelly gets away and comes back here, I'll kill her myself."

"No, you won't," he said, concerned that she was getting out of control. "If by some miracle Kelly should return, we'll plan our next move—*together.*"

"You're too passive. I need someone strong—someone like Logan McCord."

He stared at her, knowing she was deliberately goading him, but he couldn't help seeing red. Woody acted as if Logan was some damn superhero. Just wait until Woody heard that Logan been killed while trying to elude a drug trafficking arrest.

"You want someone strong, someone take charge." He advanced toward the bed.

She jumped up and rushed for the sitting room adjacent to her suite. "Don't be angry. I was just joking."

He stalked her into the ultra-feminine room with a television and a small French writing desk where she pored over Neiman Marcus catalogues. This was a game they often played.

She would taunt him, forcing him to subdue her, but this time something had changed. Logan had proven to be more challenging to eliminate than he had anticipated. Having her compare him—unfavorably—to Logan stoked the fire already smoldering in his gut.

"Don't touch me." Lust flared in her blue eyes along with a trace of fear. She must have sensed the anger gnawing at him.

He strode forward, his cock already a hot poker, a physical manifestation of the fury mounting inside him. Her eyes widened and she sprinted buck naked for the marble bathroom. She slammed the door shut, then locked it.

Banging on the door, he cursed her. He stood there, huffing like one of Woody's damn stallions. He imagined the gloating smile on her beautiful face.

The bitch! She had his number. If they'd been in a hotel, he would have busted down the door, but he couldn't do that without calling attention to their relationship.

He backed away, his penis, hot and throbbing, pressing incessantly against his fly. Retreating to the door that opened onto the terrace, he cracked one blade of the plantation shutters to see if anyone was around. No one was in sight, so he opened the door then slammed it hard.

He tiptoed across the plush carpet and hid in her mammoth closet. He knew exactly where she kept her expensive panty-hose. Pocketing two pairs of sheer black silk stockings, he waited, ready to give her exactly what she deserved.

A minute passed and she ventured out of the bathroom. From his hiding place, he saw her peer around the corner to check out the bedroom. She didn't spot him, so she sauntered forward, obviously delighted with herself.

He vaulted out of the closet and pounced on her from behind. "You bastard," she cried as he threw her facedown on the unmade bed. "Don't you dare—"

He whacked her naked fanny—hard. That shut her up. In a few seconds he had her hands and feet tied to the bed, spread eagle.

"Don't ever, ever lock me out, you hear?" He unzipped his trousers, then pulled them off along with his briefs. Facedown, her head buried in a pillow, she didn't respond, so he slapped her ass again with one hand while his other hand stroked his penis.

Her whole body trembled, and she strained at the nylons binding her to the bed, twitching her butt. He'd never been so rough with her.

They had crossed some invisible line that he liked to think of as a higher plane. She wasn't bossing him around, and for damn sure, she wasn't throwing Logan McCord in his face.

"I'm sorry," she whimpered.

"Really? Show me just how sorry you are."

He jammed his hand between her thighs and fondled the mound she had lasered—just for him. She was slightly moist, nothing like her usual self. He probed a bit, but his cock refused to wait.

Thrusting into her from behind caused her to cry out—in surprise or pain—he couldn't decide and didn't give a damn. They'd experimented with kinky sex for years, but this went beyond anything they had ever done because he meant business.

"Never, ever compare me to the likes of Logan McCord, understand?"

He suddenly felt like one of Woody's powerful stallions, mounting a mare, and he leaned forward and lifted her blond hair. Then he nipped the back of her neck just the way stallions bit the mares to subdue them.

What a turn on! All those years of being forced to watch Woody and his prize stallions had paid off. He had never been this aroused.

Beneath him, she bucked, struggling to free herself. He held her in place with his hand while he slowly withdrew until only the tip of his cock was inside her. Then he surged forward ramming into her with all his might. Over and over his hips jack-knifed until he climaxed, pouring hot seed into her.

She didn't utter a sound as he collapsed on top of her and waited for his pulse to return to normal. Finally he rolled to one side, but he had no intention of freeing her yet. He was having too much fun.

She turned to face him, her pupils fully dilated, making her eyes appear almost black. "Do it again, harder this time."

Thunderheads were stacked like ebony pyramids, darkening the buttes and mesas visible from Pop's terrace. Kelly sat in a chair, watching Rafi play with Jasper, hardly noticing the rising breeze that brought the scent of rain. It had been almost a week since she'd last seen Logan.

The Silver Bullet had whisked her to Cravo Norte, Colombia where the Anti-Heroin Task Force had its closest base to Venezuela. Without an explanation, they hustled her onto a jet that took her to the Marine facility in Puerto Rico.

There she was debriefed, and she stuck to Logan's story. No matter how much she pleaded for them to get Logan help, they seemed more interested in the heroin cartel leader, Miguel Orinda than they did Logan.

"The Cobra Force didn't lift a finger to help him." Bitterness underscored every word. It wasn't the first time she'd complained to Pop. She had been home two entire days now. He'd heard this over and over.

Cursing the Cobras and the idiotic bureaucracy didn't change things. She had absolutely no idea what had happened to Logan. Despite numerous phone calls to the Pentagon, she still didn't have an answer.

"I know you're upset," Pop said quietly. "So am I, but we can't give up hope. Logan is a man accustomed to tough situations. I'm confident that he'll survive."

The heartfelt emotion in Pop's voice echoed her own feelings. Her grandfather genuinely cared about Logan.

"Kelly," called Uma from the doorway leading into the house. "Matthew Jensen is on the telephone."

Kelly had been trying to reach Matthew, but he'd been impossible to contact. "Pop, keep your eye—"

"Don't worry. I'll watch Rafi carefully just the way I watched you."

"Thanks, Pop." Tears welled up as they so often did now. As bad as things were, she had Pop and Rafi. It was impossible to imagine a life without anyone to love you and share the good as well as the bad times, yet that was the only life Logan had ever known.

Inside, the house seemed unusually silent, like a tomb. Uma had been devastated that Logan hadn't returned with her. Like Pop, Uma had fallen under Logan's spell.

The older woman had welcomed Rafi and had been invaluable in helping Kelly, but she'd withdrawn into her spiritual, traditional Native American world. She had stopped watching the soaps she loved so much, making the house strangely quiet without the constant chatter coming from the television.

"Kelly," Matt said, his voice upbeat. "What's up?"

Obviously, he didn't know what had happened. It didn't surprise her. The government had kept the story under wraps. Not one word had leaked to the media.

"I went to Venezuela with Logan and adopted Daniel's son."

"Great," he said, but she knew him well enough to detect a false note. He'd told her he loved her and offered to marry her, but she'd refused. He was still hurt.

"A social worker called me and said you'd given them my name as a reference," Matt continued.

"Oh, my God." Kelly sank into the chair beside the telephone. "What else did she say?"

"Is something wrong?"

"I never gave them your name."

A taut silence followed, and she braced herself for his answer.

"Kelly, I'm so sorry. It seemed logical that Social Services would call me. I told the woman all about Rafi."

Knowing it had been an innocent mistake and blaming herself, didn't make this less painful. She explained the situation and asked Matthew to keep it confidential. He assured her that he would, then she realized he sounded, different, troubled.

He had been her friend for years. She understood what had happened. It had been her fault, not his. "Something's wrong, Matt. What is it?"

The long silence at the other end told her Matt was weighing his problems against hers. "Tell me, please."

"I met a woman." His voice was flat, telling her this wasn't good news. "She's crazy about me."

"What happened?"

"She couldn't take no for an answer. She's been following me everywhere, threatening any woman I even look at. I had to get a restraining order."

"Oh, Matt. Be careful. Stalker types are dangerous."

"She says she's going to love me until I die."

"That's sick." It reminded Kelly of Zoe. Women could be just as dangerous as men. "Please take care, Matt. I don't want anything to happen to you."

He assured her that he was being very careful, and they hung up. Walking back out onto the terrace overlooking Oak Creek, it was all Kelly could do to stop the floodgate of tears.

If only, if only, she had thought to call and warn Matt. Logan might have been sitting beside her. Safe.

She sank into the bent willow chair and watched Rafi. He was snuggled up to Jasper, almost dozing off. The pediatrician who checked him when they returned to Sedona had detected a mild viral infection that was making Rafi slightly listless and

sleepy. He was taking medication for the problem, and it seemed
to be working. He became more active with each passing day.

"*Papi*," said the little boy half asleep "*Mi nuevo papi.*"

It was all she could do to control her emotions. Rafi had
known Logan just a short time, but in some inexplicable way
the child had bonded with him. He continued to ask where his
"new" father was.

A father Rafi might never see again.

The next morning Kelly was having breakfast inside with
Pop at the *equiipale* in the breakfast area of the kitchen. Rafi
sat at her side at the hacienda-style table in the booster chair
that had once been hers.

"The wind is blowing out of the north," Uma observed as
she set a platter of fresh fruit on the table.

The weather had taken a turn for the worst, the wind blowing—howling—out of the north. Kelly told herself not to be
superstitious, but nothing good came from the north, according
to Navajo tradition. This harked back to olden times when the
icy fingers of winter ravaged the Navajos, blowing in from the
north.

The direction of evil.

A knock on the front door took them by surprise. Pop raised
one grizzled brow and Uma crossed herself. Only Rafi continued to eat his banana slices, sharing them with Jasper.

"The north wind brings trouble, big time," Uma said, crossing herself again.

Kelly answered the front door and found a man with a reced-
ing hairline and intelligent brown eyes. He was dressed in a
conservative gray suit, but his erect posture and the set of his
jaw told her that the stranger had a military background.

"I'm Philip Wilson," he said, extending his hand.

She shook his hand, wondering why the name didn't seem
the least bit familiar. From the way he was looking at her, she
thought he knew her.

"I'm Logan McCord's contact at the command center."

Raptor, she knew immediately, but didn't say anything because she wasn't supposed to know he existed.

"May I come in?"

"Have you heard anything? Is Logan all right?" she asked as she led him inside to the living room.

"The Venezuelan government has contacted us."

"What did they say?" She gestured for him to sit on the sofa, and she sat beside him. When he didn't immediately answer . . . she knew.

"I'm afraid the news wasn't good," he said, his voice pitched low, then he paused for a moment. "Logan was killed just after you left him."

"Are you sure?" she cried.

Even though it had seemed impossible for Logan to have escaped the hail of machinegun fire, some part of her refused to give up hope. He had survived so many ordeals—from the time he was a child until he selected a high-risk career. She kept praying that he had somehow managed to get away.

Philip slipped his hand into his pocket, saying, "The Venezuelan government is returning his Cobra Force backpack to us. They sent this in their diplomatic pouch yesterday."

He handed her a gold wedding band. Her vision blurred as she remembered Logan putting it in his pocket. Her throat worked hard, sliding up, then down as she attempted to speak.

"Where's his body?" she asked, raw emotion choking her, making her sound hoarse.

"The Venezuelan authorities haven't released it yet. When they do, we'll have the service in Washington. He'll be buried at Arlington, if that's all right with you."

She wanted to scream that he belonged here—near her. But it wasn't true. He'd been in Sedona for a brief time. His heart wasn't irrevocably linked to Red Rock country the way hers was.

Still, she wanted him to be buried here for selfish reasons. Even if he was dead, she wanted him near her where she could put flowers on his grave every week. Where she could visit him whenever she wanted.

Looking ahead at the lonely years to come, she longed to

be close enough to him to go to his grave and discuss problems she might be having. There would be light moments, too, times when Rafi did something special. She wanted to share these things with Logan. With his spirit.

But he'd lived his life, bravely facing danger. He'd represented his country as a member of the elite Cobra Force. Logan McCord deserved a hero's funeral and the special honor of being buried among other men who had fearlessly served their country.

"Logan would want to be buried at Arlington."

Pop appeared at the door and gazed at her. Tears sheened his eyes, and he suddenly looked very old, the way he had just after his surgery.

She barely heard Philip Wilson explaining the situation to Pop. All she could think about was Logan on the last day they'd been together. He must have known he was going to die, yet he'd devoted his final hours to her.

On the verge of tears, she managed to hold them back, catching the sound of Rafi's laughter coming from the kitchen. She knew Uma was distracting him somehow to protect him from the scene in here. No one had been there for Logan as a child. No one.

Her grief suddenly became too deep for tears. Crying wouldn't bring Logan back. Neither would revenge, but at least the Stanfields wouldn't have gotten away with it.

"Kelly, honey, Mr. Wilson is talking to you."

She turned to the older man. "Sorry, my mind drifted."

"I was saying that Logan was my best man. He didn't realize we had met because our communications were always by computer. But I was curious enough about him to go down to Chile to debrief him after a mission. I never told him I was his contact in the bunker." He shook his head, his dark eyes mirrored his sadness. "Logan was one of a kind."

"If he was so good, why didn't you try to help him? All they did—"

"Kelly," Pops cautioned, interrupting her, before she lashed out even more.

"Next to losing my own son in Desert Storm, this is the

worst thing that's ever happened to me." His grim expression and world-weary tone assured her of his sincerity. "It's taken years to get Colombia to allow our Anti-Heroin Task Force to set up on their soil. Most Americans think Colombians deal only in cocaine. Heroin has taken over, and it's much, much more deadly."

"Because of the demand in this country," Pop added.

"True. There are those who argue that we should treat the problem here. Who am I to say? My job is to guide Cobra Force members in the field. Often they are on loan to the DEA, helping control drug smuggling."

"Is that how Logan got in trouble with Miguel Orinda and his Colombian cartel?" Kelly asked.

"Yes, but don't think I was fooled when I got the message that one of Orinda's men just happened to be in some remote village in Venezuela and spotted Logan. It gave me the excuse I needed to contact the nearest base to help him.

"But I had to think of the thousands of lives that will be ruined by heroin if we don't stop it. I was taking a huge risk by authorizing the men to cross into Venezuela. If they'd crashed or killed any Venezuelan soldiers, it would have jeopardized the entire anti-heroin program in Colombia."

"I know," Kelly said. "Logan explained, but dealing with his death is difficult."

"I warned Logan to watch his back. One of the Stanfields was gunning for him. I'm surprised he let them—"

"It was my fault that one of them discovered where we were going," Kelly said. She briefly explained what had happened.

"Is there any way to find out exactly which one of the Stanfields wanted Logan dead?" Pop asked Philip.

"I doubt it. They've covered their tracks well."

"I have an idea. Logan and I discovered Suzanne Stanfield—she was Tyler's wife—died mysteriously. Logan thought brucine might have killed her. He said that an expert might be able to tell by looking at the autopsy report."

Philip nodded. "It's possible. If you can get me the—"

"In the other room, I have a copy of the report done by the Phoenix coroner."

"Okay, assuming we discover she was poisoned, what are you going to do?"

"You still won't know who is responsible," Pop added gently.

"True, but Logan and I downloaded a lot of information on brucine. We reviewed it on the flight to Caracas. We could check records to see who purchased it."

"I could help there," said Philip. "Brucine is one of the most tightly controlled substances. Just about the only legal use for it is in producing denatured alcohol. I could quickly check records around the country—overseas if necessary—and see which one of the Stanfields purchased it."

"Look for Benson Williams's name as well," Kelly told him. "There's something very odd about his relationship to the family."

Philip didn't stay much longer. When she walked him to the door, a bolt of thunder rocked the house, then blue-white lightning cursed them in a blistering flash. Instantly, rain pelted down in torrents, blown sideways by the wind. He streaked for his rental car and drove off.

The weather matched Kelly's mood, and she stood in the doorway. She kept hearing Logan's raspy voice. Seeing his high-dimpled smile. Feeling his strong arms around her.

In a suspended state, she gazed out at the storm, protected by the overhang. Something had shattered inside her, leaving hundreds of knife-edge pieces. Jagged, hard to fit pieces. Could she put her life back together, knowing her carelessness had caused Logan's death?

Her answer was another blast of thunder followed by a searing lance of lightning that split the heavens in half. The power of Mother Nature, so often seen in Red Rock country, was awesome. Even beautiful. Especially when she was furious.

Mother Nature echoed Kelly's anger and frustration. She must have taken to heart Uma's Navajo teachings. Thunderstorms were the gods' way of showing their vengeance.

Kelly, you're the only woman I've ever met worth dying for.

"Darling, I promise you that I'm going to get the person

responsible for your death.'' The words were hardly out when tears came, falling as fast and hard as the rain.

"Mami, mami."

Rafi had come up behind her and was tugging on her skirt, his concern showing on his sweet face. She'd been terribly upset lately, and she knew it frightened him. He'd been through a tremendous ordeal, yet he'd never whined or complained. For his sake, she had to pull herself together.

She leaned down and picked him up. His little arms circled her neck, and he hugged her. The tears slowed and a warm surge of love seeped through her.

Thank you, Logan. I wasn't worth dying for, but saving Rafi was so important. You wanted him to have a better life, the kind of loving family you never had. I promise that he will. I'll never forget the sacrifice you made.

God bless you, and God keep you, darling. You are beyond pain at last. Your body will be buried in Arlington, but I honestly believe your soul is free. It will be here in Red Rock country where you will have what you never had in life . . . people who love you.

Chapter 36

Kelly sat on the floor with Rafi, helping him put together a puzzle. It was still raining, so they were playing inside. With a little help, Rafi jammed the last piece into place.

"*Gato*," he cried, then clapped his hands, delighted with his accomplishment.

"Cat," she told him. In the twenty-four hours since Philip had told her about Logan's fate, only her determination to devote herself to Rafi had kept her from breaking down.

Rafi jumped up and straddled the fire engine Pop had given him and began to tinker with the hoses. He was thrilled with his new home. She didn't want to diminish his happiness by letting him see how sad she was. She wished that she had a dozen children to occupy her time.

But last night, she had discovered that she wasn't pregnant after all. There wouldn't be a baby to carry on Logan's name. She was left with nothing but his memory to cherish.

"Kelly," Pop called from the doorway, interrupting her thoughts. "Woody Stanfield is here."

"I don't want to see him," she replied. Philip Wilson had yet to get back to her with the expert's opinion on Suzanne

Stanfield's autopsy report. As far as she was concerened any one of them could have killed Tyler's wife—then Logan.

"What about Rafi?" Pop said, his voice low. "Social Services approved you and Logan for adoption. You're a single parent now. Don't give them any reason to take him away from you."

"Just let them try." An upwelling of fierce maternal protectiveness swept through her with astonishing intensity. No one was taking Rafi away from her.

Pop stood there, not saying anything, the way he often had when she'd been a child, behaving stubbornly. Woody could make certain that Logan's death did not become an obstacle to the adoption.

"You're right," she told her grandfather. "I'll see Woody."

She left him with Rafi and walked down the hall into the living room. Woody was on the sofa in the place where Philip had been yesterday.

Woody looked so much like Logan that it was all she could do not to burst into tears. Had Logan lived to be an older man, this is exactly how he would have looked. A full head of hair, no longer a rich chestnut, but a mellow pewter. The lines on his face would have added more character. The intelligent blue eyes that missed nothing would not have changed. Neither would have the high-dimpled smile.

"Kelly, I'm so sor-sorry."

The hitch in Woody's voice and raw emotion he was holding in check startled her. He genuinely cared about Logan, she thought as she sat down.

"How did you know?" she asked in the flat, lifeless voice that had become her own.

"I chaired the Armed Services Committee for years. I still have contacts. When the news came in from Venezuela, they called me. What happened?"

She parroted Logan's version just as she'd done at the debriefing. Finishing the edited version, she told him, "I saw the gunfire from the helicopter. He never had a prayer of a chance."

Woody looked at her for a moment. "He must have loved you very much."

He'd never said he loved her. Was the *word* "love" necessary? *You're the only woman I've ever met worth dying for.* Logan had loved her enough to die for her.

"I loved someone like that . . . once. It changes your whole life overnight. Suddenly, career goals aren't important. Personal happiness is all that matters."

"I take it that the great love of your life wasn't Ginger." The words blurted out of her with startling frankness.

He rose and she thought he was going to leave, put off by her bluntness, but he walked over to the window. The storm was passing, leaving the water on Oak Creek at a much higher level. He gazed out for a moment, then turned to her.

"My father worked in the oil fields in Oklahoma until he was killed in a drilling accident. I was in the eighth grade and had to quit school to support my sick mother."

His tone was earnest, yet a little forced. She had the distinct impression he was a man who was unaccustomed to sharing his personal feelings with anyone. Like father like son.

"A year later my mother died. She made me promise to leave the oil fields and make something of myself. She said she would be standing next to St. Peter the day they swore me in as president."

The heartfelt emotion in his voice touched her in a way she hadn't anticipated. It was totally obvious that he loved his mother. She had been a major influence in his life, and all these years later, despite wealth and success, he still missed her.

This was exactly how she felt about Pop. She hoped that one day, when she was no longer alive, Rafi would have such fond feelings for her.

"I came to Pheonix and worked three jobs, hardly sleeping until I had a nest egg. I bought a rundown apartment building. It took me a few years to profit from a rising real estate market and buy a chunk of land with a quarry."

She listened to him describe turning the worthless quarry into Finicky Feline Flakes, the country's most popular cat box litter. It was a story she already knew—thanks to Pop, but others did not. Benson Williams had carefully cultivated an image of a poor boy making his fortune mining gemstones.

"Suddenly, I was thirty-two and rich. It only seemed natural that I should marry. Ginger was beautiful, the perfect choice. It wasn't until later that I realized beauty isn't important.

"I should have divorced her, but I wanted a political career. Back then being divorced was the kiss of death. I had affairs; Ginger had affairs."

Kelly couldn't imagine living her life like that, but she knew people did.

"Ginger became pregnant with twins. I knew I wasn't the father, but my career was hot. I expected her to divorce me and marry the Vegas gambler who had gotten her pregnant. Then the man changed his mind and left the country.

"It devastated Ginger. In a way, I don't think she has ever recovered. She withdrew into herself. There was no way I could have deserted her."

Kelly was oddly and unexpectedly touched. Again, like father like son. Woody couldn't bring himself to leave Ginger just as Logan refused to reveal his mother's involvement in his disappearance.

Logan's father seemed a great deal more compassionate than she had anticipated. Raising the twins as his own was unexpected. What kind of person was he?

Woody walked back to the sofa and sat down. "It wasn't an ideal marriage, but it helped me politically. I had my sights set on the United States Senate. That's when I met Amanda McCord."

Kelly already despised Logan's mother for the way she'd treated him as a child. Still, she couldn't help being curious about the woman.

"Amanda had something special about her. She had a combination of wit and intelligence."

Kelly wondered how father and son could have such different impressions of the same woman. Who knew? Maybe her pregnancy and life in the camp had changed Amanda McCord for the worse.

"I persuaded Ginger to adopt Logan. He was a cute little kid, but I didn't have much time for him."

How could a father not have time for his own son? "Logan had too many accidents to be a coincidence." Kelly could not keep the bitterness out of her voice. "Were you aware that someone was abusing him?"

"No, not at first. I thought Luz was a bit hyper, that's all. But when he fell down the ravine and vanished. Well, I figured it out. Native Americans are terrible liars. I realized that Luz and Jim Cree knew where Logan was, but they denied it. I assumed they had taken Logan back to his mother."

The bite-like taste of utter disgust rose up from her throat. "You never bothered to check to see if he was all right?"

"Don't be too hard on me, Kelly. I thought Amanda would contact me again—for more money. When she didn't, I tried to find them, but I couldn't." His brows drew together in a self-deprecating frown. "Over the years, I wondered and worried."

She refused to feel sorry for Woody. If he'd behaved differently, Logan would not have been subjected to the horrors of that camp, never knowing love.

"Did you know Alyx and Tyler pushed him into the ravine?"

Despite usual self-composure, Woody's jaw dropped. "Logan told you that?"

"No. Logan doesn't—didn't—remember the incident. But when Luz and Jim found him, Logan told them he had been pushed. He didn't see which of the twins did it."

"By, God, why didn't Luz tell me?"

"She had come to you before, but you ignored her warnings. You didn't give her any reason to believe things would change."

"I can assure you I would have taken care of the matter." He thought for a moment, then added, "Ginger and Benson must have known something. They lost too much time before calling me."

"This just now occured to you? It didn't seem strange then?"

"No. From the moment Ginger discovered Logan was my son, she was terrified people would discover the truth. She believed media attention would destroy my career, and we would be forced to leave Washington. At the time, I thought Ginger and Benson wanted to find Logan without calling the authorities to keep the situation quiet. Now, I wonder.''

"It's a little late to be realizing this," Kelly snapped. "I don't know why you put up with the lot of them."

"Life in Washington was difficult. Having twins live with me as well as Ginger and Benson made it easier. Political functions and endless parties become boring. I could always send a pair of them in my place.

"They allowed me to concentrate on other issues. I suppose it appears odd to outsiders, but Benson has lived with us for years, just the way the twins have. I can't imagine life without them.''

Kelly was convinced they were worthless. It was impossible to conceive of Logan hanging around, attending parties. Letting his father support him.

"Excuse me, Kelly," Uma said from the doorway. "There's some dude on the phone. He says it's important.''

Kelly hesitated a second, hoping Woody would volunteer to leave, but he showed no sign of departing. In a way, she didn't mind. He reminded her so much of Logan that it didn't seem as if he were gone forever when she looked at his father and saw Logan's face.

She excused herself and picked up the telephone in the kitchen. It was Philip.

"Logan was right," he told her. "Brucine did kill Suzanne Stanfield. Actually, if someone had really known what they were doing, they would have used less.''

Kelly leaned against the counter and closed her eyes. Killers. Cold-blooded killers. Some part of her had been determined to believe that Logan's being pushed into the ravine was a childish prank that had been exploited by Ginger and Benson.

Now she knew better. Suzanne had been Tyler's wife. He must have been the one to push Logan, then years later kill his own wife. The only question remaining in Kelly's mind was who else was in on it—if anyone.

"Kelly? Kelly?"

"I'm here. I'm just in shock. Today, would a coroner be able to determine the cause of death?"

"Not without knowing to look for it. Brucine poisoning is extremely rare. I have my men working on the sales records now."

"Let me know as soon as you find out," Kelly said, then thanked him and hung up.

A prickle of unease tiptoed down her spine. Someone had seen Logan—who wanted no part of the family—as a threat. She was his widow. Could she possibly be in danger?

Part of her didn't care and welcomed the challenge to confront the coward who had caused Logan's death. Think of Rafi, cautioned an inner voice. Whoever had planted the drugs had killed Suzanne in a very sneaky way.

This was not an enemy that she could challenge out in the open. She might never know who was behind this unless she was very clever. And equally as devious. Woody might unknowingly give her the clues she needed to solve the puzzle.

She returned to the living room, unsure of how to get the information out of Woody. She couldn't decide if she should ask him about Benson or Suzanne first. Woody decided for her.

"I know this seems like a long story. You asked about the love of my life. I wanted you to understand that we are very much alike. I discovered a unique, fulfilling love with Suzanne after many years and another marriage. Your situation isn't much different from mine, is it?"

His question caught her off guard. She had thought she loved Daniel, and she'd mourned for him for a long time. Yet what she had discovered with Logan had opened up an entirely new realm of feeling.

"You're right. What I feel for Logan is completely different and all consuming. I don't know what I'm going to do without him."

"I felt the same way when Suzanne died. Suddenly, life wasn't worth living. I—" His voice faltered, stark emotion evident in each syllable. Even the most jaded cynic could not doubt Woody adored Suzanne.

"I guess you know all about Suzanne," he said, regaining his composure.

"She was Tyler's wife. That's all I know. Why don't you tell me the rest?"

His intense expression reminded her so much of Logan that it was heartwrenching. "You must think I'm a dirty old man. Suzanne was young enough to be my daughter, but her age had nothing to do with it. She was intelligent and interested in political issues the way I was.

"At first, it was very innocent . . . then we realized we were in love. I examined my life very closely. Politics no longer seemed as appealing as it once had. I wanted to move back to Sedona with Suzanne and enjoy life with our children."

Kelly could not doubt his sincerity. His eyes, his face echoed the heartfelt emotion in his words.

"I knew it would cause a scandal. After all, I had harped on family values for years, yet I was divorcing my wife to marry my son's wife. I didn't hesitate, especially after we learned Suzanne was pregnant.

"When Suzanne died of a genetic heart condition, I didn't know what to do. I hadn't yet asked Ginger for a divorce, so my life just . . . went on. But I have never been the same."

"Did you ever suspect Suzanne's death was not from natural causes?" Kelly ventured the question in what she hoped was a casual tone.

He shook his head dismissively. "Her parents insisted on a second autopsy, but the Phoenix coroner confirmed the original results." He studied her a moment in the intent way that Logan so often used. "Why?"

"I have information that confirms Suzanne was poisoned."

"That's ridiculous! Neither coroner reported any evidence of poison," Woody shot back, but she saw a flicker of doubt in his eyes.

She explained brucine wasn't easy to spot even today and led Woody to believe that Logan had used his sources to obtain the information before they went to Venezuela. She did not want Woody to know Philip was involved.

The stricken expression that came over Woody's face

alarmed her. A purple vein beat wildly along the side of his throat. He sagged back, suddenly breathing heavily as if he'd finished a long race.

"Why? Why? Why?" he muttered over and over, still gazing up as if the hand-hewn beams had the answer. He finally looked at Kelly, his voice becoming stronger. "Suzanne was an angel. She never did a thing to anyone."

"Did anyone know you planned to divorce Ginger and marry Suzanne?"

"No. It was our secret. We told her parents, of course, but they were the only ones who knew."

"Suzanne was pregnant. Did she go to a doctor to confirm it? Could the doctor's office have called your house?"

"She used a home test kit."

Kelly had no doubt he was telling the truth. She was equally certain that Suzanne's parents had not told anyone.

"Do you know what an infinity transmitter is?" she asked, recalling the tiny listening devices that Logan had discovered.

"Of course, I was on the Armed Services Committee when funding was approved for their development years ago. You're not suggesting—"

His words hung in the air, and Kelly let them, giving Woody time to mull over the situation.

"I told Suzanne I was changing my will. I wanted our child to inherit my estate. We were in my bedroom in Washington when I told her. The rest of the family was in Sedona. She flew home without me, and two days later, Suzanne was dead."

"Infinity transmitters can be hidden anywhere, not just in the telephone, right?" she asked and he nodded. "They transmit over the phone lines, but Logan said the receiver itself can be moved easily from location to location."

"He was right. Someone in my own family must have been using one the night I thought Suzanne and I were alone. They didn't want me to change my will." He stared at her for a long moment, but she didn't think he was actually seeing her. "They still don't. My lawyer was driving up here from Phoenix last week to work on my will. The brakes on his new BMW went out, and he was nearly killed. Turns out the brake line had been cut. He suspected a disgruntled client, but now I wonder.''

"I don't." Kelly sucked in her breath and decided to roll the dice. "Logan wasn't killed by Miguel Orinda's men.''

She took her time and explained about the infinity transmitters Logan had predicted they would find in Pop's telephones. Woody's eyes narrowed as she described Logan deliberately telling everyone they were going to a different part of Red Rock country than where they were actually going on their wedding night.

"Logan thought someone would try to kill him,'' Woody said.

"Yes. He tried to prevent anyone from finding out we were going to Venezuela. I didn't warn Matthew Jensen. Some woman called him, claiming to be with the Social Services department. That's how they knew.''

"They had my son killed." Woody slowly shook his head.

Interesting, Kelly thought. They. Not he or she. They.

"The twins were together when one of them pushed Logan into that ravine,'' she quietly reminded Woody. "Do you suppose?''

It was over a minute before Woody responded. When he did, his eyes were intent, determined. Logan's eyes.

"Kelly, you and I are going to find out the truth.''

Chapter 37

"I need to talk to you. It's important."

Her cool blue eyes were trained on Woody's guests, honchos from the NRA. Woody had just informed the rifle association board that he had absolutely no intention of running for president. The men had been openly disappointed. After all, Haywood Stanfield had been their champion in the senate for over a quarter of a century.

They slipped away, walking down to the stallion's stable. Everyone expected them to be enthralled with the horses, the way Woody was. They wouldn't think twice about them going to the stables together.

"Have you heard from the Israeli agent you sent after Logan?" she asked in an undertone as they walked away from the gathering.

"Not a word yet. If I hadn't been monitoring Woody's calls, it might have been days before I learned Logan had been killed."

"I want all the gory details. I hope Logan died slowly."

They passed the mares' stable, and he said, "Kelly's idea about moving the new colt in with the mares has worked. He's eating normally now."

"You dragged me all the way down here to tell me that?" she snapped.

Since Kelly had reappeared, she had gone ballistic at the slightest provocation. If he had any sense at all, he wouldn't share his latest news with her. But his plan was bold, a preemptive strike to secure their future. He needed her help, if they were going to pull it off.

"Kelly called Woody this morning. Apparently he visited her yesterday. She told him she might be pregnant. When she phoned today, she said her pregnancy test was positive."

"I knew it. Kelly will use that baby to get money out of Woody. It's Suzanne all over again. This time I'm going to be the one to kill her. I—"

"Kelly had more to say. She told Woody that she has proof Suzanne was murdered."

"She's lying! Two coroners agreed. Suzanne had a heart condition."

He let her rant for a few minutes, venting her anger so she would listen to him closely. "Kelly insists Suzanne died of brucine poisoning."

She stared at him, her delicate nostrils flaring. "You swore it couldn't be traced. How could Kelly possibly discover—"

"Lydia Hartley put the idea in Kelly's head, so she investigated."

"Woody hasn't said a word. He seems perfectly normal."

"That's because I intercepted the message. We must act quickly," he said and she nodded, a flare of excitement in her eyes. "Kelly asked Woody to meet her tonight on the Snoopy trail."

"Out in the dark by those rocks, why?"

"She claims to have proof Suzanne was murdered, and she wants to give it to Woody where no one can see them. She sounds really paranoid."

They made small talk for a moment while two of the stable hands carried a sack of feed into the stable.

She turned to him, saying, "Kelly's expecting Woody. Won't it be a delightful surprise when a hunter mistakes her for a elk? I could hide in the trees and blow her away with one shot.''

She was a crack shot and a lot of fun during hunting season. Trouble was, killing animals had made her bloodthirsty. She loved seeing an elk or deer hit the ground, mortally wounded, yet not dead. She would stand over the fallen animal, its life-blood seeping from her bullet wound, enjoying the creature's suffering.

She smiled at him, a sadistic grin that he'd seen once before when Suzanne pleaded with them to call an ambulance. They'd both stood there, smiling. Waiting for Suzanne to gasp her last breath.

''I'll use my Walther. I've been dying to kill someone with it.''

He liked her spirit. It was a side of her few people saw. He'd noticed it, of course, early in their relationship. But just like the first time that he'd helped her after she'd botched things, he was going to have to carefully guide her now.

''Kelly is a lot smarter than Suzanne. There are things we must find out *before* we kill her.''

''Agreed, but this isn't a 'we' deal. I am going to do it.''

He knew better than to argue with her. Having anticipated her reaction, he intended to play the moment and get her to do it his way. ''You'll kill Kelly, but first, you need to find out who else knows. She may have stashed copies of the information she has. Tell her that I've gone to her house, and I'm going to kill the kid and her grandfather if she doesn't tell.''

''That's sure to work. You go after them while I take care of Kelly.''

He had no intention of going near Farley unless it was abso-lutely necessary. His plan was to hide along the trail and make certain she didn't screw-up.

''Now are you convinced Woody is never going to run for president?'' he asked her. ''Even before Logan reappeared, Woody told us he didn't want to run. Telling his biggest backers, the NRA, makes it final, doesn't it?''

''Yes, damn him. I'm never going to live in the White House.''

Disappointment rang in every syllable. She adored the glamorous life in Washington. The endless parties, the gossip, and, of course, the clothes. The White House had been her fondest dream.

No denying it, he had always seen himself at the pinnacle of power, too. He had hung around, assuming that one day Haywood Stanfield would be president.

"We no longer need Woody," he told her. "He's useless."

Her reaction was a slight widening of the eyes, then the malicious smile he loved so much. "Let's get rid of Woody. He hasn't changed the will yet. We'll be rich. We won't have to stay in a backwater town surrounded by rocks the color of dried blood."

"We can live together and not care what anyone thinks," he said. "I say we kill Woody, then make sure Kelly gets blamed."

"Kelly has to die, too. I'll take care of her."

"Absolutely, but we need to lure Woody out there as well. That way, we won't be stuck with the problem of transporting a dead body. They'll both be found in the same place."

"How are you going to get Woody out there?" she asked.

"I can electronically alter Kelly's message, so she asks Woody to meet her, but doesn't mention Suzanne's death. You know how much Woody wants a grandchild. He'll meet her."

"Except when he gets there, she'll already be dead."

"Exactly. It'll be a murder—suicide. I'll fix the message so Woody arrives an hour later than Kelly expects. That will give you enough time to get the information out to her."

She slowly ran the tip of her tongue across her full lower lip, relishing the idea the way he knew she would. He detested hands-on encounters like this. Anything could happen, but he had no choice. They had to act quickly.

"You must shoot Kelly in the head, so it looks as if she shot Woody, then turned the gun on herself."

She thought a moment, then asked, "What reason would Kelly have to kill Woody?"

"That's where you and I come in. We're going to swear Kelly was trying to extort money from Woody. We knew al-

about it and warned him not to meet her. But he insisted on
going and we followed. That way, our footprints or any other
physical evidence will seem perfectly normal.''

"I can cry with the best of them," she assured him. "I'll
sob hysterically because we didn't get there in time to save
dear, dear Woody."

Darkness had long since descended on Sedona, when Kelly
made her way along the trail to the clearing under Snoopy
Rock. Like lonely sentinels the spires of red rocks jutted upward
around a rock formation that reminded everyone of the cartoon
character, Snoopy. Along the trail, alligator-bark junipers were
interspersed among huge boulders.

Plenty of places to hide.

That's why she had suggested this area when Woody told
her about his plan. There was an element of risk, of course,
but a small one. She held the flashlight steady with one hand
and used the other to pat the small canister of Mace she had
concealed in her jacket pocket. Just in case.

Capitalizing on Woody's desire for a grandchild, she had
left a message on Woody's answering machine, saying she was
pregnant. How she wished it was true! But it was merely another
incentive to lure the killer or killers out into the open.

Covering all her bases, Kelly had sent Pop and Rafi to stay
with friends in Phoenix. Rafi had been a little calmer this time
when he left her. Going to a special place with his *abuelo*—
grandfather—had pleased him.

"This is it," Kelly said, half under her breath as she reached
the clearing.

She flicked off the flashlight and let her eyes adjust to the
darkness. It was one of the many lessons Logan had taught
her. Don't rely on a flashlight that could go out or be taken
away.

A sharp blade of the moon cast creamy light on the clearing,
sheening the rocks and trees and deepening the shadows. The
only way out was down the trail she had just ascended. If she

went up the trail another ten yards, she would have to climb Snoopy, a challenge even for expert rock climbers.

It was possible to forge through the rocks and trees surrounding the clearing, but it would be rough going. If there was anyone hiding nearby, he would have had to come earlier and be lying in wait.

Once, the thought would have made her shudder, but not after the ordeal in Venezuela. *What doesn't kill you makes you stronger.* Logan had been forced to live with that motto. Sad as it was for a young child, it was true.

"I'm stronger now. I'm ready for them."

She listened intently, trying to pick up the sound of someone coming along the trail or noises in the brush. Hoo-hoo, hoo-hoo. Nothing but the distinctive hoot of a barn owl.

She waited, her back resting against a boulder. Down the trail she detected a flicker of light. Then darkness. Maybe her imagination had kicked in, she thought when she didn't see another flash of light.

She waited, her senses tuned in to her surroundings. A minute later, another spark of light lanced through the trees. Closer now. From her position, she could see flashes, but not the person.

"Logan, your death will not go unpunished," she said under her breath.

Kelly took a mental bet with herself that Tyler would be the one coming up the trail. Slim legs clad in black slacks and petite, white sneakers.

Alyx, not Tyler.

Why are you surprised? Women were more evil, more deadly than men, warned some distant part of her brain. Be careful. Alyx was only fifteen when she or her brother pushed Logan down a ravine, intending to kill him.

"You're just the person I wanted to see." Alyx aimed revolver at Kelly.

"Where's Woody?" she asked as if she didn't have a clue what was happening.

"Woody sent me. He wants to know exactly what evidence you have."

Did Alyx think she was totally stupid? She was one of the suspects in Suzanne's murder. "What evidence?"

Alyx stopped directly in front of Kelly, and pointed the gun at her temple. "Stop lying, or you're dead."

Kelly gazed down the barrel of the Walther, unfazed. "I have no idea what you're talking about. I asked Woody to meet me here, so I could tell him that he's going to be a grandfather."

"If you're counting on living long enough to have a baby, you'd better tell me exactly what you know."

Alyx was dead serious, so Kelly pretended to be frightened. "I-I bribed someone to get me a copy of the Phoenix coroner's report. Then Logan had it sent to a specialist he knows—knew. The analysis just came back. I have it in my pocket."

"Give it to me—now."

Kelly had no doubt that the second she handed over the dummy report she'd done on the newspaper's computer that she would be dead. Where was Woody? He had promised to follow whoever came up the trail and get the drop on them.

Kelly slowly withdrew the folded piece of paper from her pocket and handed it to Alyx. "Maybe you should read it."

It was a stalling tactic, but it worked. Alyx kept the gun trained on Kelly while she fumbled with the two pages of paper that had been folded down to wallet size to make them harder to open. Awkwardly, Alyx kept the flashlight under one arm as she read the report that had been deliberately written in a small font.

Kelly hoped for a chance to catch Alyx off guard, but the woman kept the gun inches from Kelly's body as she scanned the report. Come on, Woody. Come on. The only sound was the lonely wail of a coyote on a distant ridge.

"Unidentified female? What does that mean?" Alyx asked.

Alyx wasn't too bright or she would have figured it out for herself, so Kelly slowly explained, buying time. "Logan didn't want his superiors to know he was using government technicians for personal business. He submitted the data from the Phoenix coroner, but left off Suzanne's name."

"Perfect, just perfect," Alyx said, jamming the report into

her pocket. "Then we don't have to worry about the government coming after us."

We. Us. Woody had unconsciously indicated that more than one person was involved. Now Alyx had confirmed it. Where was the second the person?

What was taking Woody so long?

"Who's your partner?" Kelly asked.

"Wouldn't you like to know?"

"Yes, there's a genius behind all this. You aren't smart enough to have done it alone."

In the backwash of light from the flashlight now in Alyx's left hand, Kelly saw feral hatred in Alyx's blue eyes. "I'm a lot smarter than anyone has ever given me credit for."

"Then you were the one to push Logan down the ravine."

"You bet. I wanted to shove boulders down on top of him, but Tyler wouldn't let me. He thought a snake or a mountain lion would kill him and nobody would be suspicious. If he'd listened to me, none of this would have happened."

Alyx spun around as a noise came from the thicket flanking the trail. A hulking shadow loomed into view. Woody! Finally! Kelly muffled a sigh of relief, her eyes on Logan's father.

For one heart-stopping second he looked exactly like Logan. The determined, grim set of his jaw and the way he had the gun leveled at Alyx reminded Kelly of his son.

"Woody, what are you doing here?" Alyx cried.

"Drop your gun!"

The catch in his voice betrayed emotions his face didn't reveal. Kelly imagined how upsetting this must be for him. He'd raised Alyx as his own child and given her everything only to discover she was a cold-blooded killer.

Alyx quickly glanced around as if she expected a white knight to come charging out to rescue her. She slowly tossed the revolver onto the ground. Kelly went on full alert, certain Alyx had an accomplice.

Woody kept his gun trained on Alyx as he walked to Kelly's side. He slid his arm around her, silently comforting her. Kelly allowed herself the luxury of leaning against him, pretending for a moment it was Logan.

"Tell us about Suzanne," asked Kelly when Wooody didn't say another word. "Did you poison her?"

"She was such a bitch! She deserved to die. Suzanne was always prissing around, dabbling in politics, acting as if she was smarter than the rest of us."

Woody's arm across Kelly's shoulder quivered. She knew this must be hard for him. It might have been a May-December relationship, but he had truly loved her.

"Brucine is not a widely known poison, and it's hard to get. You're not smart enough to know about it," Kelly said, deliberately goading Alyx.

"We discovered brucine together," said a voice from the deep shadows beyond the clearing.

Kelly cursed herself for not picking up on some sound, some movement. Logan would have, but, of course, his father was accustomed to the world of politics and wasn't alert, the way Logan had been.

Benson Williams emerged from the darkness, a gun pointed at Kelly and Logan's father. "You're as good as dead, both of you."

Chapter 38

"Benson?"

The word shot from Woody's lips, a taut, ragged sound. Evidently, he was as shocked as Kelly to see Benson Williams bearing down on them, a gun in his hand and a lethal smile on his face. She had been convinced Tyler had been helping his sister.

Woody kept his gun trained on Benson. It was a classic Mexican standoff. Neither man was willing to drop his weapon—or shoot. The moon had disappeared behind a cloud, and the only light came from the flashlight in Alyx's hand. Evidently, the men were concerned about accidentally hitting one of the women in the dim light.

Woody's left arm was still draped over Kelly's shoulders. It trembled slightly, more of a tremor or muscle spasm, she thought, not fear. His right arm was steady, his jaw rigid with determination.

Benson walked over to Alyx. "Surprised, Woody? We've been carrying on under your nose for years. Years."

Alyx smiled with a glint in her eye that curdled Kelly's blood. "Years. It all started when I was fifteen, the day cute little Logan vanished."

"That's sick," Kelly blurted out.

"No, it isn't. I had been flirting with Benson for months. He thought I was just a child until I told him that I had shoved Logan into a ravine and left him to die. I promised to do anything—anything—if he would help me.''

"I guess we know what 'anything' was." Kelly ground out the words, amazed that such a young girl could have been so calculating, and even more astounded a grown man would take advantage of the situation.

"I've never been ashamed of our relationship," Benson said, his eyes on Woody, his gun aimed at Woody's heart. "I was good enough to be your flunky, but I was too old for Alyx and not rich."

Woody continued to glare at Benson with the coolly challenging expression that reminded her so much of Logan.

"Of course, hopping in the sack with young girls was your specialty," Alyx said. "First Amanda McCord, then Suzanne. But you refused to let me date Benson when I asked. You threatened to throw me out of the house, remember?" Alyx linked her arm with Benson's free arm. "We were forced to keep our relationship a secret."

"As long as you were in Washington on the track to the White House, it was worth it to sneak around, but now . . .'' Benson's words hung in the air like toxic fumes.

Power was an aphrodisiac as potent as any narcotic, Kelly knew. She'd seen more than her share of people on power trips when she'd been in New York. Washington would be even worse. Still, it didn't seem possible two people could love each other all these years and be content to sneak around.

"What about Tyler?" Kelly asked. If he were to leap out of the bushes, the delicate balance of power would shift.

"He's always been worthless," Alyx said with a sniff of disgust. "We talked about killing Logan lots of times, but Tyler never did anything more than break a tree branch so Logan would fall. Once he tripped him and Logan stumbled against the barbeque and burned his shoulder."

"When Alyx told me she'd pushed Logan down the ravine,

I told them what to say and do,'' Benson informed them. "Tyler did exactly what he was told and he always has.''

"When we had to take care of Suzanne, we told Tyler to find business in Dallas, and he did.''

The evil satisfaction in Alyx's voice and Woody's silence heightened the tension mounting in Kelly with each passing second. Something else was wrong here, but she couldn't quite decide what it was. Benson and Alyx were enjoying telling Woody what they had done, taunting him, but he wasn't taking the bait.

"What about Ginger?'' she asked.

"What about her?'' Benson responded with a sly smile at Alyx. "She lives for booze and pills and clothes. Ginger's in another world.''

Kelly glanced down at Alyx's gun and saw it on the ground nearby, but it was too far away to get it. The small canister of Mace was still in her pocket. It would be no match for a gun.

She didn't see a way out of this. Woody certainly wasn't helping. He still had his revolver aimed at Benson, but that was all he'd done. In a way, she supposed Woody's not reacting to their revelations robbed them of a sense of satisfaction. Maybe he'd done it on purpose.

Benson shifted his stance, brushing aside Alyx's arm. "This little chat has been interesting. Let's get down to business.'' He aimed his gun at Kelly, and Alyx flashed the light on her, so Benson wouldn't miss the target in the darkness. "Woody, drop your gun or your grandchild will never be born. And don't try to fool me by saying you'll shoot me. We both know you're piss-poor with a gun. I had to teach both Tyler and Alyx to shoot.''

In one swift movement, Woody's arm dropped from her shoulder and he stepped in front of Kelly. Without saying word.

Kelly pulled the canister of Mace out of her pocket. She peeked around Woody's massive frame, asking herself what had happened to the police. Woody was supposed to call them.

Alyx and Benson were huddled together, whispering, the flashlight now dangling downward. Obviously, this scenario did not fit whatever plan they had. A blast of Mace would disable Alyx and Benson, giving them a chance to sprint into the cover of the trees. On the other hand, Benson might be able to get off a shot.

You're the only woman I've ever met worth dying for.

She couldn't allow another man to die because of her. Shifting onto one foot, ready to spring out from behind Woody and blast Mace at them, she caught a glimpse of Woody's wrist. His jacket had pulled back slightly, exposing his wristwatch.

A titanium band. A face with several dials.

Couldn't be! Yet it was the watch she remembered so well. How had Woody gotten Logan's watch? Why would he wear it? Woody had a showy gold Rolex.

Her brain began to process bits of information that hadn't quite registered. The man standing in front of her was slightly taller than Woody. His arm had trembled because it hadn't quite healed. He had said little, knowing his distinctive voice would give him away.

Her stomach lurched, then dropped to her toes. By some miracle Logan had escaped. She couldn't imagine why he was pretending to be Woody. Suddenly, she was weak-kneed with relief that he was still alive. Miraculously, he'd cheated death yet again.

"You're the only man I've ever met worth dying for," she whispered under her breath.

She didn't give herself a second to think. Knowing his left arm couldn't have healed completely, she yanked it back, hard, while hurling her weight against the back of his knees. He pitched forward and she threw herself on top of him, furiously blasting Mace at the couple nearby.

She lunged over Logan, desperate to get the gun Alyx had dropped. Too far away. She scrambled toward it as a blast of light hit her.

"Shoot her! Shoot her!" screamed Alyx.

Kelly grabbed for the gun, her fingers finding the cold barrel and closing around it. A bullet singed her shoulder, knocking her sideways. Somehow she managed to fire another round of Mace.

"Stop! Police! Nobody move," a strange voice ordered.

Everything was swimming around Kelly, a hazy blur of trees and rocks and faces. Woody broke into the clearing, several police officers at his side, their guns drawn. The acrid smell of Mace filled the air, making her eyes burn and gagging her.

Where was Logan? She hadn't imagined him, had she?

"Shit! It's a trap," hollered Benson. "That's not Woody. It's Logan."

"Logan McCord! What does it take to kill you?" Alyx screeched.

Kelly wanted to shriek, "You heartless bitch," but pain seared through her shoulder into her chest.

The metallic smell of blood, her blood, filled her nostrils. She sucked in the noxious air, struggling to supply oxygen to her starving lungs. Cold sweat sheened her forehead.

There was a lot of shouting and another shot, but it hurt too much to open her eyes and see what was happening. Suddenly, her world was silent and as black as hell, but ice cold.

Logan sat outside the operating room with Kelly's grandfather at his side. She had been in surgery for over two hours to remove the bullet lodged in her shoulder. Under normal circumstances, such a wound wouldn't have been considered life-threatening.

But Kelly had lost a tremendous amount of blood. He remembered how powerless he'd felt when Benson had refused to surrender, leaving Kelly facedown in the dirt, bleeding to death. Logan gave the police a second to shoot. When they hesitated, he'd killed Benson with a single shot between the eyes.

"Self-defense," Woody had assure him.

Logan didn't give a damn. He hadn't felt threatened, but he'd known that Kelly didn't have a prayer of surviving if she didn't get to a hospital immediately. The trek down the trail with her in his arms, bleeding, had almost cost them valuable time.

When they wheeled her into the Coconino Emergency Room, Kelly barely had a pulse. The surgeon's grim face as he examined her made Logan's guts twist. Reaching Pop in Phoenix and telling him to come home fast had been the worst call Logan had ever made.

"I don't understand why she did it," Logan said to Pop as he wiped his eyes with the back of his hand. Maybe he was crying, maybe the Mace was still making his eyes water. He didn't care which. He just wanted Kelly to survive.

"I had the situation covered," he continued. "I knew Woody would be along with the police in a matter of seconds."

"But Kelly didn't. She didn't want you to be—"

"I didn't think she realized it was me. The makeup and the darkness fooled the others. They believed I was Woody. I could tell by the way they bragged about things they'd done."

"Kelly's a whole lot smarter than they are. She knew it was you. She's been heartsick because she didn't warn Matthew Jensen not to tell anyone about Rafi. That's how they discovered where you were. She blamed herself."

Logan hadn't known, but it no longer mattered. Please, don't let Kelly die, please.

Pop gazed at Logan and gave him an encouraging smile. "You can't imagine how much she loves you. When she thought you'd been killed, she nearly collapsed. Only Rafi kept her going."

Logan didn't question Kelly's love. He remembered everything she'd done for him when he'd been shot. He could still see her beautiful mouth, the lower lip trapped between her teeth as she removed the bullet. He could still see ... aw, hell, he remembered every moment with her.

For the first time in his life, he truly enjoyed being with someone. And he never wanted to leave her. He hadn't come all the way back to Sedona to get her killed. He'd returned to find out the truth.

"I love Kelly, too," he said to Pop.

"Did you ever tell her that?"

"No. She asked me to marry her because she needed help. Daniel had meant so much to—"

"Forget Daniel. Kelly had trouble letting him go because she wanted to mother him. He was a little boy in many ways.

and that appealed to Kelly. I never liked him and knew their marriage was doomed.''

He put his hand on Logan's shoulder. ''You took Kelly by surprise. She's used to being smarter than most men, able to manipulate them. She had to deal with you differently. By the time you left for Venezuela, she loved you. She just hadn't admitted it to herself yet.''

Logan knew Pop was right. He'd detected a change in Kelly on the flight to Caracas. Several times, he'd caught her looking at him in a certain way. She'd never had that tender expression before then.

He'd been proud of himself in a conceited, arrogant way that disgusted him now. Never having been loved before, he didn't know how precious a gift love was. Later, in the jungle he discovered the depths of Kelly's love.

''If only I'd had time to warn Kelly.''

Beyond his initial explanation on the telephone, Logan hadn't given Pop any details. The older man had hung up and raced like an Indy driver from Phoenix back to Sedona.

''I needed to sneak into town and talk to Woody. I didn't want to put Kelly in danger again until I knew who was after me. Woody told me the plan he and Kelly had concocted.'' Inwardly, he smiled. It was just like Kelly to confront his enemies, trying to get justice for him.

''I convinced Woody to let me take his place and carry a small tape recorder in my jacket pocket. That way we would have solid evidence against them. I'm trained for these situations, so he agreed to give me some time, then arrive with the police.''

''It was the logical thing to do.''

Logan could tell Pop didn't entirely agree. He wasn't the kind of man to allow someone else to take on a dangerous mission in his place. Logan wouldn't have done it either, but Woody had more than one character flaw.

''Why didn't you call Kelly to tell her you'd survived?''

''Pop, I had no idea if the phones were still bugged or not. I haven't slept in seventy-two hours. I barely got here. I hid outside the stable to catch Woody and talk to him without anyone seeing us or using some electronic device to eavesdrop. I had just enough time to disguise myself and meet Kelly.''

''I didn't mean to criticize. I know you were trying to protect Kelly. I love her so much I don't know if I could face losing her.''

''I know I can't.''

The surgeon shouldered his way through the swinging doors into the small waiting room. His greens were splattered with blood. Kelly's blood.

Logan had seen blood since he was a kid. He'd skinned rabbits, dressed deer. As a Cobra, blood had been part of his chosen career.

Still, his gut twisted in sheer agony at the sight of Kelly's blood.

Chapter 39

"She made it through the surgery, but we're not out of the woods yet," the surgeon told them. "Surviving the night will be crucial."

"May we see her?" Pop asked when Logan couldn't find his tongue.

"Yes, but she's heavily sedated. She won't know you're here."

Pop nudged him. "You go first."

A nurse led him down the corridor into the recovery room and left him alone. Panic hurtled through his body, hammering his temples until he became a cement block of rigid fear. The room blurred before him, shimmered like a mirage, then morphed into Kelly's captivating smile.

Except she wasn't smiling now.

All color had been leached from her face, leaving it a pallid white. Her exquisite petiteness had always appealed to him in sensual way. A phalanx of machines and tubes were attached her body, making her look fragile, delicate, not strong enough survive.

"Oh, darling. I'm so sorry. This is the last thing I meant to have happen."

His words were stolen, twisted and garbled by the myriad of machines in a deathwatch over Kelly. He stood there, frustrated at his helplessness.

There was a fracture somewhere deep inside him, a secret place that he kept well hidden, even from himself. Kelly had touched him there and made him realize that he desperately longed for two things he'd never had. Faith and trust.

With Kelly, he'd found them both. If he lost her, he would lose himself. Somehow he had to will into Kelly the strength, the mind-altering concentration that had given him the guts to make it out of Venezuela against all odds.

"Strength has nothing to do with size, Kelly. You're a fighter. Hang in there . . . for Rafi."

Logan couldn't quite bring himself to tell her that he needed her as much as the child did. He'd told her he was ready to die for her, but he'd never said how much he needed her. Aw, hell, why was he holding back now?

"Kelly," he said as he stroked her hand with his fingertips, careful to avoid the IV, "fight hard . . . for me. I need you much, much more than you could possibly know."

Her hand was cold, the fingers icy. He warmed her hand between both of his, silently willing strength into her. "Think of all you did in Venezuela. You're stronger than you realize. Don't let this get you."

He couldn't bring himself to say the word—kill. It was impossible to imagine a world without Kelly. His Kelly. There had never been light in his life. Until Kelly.

Whispering into her ear, his lips brushing her soft skin, he gave her another encouraging instruction. "Think of Rafi. Think of Pop. Think of all the reasons you have to live. Think of me."

Logan reluctantly left her, knowing how much Pop wanted to see her. When Pop was finished, Logan returned and sat by Kelly's side. For the first time in his life, Logan prayed.

In the middle of the night, she whimpered, a low moan that was barely audible above the gurgle and clicking of the machines. He vaulted to his feet and hovered over her.

"Kelly, Kelly, do you need something? Are you in pain?"

Her eyelashes fluttered and finally opened. He gazed down
t her and saw stark terror in her eyes. He knew she expected
o die and was pleading for him to care for Rafi and Pop.

Her fear was nothing compared to his. He honestly had no
lea what would happen to him if he lost her.

"Darling, don't give up. You're going to make it."

Her long lashes slipped shut. He waited, hoping she would
pen her eyes again, but she didn't. The machines continued
o spew out updates on her body while he held her hand and
rayed.

Through the hours, he kept his eyes on the cardiac monitor.
er body was pathetically still, nearly lifeless. Only the
achines in their cold, clinical way assured him that Kelly was
ill clinging to life.

Finally, the warm gold dawn light seeped between the crack
the drawn curtains, heralding a new day in Red Rock country.
he'd made it through the night.

"Thank you, God," Logan said, his voice sounding unusu-
ly harsh even to his own ears. "Thank you for helping her
t this far."

The nurses made their rounds, making enough noise to wake
e dead. But Kelly showed no signs of waking. It was another
ur before Kelly finally opened her eyes. This time she man-
ed to whisper, "Logan—Woody?"

"It's me, Logan. I sprayed gray stuff on my hair so I would
ok like Woody, and put on makeup, but it's me."

He heard the tears in his own voice and thought he might
y. It had been an agonizingly long night, half seconds ticking
as though they were hours. The whole time he'd thought
might never hear the sweetest sound in the world again—
lly's voice.

"H-how?" she asked.

He knew she wanted to know how he'd managed to escape.
began talking. If he didn't, he'd break down and bawl.

"Sometimes you just get lucky. You'd have to know more
ut local politics, but there's a lot of tension along the border.
Colombian helicopter in their territory set them off, and they
d, not at me, but at the chopper.

"Then the guys in the chopper hurled the flash-bang. There was a lot of yelling and confusion. I managed to hide in the underbrush. I heard some guy trying to give orders to the soldiers in butchered Spanish."

Hearing the door open, he turned his head. Pop walked in, saw Kelly was awake and smiled the way he had when Logan had kissed Kelly in front of everyone at the wedding.

"Pop," Kelly cried in a voice that barely carried to Logan.

The older man rushed to her side and took her hand. Kelly's eyes snapped shut, and her grandfather held one hand while Logan held the other.

"I'm listening," she whispered when Logan didn't continue.

"I knew the Israeli was one of those former Moussad agents who freelance. They're good, but they're out of their league in South America. One of the men with the Israeli was Enrique Thomasina, a soldier of fortune from Argentina.

"I'd met him the only time I'd worked in Venezuela. He'd been guarding an oil executive who was kidnapped. You remember, I told you about that mission.

"We got the man out alive. Thomasina owed me one. A bottle of expensive Glenlivet Scotch and the Levis was all it took to convince Thomasina to turn on the Israeli.

"One of his men was a hothead. He shot the Israeli before I could find out who hired him. I left my ID and your ring on his body to buy myself time to get out of the country."

What is that sound? she wondered. Blip-blip. Blip-blip. machine answered some disembodied voice. The metallic sound of blip-blip, blip-blip and gurgling noises.

She cracked one eye a slit to check the source of the unusual sounds. The fuzzy, watercolor softness of drugs dimmed her mind. It took a moment for things to register.

An IV. Drip, drip, dripping life-giving fluids. A heart monitor. Clicking away, spitting out information about her.

Alive. Not six feet under, but still alive—and yes, breathing. Thank you, God. Thank you.

Logan. She vaguely remembered him talking to her, telling about how he'd escaped. Where was he?

She tried to sit up. Searing pain exploded, arcing through her shoulder into her chest, leaving her weak. Every inch of her body ached, even her toes.

The door swung open and Logan strode in, "How do you feel, darling?"

He moved the chair beside her bed closer and sat down. Whiskers bristled across his jaw, leaving a dark shadow that was echoed by the circles under his eyes. Streaks of gray still colored his hair, flaking off in places. He looked exhausted, ready to drop in an instant, yet she knew he had spent the night at her side.

"Kelly, you had me scared to death. I don't know what I would have done if I had lost you."

"You're alive. Thank God." The words croaked out of her dry mouth. She looked at the water bottle on the stand. He understood what she wanted and poured her a glass of water.

"I'm a survivor," he told her as he gently put the straw between her lips.

She gazed into the cobalt blue eyes she loved so much, past and present merging in a heartbeat. The look in his eyes gave her strength, the way he had so many times.

"Benson is dead and Alyx is in jail. She confessed to poisoning Suzanne and hiring someone to kill me."

Kelly stopped sipping the water. She didn't care about them. She wanted to know if he loved her and planned to stay with her.

"Darling," he said, his expression serious, yet uncharacteristically tender. "Whatever possessed you to tackle me like that? You were almost killed."

She whispered, "You're the only man I've ever met worth dying for."

"Oh, Kelly." He set the glass aside. She could see how he felt in his eyes, but she wanted to hear it. "I don't know what to say. I'm no good with words."

Say you love me. Say you're staying.

"I've never met anyone like you," he said and she thought

she detected a hint of moisture in his eyes. "I love you so much."

The three little words—such powerful, meaningful words—made her heart swell with pleasure despite the pain. She knew he loved her. He'd proven it, but she still had needed to hear him say it.

"Logan, you know I love you. I made a terrible mistake. I—"

"Pop told me about Matthew. Those things happen. I never met a woman with your courage." He kissed her forehead and fondly gazed into her eyes. "I'm not sure when I first started to love you, but I knew for certain the night we went to dinner at the Stanfields. I tried to deny it, to pretend it was just sex, but it was much more than that."

"I didn't expect to fall in love either," she replied.

He stood up. "I have special surprise for you. Don't go anywhere. I'll be right back."

Don't go anywhere? She gazed at the machines that had turned her into a human octopus and chuckled despite the pain. A few minutes later, Logan came through the door, Rafi in his arms.

"Mommy, Mommy," he cried, stretching his little arms out to her.

Logan said something in Spanish, then gazed at her. "I explained that you can't hold him yet. I've taught him to say *mami* in English." He sat down beside her bed and balanced Rafi on his knee. "He can say Papa, too."

Right on cue, Rafi said, "Papa." Then he pointed at Logan with his cute little index finger. "New Papa."

Logan brushed the boy's hair with his fingertips, his touch soft and gentle. Loving. Like warm honey, Kelly's heart melted and her throat became tight. She blinked back tears. This was exactly what she had been praying for.

"I don't know squat about being a father," he confessed.

"I've never been a mother before."

"We'll learn together, then. Pop will help us."

Mist fogged her vision, she asked, "So you're staying?"

Logan cradled Rafi in one arm and leaned closer to Kelly.

"I willed myself out of Venezuela. One arm was useless. I had no pack to help me. But I made it—because I was determined to see you again.

"No one has ever understood me the way you do. You were right when you said my own experiences made me believe you wouldn't be a good mother. And you were correct when you said I was living for danger."

He moved closer and kissed her cheek. "But I meant what I said when we were waiting for the Silver Bullet. I hadn't called for a small helicopter just to see if I could make it out of the jungle alive."

He winced as he lifted his bum arm, and she remembered being in the clearing near Snoopy Rock with him, his arm around her. Spasms had wracked it, but he hadn't given into the pain.

"Hell, my arm is still worthless. I wanted the chopper because I honestly had no other way of getting you and Rafi out of there."

"I know. It wasn't the Haas Factor. You were very noble."

"Getting you two out of there was all that mattered to me."

His voice was charged with stark emotion now. Rafi stopped playing with his watch and stared at Logan, obviously picking up on the distressed tone.

"During the trek from hell, I did a lot of thinking. I've missed so much of life." Logan kissed the top of Rafi's head. "I'm not giving up anything more. I want a future with you. When you love a woman enough to die for her, your world changes. I've changed."

"I'm so happy. You have no idea. When I thought you were dead, I—"

"There is one thing you should know."

The tight frown furrowing Logan's brow sent a fission of alarm through her. Oh, no. What could possibly be wrong? They were all together now.

"I wasn't just winging it when I said the mumps settled in my testicles. I may not be able to father a child."

"Oh, Logan, it doesn't matter to me."

"You're sure?" he asked cautiously.

"We love each other. That's what counts, isn't it?"

"Yes, that's what is important." He offered her a shy smile. "I keep thinking of the orphanage in Elorza. There are so many children like Rafi who need a home."

She gazed at the little boy who was now playing with the collar on Logan's shirt. "We could adopt another child."

"I want a big family. Lots of kids running around everywhere. We'll adopt and"—he flashed his devilish smile—"we'll keep trying for one of our own. Who knows? We've beaten tougher odds. We already have what counts each other. And Rafi."

The upwelling of emotion obliterated the pain as she gazed at the man she loved, holding the little boy who had stolen her heart with a single word: Mommy. Tears seeped out of her eyes and spilled down her cheeks.

"Papa, Papa," cried Rafi, seeing her tears and turning to Logan for help.

"Tell him, I'm crying because I'm so happy. Explain that I love him . . . and I love you so much. These are happy tears."

<u>BOOK YOUR PLACE ON OUR WEBSITE</u>
<u>AND MAKE THE</u>
<u>READING CONNECTION!</u>

We've created a customized website just for our very special readers, where you can get the inside scoop on everything that's going on with Zebra, Pinnacle and Kensington books.

When you come online, you'll have the exciting opportunity to:

- View covers of upcoming books
- Read sample chapters
- Learn about our future publishing schedule (listed by publication month *and author*)
- Find out when your favorite authors will be visiting a city near you
- Search for and order backlist books from our online catalog
- Check out author bios and background information
- Send e-mail to your favorite authors
- Meet the Kensington staff online
- Join us in weekly chats with authors, readers and other guests
- Get writing guidelines
- AND MUCH MORE!

Visit our website at
http://www.zebrabooks.com

ROMANCE FROM JANELLE TAYLOR

ROMANCE FROM HANNAH HOWELL

SPINE TINGLING ROMANCE
FROM STELLA CAMERON!

PURE DELIGHTS   (0-8217-4798-3, $5.99

SHEER PLEASURES   (0-8217-5093-3, $5.99

TRUE BLISS   (0-8217-5369-X, $5.99